THE HELVETIAN AFFAIR

Also by Ray Gleason:

The Gaius Marius Chronicle
De Re Gabiniana: The Gabinian Affair
A Grunt Speaks: A Devil's Dictionary of Vietnam Infantry Terms
The Violent Season

THE GAIUS MARIUS CHRONICLE
BOOK II

THE HELVETIAN AFFAIR

De Re Helvetian

Ray Gleason

New York

THE GAIUS MARIUS CHRONICLE BOOK II
THE HELVETIAN AFFAIR
De Re Helvetian

© 2016 RAY GLEASON.

Published in New York, New York, by Morgan James Publishing. Morgan James and The Entrepreneurial Publisher are trademarks of Morgan James, LLC. www.MorganJamesPublishing.com

The Morgan James Speakers Group can bring authors to your live event. For more information or to book an event visit The Morgan James Speakers Group at www.TheMorganJamesSpeakersGroup.com.

A **free** eBook edition is available with the purchase of this print book.

CLEARLY PRINT YOUR NAME ABOVE IN UPPER CASE

Instructions to claim your free eBook edition:
1. Download the BitLit app for Android or iOS
2. Write your name in **UPPER CASE** on the line
3. Use the BitLit app to submit a photo
4. Download your eBook to any device

ISBN 978-1-63047-702-8 paperback
ISBN 978-1-63047-703-5 eBook
Library of Congress Control Number:
2015911276

Cover Design by:
Rachel Lopez
www.r2cdesign.com

Interior Design by:
Bonnie Bushman
The Whole Caboodle Graphic Design

In an effort to support local communities and raise awareness and funds, Morgan James Publishing donates a percentage of all book sales for the life of each book to Habitat for Humanity Peninsula and Greater Williamsburg.

Get involved today, visit
www.MorganJamesBuilds.com

Habitat
for Humanity®
Peninsula and
Greater Williamsburg
Building Partner

To BJ Rahn
Teacher, Mentor, Friend

*"Gratitude bestows reverence, allowing us to encounter
everyday epiphanies, those transcendent moments of awe
that change forever how we experience life and the world."*
—John Milton

TABLE OF CONTENTS

De Hospe Subito Praefatio   3
Preface: An Unexpected Visitor

I.   *De Spatio in Tartaro*   7
        Time in Hell

II.   *Hostes apud Amicos*   30
        Enemies among Friends

III.   *Ego Miles Romanus*   49
        I Become a Soldier of Rome

IV.   *De Itinere inter Alpes*   67
        We March across the Alps

V.   *Sub Patrocinio Caesaris*   83
        Under Caesar's Patronage

VI.   *De Consequente Helvetiorum*   91
        Pursuit of the Helvetians

VII.   *De Clementia Caesaris et Offensione Antiqua*   118
        Caesar's Clemency and an Ancient Provocation

VIII.   *De Calamitate Prima*   134
        The First Debacle

IX.   *Lente Festinamus*   149
       We Hurry Slowly
X.   *Scaena Caesaris*   181
       Caesar's Drama
XI.   *Calamitas Itera*   209
       Another Disaster
XII.   *Bibracte*   228
       Bibracte

       Post Scriptum   269
       Military Latin   273

DRAMATIS PERSONAE

Gaius Marius Insubrecus Tertius, our hero, known variously as follows:
- Arth Bek: "Little Bear," by his grandpa
- *Pagane*: "The Hick," by his Roman army mates
- Gai: by his family, close friends, and his few girlfriends
- Insubrecus: by his army colleagues and casual associates
- *Blatta / Vermiculus / Bestiola*: "Cockroach / Maggot / Insect," by Strabo, his training officer
- *Prime*: "Top," but that's much later in his military career

The Basic Training Squad:
  Cossus Lollius Strabo, "Squinty," an Eighth Legion *optio*, the training officer, later promoted to centurion in the Tenth Legion
  The *Veterani*, "Old Men":
    Lucius Bantus, acting *decanus*, squad leader
    Tullius Norbanus, "Tulli," assistant squad leader
  The *Tirones*, "Rookies":
    Mollis, "Softy"
    Rufus, "Red"

Pustula, "Zits"
Minutus, "Tiny"
Loquax, "Gabby"
Lentulus, "Slow Poke"
Felix, "Lucky"

Gaius Iulius Caesar, *Imperator* and commander of the Roman legions in Gaul; proconsul of Cisalpine Gaul, Transalpine Gaul, and Illyricum; ex-consul of the Roman Republic and *Triumvir* with Gnaeus Pompeius Magnus and Marcus Licinius Crassus; *Patronus* of our hero, Gaius Marius Insubrecus

Caesar's Legates in Gaul:

Titus Labienus, a professional soldier and Caesar's right-hand man; second in command of the army; saves Caesar's bacon at Bibracte

Caius Claudius Pulcher, "Pretty Boy," a self-conscious Patrician and no fan of Caesar; he would probably have been involved in the plot against Caesar—had he the brains or the energy

Publius Licinius Crassus, one of the two sons of Caesar's colleague and fellow *triumvir*, Marcus Licinius Crassus; appointed to Caesar's staff as a favor to his father and sent to Gaul by his father to keep an eye on his partner, Caesar

Quintus Pedius, Caesar's nephew—need I say more?

Servius Sulpicius Rufus, a lawyer in armor; every army has a few of these, unfortunately

Publius Vatinius, served Caesar in Rome as his pet tribune of the Plebs, a political appointment

Lucius Aurunculeius Cotta, serving in Gaul seems to have been his only claim to fame

Caesar's Military Tribunes:

Lucius Vipsanius Agrippa, an Italian from Asisium; an equestrian; a social and political nobody, but a good officer; his kid brother, Marcus, will eventually make it big

Tertius Nigidius Caecina, an *angusticlavus*, a junior tribune; a Roman and the nephew of Senator Publius Nigidius Figulus, on whose support Caesar depends

Publius Considius, been around in the army since Romulus was a corporal; in bad need of a pair of specs, but they haven't been invented yet

Fabius, a *laticlavus*, a broad-striper; a senior tribune assigned to the Eleventh Legion

The Centurions:

Decius Minatius Gemellus, *praefectus castrorum*, the prefect of camps of Caesar's army

Tertius Piscius Malleus, "The Hammer," *centurio primus pilus* of the Tenth Legion

Mamercus Tertinius Gelasius, *centurio prior pilus*, commander of the Tenth Cohort of the Tenth Legion and officer in charge of recruit training

Nerva, *primus pilus* of the Twelfth Legion

Sanga, *centurio prior pilus*, commander of the Third Cohort of the Twelfth Legion

Mettius Atius Lupinus, "Lotium," commander of the Third Century, Second Cohort, Tenth Legion; no one dares call him *Lotium* to his face

Spurius Hosidius Quiricus, "The Oak," *centurio primus pilus* of the Ninth Legion

Marcus Sestius, "Iudaeus," *centurio primus pilus* of the Eleventh Legion; his nickname has nothing to do with his religious affiliation, but rather a wound he received in a rather awkward spot

Other Roman Officers:

Decimus Lampronius Valgus, "Bowlegs," *decurio* in command of the cavalry of Caesar's Praetorian Guard

Rubigo, "Rusty," *decurio* in the legionary cavalry of the Tenth Legion

Flavus, "Whitey," a Roman soldier from Cisalpine Gaul serving in the Twelfth Legion and briefly assigned to the Sequani Cavalry under Agrippa

GAH'ELA, THE GAULS

The Aedui, the *Aineduai*, the "Dark Moon" People:

Duuhruhda mab Clethguuhno, *uucharix*, tribal king of the Aedui, and *pobl'rix*, clan leader of the *Wuhr Blath*, the Wolf Clan of the Aineduai; known to the Romans as Diviciacus

Deluuhnu mab Clethguuhno, brother of Duuhruhda, *dunorix* of the Aedui, commander of the garrison of Bibracte; known to the Romans as Dumnorix

Cuhnetha mab Cluhweluhno, *buch'rix*, "cattle king" of a small settlement east of Bibracte; *pobl'rix*, clan leader of the *Wuhr Tuurch*, the Boar Clan of the Aedui; pretender to the throne

Rhonwen, niece of Cuhnetha, a sassy redhead who catches Insubrecus' eye

The Sequani, the *Soucanai*, People of the River Goddess Soucana:

Madog mab Guuhn, *pobl'rix*, *rex gentium*, clan leader of the *Wuhr Wuhn*, the White Clan of the Soucanai, and commander of the Auxiliary Sequani Cavalry; known as Madocus *Dux* to the Romans

Athauhnu mab Hergest, *pencefhul*, "leader of a hundred," *ala* commander in the Auxiliary Sequani Cavalry commanded by Madog mab Guuhn; known as Adonus *Decurio* to the Romans

Emlun, Athauhnu's nephew

Guithiru, one of Athauhnu's veteran warriors

Alaw, one of the scouts

Rhodri, Alaw's companion

Ci, "The Hound," a veteran warrior and troop commander in Madog's cavalry

Idwal, a friend of Emlun; a rider in Athauhnu's troop

Dramatis Personae Aliae, **the Other Players:**

Aulus Gabinius, a senatorial mid-bencher who does well and is elected consul

Gnaeus Pompeius Magnus, a *triumvir*, a partner of Caesar and an *eminence grise* in this tale

Marcus Licinius Crassus, a *triumvir*, a political partner of Caesar; too intent on going off and conquering Parthia to pay much attention to what Caesar's doing in Gaul

Ebrius, "Drunk," Caesar's head military clerk and self-appointed taster of Caesar's wine and *posca* collection

Clamriu, a horse

Gennadios the Trader, a Greek merchant from Massalia who introduces our hero to retsina

Evra, Gennadios' woman from a mysterious island west of Britannia—not a redhead, but formidable nonetheless

De Bello Contra Helvetios Tabula

Map of the Helvetian Campaign

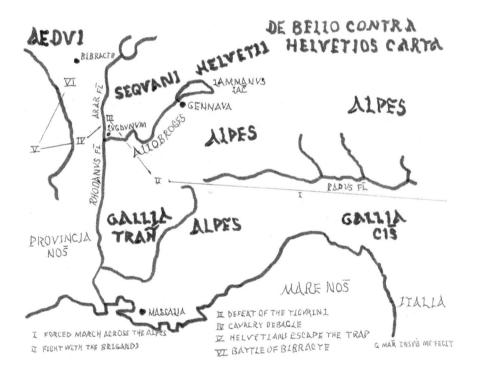

De Hospe Subito Praefatio
PREFACE: AN UNEXPECTED VISITOR

I broke my narrative to welcome a surprise visitor up from *Italia*, my former commander and comrade in the Gallic campaigns, Lucius Vipsanius Agrippa.

He is certainly grayer and a bit heavier than I remember him from our soldiering days, which is one of the reasons I have always refused ever to bring one of those *speculum* mirrors from the East into my home. If I do not have to see the physical evidence of my aging, I can still pretend that I am the same man I was when I was marching with the legions.

That is, until I have to move too quickly and my heart jumps up into my throat, or I try to leap a watery ditch and miss my stride by almost half a *pes*. My mind has not yet accepted the reality of my actual physical state.

Besides the physical changes, Agrippa was still the same good comrade I remember from our youth, just packaged in a somewhat rounder form. He even managed to charm Rhonwen, my darlin' wife—or Flavia, as she is now called since becoming a Roman and moving down to this side of the Alps.

Charming Rhonwen! When Agrippa showed up on her doorstep unexpectedly with an entourage that included two bodyguards, a half-dozen slaves with livestock, and baggage, gaining her favor was no easy task. But, Rhonwen is still in many ways a Gah'el and understands her duties to the gods to offer hearth, bread, and salt to guests. Besides, Agrippa managed to say to her, in his halting Gah'el, "*Festres uh bendit'ian uh duwiau uh bawb in uh ti hoon*"—"The blessings of the gods to all in this house, Missus." He said this as he tousled our son's hair, announcing that he looked exactly as I did at that age—except better looking—and thus, he had Rhonwen eating right out of his hand.

The fact that Agrippa put his entire *comitatus* up at an inn just off the forum at his own expense certainly enhanced Rhonwen's opinion of him.

Agrippa rarely leaves his family estate in Asisium these days. He broke with Caesar during the first civil war against the senatorial *Optimates*. Agrippa couldn't stomach Pompey, but Agrippa's Rome was the idealized republic of Cicero and Cato. After the war, Caesar pardoned him along with most of the junior officers who fought against him. Agrippa then retired to his farm, whether to avoid being placed on a proscription list or to shut himself off from what his Rome had become is anyone's guess.

Agrippa didn't leave his cloistered life—even after his younger brother, Marcus, went off to fight with Caesar's adopted son and heir, Octavius, first against the "Liberators" at Phillipi, then against Pompey's brat, Sextus, and finally against Antonius. Many believe that Octavius' victory at Actium was achieved by Marcus Vipsanius Agrippa, but stating such publically is at best risky when the Roman state is ruled by one who styles himself the *princeps civitatis*, the savior of the nation, the second Romulus, *Augustus*, the "exalted one."

In my military career, I have served with all four men: Caesar, Lucius, Marcus, and Octavius.

Marcus was by far the best general; Lucius the best soldier and comrade.

Octavius was no soldier at all.

Octavius was always a politician, a negotiator, a maker of deals. Despite my assessment of him as a soldier, and even as a human being, my *pietas* to the state demands I recognize him as the only man who can control those self-serving idiots down in Rome and prevent Roman armies from slaughtering each other as they did so many times during my lifetime.

So, if Octavius wishes to be called Gaius Iulius Caesar Octavianus, *filius Iuli divi*, *Augustus*, *Pater Patriae*, the Second Founder of Rome, or whatever titles those senatorial boot-licks down in Rome come up with, it's a small price to pay for lasting peace.

None of them are worth the mule shit that spattered Caesar's cloak when he marched the legions north of the Rhodanus in pursuit of the Helvetii, into Belgica against the Nervii, across the Rhenus into the forests of Germania, across *Oceanus* into the land of the Britanni, across the Rubico, the river of blood, to set things right in Rome.

Had he lived, peace with Parthia would have been bought with steel, not gold.

Had he lived, had only I insisted on accompanying him to the Senate meeting at Pompey's theater that day!

I'm not sure that Caesar's *lemur* is at peace, despite the apparent success of his "son" and "heir" down in Roma. Or, it may just be my sense of guilt at not having been there when Caesar, *patronus me'*, needed my strong arm protecting his *latus apertum*, his unprotected side.

Obviously, Agrippa's sudden appearance stirred up many things for me.

Agrippa said that he had come to me with a request from Octavius, which was passed to him through his brother, Marcus. Octavius is now my *patronus*, so a *request* from him is not quite a request. The fact that he used my old comrade from Gaul, Agrippa, as his messenger, is a sign that Octavius expects my concurrence in this matter.

But, more about that later.

Agrippa's appearance reminded me of when we first met during Caesar's campaign against the Helvetii. For both of us, it was our first military campaign. We were *virgines*, "cherries" as we say in the legions. He had just been assigned to the Tenth Legion as an *angusticlavus*, a narrow-striper, a junior tribune, and I had just finished my basic military training in Aquileia. As soldiers, we were green as grass; we still smelled of the farm. Real *pagani*.

Reviewing my notes, I see that I had broken my narrative just after I had run off to the legions in order to escape being arrested by Consul Aulus Gabinius on the charge of *sacrilegium* against a Roman magistrate and for an insult to his family's *auctoritas*—charges which I was unlikely to survive. This, of course, was all a smoke screen to obscure the fact that I had severely injured his son, Aulus Iunior, in a fight to protect myself from his bungled attempt to murder me. Iunior thought I had been the lover of his sister, Gabi, a pleasure which I had missed, despite my best bumbling efforts. So, he had decided to decorate the *rostra* in the *forum Romanum* with my *coleones* to recoup his family's *dignitas*.

I joined a little band of returning veterans and legionary recruits and trudged through the winter landscape of the Padus Valley. We arrived at the legionary camps around Aquileia on the day before the Ides of *Februarius*, during the consulship of Lucius Calpurnius Piso Caesoninus and Aulus Gabinius, the winter of my sixteenth year.

Cossus Lollius Strabo, our officer, an *optio* returning from leave to the Eighth Legion, brought us to the *castrum* of the Tenth Legion, to which we were assigned. After some confusion over the daily password and Strabo's authority as an officer, which the soldiers of the Tenth Legion seemed somewhat reluctant to grant to an *optio* of the Eighth Legion, we were escorted to the *principia* the military headquarters of Gaius Iulius Caesar, the army commander and proconsul of the province.

I.

De Spatio in Tartaro
TIME IN HELL

We were ushered into the *principia* tent, where a soldier in a brick-red tunic was sitting behind a small field desk working with a pile of *tabulae*, wax slates. He looked up and told Strabo, "You may pass through, *Optio*."

We passed into a large compartment behind the clerk. There were a couple of braziers warming the area and lamps illuminating maps hanging from the walls. A soldier with short, graying hair was briefing two younger soldiers while gesturing at one of the hanging maps. A fourth soldier seemed to be taking notes with a *stylus* in a hinged, diptych *tabula*. The older soldier looked over when we entered and snapped, "I will be with you presently, *Optio. Laxa*! Stand at ease!"

Strabo bunched us into a dark corner, out of the way. "The *praefectus castrorum*," Tulli, one of the *veterani* who had reenlisted, hissed into my ear.

Finally, I heard the older soldier ask, "Any questions?"

Both younger men came to the position of attention and each responded, "*N'abeo, Praefecte!*"

"*Bene!*" Then, the *praefectus castrorum* instructed, "Have your cohorts ready to march by the end of the fourth watch . . . the Fifth Cohort assembled in full marching kit outside the *Porta Dextra*, the right-hand gate, and the Seventh outside the *Porta Decumana*, the rear gate. I want you to move out at the signal for the end of watch. Dismissed!"

Both men nodded to the *praefectus*, executed an about-face, and marched out of the tent.

Then, the man walked over to our group. Strabo and both our *veterani* stiffened noticeably as he approached.

"What have we here, *Optio*? They call you Strabo . . . "Squinty" . . . right?" he asked.

"*Praefecte*," Strabo announced, "Cossus Lollius, *optio* of the Eighth Legion, reports with a detail of two *veterani* and eight *tirones* for the Tenth Legion!"

"*Laxa, Optio!*" the *praefectus* directed.

Then he turned to us. "Men, I am Decius Minatius Gemellus, *praefectus castrorum* of this army and, until Caesar *Imperator* assigns a *legatus*, the commander of the Tenth Legion. That means, as far as you're concerned, I'm a god. I have the power of life and death over you. You do not want to piss me off or even disappoint me. You *veterani*, I welcome you back to the eagles. You will undergo the first weeks of conditioning training with the recruits. My cadre will then assess your skills with *gladius*, *pilum*, and *scutum*. If you show us you haven't forgotten the fighting skills of a Roman soldier, you'll be assigned to a century in one of the second-line cohorts until we know what you have. You *tirones*, a word of advice! Although you have raised your hand in the *sacramentum*, do not consider yourselves *milites*, or members of my legion. You have yet to prove your worth for such an honor! But, you will soon have the opportunity to do so! Over the next eight weeks, we will make soldiers out of you—or we will break you and send you back to whatever civilian shit-hole you crawled out of. You will demonstrate to me, with your sweat and your blood, that you are worthy of this legion and worthy of the honor of serving the Roman people!"

Then, Gemellus demanded, "*Scriba*!"

The soldier we had seen outside burst into the room and assumed the position of attention, "*Praefecte*!"

"Get the records these men are carrying! Enter them on the legion roles; then send them down to supply for initial issue!"

Before the clerk could respond, Strabo said, "*Praefecte*! There is one thing."

Gemellus responded, "What is it, Strabo?"

"*Praefecte*! One of the recruits needs to see a *medicus*," Strabo answered.

"A doctor?" Gemellus questioned. "Is he injured?"

"No, *Praefecte*!" Strabo continued. "It's his . . . well—"

"Spit it out, Strabo!" Gemellus ordered. "Straightforward report, like a Roman officer!"

"His feet are flat, *Praefecte*," Strabo reported. "I don't think he can stand up to the marching."

Gemellus snorted, "Flat feet, is it? This is what those *podices* in recruiting are sending us for soldiers? Very well . . . *Scriba* . . . get one of the orderlies up here from the medical section to take . . . uh . . . which one is it, Strabo?"

"Mollis . . . I mean . . . *Tiro* Tertius Melonius, *Praefecte*," Strabo corrected himself.

"Send *Tiro* Tertius Melonius to be examined by the chief medical officer," Gemellus instructed his clerk. "And, Strabo! You stay behind when I dismiss the others. You and I need to talk. . . . The rest of you get out of my sight. . . . Move!"

We got out of the *praefectus'* office as quickly as we could, the *veterani* leading the way. When we reached the anteroom, the clerk collected our records and directed us to wait in a corner, "out of his way." Then, he sent a runner over to the medics to collect Mollis and another to the supply tent to collect us.

As we were waiting, Strabo rejoined us. "Looks like we're going to be stuck with each other a little longer," he announced to us. "The Eighth's already over the Alps, and the passes are closed. So, I've been seconded to the Tenth and assigned as your training officer."

He turned to the *praefectus'* clerk, "Supply, where is it supposed to be?"

The man replied, looking up from one of his wax *tabulae*, "Behind the *praetorium*, *Optio*, right across from grain storage. I've already sent a runner."

"And, I'm sure your supply sergeant will jump right on that," Strabo sneered. "You done with this bunch?"

"*Perfeci, Optio!*" the clerk started.

"*Bene!*" Strabo interrupted. "*Exeamus nos!* I'll get you people kitted up and settled in! Mollis! You wait here for the medics!"

That was the beginning of my eight weeks in hell.

Strabo organized us into a *contubernium*, a tent group, and put Bantus in charge as our acting *decanus*, our squad leader.

Getting "kitted out" was a process in which we were stripped of all our civilian clothes and equipment and issued a mattress, a blanket, three short-sleeved military tunics, a wide leather belt, a pair of hobnailed boots called *caligae*, a small satchel called a *loculus*, a mess tin, and a battered, tarnished bronze *galea* helmet. For the group, we were issued a "cooking kit, one each, *contubernium*," which Bantus handed over to one of the *tirones*. Each piece of equipment that was issued was notated against our names, and an officer in the supply section informed us that if we lost any of it, we would have to pay to replace it.

I was allowed to keep my own belt, *pugio*, and *sagum* cloak because they "adhered to military specifications," but I was warned that I would have to get the *sagum* dyed the appropriate shade of *carinus*, the dark, reddish-brown, that was authorized for the Tenth Legion. Tulli remarked that, in this way, the cloak wouldn't show blood stains—something I didn't need to hear just then.

Strabo then herded us, balancing our teetering piles of clothing and equipment, toward the back of the camp where we were assigned to a tent. He then told us to "drop our stuff and get into proper uniform." Bantus and Tulli helped us figure out what that meant. I noticed that we *tirones* had been issued undyed, woolen tunics, while the *veterani* wore red. I asked Tulli about this, and he told me that the white tunics identified us as *tirones*. When we were "accepted" by the legion, we would be issued red tunics like the legionaries who were considered "qualified" to take their places in the line of battle.

Strabo had been gone no more than half an hour when we heard his voice outside the tent yelling, "*Ad signam!* Fall in, you lazy, worthless maggots! Get out here on the street!"

We were looking at each other, wondering who Strabo was yelling at and what "fall in" meant, when Bantus and Tulli started herding us out of the tent, "Move! Move! Move! Grab your helmets! Insubrecus! Get your belt on! Let's go! Move!"

When we got outside the tent, the sight of Strabo stopped us dead in our tracks. He was in a full legionary combat rig. A highly polished, bronze *galea*, an infantry helmet with red horsehair plumes, was tied tightly under his clean-shaven chin beneath the shining cheek guards. A blood red *sudarium*, a military scarf, was wrapped around his neck and tucked beneath a shining chainmail *lorica*, which reached halfway down his thighs. A highly polished leather *balteus*, a sword belt, studded with shining bronze plates, was hanging from his left shoulder and passed across his chest down to his right side. From there was suspended a *gladius*, encased in a red leather *vagina*, and a scabbard, reinforced with brightly polished bronze cladding. A thick leather military belt, a *cingulum*, was tightly fastened around his waist and held his *gladius* in place on his right side. A *pugio* in a scabbard hung on the left. From beneath his *lorica* hung a skirt of thick, red leather strips, *pteruges*, each one ending in a polished bronze tab, on which was stamped the visage of the god of war, Mars.

Despite the winter cold, his legs were bare to his ankles, which were enclosed by the thick leather straps of his black, military *caligae*, infantry hobnail boots. Over both shoulders, but pulled back to keep his weapons free, he wore the military cloak of the Tenth Legion, a blood-brown woolen *sagum*, which was fastened at his left shoulder by a shining bronze *fibula*, a brooch pin in the shape of a bull's head. His right hand tightly grasped the leather-wrapped hilt of his *gladius*; in his left, instead of the accustomed *scutum* or *pilum*, the infantry shield and javelin, he held a long, thick wooden staff topped with a polished steel globe, the *hastile* of an *optio centuriae*, the "chosen one," the second in command of a legionary century of eighty men. He was now our training officer and would help us become Roman soldiers.

"Bantus! Get this goat-rope straightened out!" he screamed. "I want two ranks right here! One behind the other! Move it!"

Bantus and Tulli got us lined up in two ranks facing Strabo. As they positioned each of us, they whispered, "Position of attention . . . Feet one *pes* apart . . . Hands and arms at your sides . . . Stand up straight." Tulli tried to straighten out our helmets, which were wandering all around our heads, and to dress our tunics down through our military belts. Finally, Bantus took a position in front of our formation facing the apparition who was once our traveling companion, Strabo, and reported, "Training detail all present, *Optio!*"

Strabo announced, "*Contubernium! Lax . . . ATE!*"

Bantus slid his right foot straight back, toe to heel, and clasped his hands in front of him. We tried to emulate him. My helmet immediately slipped down in front of my eyes. When I attempted to adjust it, Strabo screamed, "Who gave you permission to move, *Tiro* Gaius Marius Insubrecus? You're supposed to be a shaggin' Roman soldier! Stop fidgeting like a *paganus Gallicus* waiting for his turn at the public latrine!"

And, there it was! From that moment on, my buddies in the Tenth Legion knew me as Gaius Marius *Paganus* . . . Gaius Marius, "The Hick."

Strabo continued, "The rest of you miserable *vermiculi,* freeze! Don't move! Don't even breathe without my permission! This cluster has got to be the sorriest excuse for a military formation I have ever seen in my entire military career!"

Strabo began strutting across our front rank. "I do not know what I could have possibly done to offend the immortal gods so badly that they would send the Furies out of the depths of Tartarus to inflict this on me! You are the sorriest excuse for Roman soldiers I have ever seen!"

Suddenly, the domed end of Strabo's *hastile* staff shot out into the stomach of a recruit in the first rank. The breath exploded out of the man and he doubled over. "Suck in that gut, *Tiro!*" Strabo ordered. "Stand up straight when standing in the presence of a superior officer!"

The man struggled to regain his composure as Strabo continued his tirade. "You are *tirones Romani,* the lowest things on earth! You are lower than sailors' shit in the ocean! You are so low that you have to call the mules '*sir!*' You will speak only when spoken to! And, your only authorized responses are, 'Yes, sir!', 'No, sir!', 'I do not understand, sir!', and 'No excuse, sir!' Do you pieces of fly shit understand me?"

There was a ragged chorus of "Yes, sir!"

"What?" Strabo yelled dramatically cupping his ear. "I can't hear you! Do you *understand* me?"

Stronger this time, "Yes, sir!"

"What in the name of *Martis* is going on here?" Strabo screamed into our faces. "Did the recruiters send a bunch of *puellulae*, little girls, to this legion? Do you understand me?"

"YES, SIR!"

Strabo stepped back. "Bantus! Prepare the detail for inspection!" he ordered.

"*A'mperi'tu'*," Bantus snapped.

Bantus executed a smart about-face and said to us in a low voice, "First, I'm going to call you to attention with the command, '*Contubernium . . . Stat!*' Then, I will give the command, '*Ordines extendit*! Open ranks!' At the command of execution, '*it*,' the first rank takes one pace . . . that's two steps forward for you civilians. . . . The second rank stands fast . . . Ready now."

Then, he said in a loud voice, "*Contubernium . . . Stat!*"

We assumed a fairly recognizable position of attention.

Then, Bantus yelled, "*Ordines! Extend . . . IT!*"

Those of us in the first rank managed to stumble forward the required distance and stop. Again, my helmet rearranged itself over my eyes, but this time I didn't dare adjust it.

Strabo, trailed by Bantus, was walking down the first rank, reeling off criticisms, "*Caligae* improperly secured . . . helmet tarnished . . . unshaven . . . belt improperly adjusted." Behind me, I heard Tulli whisper, "Second rank . . . stand at ease!" I then heard the rear rankers rustle then go silent.

Strabo stopped in front of me and demanded, "*Pugio!*"

When I didn't react, Bantus said in a low voice, "*Tiro*! Present your dagger to the *optio*!" Then, he reached over and adjusted my helmet off my eyes.

I removed my *pugio* from its scabbard and handed it to Strabo.

"Sharp . . . no rust... Good job, *Tiro*," Strabo announced, then handed me back my knife. As Bantus followed Strabo down the rank, he gave me a quick wink.

As Strabo and Bantus arrived at the second rank, he commanded, "Second rank . . . attention! First rank . . . stand at ease!"

We assumed the position, right foot to the rear, hands clasped in front of us, while Strabo and Bantus reviewed the second rank to Strabo's mantra, "Helmet tarnished . . . *caligae* improperly secured . . . haircut . . . belt improperly adjusted."

Finally, as Strabo and Bantus circled back to the front of the formation, Bantus ordered, "*Contubernium . . . STATE!*"

After we managed to close ranks, Strabo told us, "You people have a long way to go before you even start looking like soldiers! When you get back to your quarters, you will start working on those bronze chamber pots sitting on top of your heads. By the tenth hour, I want them shined and polished so that I can see my face in them! Do you rat turds understand me?"

"Yes, sir!"

"Detail! *Ad dex' . . . VERT!* Right . . . FACE!" Strabo ordered.

We all managed to shuffle about in the right direction. Bantus and Tulli positioned themselves at the head of our two files.

"*Promov . . . ET!* Forward . . . MARCH!" Strabo shouted, keeping a station to the left of our files, counting cadence, "*Dex' . . . Dex' . . . Dex', Sin', Dex'.*"

As soon as we were all moving together in the right direction, Strabo ordered, "*Gradus . . . bis! . . . Mov . . . ET!*"

With helmets going one way and heads another at the double-time, we started bouncing back up toward the *Via Principalis*. As we ran, Strabo shouted, "*Tirones*, always move at the double-time! Every place you go, you run! *Vos vermiculi*, got that?"

"Yes, sir!"

We spent the next two hours queuing up outside of various tents in the headquarters section. At one, our heads were shaved; at another, we were poked and prodded by various members of the medical staff; then, we were inspected for any undesirable critters in our body hair; at the camp bathhouse, we were dunked and scrubbed; and finally, we were allowed a meal of bread, oil, something cheese like, and water.

When we got back to our tent, Bantus set us to work on shining our helmets with oil, sand, and rags. Tulli disappeared for a while and returned with a sack from which he distributed what looked like a *pilleum*, the cap of a freed slave, but thicker. He told us to wear the cap underneath the helmet and tie the chin straps tight to keep them stable. If we needed more cushioning, we would have to double up on the *pilleum* or stuff a piece of cloth between the cap and the helmet.

While we were scrubbing and scraping our helmets, Bantus gave us our first lesson in how a legion was organized.

"Roman soldiers fight in pairs," he told us. "Each legionary has a *geminus*, a companion, a brother, a twin, who stands with him in the line battles."

"How can that be?" I asked. "I thought the legion formed a line to face the enemy."

"Three lines actually," Bantus replied. "One behind the other, eight men deep, if the terrain permits. But, individual soldiers fight in pairs. One engages the enemy on the battle line, while the other protects his flanks, supports his companion against a determined enemy rush, and relieves him when he's exhausted, hurt, or wounded. If a soldier is wounded, his *geminus* protects him and gives him medical assistance until he can be withdrawn from the line of battle."

"How does a soldier get his *geminus*?" asked a big, lunking farm boy we called *Minutus*, "Tiny."

"Strabo will start pairing you off in training once he gets a feel for you," Bantus said. "But once you're together, there's no stronger human bond—not brother with brother, not father with son—than the bond between legionary *gemini*. It's rare, almost shameful, for one to die in battle and the other to live."

"But, how's the legion organized?" asked Rufus, a tall, lanky, redheaded *tiro*.

"Simply put, a legion consists of a headquarters and ten *cohortes*," Bantus explained. "Each *cohors* has six *centuriae*; each *centuria*, ten *contubernia*; each *contubernium*, eight *muli*. At full strength, that's 4,800 *pedes*, infantry legs, plus the officers, but legions are rarely at full strength."

"So, we're pretty much a . . . what did you call it . . . a *contubernium*?" I asked.

"*Recte!*" Bantus replied. "Correct! Strabo's got you organized into a *contubernium*. That's a basic tent squad of eight *muli*. *Contubernales* live together in the same tent; they mess together in the field; they fight together in battle. This is a soldier's family within the legion . . . Hey, *Pustula!*" Bantus suddenly called over to one of our group, a kid with a bad case of acne. "Rub the sand in a circle, or you'll scratch the helmet, and Strabo'll have your ass!"

Bantus continued, "When your training's over and you get your red tunics, you'll be assigned to a *centuria,* probably in one of the *cohortes ordinis secundi.*"

"Our red tunics!" Minutus piped up. "Then we'll be *veterani* like you, Bantus?"

"*Veterani?*" Bantus corrected him. "No, you'll be a *miles.* You won't be considered a *veteranus* until you're blooded in battle."

"What do you mean by a '*cohors ordinis secundi*'?" I asked.

"A *cohors* of the second rank," Bantus started, then called over, "Hey, Tulli! Will you show Pustula over there how to rub the sand in before he carves a hole in that helmet?"

Then Bantus addressed my question. "The legion lines up for battle in three *ordines,* ranks. Cohorts one, two, three, and four are in the front; five, six, and seven in the middle; and eight, nine, and ten in the rear."

"What's the difference?" I asked.

"Since the first rank makes contact with the enemy," Bantus explained, "that's where you want your best soldiers . . . the big guys . . . guys who don't break. . . . In fact, the First Cohort is always on the legion's right flank. . . . When the legion advances, their job is to turn the enemy's flank . . . So the First Cohort guys are always your biggest and your fastest . . . the best guys to have in a scrum. . . . In most legions, the First Cohort gets extra pay and is immune from most details. At the end of a day's march, while you *muli* are humping to dig a marching camp, they're out in front providing security."

"So, that's where we want to be," Rufus interrupted. "More money, less work!"

Bantus snorted, "You're goin' to have to grow a bit before you get a chance at that, Red! But, remember, those guys earn their money! You can spend your entire military career in the third rank and never see a living enemy soldier, never get a scratch on you, but those guys in the front rank always make contact. If you're in the First Cohort, you better be good, or you're *perfututus,* completely screwed!"

Bantus grabbed my helmet and inspected it. "That's a good job, *Pagane*," he said. "Now, once you get all the tarnish off, buff it with one of the softer cloths. In fact, fog it with your breath, then polish it up, like this." Bantus demonstrated what he was talking about.

"*M'audite, infantes!*" he addressed the group of us. "Once you get these pots polished up, don't touch them with your fingers. It'll smudge the shine, and Strabo will write you up for it! Always keep a cleaning cloth with you for inspection. You can stuff it under your helmet on top of your *pilleum*. The damn pot'll fit your head better that way."

"That reminds me," Tulli butted in. "You guys owe me a *minerva* each for those caps."

Suddenly, one of our squad, a guy who had not said much to any of us all the way up from Mediolanum, so of course we called him *Loquax*, "Gabby," asked, "What about the officers, Bantus? Don't we have to watch out for them?"

"Officers?" Bantus snorted. "*Cacat!* You're *tirones* . . . and everybody knows it because of those white, vestal-virgin dresses you're wearing. . . . Everybody in this camp outranks you . . . even the shaggin' cockroaches . . . But you got a point, Loquax . . . Until you guys have your shit together, you want to avoid the centurions."

"Centurions?" a *tiro* we called *Felix*, "Lucky," piped up from the rear of the tent. "There was this guy who had a small farm a couple miles from my village . . . Used to come into my dad's *caupona* and get himself drunk a couple of times a month . . . Said he was a retired centurion . . . a real hard case."

"*Durus*," Tulli nodded, while trying to adjust the straps on Minutus' helmet so it would fit on his melon-sized head. "That's as good a description for a centurion as you can get . . . hard as a boot nail on a forced march . . . and just as sharp."

"Centurions command the centuries," Bantus nodded. "That means there's sixty in the legion, plus the *praefectus castrorum*, the camp prefect—that hard case we met this morning. My advice to you *tirones* is to stay out of their way. Compared to one of those guys, Strabo's a pussycat."

"How can we recognize them to avoid them?" I asked Bantus.

"They carry a *vitis*, a cudgel made of vine wood," Bantus told me. "If a centurion doesn't like what you're doing . . . or if he just doesn't like your face . . . he'll let you have it . . . across your back . . . on your shoulder . . . across the back of your legs . . . or right down on your head. . . . You spot a soldier carrying a *vitis*, you better decide you have business in the other direction. . . . There's nothing to be gained by getting involved with a centurion."

Bantus seemed to be talking from experience.

Strabo suddenly burst into the tent.

"*Contubernium! STATE!*" yelled Bantus.

We all jumped to our feet and assumed the position. Somewhere behind me I heard a helmet hit the ground.

"I need three volunteers for a detail," Strabo directed. "You . . . you . . . and you!"

He pointed to Minutus, Felix, and me. "Helmets, belts, and boots!" he ordered. "Tulli! You take charge of these men and report to the mess tent. Move it! You . . . Pustula . . . pick up that helmet . . . The rest of you . . . I'm looking at this shaggin' pigsty you call a tent, and I'm not liking what I see!"

The three of us spent the rest of the day working in the legion's mess tent, assisting the cooks, scrubbing the pots and cooking utensils, hauling water from the camp water point, serving the food, cleaning up after the meal, and then scrubbing the pots and cooking utensils all over again.

We didn't get back to the tent until halfway through the first watch of the night. When we arrived, we saw Loquax and Pustula standing guard at the entrance. No sooner were we three paces from the entrance when Loquax challenged us.

"*Consistite! Quis est?*" he called.

We stopped, more from surprise than obedience. Felix responded, "Cut the shit, Loquax! You know who we are!"

There were a few heartbeats of silence before Loquax said, "Advance one to be recognized!"

"*Cacat!*" Felix said and walked forward.

When Felix was about a pace away, Loquax said loudly, "*Consiste!*" Then, he said softly, "*Palus!*"

Felix stopped and said to him, "*Palus*? Swamp? What are you talkin' about? Swamp? We're tired! We want to get some sleep. Will you cut this shit out?"

By this time, Tulli had come out of the tent. "Will you two keep it down?" he hissed.

Then, he turned to Felix. "This is a guard mount, *Tiro*! He's just given you the sign. If you want to pass, you have to give him the countersign."

"Sign? Countersign?" Felix spat. "Tulli! I don't know what you're talkin' about!"

Tulli nodded. "The countersign's '*cygnus.*' When the guard challenges you with the sign *palus*, you're supposed to respond with *cygnus*, swan. If you don't, he's supposed to put a *pilum* through your chest. Then, you can sleep forever, you stupid *mentula*!"

Then, Tulli called out to us, "Bring it in here! You can relax, Loquax. I'll handle this."

When we were around him, Tulli said, "Strabo's established a guard mount around the tent at night. Each of you will pull one or two guard watches here each night, depending on the duty roster. In fact, you better get inside and get some sleep. Pagane, you and loudmouth here got third watch tonight. Minutus, you're on second watch with Rufus. I'm your *tesserarius*, sergeant of the guard. I rouse you up and brief you when it's your turn. But, remember, if you got to leave the tent to go to the latrine, the sign-countersign tonight is '*palus-cygnus.*' Repeat that!"

We did.

"*Bene*!" Tulli said. "Now, get in your bunks, and get some sleep! We eat chow at first call tomorrow, and I'm sure Strabo has a busy day planned for you boys."

And, that was the start of many "busy" days for us. We roused up just before the horn signaling the end of the fourth watch. We were double-timed to the mess tent for some bread and watered-down *posca*. Then, Strabo led us on a twenty thousand pace trudge into the hills, partly marching, partly double-timing, and sometimes outright running. We were back in camp by the seventh hour where we were fed some kind of hot porridge, boiled vegetables, bread, and more *posca*. After about an hour's rest, Bantus and Tulli trained us in close-order drill, marching, and formations. Then, Strabo was back with more physical conditioning.

One of Strabo's favorite drills was what he called *situlae*, buckets. Each of us would grab two empty buckets from the mess tent. Then, we would double-time out to the water point about a thousand paces west of the camp, fill the buckets, double-time back, and empty the water into the mess-tent troughs. Sometimes, Strabo would have us carry the filled buckets at our sides until our shoulders seemed like they were on fire; then, we'd shift them in front until our biceps were almost bursting, then behind us until our triceps burned. Sometimes our hands were under the bucket handles and sometimes on top, so our forearms got a work out.

Of all Strabo's dirty little tricks, *situlae* was the worst. I even saw Minutus, despite his size, weeping one day because of the pain in his shoulders and arms. But, Strabo kept driving us, shouting at us to move faster and to keep our buckets up, saying that in order to wield the infantryman's weapons in battle—the *gladius*, *scutum*, and *pilum*—we needed upper-body strength.

There were nights, as I hit my cot, I couldn't feel my arms and shoulders at all, and my legs ached like a bad tooth. And, the nights when I could hit my cot were the best ones. Every night, we each pulled a guard watch, sometimes two. Despite our exhaustion, we didn't dare fall asleep on guard. Bantus told us that sleeping on guard was punishable by death; it endangered everyone in the camp. An offender was cudgeled to death in front of the entire legion by his tent mates. We didn't question whether this applied to us guarding a tent full of recruits in the middle of a legionary camp; none of us wanted to find out—especially after what happened to Rufus.

We were running buckets one afternoon. We had all learned the trick of not filling the buckets up to the top to lessen the weight. We had to be careful because Strabo was wise to most soldiers' tricks, but as long as we didn't overdo it, we could usually get away with a few *ligulae* less than a full bucket. That day, Rufus was having some problems. He had hurt his back earlier in the week when he had stumbled during one of the conditioning marches, but Strabo had refused to send him to the medics, telling him he was a *puella* for even asking. So, instead of spilling a few *ligulae* of water out of his bucket, he spilled most of it. Strabo caught him. We all thought it was a joke, part of the game.

Strabo decided to use Rufus to demonstrate what happens when a "Roman soldier fails in his assigned duty," as Strabo stated the charge.

Next morning, before chow, Strabo lined us up in a small drill field near the *praetorium*. He marched Rufus out in front of the formation and announced that for failing in his duties, Rufus would suffer a *castigatio* of ten blows with the *optio*'s staff. Rufus removed his helmet and cap, unbuckled his soldier's belt, stripped off his recruit tunic, and while Bantus held his wrists, Strabo inflicted the *castigatio*.

To his credit, Rufus did not once cry out—despite the fact that we could see each blow smack across his shoulders and drive the breath out of his body. At one point, Rufus seemed to stumble forward into Bantus, who straightened him up and urged him to take his correction like a Roman. When it was over, Strabo was sweating from the exertion, and Rufus' back was striped crimson and white from the beating. Rufus slowly put his tunic back on and rebuckled the belt around his waist. He winced as he lifted his arms to pull his *pilleum* cap down on his head but managed to regain control of himself. He tied his helmet straps under his chin and took his place back in our formation.

Strabo announced to us that the *castigatio* we had just witnessed, a beating with an *optio*'s *hastile* staff, was one of the mildest forms of discipline in the legion. Had Rufus failed in his duty in the presence of or in contact with the enemy, he would have been beaten to death. Having said that, Strabo led us out of camp on our conditioning march.

After three weeks, we lost Bantus and Tulli. They were assigned to a *centuria* in the Fifth Cohort. Tulli was pleased. He said that was far enough forward in the battle line to have honor and far enough back not to be *semper immerda*. Strabo named Minutus as our acting *decanus* because he had kept his nose clean, and he was the biggest guy in our *contubernium*—far too big for us to say no to easily. I replaced Tulli as acting *tesserarius*, but this was no break for me. I still had to take my turn on the sentry duty roster, and I also had to ensure that every relief was made throughout the night. I soon learned to sleep in two- to three-hour snatches. Strabo said that was good training.

During the fourth week, we began our weapons training. Strabo lined us up and marched us over to supply to draw our combat armor. There was no point in doing weapons practice in our tunics, he told us. That was not the way we would actually fight.

"Train the way you fight; fight the way you train," he said. "That's the Roman way!"

First, we turned in our training helmets for the newer models that we would actually wear in combat. They were heavier, but they had better protection, a rear neck guard, wider cheek guards, and a reinforced "brow" above the eyes. Strabo inspected each of our helmets to be sure that they weren't rejects that the supply people were trying to fob off on us. He said the metal had to be of a uniform thickness, with reinforcement over the crown of the head and no sign of repair welds.

Loquax, noticing the socket on top of the helmet, asked when we were going to get our red infantry crests.

"When you've earned it, *Tiro!*" Strabo snapped.

At the next station, we were issued our body armor, a coat of chainmail called *lorica hamata*. When we got outside the tent, Strabo had us lay our *loricae* out for his inspection. He talked us through what he was doing so we would eventually be able to do it ourselves. First, he told us to be sure the *lorica* is iron, not brass. Iron rusts and is a pain to keep clean, but it's much stronger than brass, and that might be the difference between just getting the wind knocked out of us when some Kraut *podex* tries to stick a sword through us and having the *medicus* try to reassemble our guts so we look neat on the funeral pyre.

Next, Strabo instructed us to check the size of the rings—smaller is stronger than bigger—and to check how the rings are entwined with each other. Each ring should be entwined with a minimum of four other rings. The more connections, the more protection. There should be no broken rings and no rings missing rivets. If we found any of these, we should take the *lorica* back to supply and draw a new one.

We had to make sure the leather closure straps were present and not frayed. We didn't want a strap breaking in combat and our armor falling off. "Very embarrassing and usually quite fatal," Strabo quipped.

Next, we should check the shoulder straps for fraying. That's where we would be attaching an additional layer of mail to protect us from slashing attacks and ax blows coming down over the top of the *scutum*, a favorite trick of those long-haired Gauls on the other side of the Alps. That shoulder armor was something else we didn't want falling off when it was needed.

Next, we had to check the fit. For this, Strabo went back into the supply tent and returned with a pile of what looked like padded red jackets and a bunch of red rags.

"Take off your belts and put these on over your tunics," he told us, handing out the jackets. "This is your *subarmalis*. It gives your shoulders and body some padding from the chainmail."

We put the *subarmales* on and closed them with lacings up the front. When he was done, Minutus, who had struggled to close the jacket, looked a bit like a giant red sausage. Short leather straps sewn on both sleeves covered the upper arms, and a skirt of leather straps covered the crotch and upper legs.

Pustula started strapping his belt back on over the *subarmalis*, but Strabo stopped him. The belt went over the *lorica*.

When we all had our *subarmales* on, Strabo took one of the red rags and called Felix over to him. He threw the rag around Felix's neck, and just as we were convinced Strabo was going to strangle him, he said, "This is your *sudarium*, your infantry scarf. It's good for a lot of things: rubbing the sweat out of your eyes on the march, wiping the snot off your noses on a cold day, or plugging holes in a buddy; but its customary use is to pad the neck to keep it from being torn to shreds by the iron rings of your *lorica*. You tie it like this."

Strabo tied the *sudarium* around Felix's neck, saying, "Tie it this way so some *podex* doesn't grab hold of it in a fight and strangle you with it."

We each picked one out of the pile, and we tied them around our necks like we had been shown.

Finally, Strabo told us to strap on our *loricae*. This was a two-man job. Felix held up my *lorica* in front of me, and I put my arms through the sleeves in the chainmail jacket and moved forward until it rested on my shoulders. Then, Felix moved behind me and pulled the *lorica* tight across my body.

"How's that feel, Pagane?" I heard Strabo's voice behind me. "Should be tight enough to give you protection, but loose enough for you to breathe."

Felix adjusted my straps, then handed me the ends of my belt. Before I could buckle it, Strabo stopped me.

"Look over here, boys!" he called. "I want to show you a little infantryman's trick with these belts."

Strabo grabbed my *lorica* just below where my belt would ride and pulled it up a bit. Then, he told me to buckle my belt. When I did, he let the resulting fold of the *lorica* fall into place on top of my belt.

"Look here!" he said. "If you adjust the *lorica* over the belt like this, the belt takes some of the weight off your shoulders. That way, your *gladius* and *scutum* can move more quickly in combat. That could be the difference between walking back from a fight and being carried back."

Then, using my *lorica* as an example, he said, "Be sure the ends of the coat overlap by at least two palms in the back and extend at least three palms below your balls."

"Now, jump up and down, Pagane!"

"*Qui' vis m'agere?*" I challenged, thinking he was putting me on.

"Jump up and down, Maggot!" Strabo ordered.

I did. The *lorica* moved a bit but stayed on.

"Always test your fit," Strabo said. "When you are moving quickly, you don't want this thing shifting and exposing nice, tempting targets to your enemy, like your throat, crotch, or armpits. Now, the rest of you cockroaches suit up!"

While I was helping Felix into his rig, Strabo went back into the supply tent. I just about had Felix squared away when Strabo returned, followed by a couple of the supply clerks carrying what looked like wide strips of chainmail. They piled these on a piece of canvas lying on the ground in front of us.

When they had gone back into the supply tent, Strabo called, "Gather around me, *blattae!*"

We did, and Strabo held up one of the chainmail stoles. We then noticed it had leather straps. "These are your *chlamys*, your shoulder-armor rigs. You inspect the chainmail the same way that I showed you with the *loricae*. It attaches like this . . . Get over here, Pagane!"

I walked over, and Strabo adjusted a *chlamys* around my neck and over both my shoulders. "You attach the *chlamys* to the back of the *lorica* with these two straps first," Strabo instructed, strapping my shoulder armor down. "Then you close it with these straps. Be sure the *sudarium* is up above the edge so the chainmail doesn't chafe your neck while you're moving, which, for a Roman soldier, is always. Then, come around front and attach these three straps . . . *Bene*! Pagane! *Sali*!"

This time, I didn't question Strabo. The chainmail rig moved a bit as I jumped, but settled back smoothly on my upper body.

Strabo continued, "That's how a well-adjusted *lorica* should move on your body . . . smooth . . . no gaps . . . Stop jumping, Pagane! Now, there's a hook here on the front of the *chlamys* . . . It should be positioned about the middle of your chest . . . This is to hang your *galea*, your helmet, when the centurion lets you remove it during the march."

Strabo bent over, picked up one of our helmets, and hung it on my rig.

"Fits like that!" Strabo said. "Any questions?"

There were none, so Strabo said, "*Bene*! Get yourselves rigged out in these *chlamydes*, then helmets on and strapped!"

When we were all in our *loricae* and lined up in our two files, Strabo announced, "You're beginning to *look* like Roman soldiers, but you're not there yet . . . not by a long shot . . . But from now on, you will *act* like Roman soldiers . . . That means you're in your *loricae* and *galeae* from first trumpet in the morning until seventh hour every duty day . . . longer when there's an enemy near . . . *Bene*! It's still early . . . We can get at least a ten thousand-pace march in before chow!"

Strabo shouted, "*Contubernium . . . STATE*!"

"*Ad dex' . . . VERT*!"

"*Promov . . . ET*!"

"*Gradus . . . Bis . . . mov . . . ET*!"

Off we clinked and clanked at the double toward the *Porta Decumana* at the rear of the camp. And, Strabo was good to his word. From that day, we did everything like Roman soldiers, in full armored rig: conditioning marches; weapons training; even "buckets."

Our first phase of weapons training was with the infantry sword. Strabo double-timed us to a training field along the *Via Principalia* near the *Porta Dextra* of the camp. From Macro's drills with the *pugio*, I immediately recognized the *palus* erected in the ground. Those drills, although only six months earlier, seemed a different world to me. Strabo gathered us at the edge of the field and drew his sword from the scabbard on his right hip.

"*Audit' me, vermiculi!*" he yelled holding up the sword to us. This is the *gladius hispaniensis*, the Spanish short sword, the basic weapon, best friend, and only true and faithful lover of a *pedes Romanus*. Like a good woman, if you take care of her, she'll take care of you! The *gladius* is a carbon steel, double-edged sword with a tapered point for stabbing during combat. The blade is nine palms in length and one palm wide at its widest point. The gladius weighs just less than three *librae* . . . Pustula! You cockroach! Listen up! . . . The *gladius* possesses a solid grip provided by a ridged, wooden hilt wrapped in leather and secured by metal wire. It has a knobbed hilt which prevents your hand from sliding forward onto the blade—regardless of how much guts and blood has slicked your sword hand. It also has a knobbed pommel, which prevents the sword from being ripped from your hand when the blade gets stuck in the bone and gristle of some hairbag *mentula* you have dispatched to the ferryman. The pommel is also weighted, to give the *gladius* perfect balance, which, when you sorry excuses for Roman soldiers are properly conditioned and trained, will make the *gladius* feel weightless in combat. This sword in the hands of a trained and motivated Roman legionary—which you maggots-in-chainmail are not—is the finest weapon ever to be introduced onto the field of battle. Had Alexander the Great and his armies had these swords, we'd all be speaking Greek today. Do you *bestiolae* have any questions?"

"*N'abemus, Optio!*" we answered in unison.

"*Bene!*" Strabo continued. "The *gladius hispaniensis* is a stabbing sword, not a slashing sword. Barbarians, cavalrymen, and pissed-off wives slash. Roman soldiers stab. In this field, you will learn the proper technique for using a legionary's *gladius* on the field of battle. However, until you maggots prove to me that you are worthy of the title *milites Romani,* you will not put your meat hooks on real steel!"

Strabo dramatically sheathed his sword. He bent over and picked up a wooden replica of the *gladius*, which he held up for us to see.

"You will be learning your combat sword techniques using a *rudis*," Strabo announced. "The *rudis* is made in the exact dimensions of a *gladius*, but it's heavier than the real thing by almost two *librae*. This is to condition your arms and shoulders so that when the army finally has enough confidence in you maggots to give you real swords, they will feel like feathers in your hands. Before we start, each of you will file through the tent to my rear, where you will be issued your training swords. You will keep these *rudes* with you at all times. Awake! Asleep! Coming! Going! Walking! Running! Your *rudis* will either be in your hands or in your belts. They will be so much a part of you that, if some night you dream that a five-headed hydra pounced on you from out of your mommy's closet, you will be able to kill that scaly, slimy maggot with your *rudis*. If I ever see any of you without your little wooden swords, you will be cleaning *merda* out of latrines until you begin to enjoy it. Do you have any questions, *me' blattulae?*"

"*N'abemus, Optio!*" we shouted.

So, we began our *gladius* training. Strabo abbreviated the daily conditioning marches to ten thousand paces, but we were now doing them in armor and double-timing at least half the distance. We were back in camp by the fourth hour and on the stakes until the sixth. Chow. Rest and cleaning. By the eighth hour, back on the stakes, where we remained until the tenth—eleventh if Strabo didn't think we were "motivated" enough. The training was familiar to me. I'd been through it already with Macro. The only difference was the size and weight of the *rudis*.

Strabo was true to his word, and we always kept our practice swords with us. Lentulus left his on his bunk at the end of the day when he went to take a shit. When he got back to the tent, Strabo was waiting for him. As Strabo was beating Lentulus on the shoulders and upper arms with his discarded practice sword, he reminded Lentulus that a real soldier never walks away from his sword. Then, Strabo put Lentulus on latrine-cleaning duty. But, so that Lentulus wouldn't miss any training, or burden his *contubernales* by missing his guard shifts, he had to clean the shitters at night, when everyone else was sleeping. I remember the morning Lentulus stumbled back into our tent, less than an hour before the end of the fourth watch and the beginning of our training day, smelling like the *merda* he'd been scraping out of the latrines all night.

Strabo didn't spare the rest of us either. He told us no *contubernalis* would ever let a mate walk away from his sword. That endangers the man and the unit. He had us suit up in our armor, and until the end of the first watch, we had to double-time around the *intervallum*, the open space between the camp's wall and the soldiers' living quarters.

After two weeks of sword training, Strabo introduced us to the second basic legionary weapon, the *scutum*. Since we were *tirones*, we were not given the real thing, but a weighted wicker shield Strabo called the *vimen*, the "basket."

To my surprise, in the hands of a trained Roman soldier, the *scutum* was as much an offensive weapon as it was a defensive one. Using a *palus,* from which hung a sack of sand, Strabo taught us to "punch" an enemy with the *umbo*, the iron boss of the shield, a fighting technique he called *percussus*. On one of the padded training stakes, Strabo demonstrated how the left hand grasped a padded, metal handle welded to the back side of the *umbo*, and turning through the hips and shoulders, smashed the iron boss into an opponent. After striking the bag of sand a few times, Strabo "asked" for a volunteer to attempt the technique and immediately pointed to Minutus, "Tiny."

The weighted *vimen* looked like a dinner tray in Minutus' mitt, and the first time he attempted the *percussus*, the training pole seemed to shift a bit in the ground.

But, that didn't satisfy Strabo. "Is that all you got, *tu puella?*" he shouted at Minutus. "You little girl! Hit that pole like you have a pair!"

Minutus' face reddened a bit, but he hit the *palus* again, harder this time. I heard him grunt and thought I heard the stake crack.

"My baby sister hits harder than that!" Strabo taunted. "Hit it again, *me' puella!*"

Minutus looked hard at Strabo. For a second, I wasn't sure whether his next *percussus* was going into the stake or into our training officer. The stake lost. Minutus smashed it with a grunting shout and the stake split at ground level; its shattered fragments flew back at least three paces.

We were stunned. Even Strabo was rendered speechless for a few heartbeats.

Finally, Strabo announced, "That's the way a Roman soldier executes a *percussus!*"

He took the *vimen* from Minutus. We could all see that its iron *umbo* was crushed. Then, something happened that we had never seen in all our training. Strabo, staring down at the crushed iron boss, finally looked up at Minutus, who was panting a bit and standing next to the shattered *palus*, and said, "Minutus! Return to quarters! You have the rest of the afternoon off!"

As Minutus double-timed down the camp street, Strabo turned to us, the shattered *vimen* still in his hand, and shouted, "What are you maggots staring at? Pick up your baskets! Find a pole! Get to work!"

We spent the rest of that day, until well past the tenth hour, punching sandbags with our training shields. Despite Strabo's shouts of "encouragement," none of our repeated blows as much as shifted the training stakes. When we finally got back to the tent, our shoulders and arms had no feeling left in them at all.

Minutus was on his cot, sleeping like a baby.

II.

Hostes apud Amicos

ENEMIES AMONG FRIENDS

M ensis Martis, the month of the god of war, Mars, arrived, and activity in the *castrum* of the Tenth Legion picked up. Rumors had it that the tribes up in *Gallia Comata,* long-haired Gaul, were again on the move. The snow would soon be melting in the Alpine passes, and Caesar *Imperator* would be summoning his legions for a summer campaign against them.

The regular infantry *cohortes* of the legion were now regularly in the field on conditioning marches and training exercises. The *immunes,* soldiers with special skills who were exempted from fatigue details, remained in camp and worked daily, cleaning and repairing equipment for the expected campaign.

Strabo was pushing us hard to be ready. Our training day rarely ended before the eleventh hour, and with the change of season lengthening the hours, we tumbled into our cots every night totally exhausted, only to be roused in a matter of hours for a tour of guard duty.

In a practice field just outside the *Porta Sinistra*, Strabo had us working daily on combat techniques for the battle line with our *rudes* and *vimenes*. He constantly drilled us in two techniques: the close-order defense and the open-order advance.

The basic infantry combat formation of the *centuria* was a column of *contubernia*, one squaddie behind another, with each *contubernium* in the *centuria* lined next to each other. Typically, the distance of one *gradus*, a little less than three *pedes*, separated one soldier from another, so sword and shield were unencumbered. Soldiers typically measured the distance as an arm's length between men across the front line. The exception to the "three-*pedes* rule" was the *gemini* pairs. The partner of the man on the front line positioned himself at a distance to support his *geminus*. Because we didn't make up a full eighty-man *centuria* formation, we simulated with a four-man front line in *gemini* pairs. For most of our training, I was paired with Loquax. At times, I was on in front; at other times, he was.

The close-order defense, or the *murus scutorum*, "the shield wall," as the *veterani* called it, was used when defending against a determined assault from a numerically superior enemy. The goal of the *murus* was to hold a position or to relinquish ground as slowly as possible. In this formation, the *contubernia* were aligned in "close order," about half a *gradus* between men across the front line—so close that shields could be interlocked, forming a wall facing the enemy.

Initially, the primary role of the *geminus* of the front-line man was to place his shoulder into his partner's side and dig his hobnails into the turf so his mate isn't bowled over by the initial impact of the enemy assault. Then, as the front-line squaddies stabilized and sustained the shield wall, the *geminus* ensured that no one got to the front-line man by stabbing at him over or under his shield.

To practice this, Strabo detailed about a score of legionary slaves to charge at us, usually down a hill with us at the bottom. If Strabo was in a really perverse mood, he'd find a nice patch of mud for us to form our *murus* in. Half the slaves would be carrying sacks of sand to give their charge some momentum and produce a significant shock when they hit our shields. The others would carry blunted stakes. After the first wave of slaves crashed into our wall with their sand bags, the ones with the stakes would keep our back-line boys busy defending as they poked at us over the shield wall.

The first time we practiced the *murus*, Strabo had us formed in the mud at the bottom of a ridgeline. When the first wave of slaves, the ones with the sandbags, hit our shield wall, the feet of our first-line men went out from under them, and they went down, taking the second line, the *gemini*, with them. The first wave of slaves followed their own momentum over our falling bodies and ended up in the mud with us. The second line of slaves, the ones with the poles, tried to stop, but had too much momentum from charging down the slope, and with no footing on the slick muddy ground, they piled on top of the already struggling scrum.

Strabo watched this muddy pile of arms and legs for a while to see if we could extricate ourselves. Finally, he began dragging individual bodies out of the pile by their muddy arms and legs. When he eventually had us untangled and back in some semblance of a military formation, he congratulated us for being the first Roman military unit ever overrun by a pack of slaves armed with sandbags and sticks. He then double-timed us back to our tent, telling us we had one hour to prepare for a complete inspection of our kit, living quarters, and persons—and we would not be permitted to eat, sleep, or drink anything until he could not find one speck of mud or dirt anywhere.

Finally about halfway through the second watch of the night, we were permitted to sleep—at least those of us who weren't on guard duty.

The slaves got a charge out of knocking us flat. Typically, legionary slaves were good eggs; serving with a legion was a good deal for them. Although they were the property of the *res publica*, they got plenty to eat and were worked no harder than the soldiers were. After twenty years of service, they were freed, given a *pilleum*, the "liberty cap," and the franchise. In many ways, they were better off than most citizens, and they knew it. But, there was one rule they were never allowed to break. Ever since the slave insurrections down in Sicilia and Italia, no slave was allowed to hold a weapon. The penalty was crucifixion.

There was an old war story that went around the camp about a fight in which the enemy had breached the Roman line. A squad of legionaries from the *tertius ordo*, the "forlorn hope" of any legion, was the only thing keeping the barbarians from breaking through to the rear of the Roman formation. A *contubernium* fought alone until there were none left standing; every squaddie was either killed or wounded. That was when an army slave picked up the *gladius* of a wounded legionary and fought the enemy. He not only saved the lives of his wounded comrades, but he saved the army as well. After the battle, the *legatus legionis*, the commander of the legion, awarded the slave the Civic Crown for saving the lives of Roman citizens and standing his ground against overwhelming odds. He then immediately ordered the slave to be crucified for daring to take up arms.

Even Strabo snorted at that story. He said the Civic Crown would never be awarded to a slave. Besides, if it were true what the slave had done, single-handedly stopping the enemy and saving the lives of Roman soldiers, the legion would not tolerate his being executed—even if some pumped-up, patrician *legatus* ordered it.

The other formation that Strabo drilled was the open-rank advance, which was used against a numerically inferior enemy or one whose battle line had been broken but was not yet fleeing. The purpose of the open-rank advance was to gain ground quickly without losing the integrity of the legionary battle line. For this, our battle line assumed an "open" formation, double spacing between each man in the front line. To measure this, we'd raise our arms and align ourselves fingertip to fingertip with the men on either side. The second pair in each *contubernium* would maintain the same interval but would align themselves in the gaps between the front-line pairs. So, the *centuria* would advance in what looked like a checkerboard pattern, *in quincuncem dispositi*, deployed in the oblique, Strabo called it.

The individual combat technique used in the advance was what Strabo called the "Roman one-two punch," a combination of a forward *percussus* with the *scutum* followed by a full forward thrust with the *gladius*. The movement started with the right foot forward, facing the enemy. The *percussus* was executed when the legionary stepped forward with the left foot, punching the shield's *umbo* into the enemy's head, face, or chest. This was immediately followed by stepping forward with the right foot, stabbing forward into the enemy's throat, abdomen, or groin with the short sword. The *mulus* repeated the technique until the advance was halted or he was relieved by his *geminus* or there was no one left in front of him to kill.

This technique left the front-line man horribly exposed. In stabbing forward with the *gladius*, the soldier's entire right side, his *latus apertum*, his "open side," was exposed. His partner's main concern was to keep the enemy from sneaking in on that side when the front-line man's sword was fully extended. While there was also some vulnerability on the soldier's *latus opertum*, the left side, when he delivered the *percussus*, it was significantly less than on the sword side, so the forward man's *geminus* tended to hover on his right side during the advance. The *geminus*' other task was to relieve his partner when he became exhausted.

Strabo used the open-rank advance drill for conditioning. After lining us up in a four-man front in full kit with training swords and "baskets," he would have us advance across an open field with no opposition: step, punch, step, thrust, withdraw, step, punch, step, thrust, withdraw. The whole time, he was screaming at us:

"My sister hits harder than that, Loquax!"

"Step! Punch! Step! Thrust! Withdraw!"

"Stay aligned! Stay aligned!"

"Step! Punch! Step! Thrust! Withdraw!"

"Harder, Rufus, you little girl!"

"Step! Punch! Step! Thrust! Withdraw!"

"You hit like that, Pustula, and the only way you'll kill a barbarian is if he laughs himself to death!"

"Step! Punch! Step! Thrust! Withdraw!"

"Lentulus! You're falling behind! Move it!"

"Step! Punch! Step! Thrust! Withdraw!"

And, so it continued until we were ready to puke our guts up—or until after one of us *had* puked his guts up.

To give us the real feel of the technique, Strabo again brought in a detail of slaves with sandbags. He aligned us in a four-man front—each front-line man with a trailing *geminus*—and had us advance up a ridgeline against the sandbag-wielding slaves.

"Step! Punch! Step! Thrust! Withdraw!"

"Stay aligned!"

"Step! Punch! Step! Thrust! Withdraw!"

"Cover Loquax's open side, Pagane!"

"Step! Punch! Step! Thrust! Withdraw!"

"Hit harder, Loquax! Make that man grunt!"

"Step! Punch! Step! Thrust! Withdraw!"

"You puke on my grass, Minutus, and I'll have you for breakfast!"

"Step! Punch! Step! Thrust! Withdraw!"

About halfway up the ridge, Strabo had us execute a relief where the trailing *geminus* replaced the lead man on the front line without breaking the momentum of the advance. To do this, the trailing man swung around the open side of the lead man as he was delivering the forward thrust with his *gladius*. The trailing man would come through the gap, while delivering a *percussus* with his *scutum*. The man who had been relieved would then take up the trailing position by moving around to the open side of his partner by the time he delivered his first sword thrust. The advance continued, uninterrupted, with Strabo shouting directions:

"Step! Punch! Step! Thrust! Withdraw!"

"Get your alignment back, you maggots!"

"Step! Punch! Step! Thrust! Withdraw!"

"Hit harder, Pustula, you cockroach!"

"Step! Punch! Step! Thrust! Withdraw!"

"Loquax, cover Pagane!"

"Step! Punch! Step! Thrust! Withdraw!"

When we reached the top of the ridgeline, Strabo let us briefly celebrate our victory over the twelve withdrawing slaves with sandbags. Then, he ran us back down the slope to do it again.

It was a couple of days past the *Ides Martis*. The weather had finally broken, and we could feel the warmth of the returning sun on our faces, necks, forearms, and legs when we trained outside. There was now plenty of mud in the camp and in the surrounding fields for Strabo to make our training "interesting."

The Tenth Legion was in a frenzy of preparation for the campaign season. Entire *cohortes* of the legion were playing war games and staging mock battles against each other in the training fields around Aquileia.

At our morning training formation, Strabo told us that he had heard a rumor in the officers' mess that there was a crisis brewing in the north. A Gallic tribe, the Helvetii, had overthrown their Senate and leaders, and their warriors were on the move toward our *provincia*. The last time the Helvetii had moved south was during the great Cimbri invasions in Marius' time. Then, they allied with the Krauts, killed a Roman consul, and forced an entire Roman army to pass under the yoke. Caesar *Imperator*, our proconsul and commander, had rushed north from Rome to Gennava, an *oppidum*, a fortified trading town of a Gallic tribe called the Allobroges, *socii Populi Romani*, an ally of Rome, at the farthest extent of our *imperium* in Gaul. Gennava guarded a bridge near the mouth of the River Rhodanus where it flowed down from a great lake called Lammanus. The Helvetii wanted to seize the bridge in order to invade our lands and those of our allies. Caesar intended to stop them.

Caesar had no confidence in these Allobroges. He doubted they would stand with us and was sure they would not stand alone against the Helvetii. But, Caesar had only one legion north of the Alps, Strabo's Eighth. The Seventh, Ninth, and our Tenth, all veteran legions, and two newly recruited legions, the Eleventh and Twelfth, were encamped around Aquileia. Caesar had dispatched one of his *legates*, his senior commanders, from Rome to take command of these five legions and get them ready to march. As soon as the passes across the Alps were open, they were to move into *Gallia Transalpina* to reinforce the Eighth at Gennava before the Helvetii overran them. If the Helvetii were to succeed, the lands of our allies, the Allobroges, and the entire Roman *provincia* in Gaul would be ravaged by these barbarians.

Our training took on a new sense of urgency. We had to be ready to stand in the battle line by the time our legion moved out. So, as the sun was just beginning to pink the eastern sky, Strabo double-timed us down through the *Porta Decumana*, through the civilian *vicus*, and out into a large, flat, grassy field, where about a dozen legionary slaves were waiting for us with their sandbags.

Strabo lined us up for the open-order advance. I was on the front line for the first run-through. Minutus was my *geminus*.

That was what saved my life.

The slaves lined up opposite us with their sandbags, acting as targets for our weighted training shields and swords. We began the drill.

"Step! Punch! Step! Thrust! Withdraw!"

"Get your head in it, Felix!"

"Step! Punch! Step! Thrust! Withdraw!"

"Hit that bag like you mean it, Pustula! That slave's laughing at you!"

"Step! Punch! Step! Thrust! Withdraw!"

After about four or five repetitions, as I made my sword thrust, thus exposing my side and sword arm, I felt a blow on my forearm. I didn't think anything of it and continued the drill.

"Step! Punch! Step! Thrust! Withdraw!"

Then, I heard Minutus gasp, "Pagane! You're bleeding!"

I looked down at my sword arm, still extended in my thrust, and noticed a red, dripping rent near the top of my forearm. I froze. I noticed that the slave in front of me had dropped his bag and was moving in on my open side. There was something shining in his right hand.

Before I could react, I sensed a blurred motion from my right rear. I saw Minutus' arm shoot out and his weighted *vimen* hit the charging slave full in the face. The man crumbled like a puppet whose strings were suddenly cut. Minutus followed up his *percussus* by stabbing the supine slave in the throat with his wooden *rudis*.

It was textbook. I knew the man was dead.

Then, I heard Strabo yell, "What, in the name of *coleones Martis*, are you two doing?"

Then, the pain hit.

It shot up my arm into my brain, like a hot, red wave. I looked and saw my arm dripping with blood below the elbow. My brain vaguely registered that the blood had flowed down over my hand and onto my wooden practice sword, and I was fleetingly worried how I was going to get it cleaned up for inspection. I fell to my knees, dropping my basket. Another demerit, my foggy mind registered.

Then, Strabo was there with me. He was pulling my red *sudarium*, my infantry scarf, off my neck and stuffing it into the hole in my arm.

I heard him saying, "It's dripping, not spurting . . . That's good . . . It's a scratch . . . You'll be fine . . . Can you move your fingers?"

I wondered what my fingers had to do with anything, yet I willed them to move. It seemed to take a long time, but finally they did move for me.

Again, Strabo, "Good . . . That's good . . . That *cunnus* didn't slice any of the tendons . . . Minutus! Give me your *sudarium* here!"

I felt something tighten around my arm over the wound.

Then I heard Felix's voice, "He had this, *Optio*!"

Strabo, "A *sica*! How did that *podex* get hold of a *sica*? Is he dead?"

Rufus, "As a doornail, *Optio* . . . Minutus just about took his head off . . . not much left of the face."

Strabo was untying my *galea*. He let it drop to the ground. More demerits for inspection, my foggy mind registered.

"Get the head slave over here!" Strabo shouted.

Then, to me, "You keep your head down till it clears . . . It's a scratch . . . You'll be fine . . . Lentulus! Keep an eye on Pagane here!"

Strabo left me as Lentulus moved in.

Then, I heard Strabo, "Who is that, Demetri?"

"*Illum non cognosco, Domine*! Don't recognize him, Lord! He's new. He just joined our *domus* this morning," responded the one called Demetri.

Strabo, "You know if he killed a soldier, your whole *domus* would be crucified?"

Demetri, "Yes, *Domine* . . . The man's new . . . I don't know him . . . The only thing I can tell you is he spoke Latin like a Roman."

Strabo, "Like a Roman? That's odd . . . a slave from Rome . . . That makes no sense! Demetri, get your boys to police-up the body . . . Drop it off with the medics . . . Tell them *Optio* Strabo doesn't want them to touch it or lose it . . . Then you get back to your *stabulum* . . . Stay there until someone comes for you . . . You're restricted until further notice . . . *Compre'endis tu*?"

"*A'mperi'tu', Domine*!" Demetri responded.

Strabo walked over to where I was kneeling. "You think you can stand up, Pagane?" he asked.

"*Possum, Optio*," I answered.

The fact that Strabo didn't just order me to my feet indicated his concern. Slowly, I got up, leaning on Lentulus.

Then, I remembered my helmet and equipment on the ground. I made to pick them up, but Strabo stopped me. "Don't worry about your gear, Pagane. Your mates'll take care of it for you. Minutus!"

"Yes, *Optio*," my *geminus* responded.

"Good job taking out that *podex* that tried to stick Pagane. That's how this *geminus* shit's supposed to work in combat! Next time, don't waste a sword thrust on a dead man! Other than that . . . *bene gestum* . . . *good job*! Now, I want you and Lentulus here to get Pagane over to the medics . . . Keep an eye on him . . . Something's going on here that doesn't smell right . . . A *new* slave with a *Roman* accent? . . . Stick with Pagane till I send for you . . . Got it?"

"*A'mperi'tu', Optio*," Minutus responded. Then, I felt his hand under my shoulder, gently turning me back toward the gate of our *castrum*.

Minutus and Lentulus walked me back to the medical station in camp. When we got there, a fair number of legionaries were waiting on sick call. The legion was training hard, so it was producing its fair share of bruises and strains. Since I was bleeding, I was seen immediately by one of our assistant *medici*, a jovial chap with black hair, olive skin, and an accent that would be right at home in the depths of the *subura*. He tried to send Minutus and Lentulus away, but they insisted they had been ordered by our *optio* to stay close to me.

"I outrank yaw *optio*," the doc told them, "but if ya wanna stay, just make shoowah ya don't puke on my nice clean floor hee'ah. Dere's a bucket ovah dere fer dat!"

"Now, let's see whadawegot hee'ah," he said, unwrapping the infantry scarves around my forearm. He handed the sodden *sudaria* to Minutus, who went a bit pale when he felt the damp cloth hit his hands.

The doc looked at my arm and whistled, "Dat's some cut ya got hee'ah on y'arm! How'd dat happen?"

"Uhhh . . . training accident . . . uhh . . . *Medice*," I said, not quite sure what the military protocol was.

"Just cawl me Spina. Everybody else 'round hee'ah does," the doc said. "Training accident, huh? Looks like ya was in a knife fight in some wine dive in town. . . . I know cuts like dis . . . looks like a *sica*. Wiggle you fingahs for me!"

Again, I wiggled them.

"Dat's good . . . Can ya make a fist?" Spina asked.

I did, but I winced as pain shot through my arm.

"Dat's good," Spina said again. "Stings dough, don't it? Now, I want yas to make a fist atta one fingah atta time."

I did. Each finger seemed to work.

"Dat's good," Spina said. "Doesn't seem to be anyding wrong wid ya tendons. We get dis ding closed up and it don't festah, ya should be back to work in a couple a weeks . . . tops . . . Mahcus! Get in hee'ah! Bring a bucket of dat boiled wawdah and some wine!"

I looked over and saw Minutus still holding the sodden scarves, not quite sure how to get rid of them. Soon, Spina's attendant, Marcus, entered the *cubiculum* with a bucket of water and a pitcher of wine.

Spina took the wine from him, sniffed it, and said to Marcus, "Clean up de wound and de ahm."

Spina sipped the wine while Marcus worked.

"Why boiled water?" I asked Spina.

"When I was a novice, my *praeceptor* swaw on it," Spina said putting down the wine pitcher. "Don't know why, but when ya boil de wawdah, dere's less infection. Greeks say it chases the *daimones* outta de wawdah. I think dat's a load a crap, but it woiks, 'n' I can't argue wid dat."

When Marcus was done, Spina inspected his job. Satisfied, he told me to hold my arm over the bucket. Marcus grabbed onto my wrist.

Spina looked at me and said with a wink, "Dis is gonna sting a liddle!"

Then, he picked up the pitcher and poured the wine over my wound.

It felt like he had set my arm on fire. I tried not to make a sound, but a gasp escaped. "*Cacat!*"

"Shit, Indeed!" Spina echoed, draining the last drops of wine from the pitcher into his mouth. "Dah wine also chases de *daimones* outta yaw arm, so de Greeks say . . . and dat woiks, too!"

The pain subsided, but I noticed that Marcus had not let go of my wrist. Spina was removing something from his medical kit. When he turned around, I noticed he had what looked like a curved needle attached to a length of brownish-black lumpy thread.

Spina saw me looking. "Cat gut," he said. "It's miraculous, really. We get de stuff all de way from Egypt. I'm gonna sew yaw arm muscle back together, and yaw body'll absorb de stitches by itself. Dah Greeks're amazing with what dey come up wid . . . Oh . . . yaw not gonna like dis part."

Spina was right. I didn't like that part at all. By the time he was done, Marcus' fingers had bruised my wrist, and there were tears rolling down my cheeks. I also noticed Minutus and Lentulus had gone out in search of a puke bucket.

"*Bene*," Spina said, examining his handy work. "Woist part's ovah! Now, I just gotta close you up. Den Mahcus hee'ah can bandage y'arm and yaw on yaw way."

By the time Marcus was finishing my bandages, there was a commotion outside the *cubiculum*. A soldier burst into the room. He was in full kit, under arms without shield, and wore the thin purple sash of the praetorian detail around his waist.

"Are you *Tiro* Gaius Marius Insubrecus?" he demanded.

"Uhhh . . . yes . . . uhhh . . . sir," I stammered.

"You are to come with me to report to the *praefectus castrorum,* forthwith!" he ordered.

Spina interrupted, "If 'fort'wid' means when I'm done wid 'im, *Praetoriane*, then we got no problem."

The praetorian winced at Spina's use of the Latin language.

"Of course, *Medice*," he responded. "Are you the doctor in charge of this case?"

"Dat's me!" Spina agreed.

"Then, my compliments, sir," the guard continued. "The *praefectus* requests that you examine the body of the dead slave and report to him your findings at your earliest convenience."

"My earliest convenience," Spina repeated. "Dat's officah tawk for fort'wid, right?"

The praetorian didn't answer that question.

"*Bene*," Spina continued. "Let me finish up wid dis one hee'ah, and I'll examine yaw dead slave. Then, I'll be along fort'wid."

Spina had Marcus make me up a sling, and he told me to keep my arm in it until he examined my wound again in three days. Meanwhile, I was on restricted duties: no using the arm, no double-timing, and stay away from filth—so no latrine duty.

"And, diss is impaw'ent," Spina warned. "Ya should see some dischahge from de wound, looks like wawdery blood, and you will probably have a little fevah tonight, but if ya see any white, milky discharge, aw yaw fevah doesn't go away by the mawnin' or ya see red lines goin' up yaw ahm or the wound gets puffy and starts to stink, get right back hee'ah! And, just drink plenty of wawdah!"

"What if any of that stuff happens?" I asked.

"If yaw lucky," Spina said, "people'll be callin' you Lefty for de rest of yaw life . . . If not . . . well . . . let's just hope for de best . . . eh?"

We left the medical station and the praetorian escorted Minutus, Lentulus, and me to the *praetorium*, where we had reported weeks ago when we first arrived at the *castrum*. This time we were ushered straight into the prefect's *cubiculum*. Strabo was already there with the prefect, whose name I recalled was Decius Minatius Gemellus.

When we entered, Gemellus told us to stand at ease. Then he asked me, "Do you want to sit, *Tiro*?"

"*Nolo, Praefecte*," I said snapping to attention.

"Don't be an idiot, *Tiro*," he snapped. "You look as pale as a *lemur* with a hangover. . . *Scriba*!"

"*Praefecte*!" the voice of his clerk from the outer room.

The clerk brought in a camp chair, and I did sit down, but in the presence of the *praefectus castrorum* of at least five legions, my back never touched the chair.

I then noticed that there were two other officers in the room. Each had his sword strapped on his left side and a *vitis* in his belt—centurions! As I straightened up further in the chair, the clerk reentered the room with a double wax tabula and stylus.

The prefect nodded toward one of the centurions. "This is Tertius Piscius Malleus, known as the 'The Hammer,' *centurio Primi Ordinis*, commander of the First Cohort and *primus pilus* of the Tenth Legion. The other officer on his left is Mamercus Tertinius Gelasius, *centurio Tertii Ordinis* and officer in charge of recruit training. They are here to witness your statements and to interrogate you further concerning today's events."

The prefect paused, so I said "*Compre'endo, Praefecte!*"

"*Bene!*" He continued, "Your officer here, *Optio* Strabo, has already made his statement. Now, I'd like you to tell us what happened."

I related the story as best as I could. No one interrupted my narrative, but when I was done, the prefect asked, "Your *geminus* . . . the one who killed the slave . . . is that this big fellow here?"

"I'm called Minutus, *Praefecte!*" Minutus confirmed.

"Minutus," the prefect chuckled, "Tiny . . . eh? I don't know why the fathers of Roman soldiers bother naming their sons when they put on the *toga virilis* . . . They're not men until their mates in the legions name them. . . . So . . . Minutus . . . do you have anything to add to *Tiro* Insubrecus' account?"

"*N'abeo, Praefecte,*" Minutus responded.

Gemellus turned to the other two officers. "Do you have any questions for these men?" he invited.

Malleus, the *primus pilus*, spoke, "Have either of you ever seen the slave who attacked *Tiro* Insubrecus before?"

"*Illum non vidi, Prime,*" Minutus and I answered in unison.

"Do either of you have any idea why this man would want to kill you?" he asked.

"*No' scio, Prime!*" Minutus snapped.

I remained silent while I thought about what I should say.

Malleus picked up on my silence immediately. "You have something to add, *Tiro* Insubrecus?"

I thought about it for a few heartbeats. Telling the *praefectus castrorum* of Caesar's legions and the *primus pilus* of the veteran Tenth Legion that I was possibly a fugitive, wanted by the consul of the Republic, had a bit of risk attached to it. But, even in the midst of Caesar's army, I obviously wasn't safe. So, I told them everything: Gabinia in the arbor, the attack on the road to my parents' farm, Gabinius Iunior and his gladiators, the threat of Gabinius Senior's arrest warrant, my flight, and the gangsters in Mediolanum. I did leave out a few details about Rufia's operation. I had enough enemies as it was, and I planned to go back home to Mediolanum in about six years' time if I didn't get skewered by some foaming-at-the-mouth, seven-foot-tall, hairy, Roman-eating German tribesman.

It was rare indeed to see a look of utter astonishment on the face of a Roman officer as senior and as experienced as a *praefectus castrorum*. This was one of those times.

Gemellus burst out laughing—another rarity. "You mean to tell me that *Rufia . . . Rufia* of Mediolanum . . . *Rufia,* with the blue, Venus-door . . . hid you out in one of her private suites?"

"*Recte, Praefecte,*" I stammered out.

"I know senior officers . . . purple-stripers . . . who'd piss away their entire purse to have been in your shoes!" Gemellus continued to laugh. "Rufia of Mediolanum . . . and she's sweet on a clapped-out *optio* from Asia . . . No offense, Strabo . . . *Mammis Veneris* . . . that's rich!"

"Sir," Malleus beckoned.

"Yes . . . Yes," Gemellus chuckled, getting back on track. "I think we can rule out the consul. If he wanted you, all he'd have to do is send a warrant up here for your arrest. If he wanted you dead, he could just make sure you never made it back to Rome. Of course, Caesar as proconsul of the province and commander of the army would have to approve."

"Sir," I ventured.

"What is it, *Tiro?*" the prefect said, a bit surprised at being interrupted by a recruit. "Don't tell me that you have a passel of Athenian *hetairai* in the *vicus* who clean your underwear."

"No, sir," I assured him. "But, there is something about my family's relationship with Caesar *Imperator* that may have some relevance."

I told him about my gran'pa, Marius and Gaius Senior, how we got our farm, and how we are technically Caesar's clients.

"*Cacat*," Gemellus said. "That explains the name, 'Gaius Marius,' at least . . . I doubt the *imperator* even knows you or your family exist . . . But you're correct . . . Technically, you're *cliens genti Iuliae*, and therefore, entitled to his *patrocinium* . . . his protection. . . . He will have to be informed."

There was a commotion in the outer tent. Another of the prefect's clerks stuck his head in and announced that the *medicus* had arrived to give his report on the dead slave.

"About time!" the Prefect responded. "Get him in here!"

Spina entered the room and reported.

"What can you tell us about the dead slave, *Medice*?" the prefect demanded.

"Dead slave?" Spina repeated. "First, I can confirm he's crossed the river . . . Either de broken neck aw de damage to his head did 'im."

"How can you be so sure, Spina?" Gelasius spoke up for the first time. "He was also stabbed through the throat."

Spina looked over at the centurion. "Gelasius! Didn't see ya standin' back dere. How do I know? Easy! Dah stabbing wound to his throat pierced dee aorta. If his heart was beatin' when dat happen'd, dere would a been a fountain a blood. But dis wound hardly bled . . . *Ergo* . . . he was dead when it happened."

Gelasius grunted in the affirmative.

"Continue, Doctor!" Gemellus prompted.

"Dah second part of yaw question about a dead slave raises a problem, *Praefecte*," Spina continued. "Dis guy wasn't a slave."

"What?" Gemellus shot. "Wasn't a slave? How can you be so sure?"

"Coupl'a dings, *Praefecte*," Spina explained. "First, his hair, or what was left of it, wasn't regulation cut. Second, he had no 'SPQR' tattoo on his left shoulder blade like de rest a de government slaves around hee'ah. T'ird, his hands weren't callused like a slave's . . . A *sicarius*, a hit man, yeah . . . a slave, no. Fourt', I cut 'im open and his last meal included *garum* and eggs, not de barley porridge de slaves eat for breakfast. Finally, he had a tattoo of a *sica* and skull on his left shoulder. I've seen marks like dat when I was a kid growin' up on the Aventine . . . It's a *collegium* mark . . . Dis guy was a *grassator* . . . a gangster . . . probably a *percussor* . . . a hitter up hee'ah from Rome . . . That explains the report of his Roman accent."

"Are you sure about this, Spina?" Malleus asked. "Seems a little flimsy to me."

"Any one a dem, *Prime*, yeah . . . It'd be pretty flimsy, like ya said," Spina responded. "But, all togedder . . . no . . . Dis guy was a ringer . . . a hitter . . . He was up hee'ah to wack de kid . . . I'm shoo-a-wit."

"'Shoo-a-wit'," Gemellus said absently. "Oh . . . 'sure of it' . . . Yes . . . I agree . . . *Bene gestum, Medice* . . . Anything else?"

"Yeah, *Praefecte*," Spina continued. "I took a look at dis guy's knife . . . It's a straight-bladed *sica* . . . I seen a lot of dese back on de Aventine . . . The boys on de hill like 'em cause dere easy to conceal . . . Dis one's razor shawp . . . well taken care a . . . and expensive . . . Got an ivory grip . . . matches the scabbard I found strapped to de guy's forearm . . . But dis is de ding . . . On the blade was engraved DON MILONE SUM, 'I'm a gift from Milo.' Not only we got a hitter heah, we got one of Milo's top boys. He don't give away knives like dat to schleps!"

"Schleps?" Gelasius questioned.

"Schleps," Spina clarified. "It's a word we used back on de hill for guys who ain't too impaw'int or too bright, so they get the worst jobs . . . like a . . . like a . . . *ianitor* . . . a *baiulus* . . . only dumber."

"Yes! Yes! Very good," the Prefect interrupted. "Do get on with it, Spina!"

"Yeah . . . of course, *Praefecte*," Spina said. "Like I said, dis guy was good at what he did . . . so he had to have an escape plan after he did the kid hee'ah . . . Dat means a quick change a clothes outta de slave tunic . . . So, somewhere neah wheah he slashed de kid hee'ah, he hid 'is stuff . . . So, if ya send a few a de boys out on police call, you should find 'em . . . Maybe tell you somethin' maw 'bout dis guy."

It took Gemellus a couple of heartbeats to translate Spina's west-slope-of-the-Aventine Latin, but when he finally did, he grunted his approval, "*Bene* . . . Good thinking, Spina . . . Anything else?"

"Yeah, *Praefecte* . . . couple things," Spina continued. "I inspected dis knife real close . . . It's been shawpened recently . . . Looks like a professional job . . . Best knife-grinder 'round hee'ah is a Gaul named Aeddan. I use 'im myself to sharpen my instruments . . . First rate job he does . . . He's got a booth out in the *vicus* behind de Ninth's *castrum*. I'll bet dat's where aw boy shawpened his fancy *sica*. Doubt yaw gonna get much . . . Dis guy's too good . . . but it's worth a try."

"You said 'couple things,' *Medice*?" Gemellus prompted.

"Yeah, *Praefecte*," Spina continued. "The garum and eggs aw boy had for 'is last breakfast . . . Dat's a pretty fancy meal . . . He didn't get it in some *vicus* flop . . . My bet's he stayed at some fancy joint, a *deversorium* up in de town . . . Best place I know up deah is the *Anser Volans*, the Flying Goose . . . It's on de main drag neah de west gate . . . Run by a retired legionary named Macer . . . Dey'd have garum and eggs, fer shoowaw."

"Macer . . . Flying Goose . . . Aeddan," Gemellus repeated, "You know any of these places, Malleus?"

"I know the Goose, *Praefecte*," the *primus pilus* responded.

"*Bene*! Send a couple of your *prima centuria* boys up there to talk to this Macer," Gemellus instructed. "He used to be one of us, so I assume he'll cooperate. As far as this Gaul is concerned, this Aeddan, send a *contubernium* in full rig . . . shields and swords . . . just in case he decides to play it cute."

"*A'mperi'tu', Praefecte*," Malleus responded.

Gemellus turned to the doctor, "Anything else for us, *Medice*?"

"*N'abeo, Praefecte*," Spina responded.

"*Bene*! You may return to your duties," Gemellus instructed.

Spina inclined his head to the three centuriate officers in the room and left.

After Spina had gone, Malleus asked, "*Praefecte*! What about the slaves, the real ones, I mean?"

"The slaves?" Gemellus asked. "What do you mean, Malleus?"

"Do you want them interrogated?" the *primus pilus* inquired. "This . . . this 'hitter,' as the doctor calls him, may have bribed them to get them to conceal his presence within their *domus*."

"Hmmm . . . I see what you mean," Gemellus considered. "Are you suggesting we put them to the *interrogatio*? That means torture for slaves."

"That is the custom, *Praefecte*," Malleus confirmed.

"I see," the prefect reflected. "No . . . I don't think so . . . It's bad for morale, and we're less than two weeks from going into combat . . . The Tenth's *stabulum* of slaves are veterans . . . Most of them been with us for years . . . I don't think any of them would risk *manumissio*, their emancipation, for a few denarii . . . No . . . But, Gelasius . . . I have a job for you."

"*A'mperi'tu', Praefecte*," the Tenth Cohort commander snapped.

"Send a couple of your boys over to Spina and tell him to sew his patient up," Gemellus instructed, "Then, take the body out to the field where he attacked *Tiro* Insubrecus and crucify him. If he wanted to disguise himself as a slave, he can end up like one, feeding the crows on a cross."

"*Stat', Paefecte!*" Gelasius confirmed.

"Be sure to hang him up in his slave tunic," the Prefect continued. "Hang a sign on him, something like, 'Attacked a Roman Soldier.' Then, after last call this evening, when training's over, take the slaves out to that field, the entire *stabulum*, and file them by the cross. That should take care of any thoughts they *might* have about taking bribes from outsiders. Got it, Gelasius?"

"*Compre'endo, Praefecte!*"

"Strabo," Gemellus turned his attention to our training officer. "Will your *tirones* be ready to participate in the *significatio* next week?"

"*Parati, Praefecte*," Strabo snapped.

"*Bene*," Gemellus said. "This army will be moving out over the Alps as soon as the *imperator* summons us. So, with the Helvetii on the move, we must be sure we are all *parati*. *Tiro* Insubrecus, you are excused from all training exercises and fatigue details until further notice! I will be notifying your *patronus*, Caesar *Imperator*, of this event. This affects his *dignitas*. As far as the rest of this legion is concerned, this was just the work of a renegade slave. *Compre'enditis vos toti?*"

A chorus of "*Compre'endo, Praefecte!*" ensued.

"*Bene*," Gemellus concluded. "*Optio* Strabo, you will remain behind. We have something to discuss with you. *Tirones, miss'est!*"

III.

Ego Miles Romanus
I BECOME A SOLDIER OF ROME

S o, I spent most of my last weeks as a legionary *tiro* restricted to barracks. None of Spina's dire fears about my arm materialized. When I reported to him at the medical station three days later, he was quite pleased with his handiwork and my progress—pretty much in that order. He had me flex my fingers a couple of times; then he told Marcus, his orderly, to wash the wound with wine—after Spina had personally tested the brew for potency—and change my bandages. Spina sent me back to barracks with the advice to learn to use my left hand as it was good military practice. I wasn't sure what he meant, but he seemed to have amused himself.

Strabo had a surprise for us. When he returned to collect us the first morning after the meeting with the prefect, he had his sword hung on his left hip and a *vitis* in his right hand. He announced in formation that he had been granted a temporary appointment in the Tenth Legion as a *centurio tertii ordinis* and was in command of the Fourth *Centuria* of the Tenth *Cohors*, where the legion assigned its trainees. He then announced that he had selected our old friend Bantus as his "chosen one"; the *optio* of the Fourth *Centuria* was our new training officer. He then sent me back to quarters while he put the rest of our *contubernium* through its daily ten thousand-pace conditioning march.

Rumors about what was happening on the other side of the Alps continued to swirl through the camp.

The Germans had crossed the Rhenus. The Helvetii had stormed the bridge over the Rhodanus and had burned Gennava. Roman citizens were being massacred, and the Eighth Legion had been pushed back into our *provincia*. Roman auxiliary units had mutinied and gone over to the barbarians. Massalia had locked its gates against us, and the entire Roman army north of the Alps was being pushed back into the *Mare Nostrum*, the Middle Sea.

The Tenth Legion continued to train and prepare to move out over the Alps. It was now participating in army-level training exercises, maneuvering with, and against, the other legions of the army. Our senior officers—legates and tribunes— were arriving from Rome. But, still no word had come from Caesar *Imperator*.

Finally, on the *Nones Aprilis*, Strabo announced to us that word had been received from the proconsul in Gennava, which apparently the barbarians had not burned, that the army must be ready to march on the *Ides*. Therefore, our *significatio* would be held five days before the *Ides* so that we would be ready to march with our legion. Strabo then asked if we had any questions.

"*Quaestionem 'abeo, Opt* . . . uh . . . *Centurio*," Loquax popped up.

"*Roga*," Strabo responded. "Go ahead!"

"*Centurio*, what is a *significatio*?" Loquax asked.

Strabo stared at Loquax for a few heartbeats, trying to decide whether the *tiro* was putting him on. He decided he was not.

"Good question, *Tiro* Loquax," Strabo responded. We would come to notice that after his promotion, Strabo was more refined, more observant of proper military protocol and courtesy. He hardly ever called us maggots or cockroaches anymore.

"The *significatio* is a ceremony in which the legion demonstrates to Father Iove that you are now part of it," Strabo explained. "In front of the legion's *aquila*, the *primus pilus* asks the assembled legion whether it accepts you, and the soldiers acclaim their acceptance. Then, you are invested in the red tunic of a soldier, given the shield of the Tenth Legion, and awarded your *gladius*, your infantry sword. You renew your *sacramentum* in front of your comrades and swear you would die before you would shame our standards or let the legion down. Then, the legion acclaims you as a *miles*, one of their number. Any other questions, *Tirones*?"

We had none, so Strabo said, "*Optio* Bantus! Take charge of the training detail. Move them out to the *pilum* range . . . at the double . . . Pagane . . . you will remain in quarters!"

"*A'mperi'tu', Centurio!*" Bantus snapped and took his position in front of our formation.

"*Contubernium . . . STATE!*"

"*Pagane! Miss'est . . . A signis!*"

"*Contubernium . . . Ad Dex' . . . VERT!*"

"*Prov . . . ET!*"

"*Gradus bis mov . . . ET!*"

The day of our *significatio*, our acceptance into the Roman army, would be the fifth day before the *Ides Aprilis*, a day that was considered *fastus*, auspicious, and *comitialis*, a day on which the Roman people could assemble to conduct business.

A few days prior, Bantus had our acting *decanus*, Minutus, collect our white trainee tunics, leaving us one each to train in, and had Moelwyn, our newly-assigned *contubernium* slave, take them down to the civilian *vicus* just outside the *Porta Decumana* to be dyed infantry red. The process took two days. When Moelwyn returned from the *vicus* with them, we were excited by the prospect of finally donning them. I remember sitting on my cot, running my hands over the red fabric. Bantus told us not to try to outrun our own chariot horses, but to store them away until we had been invested.

Three days before the *significatio*, Spina had his aid, Marcus, remove the exposed stitches from my injured arm. This time Spina sampled his medicinal wine and didn't use it for washing my wound. He examined my injury and congratulated himself on a "jawb well dun." Then, he congratulated me on acquiring the first "noble scah" of my military career. He then warned me to keep the arm bandaged and go easy with it for the next few days, "No sword practice and no *pilum* chucking!"

Then, Spina offered me a swig of his pitcher.

I got back to our tent around the seventh hour. Moelwyn was outside working on a harness. I greeted him in *Gah'el*.

"Please speak Latin, *Domine*," he answered me in Latin. "That is the language of the legions."

I sat down next to him and started examining the harness he was working on. I recognized it from the time I worked in Gabinius' stable.

"What's all this for?" I asked Moelwyn.

"The *contubernium* mule, *Domine*," he answered me.

"We have a mule?" I blurted. "What for?"

"Every *contubernium* has a mule, *Domine*," Moelwyn answered. "It's used to carry things that are not essential for a legionary to carry on his *furca*, his pack pole. In this legion, the mule carries the tent, tent poles, and pegs, eight *sudes*, the sharpened wooden stakes to fortify the daily marching camp, extra rations, water, *et cetera*."

I realized that Moelwyn had been with the army much longer than I had. "How long have you been with the legions?" I interrupted.

"Me, *Domine*?" he responded. "Eight years this month."

"Eight years!" I repeated. "You're almost halfway there."

"Yes, *Domine*! Halfway there, as you say," he agreed. Then he continued, "It's not good to talk about . . . . *Domina Fortuna* does not like mortals to boast of her gifts to them."

Realizing that soon we would all be marching through the Alps to face hordes of rampaging Helvetii, I nodded in agreement, then rubbed my *Bona Fortuna* amulet, and spat toward the north.

The mule's rig seemed to be in good shape. I wondered briefly if the metal fittings on it had come from my *Avus* Lucius' forges down in Mediolanum. Then, I asked Moelwyn, "Were you brought down from *Gallia comata*?"

"Me, *Domine*?" He seemed a bit startled by the question. "*Gallia comata* . . . No, *Domine* . . . Never been there . . . I joined this legion in the *provincia* and went with them into *Hispania* . . . I was born a couple hundred miles from here, up in the foothills of the mountains to the north . . . near a great lake . . . My village is called Sarnis."

"You joined? But you're a . . . a," I stammered.

"A slave, *Domine*?" Moelwyn finished my question. "Most of us in the legions serve *voluntate ipsius*. We are voluntary slaves . . . We sold ourselves to the *res publica*."

"Why would you do that?" I blurted, not understanding why anyone would voluntarily become a slave.

Moelwyn shrugged and said, "In my village, all we could grow were rocks . . . I was starving . . . When I was fourteen, I left my family and wandered down into the valley, looking for work and food . . . The only thing I knew how to do was herd goats . . . but small farmers did that for themselves, and large farmers used slaves . . . and even they were eating better than I was . . . Then a Roman told me that I could sell myself to the state . . . serve in the army . . . Three squares a day, a roof over my head, and the work wasn't all that hard . . . After twenty years, if I did my job and kept my nose clean, I'd be released and be granted Roman citizenship . . . What did I have to lose? I wasn't a citizen . . . I had no rights . . . I was starving . . . So I did it . . . The army's even holding my purchase price . . . I get it when I'm freed . . . I've had to take a few beatings over the years, but most of the soldiers are pretty straight . . . As long as I do what I'm told . . . be respectful … they leave me alone . . . All in all, it was a good choice . . . I got no regrets . . . In twelve years, I'm free."

Moelwyn spat toward the north to ward off any misfortune.

Later that day, during the tenth hour, our new *optio*, Bantus, examined my arm and decided that I could rejoin the training, except for sword and *pilum* drills. He agreed with Spina that I'd have a nice scar to impress the *caupona* girls with, demonstrating what a *miles gloriosus* I was.

Bantus' training for us that evening was on packing the *sarcina*, the legionary marching pack. He had Moelwyn distribute two wooden poles to each of us: one about four *pedes* in length; the other shorter, about two *pedes*. Each pole was about a *palmus maior* in circumference, about three fingers short of a foot. Then, Bantus gave each of us a length of rawhide lashing.

"*M'audite, Tirones*," he called out over the noise we were making, talking about what to do with the wooden poles. "I'm going to show you how to construct a *furca*."

When we finally settled down and he had our attention, he continued, "The *furca* is a forked pole that carries your pack and equipment while you're marching *impeditus,* or as the *veterani* call it, *mulare*, muling it. I'm going to show you how to construct one."

Bantus grabbed Rufus' poles. "The *furca*'s made from a thick staff about four *pedes* in length," he said, holding up the longer staff.

"A shorter cross piece is fixed about a *pes*, a foot, from the top of the long stake." Bantus demonstrated, making what seemed to be a cross from the two stakes.

"To attach them, you carve a notch in each . . . You interlock them . . . like this . . . Then you lash them together with the rawhide bindings. . . . Any questions so far?" he asked holding up the cross in one hand and a set of rawhide bindings in the other.

There were scattered mutterings of "*n'abeo*" around the tent.

Then, still holding up the crossed stakes, Bantus joked with us by asking if we knew the difference between a criminal's cross and a legionary's *furca*. When we didn't answer, he said, "A cross carries a criminal till he's dead. The legionary carries his *furca* till he wishes he was dead."

We didn't get it, but Bantus just laughed and muttered, "Infantry humor." Later we would know what he meant. By the time we got over the Alps and chased the Helvetii halfway across Gallia, we all knew the difference between a *furca* and a cross, and I think some of us would have preferred the cross.

But, Bantus continued, "First, notch your stakes, the shorter one in the center, the longer about one *pes* from the top. Don't go any deeper than about halfway . . . a little less is better . . . The cut's no longer than the diameter of the stake . . . Remember the stakes have to fit together . . . so use them to measure your cut . . . Go ahead ... Get to work."

I pulled out my *pugio*, the knife Macro had given me for my sixteenth birthday, seemingly a lifetime ago, and laid the shorter stick across the longer in the correct position, about a *pes* from the top, centered. Using the opposing stakes, I scratched cut lines on each to mark the width of the cut and started whittling out the notches.

Bantus walked around the tent, inspecting our work. Moelwyn assisted him. "*Bene . . . bene,*" I heard him saying to my mates as they worked. "No, Lentulus . . . Go look at how Pagane's doin' it . . . He's got it right."

Finally, we had our stakes notched and fitted. I looked worriedly at the pile of sawdust and wood chips around our bunks. We would have to get that swept up before evening inspection.

Bantus was talking, "Before I show you how to lash the poles together, I want you to wet and stretch the rawhide bindings." As he spoke, Moelwyn brought in a bucket of water.

Optio . . . ad quam rationem," Loquax started. "Sir . . . why—"

Bantus seemed to have anticipated the question. "You wet and stretch the rawhide because it will shrink when it dries . . . That way you get a tight binding of the two poles . . . If you fasten your *furca* with dry rawhide and it gets wet . . . and I assure you, it will . . . the bindings will loosen, and the *furca* will come apart . . . You'll be trying to march while balancing all your shit in your arms . . . That's a real rookie mistake, boys . . . Soldiers I train don't make those kind of mistakes . . . So, wet the bindings in the bucket . . . Stretch 'em out good . . . and I'll show you how to lash the *furca* together."

We did as Bantus instructed, and he showed us how to lash the *furca* poles together. Bantus went around, inspecting the bindings and their tightness. Finally, when he was satisfied with our work, he continued.

"The *sarcina,* the infantry marching pack, is constructed by strapping the *loculus,* your leather satchel, to the cross piece of the *furca,*" he told us. "The *loculus* is primarily for carrying your marching rations . . . *buccellatum,* your hardtack . . . salt meat . . . pork and mutton usually . . . Sometimes we get some beef . . . If you can scrounge any cheese, fresh fruits, or vegetables along the way, toss them in there too . . . This way, your food's accessible to you during rest breaks . . . Wrap any cheese you get in a damp cloth . . . That helps keep it soft . . . soft enough to chew, anyway . . . What is it, Felix?"

"*Optio,* do we get rest breaks on the march?"

"Usually," Bantus responded. "When it's not a forced march or when we're not in proximate contact with the enemy, the legion takes about a quarter-hour rest break every five thousand *passus* or so. It's a good time to get the *furca* off your shoulder . . . grab a piece of *buccellatum* . . . maybe a hunk of cheese, if you got it . . . wash it all down with a swig of *posca* or water . . . Stretch 'em out . . . Then we're off again . . . Back to this *sarcina* . . . your marching pack . . . You tie your *patera*, your mess kit, and your *cochleare*, your eating spoon, to the cross piece like this . . . Some guys like to put their spoons in the *loculus* . . . Keeps it cleaner . . . It's up to you. Balance the mess kit with your *lagoena*, your water bottle . . . What is it, Loquax?"

"*Optio*! Do we carry water on the march? I thought that was carried in the baggage train."

"Always carry some water with you, Loquax," Bantus told him. "Sometimes we get separated from our supplies, and we can't find a good source of potable water at the end of the day . . . A soldier can go for a few days without food, but won't last a short summer's day without water . . . Some guys carry two water bottles, just in case . . . Keep 'em filled . . . You can carry water or *posca* . . . I recommend the water . . . Load a skin or two of *posca* on the mule for the end of the day . . . Now, back to the *sarcina* . . . In this legion, soldiers carry their *dolabrae*, their digging picks . . . You can tie them here on the *furca* and not unbalance it . . . Always tie the *dolabra* high on the *furca* . . . You don't want it digging into your back or shoulders on the march . . . The digging baskets go on the mule . . . I get that right, Moelwyn?"

"*Recte, Domine*," Moelwyn's voice sounded from the back of the tent. "The entrenching baskets go on the mule in the Tenth . . . with the *rutra*, the shovels."

Bantus chuckled. "In the field, a good *mulio*, a teamster, is worth a month's pay . . . Makes sure everything's packed right . . . Keeps the mule healthy . . . Make sure you treat 'em right . . . You don't want to be carrying all that stuff yourself . . . *Bene* . . . Your field cloaks . . . some guys like to roll them up and put 'em in a *saccus*, a cloak bag, and tie the bag to the cross piece . . . I'll let you in on a little trick . . . Wrap your cloak around the upright of the *furca,* right where it sits on your shoulder . . . That way, it'll cushion your shoulder a bit . . . Save the cloak bag for whatever fresh food you can scrounge, or if we get lucky, any swag we can pick up . . . While I'm thinking about it . . . even cushioned with a cloak, the *furca's* going to press the chainmail of your *lorica* down into your shoulder . . . After a couple of days on the march, you'll be in agony . . . So, when you're suiting up in the morning, slip some cloth, a towel if you got one, between the *lorica* and your *subarmalis* jacket on your left shoulder . . . What is it, Felix?"

"*Optio*! Why the left shoulder?"

"On the march, the *furca's* carried on your left shoulder. You'll hang your helmet on your lorica . . . You'll be carrying a *pilum* or two in your right hand," Bantus explained. "You guys are lucky . . . The Tenth marches light . . . In my old outfit, we each carried two *pila* and an entrenching stake on our right shoulders and had to strap our unit mess gear, digging baskets, and even extra darts for the *ballista* on our *furcae* . . . We were humping more stuff than the mules . . . That's why we were called *muli Marii* . . . Marius' mules. . . Your namesake invented the *furca*, Pagane."

"*Intelligo, Optio*," I said, not really knowing how to respond.

"*Bene*," Bantus concluded. "For our conditioning march tomorrow . . . ten thousand *passus* at first light . . . You'll march *impediti* . . . Fall in with your *furcae* packed and ready to go . . . We march under full kit . . . *lorica* and *galea* . . . but without shields and swords . . . We'll swing by the range on our way out, and each of you will pick up two practice *pila* . . . And remember to pad your left shoulders . . . We're in the field soon, and you don't want to start a campaign with a bum shoulder . . . It won't get any better . . . Any questions?"

Scattered responses of "*n'abeo.*"

"*Bene*," Bantus started. "Before I forget . . . another piece of *veterani* lore for you rookies . . . We'll be marching over the Alpine passes in a few days . . . It's still winter up there . . . colder than a centurion's heart . . . And the sun shining on the snow'll blind you . . . Scrounge yourself up a couple of extra *sudaria* . . . Use one to wrap around your head and ears . . . The cold up in them mountains'll freeze your ears off . . . I swear . . . Use the other scarf as a mask . . . Cut some narrow eye-holes in it . . . It'll keep you from going snow blind . . . Grease helps too . . . Rub some on your face and lips . . . It'll keep 'em from chapping . . . You guys getting this?"

Scattered mutterings of "*compre'endo.*"

"*Bene*," Bantus continued. "Collect up some money among yourselves and send Moelwyn down into the *vicus* . . . Have him buy you some woolen socks and some *manicae*, gloves, if there are any left to buy . . . If he can't get the gloves, you can cut finger holes in an extra pair of socks . . . Wear socks under your *caligae* . . . I've seen guys lose fingers and toes up in them high mountains . . . And each of you get a good, sturdy pair of leather *bracae* to wear underneath your tunics . . . What is it, Rufus?"

"*Optio*, are *bracae* authorized? They're *inromanitas*, un-Roman," protested Rufus.

Bantus chuckled, "Having your balls freeze off is un-Roman too, Rufus . . . We all wear 'em when it's cold . . . Only the patrician snobs, the purple-stripers up from Rome, worry about that being 'un-Roman' shit . . . Most of 'em have no balls to freeze off anyway . . . Their wives've already removed them . . . Get yourself each a good, solid pair of *bracae* . . . None of that Gallic wool shit with the colors and plaids . . . leather . . . They'll keep you warm up there in those passes . . . Any more questions?"

We had none.

"*Bene*," Bantus said getting up and looking around our tent. "This place looks like some drunken carpenter's workshop! Get it cleaned up before the start of the first watch! I'll be back to inspect."

I was lucky. The quartermaster still had the *bracae*, gloves, and socks I had turned in when I received my clothing issue. For a couple of *minervae*, Moelwyn was able to get them back for me through one of the slaves that worked in the supply tent. The rest of the guys had to compete with over four thousand other *muli* for the limited supply of leather trousers and woolen socks to be had in the *vicus* and in the town. Luckily, the civilians seemed to know months in advance where we'd be going and what we'd need to get there, so they had had some time to lay in a good supply—with which they were now happy to part for a prime price.

The evening before the *significatio*, the legionary *haruspex* pulled the liver out of a healthy, black goat and declared that its appearance indicated that the gods favored the acceptance of the trainees into the legion. Strabo could hardly conceal his skepticism and contempt when he told us this news.

Bantus seemed more terrified by his centurion's irreverence than relieved by the propitious omens.

Our *haruspex* was an *immunis* soldier from the Second *Centuria* of our own *cohors*, whose only qualification for the job seemed to be that he was born in a barn just outside the town of Veii and had black, curly hair like a genuine Etruscan. So, of course, everyone called him Crispus, "Curly."

The *haruspex'* job certainly did have its perks. He pulled down extra pay. On top of that, Crispus was not only exempt from all fatigue details, but he and his mates also got to keep most of the meat from the sacrificial animals. I later found out that Crispus had a healthy side business with the purple-stripers, who were known to slip him a *quadriga* or two so that he might claim to see propitious things in the entrails of chickens or the viscera of goats.

Strabo wondered out loud whether a cow farting in a northerly direction during the dark of the moon meant the gods were against long sea voyages. That made Bantus go pale. I rubbed my *Bona Fortuna* and spat. I made a note to myself that if we ever went into battle, I wouldn't stand too close to Strabo. I should have spat twice.

But, Strabo reported that the goat's liver was a healthy pink with a well-formed right lobe that was larger than the left lobe. So, the gods must be happy with what we had planned for the next day. That night, we anticipated our induction into the Tenth Legion and salivated over the aroma of roasted goat wafting over from a tent in the Second *Centuria*.

Bantus roused us before first light. He had us dress in our white trainee tunics, without belts. Carrying our newly dyed red tunics under our arms, he marched us toward the *Porta Principalis Dextra* of the camp. We were assembled just inside the gate in the *intervallum*. We were surprised to discover that we weren't the only ones being integrated into the legion that day. Organized into four *contubernia,* there stood almost thirty other *tirones* in white tunics. Although we could see nothing outside the walls of the camp, we could hear the stirrings and murmurings of a large gathering. When Bantus stood us at ease, I realized that, except for the guard detail manning the ramparts, the camp of the Tenth Legion was deserted. Bantus collected the red tunics from us and handed them over to a soldier who carried them out through the gate.

As the first glimmers of the sun began to glow faintly beyond the camp walls, a trumpet sounded in the field beyond. All movement outside the wall ceased. We heard commands shouted, the sound of metal and movement in unison, then silence. We were then called to attention by our officers and filed through the gate of the camp.

The sight that greeted us there is one I have never forgotten even to this very day.

To our right, the entire Tenth Legion was assembled in parade formation in full-dress kit. Ten cohorts formed a single rank, stretching off into the paling horizon, their centuries assembled in columns behind them. My first impression was of ranks upon ranks of ghostly Roman soldiers waiting for us to join them in the shadows. Nothing moved. Even the scarlet plumes on the legionaries' helmets were still in the darkling airs. From beneath the overhanging brows of bronze helmets, I felt the eyes of the over four thousand soldiers assembled on that silent plain, boring into us, measuring us, and assessing our worthiness to join their ranks.

In front of each cohort, a *centurio pilus prior* stood at attention. Their transverse crests radiated from polished bronze *galeae* like fiery red nimbuses. Combat decorations, suspended by leather harnesses on polished breastplates, caught the first faint glimmers of the new sun: gold and silver *torcs*; gold, silver, and bronze *phalerae* disks; and silver *hastae purae*, awarded to those who have blooded an enemy of Rome.

To the left of each centurion stood the cohort's signifer, a wolf's head pulled over a shining bronze *galea*. The *signum* of the cohort, an open, silver hand paying perpetual tribute to Father Iove, was held upright above the heads of the assembled soldiers.

Behind the command groups, the soldiers themselves stood silently behind a low wall of red shields, their bronzed bosses polished to a mirror finish, from which radiated the golden-yellow winged thunderbolts of Father Iove. Each shield displayed a rampant boar, the symbol of the Tenth Legion.

To our left, on a low, wooden platform, stood the golden *aquila* of the legion, the sign of Father Iove, the totem of the legion, the spirit of its resolve. Beneath the golden eagle, the *vexillium rubrum*, the red flag of the legion, hung in the still air. I could clearly see the image of the rampant boar and the symbols LEG X.

To the eagle's right, the *aquilifer*, the legionary entrusted with the *anima* of the legion, its very spirit, stood as a silent sentinel. Next to him, I recognized Tertius Piscius Malleus, "The Hammer," *primus pilus* of the Tenth Legion, with the leaves of a Civic Crown, the highest award for valor bestowed by the Roman nation, entwined into the red traverse crest of his helmet.

In front of the platform was set a row of legionary *scuta*, red oval shields identical to those held by the soldiers of the legion. Against each leaned a sheathed *gladius*, the infantry sword, with its baldric draped over the shield. In front of each of these was a folded, red tunic.

Before the *aquila*, praying over a sensor that misted the golden standard and the red pennant of the legion in clouds of sweet-smelling incense, stood a man, his pure white toga covering his head.

As we drew closer, the words of his chant became clear to me:

Divum empta cante,
Divum deo supplicate,
Cume tonas, Leucesie,
Prae tet tremonti.

I remembered the *magister* telling me that Roman priests spoke to the gods in an obscure tongue, an archaic Latin, a language no one now understood. The priests had to recite these chants verbatim, without error, or a terrible curse would be incurred.

Quot ibet etinei de is,
Cum tonarem osculo dolori ero,
Omnia vero adpatula coemisse.

We were filed before the standing shields to face the priest hovering above us on the platform. The commands of our officers were hushed, awed. The incense began to swirl around us. Behind us, I could feel the presence of thousands of silent men, watching.

Ian cusianes duonus,
Ceruses dunus Ianusve,
Vet pom melios eum recum.

The hooded priest in the white toga raised his hands to the sky, speaking in a loud voice:

Cume tonas, Leucesie,

Prae tet tremonti

Quom tibi cunei

Decstumum tonaront.

He bent over the brazier and whispered something I could not hear.

Then, the priest turned toward the assembled legion and removed the hood from his head. In a loud voice, he proclaimed, "Father Iove has heard the prayer, has heard it sanctified in the sacred name of Rome, and accepts your petition! Let these acolytes join your ranks as his soldiers!"

From behind us, thousands thundered in one voice, "*Fiat! Fiat! Fiat!* Let it be!"

I looked up at the priest. He wasn't that tall, but his long, slender body gave the impression of height. The hair behind his receding hairline was sandy brown, sparse, and graying. His forehead was broad, descending into thin eyebrows. His eyes were blue, piercing, and cold. His nose was thin and prominent. His mouth a black line slashed across his face. His appearance gave the impression of a dangerous weapon: a slender, razor-sharp *sica*.

Malleus, the first spear, stepped forward to the edge of the platform and commanded, "*Legio!*"

Behind me, I heard echoing commands, "*Cohors!*"

Then Malleus, "*Imperatorem . . . Adclamate!*"

Thunder from behind me, "*Ave, Imperator! Ave, Imperator! Ave, Imperator!*"

"*Ave, Imperator?*" This priest was Caesar himself! Our commander! The *pontifex maximus* of the Roman nation.

Caesar inclined his head slightly in response to the legion's acclamation. He turned, nodded to Malleus, and left the platform.

Malleus waited while Caesar mounted a white horse that was being held by a legionary behind the platform. Then, he rode off toward the town. After that, the *primus pilus*, in a theatrically loud voice, asked Strabo, who was standing behind our file, "*Centurio!* Do you attest before the eagle that these *tirones* have successfully completed their training and are ready to be welcomed into the ranks of this legion as *milites Romani*?"

"*Confirmo!*" I heard Strabo's voice from behind our rank.

"*Legio!*" the Primus Pilus continued. "These *tirones* have completed their training. Will you accept them into your ranks as soldiers of Rome?"

"*Fiat!*" thundered the voice of the legion.

"*Tirones!*" the Hammer addressed us. "Remove the white tunic of the acolyte and assume the red tunic of a soldier of Rome."

We hesitated, not sure what to do. I heard Bantus' voice hiss, "Strip!" We did, down to our loincloths.

Again, I heard Bantus: "Put on the red tunics!"

I stepped forward, picked up the tunic in front of me, and threw it on over my head. After a few heartbeats, our entire file settled down.

"*Milites*," Malleus continued, "assume the weapons of a Roman soldier!"

Again, I stepped forward. I picked up the sword. I threw the baldric over my head and put my right arm through it so the sword was positioned on my right hip. Then, I picked up the shield, threading my left forearm through the leather support strap and grasping the leather grip. I stepped back into line with the rest of my *contubernales*. For the first time, I could feel the weight of the sword pressing on my shoulder and against my hip, and I could smell the fresh leather from the bands of my new shield. I grasped the pommel of the sword with my right hand.

Malleus told us, "*Milites!* Raise your right hands open to the eagle and repeat after me."

I did, and again I repeated the words of the *sacramentum* in front of my new comrades:

I, Gaius Marius Insubrecus Tertius, do solemnly swear by Father Iove, greatest and all powerful, whose eagle I now follow, and by all the gods, that I will defend and serve the Roman nation. I will obey the will of the Senate, the people of Rome, and the officers empowered by the Senate over me, and my general, Gaius Iulius Caesar, *Imperator*. I swear that I am a free man, able to take this oath, and obligated by bond or debt to no Roman. I will remain faithful to the Roman people, the Senate, to the officers empowered over me, to the army of Rome, and to the Tenth Legion until legally discharged by my time of service, by the will of the Senate and People of Rome, by the will of my general, Gaius Iulius Caesar, *Imperator*, or by my death. I offer my life as the surety of my oath.

Then, the *primus pilus* commanded, "*Milites! Contra . . . VERT!*"
When we were facing the legion, Malleus acclaimed, "*Infantes! Salvete novos!*"
The legion thundered, "*Salvete! Salvete! Salvete!*"
When the echoes of the acclamation had died, Malleus commanded, "*Centurio Strabo! Miss'est!*"
Strabo ordered:
"*Ad Dex' . . . VERT!*"
"*Promov . . . ET!*"
"*Dex' . . . Dex' . . . Dex', Sin', Dex!*"
"Pick up your feet, Pagane!"
"Right . . . Right . . . Right, Left, Right!"
"Get in step, Lentulus!"
"*Dex' . . . Dex!*"

When we got back to our tent, we were energized by the ceremony, our *significatio*. The cry of "*salvete*" by the thousands of our new comrades rang in our ears. And, Caesar *Imperator* was here among us. Caesar himself! Something was about to happen, something big. We were part of it; we were finally wearing the red infantry tunics of the Tenth Legion. We were soldiers of Rome.

I sat on the edge of my bunk, my new *gladius* across my knees. I loved the substantial feel of its weight in my hands. I pulled it partially out of its sheath; it slid out smoothly and silently. For a moment, I felt I was violating it. As the light coming in through the tent flap enflamed its edges to glowing white, I knew it had been honed razor sharp, and it was mine. *Miles Romanus*, a *mulus*, a grunt in the Tenth Legion, the best legion in Caesar's army—in any army—and I was part of it.

Bantus burst into our tent. Loquax saw him and tried to call us to attention, "*Ad, Pedes!*"

Bantus told us to be at ease, *laxate,* "You're soldiers . . . You don't have to bounce to your feet for an *optio.*"

"Boys, I got some good news for you and some other news, so listen up," he started. "Let me give you the good news first! As soon as you get your quarters squared away, you have a pass to leave the camp . . . Go up to the town, have a few drinks, celebrate your *significatio* . . . You worked hard . . . You deserve it. Uniform's tunics and belts . . . Wear your *pugiones* . . . That's so these sorry civilians know you're Roman soldiers . . . Be back here by the first call for night watch . . . Other than that . . . go relax for a couple hours . . . Enjoy yourselves!"

We all sat there stunned, silent. Since we had reported over two months before, we had not had a moment off, had not been outside the camp walls, except for training. "Have a few drinks . . . Celebrate . . . You deserve it." Bantus could have said it in Greek, and it wouldn't have sounded more foreign to us.

Finally, Rufus broke the silence, "*Mammis Veneris*! It's about time!"

I snapped him with the end of my *sudarium* before he could continue.

"*Tacet*! *Tacet*!" Bantus interrupted. "Settle down! Let me tell you the other news before the celebrations begin."

We settled down to listen.

"*Bene.*" Bantus continued, "We have orders to break camp and move out the day after tomorrow. We're headed for *Gallia* with the army."

Mutterings around the squad bay: "*Mercule!*" "*Cacat!*"

"Settle down!" Bantus continued. "There's been a fight up near Gennava . . . The Eighth held the barbarians off, and they retreated back over the Rhodanus . . . The general wants us up there quick . . . so he'll be running our asses off to get there . . . You guys are goin' to stay together as a *contubernium* in the Tenth Cohort—at least until we get over to *Gallia Transalpina*, Gaul-Over-The-Alps . . . We're bringing Tulli back to be your *decanus* . . . He'll be moving in with you guys tonight."

We were a bit shocked: a fight near Gennava; got to get up there quick. It was starting to hit us that we were going into combat, going up into *Gallia comata*, a place of nightmares and cold, dark forests, with giant savages screaming for Roman blood. I felt my hand tightening on the hilt of my new sword. Somehow it didn't seem as substantial as it had only moments before.

Bantus was talking, "Before you guys head to town, go by supply and draw your *tegimenta*, your shield covers . . . Got to keep those nice, new shields bright and shiny to impress those hordes of hairy barbarians you'll be meeting soon . . . Get this place squared away before you leave . . . Oh, yeah . . . before I forget . . . Scratch your initials or your sign somewhere on your sword hilt or near the bottom of the blade . . . They all look alike after a while."

IV.

De Itinere inter Alpes

WE MARCH ACROSS THE ALPS

Bantus was wrong. We didn't leave camp the next day, the day of Mars, or even the day after that, Mercury's day. It was Iove's day before the *augur*, the *haruspex*, and priest all agreed it was *faustus*, propitious to march. Rumor had it that Caesar *Imperator* was fuming, but as superstitious as soldiers are, even he did not dare to initiate a campaign without the favor of the gods. Rumor also had it that the delay had something to do with Crispus' girlfriend in the town.

Bantus just shrugged and repeated the age-old wisdom of the Roman army: "*Festina lente* . . . Hurry up and wait!"

When we did leave, the general had us hotfooting down the road at the double, thirty to forty thousand *passus* a day, *impedimenti*, loaded down like the *muli* we were. Bantus told us the mountain passes would slow us down, and we might have some trouble with the highland tribes, a bunch of thieving brigands who notoriously showed no respect for the Roman *imperium*, so we had to go as fast as we could while we were on flat ground in "friendly" territory. Although the march to *Gallia* normally took an army marching *expediti*, unburdened with a supply train, over thirty days, the general was determined to have us in position along the Rhodanus in less than twenty.

The first day out we passed through Patavis; by the second, Vicetia had seen our backs; the third day, we marched around Verona, where we had been snowed in last *Ianuarius*.

Despite being in "friendly" territory within the *Imperium Romanum*, each night we dug a marching camp. Most of our mates in the *centuria* were *immunes*, exempt from fatigue details, so they went off to perform whatever duties they had, while the rest of us dug and piled dirt. Our assignment was a portion of the *fossa et vallum*, the ditch and the rampart, to the right of the *Porta Decumana*, the rear portal of the camp. By the time we were done and the *sudes*, the entrenching stakes, were lashed together and in place, the baggage train was pulling in through the gate we had just constructed.

Moelwyn had our tent erected in its assigned place, but we had little time for it. Our *contubernium* was assigned sentry duty on the rampart to the right of the gate, and since most of our mates were exempt from that too, we had one watch on, one watch off, through the night. At the first glimmer of dawn, we pulled everything down. The entrenching stakes went back on the mule, and the dirt ramparts were pulled down into the ditch, filling it. Entrenching baskets went back on the mule with the squad tent Moelwyn had pulled down. *Dolabrae*, our entrenching tools, were cleaned and strapped to our *furcae*. Then, back on the road, double-time, we truly understood what it meant to be a *mulus Romanus*.

Along the paved military roads, we marched four abreast at the rear of our cohort, which marched at the rear of the legion. So, *furca* on the left shoulder, *pilum* in the right hand, we ate the dust stirred up by over four thousand pairs of *caligae* and a few hundred horses and mules. About every five or six thousand *passus*, we got a break and a couple of mouthfuls of water to wash down a piece of *buccellatum*. Then, back on the road, double-time, about a thousand *passus*, regular pace for a thousand more, and then back to the double.

We double-timed through Brixia, camped near Bergomum, and passed north of Mediolanum. I remember looking to the south. There was a slight smudge of smoke marking where the city lay. I wondered briefly what Mama was doing at that very moment, whether she was thinking of me.

In camp that evening, Tulli told us that we'd cross the mountains near a tiny piss-ant town called Ocelum, where the pass opened that would bring us through to *Gallia*, south of Gennava. Rufus and I were boiling up some porridge. We didn't have to be on the ramparts until second watch. We hoped to fill our bellies and get a couple of hours of sleep before that. Despite the extra padding where I carried the *furca*, my shoulder was aching. I hoped it wouldn't keep me awake, but after humping over thirty-five thousand *passus* that day, once I wrapped myself up in my woolen cloak, I doubted Hannibal and all his elephants could keep me awake.

Tulli had told us that once we got up into the mountain passes, all bets were off as to how many *passus* we made each day. Snow drifts, avalanches, bandits—we'd have to get through all that *merda* to get to *Gallia*. In the mountains, our cohort would be detailed with securing the *impedimenta*, the baggage train. The good news was that we could dump our packs in a wagon and march *expediti*, with just combat gear. The other news was that if the wagons got stuck, we were expected to "unstick" them, so we'd better keep our shovels and digging picks handy. The bad news was that the baggage train attracted bandits like a tavern attracts drunks. So, we'd better keep our shields, swords, and *pila* close at hand—even when we were digging some teamster out of a snow drift.

We pulled into Ocelum during the fifth hour of the sixth day of the march. It wasn't much of a place, more goats than people. The Seventh and Ninth Legions were already encamped in the valley. The Eleventh and Twelfth were strung out a couple of hours behind us. The Alps stood before us like a wall of snow-covered granite. As we were marching down into the valley where we would dig our marching camp, I shivered as I noticed the looming mountains still covered with snow.

After we dug our *castrum*, we spent most of the afternoon on our butts. When Bantus arrived at our tent, we were blissfully racked out, bellies full. He roused us for a quick briefing.

Things over in *Gallia Transalpina* were developing quickly. After being repulsed at Gennava by the Eighth Legion, the Helvetii withdrew west, down the Rhodanus through some narrow passes in the Iura mountains. Roman allies in *Gallia*, tribes called the Sequani and the Aedui, were now directly in the path of the Helvetian horde. That, and the Helvetii being such a threat to the most fertile lands of the Roman *provincia* just across the river, was unacceptable to Caesar *Imperator*. Our objective, then, was to stop the Helvetii and force them to return to their homeland, where they would continue to serve as a buffer between *Gallia*, our *provincia*, and the German barbarians east of the Rhenus.

The goal of our march was no longer just to reach Gennava, but our goal was to reach the Helvetii themselves.

Later that afternoon, Strabo called the *centuria* together to give us our marching orders. There were only about fifty of us assembled. Many of our *immunes* soldiers were off on various details around the *castrum*.

"The army'll move out tomorrow morning at the second hour and pass through the Alps in a column of legions," Strabo began. "Caesar *Imperator* is interspacing the new legions with the veterans. The Seventh will lead out, followed by the Eleventh . . . then the Ninth, followed by the Twelfth . . . We'll take up the rear."

Strabo paused to see if there were any questions. There were none, so he continued, "The Seventh will move out at the second hour, but the Eleventh won't follow until the fourth hour . . . Yeah . . . What it is?"

I heard a voice from the back of the formation ask why the delay for the Eleventh.

Strabo responded, "The Seventh will have to do most of the route clearance through the passes, and if any of those mountain tribes decide to kick up a fuss, the boys in the Seventh will have that to take care of, too. So, there'll be delays . . . stop and go . . . especially in the narrow passes . . . The general doesn't want us to bunch up . . . The Eleventh will probably catch up to the Seventh anyway . . . The general wants them far enough back so both legions won't be caught in the same ambush, but close enough so they can support each other . . . Besides, the Seventh is marching *expediti* . . . light and ready for combat . . . Their baggage train'll be moving with the Eleventh . . . Any other questions?"

When Strabo mentioned ambushes and marching "combat ready," I felt a stirring in my belly, almost a weakness in my legs. That was it; we were going into a fight.

Strabo continued, "After the Eleventh moves out, the rest of the legions will depart at one-hour intervals . . . The Ninth at the fifth hour . . . the Twelfth at the sixth . . . then us at the seventh. The *equites*, the legionary cavalry, will be positioned between the legions so it can coordinate communication and maintain the marching intervals . . . I doubt those horses'll be much use in the high passes . . . Their mobility will be limited . . . A real shame, cavalry having to walk . . . We should anticipate delays during the march . . . stop and go as we move through the mountains. The cavalry's supposed to coordinate our spacing so we don't bunch up or get too far behind."

Strabo repeated that our departure time was the seventh hour the next day. Then, he concluded, "We'll march in a column of cohorts . . . The first-line cohorts, the First through the Fourth, will be our *primum agmen*, the vanguard . . . The Fifth and Sixth Cohorts, from the second line, will act as our *novissimum agmen*, the rear guard. Our cohort is detailed to guard the legion's baggage train, which'll follow the Ninth cohort out."

Still no questions, so Strabo continued, "Caesar *Imperator*, will be marching with the point legion, the Seventh, along with most of his party. The *primus pilus*, Malleus, is commanding our legion on this march. He'll be with his *centuria* in the First Cohort. The general hasn't assigned a *legatus legionis*, a legionary commander, to us yet, and we won't be dragging any wet-behind-the-ears, somebody's-wife's-cousin, Patrician brats as military tribunes with us." Some snickers come from the back of the formation. "So, the good news, we don't have to drag wagons full of their useless shit over the Alps." Some guffaws this time. "The other news is we can't help ourselves to their wine and *garum* supplies." Some theater groans. "So that's about it . . . Any questions?"

There were none, so Strabo dismissed us back to our tents.

We didn't have any duties until guard mount that evening. Since we weren't going to drag any livestock over the Alps with us, except for the *contubernium* mules and the cavalry horses, Malleus had ordered the cooks to brew up a feast for us. We could smell the aroma of the roasting meat and baking bread wafting over from the cook tents in the middle of the *castrum*. Meanwhile, in the age-old tradition of the Roman infantry, we decided to crap out until chow time.

Tulli, our *decanus*, seemed determined to talk to us, however.

"We caught a break on this one, guys!" he started.

"*Quómo?*" Rufus mumbled, half-asleep.

"Think about it," Tulli lectured. "The Seventh has to do all the heavy lifting on this one . . . clearing the passes and taking care of any barbarians stupid enough to get in our way . . . By the time we go through the passes, the route'll be clear, and there won't be a single, living *podex* for miles to mess with us."

"Makes sense," Loquax mumbled from somewhere deep in his woolen cloak.

"Sure it does," continued Tulli, not wanting to let go of it. "And, we get to march with the baggage train . . . That means no faster than the slowest cart . . . and we march *expediti* . . . just swords, shields, and one *pilum* each . . . The rest of our equipment can go on one of the carts . . . Except for the cold and having to push a cart or two up a steep incline, this'll be a piece of cake."

Tulli was begging *Fortuna* to screw us. I should have rubbed my amulet and spit, but I decided just to turn over and go to sleep instead.

The next day, getting the army moving was a complete cluster, and we didn't cross the line of departure until well into the eighth hour. Tulli's assessment seemed right, though. We were marching light, with troops in front of us and to our rear. The oxen pulling the supply carts didn't seem to be in any hurry to get up into the mountain passes. Tulli said when we get over into *Gallia*, the baggage will move independently of the legions, so we can move quickly. But, if we tried that up in the passes, the mountain tribes would steal the hooves off the horses.

That first day the climb wasn't bad, but we only made about ten thousand *passus*. We camped next to a small mountain river in a narrow, ascending valley. By the time we pulled in with the *impedimenta*, the camp was already constructed—another benefit, Tulli winked—so all we had to do was settle the baggage in and pull our guard shifts that first night.

The next morning, the legion was up and moving before the fourth watch was over. We continued to climb. By the fourth hour, we passed through some piss-ant village of stone and lumber huts. It was abandoned. No fires burning.

Even the livestock was gone. By the sixth hour, we swung west and north, still following a mountain river upwards. Four more hours found us at the junction of two streams: one flowing down from the north; the other, the one we seemed to be following, still led toward the northwest.

We halted there. When we realized that this wasn't just a break from the march, our *centurio pilus prior*, Gelasius, the cohort commander, deployed four of our *centuriae* on the uphill side of the baggage train, and the remaining two, including us, on the downhill side. Eventually, the word came down that there was some sort of delay up ahead. After being in position for almost an hour, we even began to imagine that we'd spend the night there. No sooner had we entertained that hope than the column started moving again.

We continued to climb. The twelfth hour came and went. I estimated we had at least thirty thousand *passus* under our boots. The sun went down, and we still continued to climb. We stumbled up the incline, starting, stopping, and starting again. Finally, the word came down we were staying put where we were for the night. No camp. Since we were headed uphill, Gelasius deployed two centuries forward, one century to the rear, and split the rest of us equally on both sides of the baggage. He ordered "half and half" for the night—one man slept while the other kept watch. Strabo broke us down into shifts by *contubernia*.

It was starting to get cold in the passes. Gelasius forbade the building of fires. He said it would silhouette our positions for any enemies up in the hills. He had a bit of difficulty convincing some of the civilian teamsters. But, after he emphasized his orders with a liberal application of his *vitis*, the centurion's vine cudgel, the rest fell quickly into line. Most of us had broken out our *bracae* trousers and woolen socks. Still, I was shivering so hard, it was difficult getting to sleep. I was almost grateful when I was roused up for guard duty because it gave me a chance to move around and warm up a bit.

We were moving before sunrise the next morning. When the sun finally came up, I could see we were marching directly up toward a huge mountain. The rising sun behind our backs was changing the snow on the mountain's flanks from a glowing blue to a pale white.

Tulli caught up with me. "That's *Alba Magna*," he said. "Don't look at it. You'll go blind. Here!" He offered me what seemed to be a burned-out lamp.

"Rub the soot around your eyes and on your cheekbones . . . It'll cut down the glare."

I had no idea how a snow-covered mountain could make me blind, but I did as Tulli suggested. "If that doesn't seem to help . . . if you feel your eyes get dry or they start to hurt . . . tie a *sudarium* around your face like a mask . . . In a couple of hours, we'll be turning south, so the mountain will be over your shoulder."

As we continued to climb toward *Alba Magna*, the sun rising behind us set the mountain ablaze like a brilliant, white flame. I found that even with the lamp soot around my eyes and the scarf tied up around my face, I couldn't look at it. I grabbed the tailgate of one of our carts and let it lead me up the pass while I kept my eyes fixed on the ground to keep from tripping.

Tulli was right about one thing. The legions marching ahead of us had cleared the passes. Our path was free of snow and rubble. We hadn't seen a native since we left Eporedia.

By the fifth hour, I thought we had reached the top of the pass at the foot of *Alba Magna*, but we turned south and continued to climb. The mountain was now on our flank, and the sun was no longer at our backs. I was able to see again. My eyes felt like they were full of sand—a bit achy, but I was able to see.

The air in the pass was still, but frigid. It was colder up here in *Aprilis* than it was down in the valley in the middle of winter. My breath steamed out of my mouth and nostrils like mama's kettle on a cold morning. We were allowed to march without our helmets, so I had the hood of my cloak up over my head and a *sudarium* wrapped around my ears. I had pulled my woolen socks up and stuffed the bottoms of my leather *bracae* down into them, so no part of my legs was exposed.

Still we climbed; still it seemed to get colder.

We topped the pass by the seventh hour. I could swear we had twenty thousand *passus* of climbing under our belts since we started out before dawn. But, I was glad to be moving in that cold. Now that we seemed to be on the downhill side and headed into warmer temperatures, I was happy that we were pushing on.

Bantus, our *optio*, came down the line of march. "Another ten thousand *passus* before our day's done, boys," he announced. "The valley opens up down below . . . That's where we'll spend the night . . . The First Cohort boys should have the camp all set up for us by the time we get there . . . hot chow and a warm tent . . . It's all downhill . . . so hang in."

We made it into camp after nightfall. The little valley seemed more like a hole that the gods had blasted between the mountains. There was high ground all around us. It was warmer than the pass, but not much. Since we were in a fortified camp, we were allowed to build fires. Somehow, the first cohorts in camp had managed some hot chow and warmed *posca*, which was waiting for us when we corralled the baggage train. I couldn't remember ever drinking anything as comforting as that steaming cup of *posca*.

Later that night, when I took my turn on the ramparts, a cold wind was blowing down out of the pass from the northeast, the frigid breath of *Alba Magna*. I saw some fires glowing about two thousand paces across the valley to the southwest. When I asked about it, I was told that it was the camp of the Eleventh Legion. Where the rest of the army was that night, we had no idea.

The next morning, we didn't move out until the first hour of the day. Malleus had decided to give the Eleventh a head start down the next pass. But soon, we too were descending down the narrow valley behind them. Tulli was still feeling good about the whole thing. A few more zigs and zags, but it was all downhill from here, as far as he was concerned.

That day's march seemed to prove him right. The passes and gorges were narrow, but the leading legions had done a good job clearing the route of the march. We did over thirty thousand *passus* and arrived in another little valley at nightfall. There, we got our first indication that things would be different on this side of the Alps. There had been a village near the intersection of two small rivers. What people did to stay alive so far up in the mountains was anybody's guess, but whatever it was, it was no longer a concern for the people who had lived here. The village was destroyed, burned out. When we arrived, the ashes were cold, but we could still smell the odor of wet, burnt lumber and thatch. There were no bodies. Perhaps whoever had lived here had escaped.

"My guess is this is the work of the boys in the Seventh," Tulli said as we marched past.

"Why'd they do it?" I asked.

"Who knows?" Tulli answered with a shrug. "Don't see any bodies, so I guess most of them are up in the hills. They must have done something to piss off the general."

The next morning, we followed a river descending toward the northwest. Around the third hour, we passed another burned-out village. Again, the fires were long out and the ashes cold.

We were about two thousand *passus* beyond the village when the column came to sudden halt. We didn't think too much of it until we heard a *cornu*, a signaling trumpet at the head of our column, calling, "*Ad Signa!*" I immediately heard Strabo's voice repeating the call to fall in and spotted our century's standard raised on the other side of the baggage train. We quickly assembled around the standard, and Strabo called us to attention. We waited, but there were no more trumpet calls. Strabo had us stand easy and check our combat equipment.

I was just deciding that this was some kind of drill, when Gelasius, our cohort commander, arrived to brief Strabo. After the two centurions finished talking, Strabo came over to talk to us.

"Seems there's a roadblock set up in front of the column," Strabo said. "Must've gone up after the Eleventh passed through and before we arrived, so it's deliberate . . . Not sure what's going on . . . The natives are probably trying to pick off a wagon or two . . . The valley opens up about two thousand *passus* farther down the road, so this is their last chance to get to us . . . The First Cohort's clearing the road, and then we'll be moving . . . Meanwhile, we're going to move straight toward that line of spruce and pine trees to see if any of them *mentulae* are hiding in there . . . The Third Century will stay close to the *impedimenta* and support us if we need it."

We had already assembled in the basic combat formation, a ten-man front at normal intervals with the *contubernia* in column, so Strabo marched us straight forward, toward the tree line. I was positioned in the front rank with Minutus behind me as my *geminus*. The rest of our *contubernium* was in file behind us. I could see Strabo and our *signifer* marching on the right flank of our first rank. I knew Bantus and our *tesserarius*, a legionary everybody called Brevis because he was almost six *pedes* tall, would be to our rear.

As we got closer, I noticed that the trees to our immediate front receded a bit and the ground in front of them dipped, creating the semblance of an amphitheater with the evergreen forest on three sides. Strabo halted us before we entered the low ground. There didn't seem to be any movement in the trees. Despite that, Strabo decided to gain width and sacrifice depth. He ordered us to open our intervals, and he doubled the *contubernia* front. Now I had Tulli, our *decanus*, on my left, with Rufus backing him up. The *centuria* now had a twenty-man front, but we were only four men deep.

Strabo ordered us to stand at ease.

We waited. Nothing happened. No enemy appeared to our front. No recall back to the line of march sounded.

I heard someone behind me mutter, "Another goat rope!" A few guys guffawed at that. Strabo must have heard, but he said nothing.

Suddenly, we heard a *cornu* at the head of the column signal, "First Cohort," then, "Advance!"

Then we heard calls for the Fifth and Sixth Cohorts at the rear of the column.

Still we waited. But, nothing for us.

Then, one of our guys near the left flank yelled, "*Centurio!* Movement in the trees!"

I looked down the column and saw the man pointing with his *pilum*. I looked toward where he was pointing. At first I saw nothing. Then, as my eyes adjusted to the gloom under the evergreens, I saw movement. Men. Dozens of them. They began to come out of the forest in front of us. They weren't armored like us. Most of them seemed wrapped in animal firs. I could see no swords, no spears. I couldn't understand how such a rabble could be any threat to us.

Strabo was walking across our front, slightly down the incline. Without taking his eyes off the enemy, he called us to attention, "*Centurio . . . State!*"

The enemy remained well out of *pilum* range. There was now a mass of a couple of hundred of them, standing just outside the tree line. They made no attempt to advance on us. Then, a few dozen of them ran forward, twirling something over their heads.

Strabo screamed, "*Scuta . . . Erigit!*"

No sooner did we raise our shields to cover our heads and bodies, than sling-bullets rained down on us. We had taken two or three volleys to no effect when one of the legionaries on the left shouted a warning, "*Centurio*! Flank! Left!"

I stole a peek around my shield and saw the enemy working their way through the trees on our left flank. Then, from our right, I heard, "*Centurio*! *Hostes a' dex*!"

The slingers were trying to hold us in place while their mates got around our flanks. If they got some slingers on our right, our open side, they could do some damage.

Strabo had to pull the *centuria* back. If he pulled back quickly, he would expose us to the slingers to our front. If he withdrew slowly, the enemy might get around on our exposed flank.

"*Centurio*! *Ad testudinem*! Form the turtle!" Strabo commanded.

The extended ranks withdrew backward, shields up, and fell in at the rear of their *contubernia*. The *contubernia* side-stepped to a close interval. Front and flank shields came up and interlocked, forming a wall around three sides of the century. The legionaries in the interior of the formation lifted their shields over their heads and locked them to form a roof.

We waited. The command to withdraw didn't come.

Where was Strabo?

I peeked around my shield. He was down! He was on his hands and knees in the grass. His helmet was off. He was bleeding from his nose and from his head.

"Centurion down!" I shouted.

I heard Bantus' voice from the rear, "*Centuria* . . . take my command! *Ad tergum* . . . *It*! Backstep . . . MARCH!"

As we began to backstep out of the trap, I again looked and saw about six of the enemy running across the field toward Strabo.

Without thinking, I broke the formation and ran down into the bowl toward my centurion. When I reached him, the first of the barbarians was well within *pilum* range. I let loose! The weighted spear hurtled forward, taking the man full in the face. I drew my sword. I sensed another *pilum* fly from behind me and saw it bury itself in a barbarian's chest. I glanced back quickly to see that my *geminus*, Minutus, had followed me.

The four remaining enemy were almost on top of us. The closest raised a knife. Without thinking, I stepped forward and delivered a *percussus* with the boss of my shield. My *umbo* made contact. I heard the man's neck break. I stepped forward with a sword thrust, and the next man impaled himself on my *gladius*. His momentum pushed me back. I couldn't withdraw my sword from his abdomen. Minutus moved around my right side. He took the next barbarian with his shield. The man literally flew backward as the *umbo* of Minutus' shield smashed into his head.

Then, it was over.

The sixth man, seeing his five mates killed so quickly, was having none of it. He fled back to the mass of barbarians at the edge of the forest. They seemed to hover there for a few heartbeats. Then, they began to melt back into the trees.

For a few heartbeats, all I could hear was the sound of my own breathing. I looked around me. Two barbarians lay dead, pinned to the grass with our *pila*. Another man lay in front of me, his head at an impossible angle. Another had a face that was a mass of blood and shattered bone. A fifth man was on the ground, screaming and trying to keep his guts from pouring out of his belly. Minutus relieved him of his agony with a quick thrust into his throat.

I could still hear moaning. Then, I remembered. Strabo! The centurion was sitting upright on the ground, holding his head. Blood was pouring down his head over his right ear. I spotted his helmet on the ground next to him. There was a dimple, the size of a baby's fist, above the right cheek guard.

Our *centuria* had halted about a fifty paces away. They were out of the turtle and standing in the standard formation.

"*Capsarius!*" I shouted. "I need a medic! Man down!"

Minutus walked up and dropped our two *pila* on the ground. "Not even bent," he observed.

I looked up toward our *centuria*. They were still stationary, but Bantus was striding toward us. I imagined for a moment that he was going to congratulate me, maybe I'd get a decoration—at least a silver torc.

When he got to where I was standing, he said, "*Miles!* Remove your helmet!"

I didn't know what he meant.

Again, he ordered, "I told you to take off your shaggin' helmet, *Podex!*"

Quickly, I fumbled with the bindings under my chin. I removed my *galea*.

No sooner did I have it off than Bantus slugged me on the jaw. I fell on my ass next to Strabo.

"*Sta, miles!*" Bantus shouted at me. "Get back up on your feet, soldier! Get your helmet back on!"

While I was sitting on the ground, searching for my helmet, the *capsarius* arrived. He looked at the two legionaries sitting on the ground and asked, "We got two casualties?"

"Just the centurion!" Bantus snapped. "Get on your feet, Insubrecus!"

I got up and put my helmet back on and laced it up. Bantus wasn't done with me.

"You stupid son of a whore! You never break formation!!" He continued to shout in my face, "Never! For no reason! You break formation, you endanger your mates . . . the entire *centuria* . . . I don't care if your mother's being raped by a cohort of hairy Krauts right in front of you! You *do not break formation*! Do you understand me, you shit?"

"*Compre'endo, Optio!*" I snapped.

While Bantus was ripping me to shreds, Spina, the *medicus*, arrived on the scene. He bent down over Strabo and ran his fingers over the centurion's skull. "*Bene,*" he muttered to himself. "Skull's in one piece."

"Centurion! What day is it?" Spina asked Strabo.

Strabo just stared up at Spina.

Meanwhile, Bantus was "fixing" me: "Breaking formation in contact with the enemy . . . You could suffer *fustuarium* for that . . . Do you want to be beaten to death? Did you know that, *stulte*? What you got going for you is only that you ran *toward* the enemy and gutted three of the bastards! And, you may have saved your officer's life . . . but that's no excuse for what you did . . . *Compre'endis me, miles?*"

"Excuse me, *Optio,*" Spina interrupted.

"*Qui' vis tu, Medice?*" Bantus turned.

"I need tah move dah centurion hee'ah back to my wagon, so's I can treat 'im," Spina explained. "Could I borrow a couple a ya guys hee'ah to help?"

"Of course, *Medice*," Bantus responded. "Brevis! Detail a couple of the boys to help the doctor here!"

"*A'mperi'tu', Optio!*" I heard Brevis respond.

Suddenly, Gelasius, our cohort commander, arrived on the scene. He saw Strabo on the ground and the *capsarius* bandaging his head. Then, he looked at the dead barbarians lying in the grass.

Ignoring Spina and me, he asked, "What's going on, Bantus?"

"*Centurio!*" Bantus reported. "This bunch of *mentulae* tried to rush the wagons . . . We stopped them . . . Strabo was hit by a sling-bullet."

"*Tota?*" Gelasius asked examining the reddening welt on my jaw. "That it?"

Bantus hesitated for a few heartbeats, then said, "*Tota, Centurio!*"

Gelasius gave him a long look. Then he turned to ask Spina, "How's Strabo, *Medice?*"

"Don' know, Centurion," Spina answered. "May just be a *concussus*, but head injuries aw tricky. I wanna get 'im back to my wagon."

Gelasius grunted and said, "Carry on, *Medice!*"

He took one last look at the dead raiders and turned to Bantus, "*Bene gesta, Optio!* I'll need your after-action report when we get into camp tonight. You have the *centuria* until Strabo gets back on his feet!"

"*A'mperi'tu', Centurio,*" Bantus responded.

As soon as Gelasius was out of hearing range, Bantus hissed at me, "I just saved you, Pagane! Don't forget it! You saved Strabo's bacon . . . a life for a life, eh . . . And don't forget what I told you about breaking formation . . . You try that shit again, and I'll beat you to death myself . . . Now get your sorry ass out of my sight!"

I double-timed back to the *centuria* with Minutus in my wake.

The column started moving again at the sixth hour. Soon, we turned southwest down a wide, fertile valley. Here, there was no sign of war. There was a town at the head of the valley, rather large and prosperous for the region, totally unfortified. In the fields there were cattle, who watched us pass with total indifference. We saw some people, too. None of them seemed the least concerned by the presence of a Roman legion in their valley.

We moved into camp at the eleventh hour. The legion had hot rations waiting for us: a hot stew of pork and vegetables with fresh bread and plenty of *posca*. Before the first watch of the night, Bantus briefed us that this was the valley of a Gallic tribe called the Vocontii, a people at least nominally under the Roman *imperium*. Since they grow fat on money extorted from Roman merchants in tolls, protection, and "hospitality," they were quite content with Roman rule. The general had passed down the word that the natives were not to be harassed in any way: no stealing crops, livestock, or anything else not nailed down, and leave the women alone!

We were going to consolidate with the rest of the army the following day. The other legions were camped near a Gallic town called Leminco, about fifteen thousand *passus* down the valley.

As Bantus left us, he announced, "*A' Galliam comatam beneventi, infantes*! Welcome to long-haired Gaul, guys!"

V.

Sub Patrocinio Caesaris

UNDER CAESAR'S PATRONAGE

We pulled into Leminco by the sixth hour on the next day. It was an easy march down the valley of the Vocontii, more of a parade than a march. In fact, as we marched, children and civilians looked up from their work in the fields and waved as we went by. About two thousand *passus* out, Malleus, our *primus pilus*, pulled us off baggage train duty and lined us up with the rest of the legion. We marched into the valley where the rest of the army was camped as if it were a military parade and not the end of a trek over the Alps. Caesar *Imperator*, along with his entire staff, met us as we marched down into the encampment. Mounted on a white stallion, Caesar was bareheaded and draped in a *sagum rubrum*, a bright red general's cloak. We passed in review before him.

We were guided to a section of the valley where we were to camp, and there we began to dig in. By the ninth hour, we had the *fossum* dug and the *vallum* erected for our marching camp. Although we were surrounded by the other legions of the army, we still had our *sudes* lashed and positioned in our section of the ditch.

As usual, our *centuria* was billeted near the rear gate, just to the left of the *Via Praetoria*, Headquarters Street. When we arrived, Moelwyn had our *contubernium* tent set up. When we arrived, he wasn't about, so we assumed that he was off tending to our mule. Tulli went to find Bantus to learn where the bath point was, when it would be our turn to wash up, and what the arrangements were for chow. The rest of us decided to take advantage of the lull and crap out for a while.

Anyway, that was the plan.

I was about halfway down a deep, dark hole, on my journey to the realm of Morpheus, when a *caliga* nudged my shoulder. I opened my eyes expecting to see Tulli, but then I realized I was looking up at a soldier wearing the purple waist-ribbon of a praetorian.

"*Gaius Marius Insubrecus, miles, es tu?*" he demanded. "Are you Trooper Gaius Marius Insubrecus?"

"*Sum!*" I answered getting to my feet. "I am!"

"You are to accompany me to the *praetorium*," he stated. "*Stat!*"

"Uniform?" I asked.

"Full kit! Sword, no *scutum*, no *pilum!*" he again stated flatly. "I will wait for you outside the tent."

What was this about? I wondered. *Did Bantus rat me out in his report and say that I broke formation?* I was carrying my own sword, and the praetorian was waiting outside for me. At least I wasn't under arrest.

I had to wake Rufus up to get back into my *lorica*. He wasn't too pleased about having his siesta disturbed, but was glad it was me being dragged over to headquarters and not him. As I left the tent, I told him to let Tulli know where I was. I doubt he heard me over his own snoring.

As soon as I emerged from the tent, without a word to me, my escort turned and began marching toward the *Via Praetoria*. As expected, he turned right on the main street of the camp toward the *praetorium*. Then, surprisingly, he walked right by our legionary headquarters and continued toward the main gate of the camp. He passed through with barely a nod to the sentry on duty.

We marched west across a field to another of the legionary *castra* in the valley. When he approached the gate, the sentry challenged him with the sign, *malus*, apple. He responded immediately with the countersign, *quercus*, oak, and without stopping, he stated, "He's with me."

When we turned through the portal and entered the camp, I realized that we were on the *Via Principalis*, the main street of the camp. The *praetorium* of that camp was straight ahead, but I had no idea why I was being summoned to the headquarters of another legion.

When we arrived at the headquarters tent, my escort pointed to a spot on the ground and said, "Wait here until you're summoned." Then, he entered the tent.

I didn't know how literal the praetorian was being, but I didn't wander far from the spot on the ground he had indicated.

It was a good thing I was away from the entrance. Soldiers with the thin, red sashes of the general's staff bustled in and out. Runners, I assumed. Periodically, senior officers, *tribuni angusticlavi;* junior, "narrow-band" tribunes; and even a *legatus legionis*, a legionary commander passed me by. But, to these men, I was invisible, just another *mulus* among thousands. That was fine with me. I had nothing to gain from being noticed by senior officers—and much to lose.

Finally, a clerk on the general's staff stuck his head out. "You Insubrecus?" he asked.

"*Sum!*" I answered.

"*Bene!* Get in here!" he demanded.

I entered the headquarters tent, still with no idea what was going on. I was hoping it was all just some mix-up, but they seemed to have my name. And, if this had anything to do with my breaking ranks to save Strabo's bacon, this seemed to be the place where death sentences were passed.

When my eyes adjusted to the gloom inside the tent, the *scriba* who had summoned me pointed to a cubicle on the right and said, "Report to the legate, Insubrecus!"

The legate, my mind screamed! This was worse than I had imagined. A shaggin' legate?

I entered the *cubiculum* and reported to a man seated behind a field desk, "*Legatus*, Gaius Marius Insubrecus, *miles*, reports as ordered."

The man looked up from some *tabulae* he was scanning and gave me a long look. He didn't look like a legate to me. He looked more like a guy you didn't want to mess with in a cheap *caupona* in a bad neighborhood after drinking half the night. He had short, curly black hair, which matched his bushy eyebrows. His eyes were deeply brown, but alive, the kind of eyes that see everything, assess it, and find it amusingly lacking. He had a couple of days' worth of dark stubble on his chin and jowls. He had discarded his officer's *lorica*, which was lying against the side of the tent. His sword and his helmet were deposited on top of it. He wore the faded, red tunic of an infantry *mulus*.

When he stood up, I was again surprised. He was half a head shorter than I was.

"I'm Labienus," he told me, "the old man's *legatus ad manum*, his chief of staff. Let me take a look at you."

He inspected my uniform and equipment, adjusting invisible defects and centering my belt.

"Let me see your *gladius*!" he demanded.

I unsheathed my sword and handed it to him. He inspected the blade, grunted, and handed it back to me.

"*Bene*," he continued. "When you report to the *imperator*, don't mumble . . . Speak up like a man . . . The old man hates it when people mumble . . . And look the old man right in the eye when he talks to you . . . Don't look down . . . Roman soldiers never look down . . . Speak when spoken to . . . Be short and to the point: 'Yes, sir,' 'No, sir.' No explanations unless the old man asks you . . . Got it?"

"Yes, sir!" I answered.

"And, this is very important," Labienus continued. "Don't stare at the old man's hairline . . . He's very sensitive about that . . . *Compre'endis tu*?"

"*Compre'endo, Legate*!" I replied.

"*Bene* . . . Let's get this over with . . . Any questions?" he asked.

"Yes, sir," I said.

Labienus waited a few heartbeats and said, "Are you going to ask it or just leave me here guessing?"

"Sir! To whom am I reporting?" I asked.

Labienus gave me a long, quizzical look, then snorted. "Son, you are about to meet the proconsul of all the Gauls, the commander of this army, and the great-great grandbaby of the goddess Venus herself. You are about to meet Gaius Iulius Caesar."

Labienus made an overly dramatic gesture toward a doorway in the rear of his cubicle. I marched through.

I entered a larger area of the tent. Most of the tent walls were covered by maps with various military symbols etched in chalk over the representations of the terrain. There were soldiers dressed only in their red tunics fussing over them. A tall, thin man in a white tunic with the thin, purple stripes of an Equestrian seemed to be supervising them. I began to walk toward him when Labienus put his hand on my shoulder and guided me toward the back of the tent.

There was another partition there and behind it, a man, the same man I had seen acting as the priest during my *significatio*. He sat reviewing stacks of *tabulae* arranged before him on an oversized field desk. A *scriba* stood in attendance at the man's left shoulder. When the man saw me approach, he sighed.

He closed the tabula he had been reading, passed it to the clerk, and said, "Ebrius, inform the quartermaster that it is my decision that we will not wait for the supply train from Massalia to reach us. We will pursue the enemy as the situation demands. We will draw supplies from our Gallic allies if necessary."

"*A'mperi'tu', Imperator*," the clerk snapped, taking the *tabula*. Then, he posted out of the tent.

The way was now open. *My turn*, I thought.

"*Imperator*! Gaius Marius Insubrecus, *miles*, reports as ordered!" I snapped. I felt Labienus hovering behind my right shoulder.

While Caesar began to search through the *tabulae* on his desk, he said, "*Laxa*, Insubrecus!"

I willed myself to unstiffen a bit, but I was hardly "at ease."

Finally, he drew two *tabulae* before him. He opened the first and said, "This is the daily operations log of the Tenth Legion that reports a slave attacked a soldier . . . you, as a matter of fact . . . during a training exercise . . . The slave was killed, and you suffered a minor cut to your right arm."

Caesar had not asked me a question, so I did not respond.

He took the second *tabula* and opened it. "This is a confidential command report to me from my *praefectus castrorum* . . . very curious . . . It says the slave was not a slave, but a Roman *grassator*, a street gangster . . . one of Milo's *collegium* . . . Milo's a major player in the Roman underworld . . . What could a legionary grunt in *Gallia Cisalpina* have done to get such attention from a Roman gangster? . . . Do you have any idea, Insubrecus?"

I didn't know how to respond. Labienus warned me against talking too much. The question was straightforward, so I just said, "*Non cognosco, Imperator!*"

Caesar nodded slightly and kept reading. "There's some nonsense here about the involvement of the consul's family . . . Hmmm . . . ah . . . Here it is . . . This has been sent to me because you claim to be a client of my family, the *gens Iulia* . . . Would you be so kind as to explain that, Insubrecus?"

I did. I explained my grandfather's involvement with Gaius Marius, the granting of citizenship, the awarding of the farm, and Caesar Senior explaining to my grandfather that Marius' *patrocinium* had reverted to his family, the *gens Iulia*.

Caesar listened and said, "Yes . . . I do recall some stories about Marius and your grandfather . . . He was a Gallic cavalryman . . . quite colorful, if the stories are accurate . . . practically a part of Marius' *familia* . . . Marius swore *Bona Fortuna* always smiled on the man . . . So . . . you're his grandson?"

Caesar looked over at Labienus, "We have anything for this trooper on the staff?"

Labienus asked me, "Can you ride, soldier?"

"*Possum!*" I responded without turning my head away from Caesar.

"We could mount him as part of the mounted praetorian detail, Caesar," Labienus stated.

"Yes . . . we could," Caesar started. Then, he asked me, "Can you read and write Latin, Insubrecus?"

"*Possum, Imperator,*" I responded.

"Μπορείτε να διαβάσετε Ελληνικά;" Caesar asked abruptly.

It took my mind a heartbeat to adjust. He was asking if I could read Greek. "Διαβάζω, στρατηγε," I stammered. "Yes, General!"

"Interesting . . . Do you have any more hidden talents I should know about, Insubrecus?" Caesar asked.

"Yes, sir," I responded. "I speak Gah'el, I mean, *lingua Gallorum.*"

Caesar spoke to his aide, "Labienus, I think we have more here than just another sword on a horse . . . Go ahead and assign him to my praetorian cavalry *turma* for administrative purposes, but I think I may have a further use for this young man here . . . When are those Gallic chiefs supposed to get here?"

"They're already here, Caesar," Labienus responded. "I have them cooling their heels, waiting for an audience. I like to build up the anticipation a bit . . . Good theater . . . even better politics."

"Splendid!" Caesar said. "Erect an audience tent just outside the *Porta Praetoria*. I will receive these petitioners tomorrow at the first hour, the time when clients traditionally pay their obligatory call on their patron. I hope they understand the significance."

"*A'mperi'tu', Caesar,*" Labienus nodded. "Refreshments?"

"No . . . I don't think so," Caesar stated. "I don't want them feeling too comfortable . . . Not yet, anyway . . . And you, Insubrecus . . . you will be part of my security detail at that meeting . . . No one knows you understand . . . what did you call it . . . 'Gah El'? See what you can pick up."

"*A'mperi'tu', Imperator!*" I snapped.

"As far as this other issue is concerned," Caesar continued, "I doubt this attack was aimed at me. Our connection is too remote. But, one can never be too careful. You are now *sub patrocinio Caesaris*. Outside this tent, you will address me with full military courtesy, but here you may address me as *patrone*. Understood?"

"*Compre'endo, Imper . . . Patrone!*" I corrected myself.

"*Bene!*" Caesar concluded. "Let's see how this encounter works out tomorrow. I may have a special task for you, Insubrecus. But, for now, let me get back to this pile of administrative *merda* that's piled up on my desk. Labienus! Get young Insubrecus squared away."

The interview was concluded. I had no idea at the time, but that was one of the most significant moments in my life. From that moment on, I have been *sub patrocinio gentium Iuliarum Caesarum—pro bono et pro malo*, for the good and for the bad.

VI.

De Consequente Helvetiorum
PURSUIT OF THE HELVETIANS

Helvetii iam per angustias et fines Sequanorum suas copias traduxerant et in Haeduorum fines pervenerant eorumque agros populabantur Haedui cum se suaque ab iis defendere non possent legatos ad Caesarem mittunt rogatum auxilium.

"The Helvetians had already led their forces through the defile and into the territory of the Sequani. They then invaded the territory of the Aedui and were ravaging their lands. Since the Aedui could not defend themselves and their possessions from the Helvetians, they sent envoys to Caesar and requested assistance."

—(from Gaius Marius Insubrecus' notebook of Caesar's journal)

*W*hen I got back to my *contubernium* in the Tenth Legion, I quickly found out I had no unit to leave. Bantus informed me that our tent squad was to be broken up and assigned around the legion as individual replacements. When I informed Bantus of what had happened to me, he shook my hand and wished me well. He promised that our *signifer* would forward my pay records and allotments to my new unit.

Bantus then shared with me that Strabo was recovering. Bantus had been over to the medics, and Spina had assured him that, under his professional and expert care, our centurion was going to make a full recovery and would be back on duty in less than a week.

Bantus had told Strabo what I had done. After making sure that Bantus had disciplined me for breaking ranks, Strabo said, "Tell the kid thanks. I owe him."

I packed my personal gear up, shook hands all around, strapped my shield to my back, threw my *furca* over my shoulder, and trudged back to the camp of the Seventh Legion to report to Labienus.

When I got back to Caesar's headquarters, one of Labienus' assistants walked me over to where the praetorian *turma*, the cavalry troop, was housed. I was shown a bunk to dump off my kit. Then, I was taken over to report to my new officer, a *decurio* named Decimus Lampronius, who had been in the cavalry so long that everyone called him *Valgus*, "Bow Legs."

Valgus looked me up and down, then asked, "Can you ride?"

When I answered yes, Valgus just grunted and said, "We'll see. Get that infantry gear off, and I'll take you down to the horse line."

I dropped my *gladius* and *galea,* and Valgus helped me out of my *lorica.* We walked down to the horse line, and Valgus picked out a horse for me, a black mare with a white snip. The stable slave bridled and saddled the horse for me.

"The old man likes his praetorian escort all mounted on black horses . . . looks smart," Valgus explained. "Mount up, and walk him around the corral a couple of times . . . Get him warmed up."

I hopped up and walked the horse around the corral. Valgus had me execute some turns. Then, he called out, "Trot!"

I dug my heels into the horse's sides, and it responded immediately. Valgus watched us for a while, then commanded, "Canter!"

We picked up speed, making a few circuits around the corral until Valgus called, "Come on over here, Insubrecus!"

I complied and dismounted in front of him.

"You got a good seat," Valgus told me. "I'm going to have you work with our training officer until he's satisfied that you're ready for tactical training with the *turma*. My understanding is that you're on *immunis* status to the old man's headquarters, so that will have to take priority. Meanwhile, I'll walk you over to the armory to draw a *spatha*, a cavalry sword. It's longer than that infantry pig-sticker you have now. Keep both. The *gladius* comes in handy if we have to fight dismounted. Most guys hang the *spatha* from the horn on their saddle and keep the *gladius* on their bodies. If you take a tumble, it's nice to know one of your swords stays attached to you. We also have to get you a *parma*, a cavalry shield. We'll send that table top you're carrying back to your former legion. I see you already have one of the new *galea* with the long neck guard . . . That'll work just fine in the cavalry . . . so keep that."

Valgus and I walked back to the headquarters tent of the praetorian detail. Before he dismissed me, Valgus handed me a *cingulum purpureum*, a thin, purple sash.

"Tie that around your waist," he said. "Wear it outside your *lorica* when you're on duty . . . It indicates who you work for . . . Even centurions won't screw around with you when they see that sash."

When I got back to my tent, I discovered one of the benefits of being an *immunis* praetorian. No guard duty. For the first time since I joined the army, I slept through the entire night.

I was awakened in the dark by someone kicking my cot. I grunted, "*Qu'accidit?*" I then heard a voice out of the darkness, "You, Insubrecus?"

"Yeah . . . that's me," I answered, sitting up.

"You're on the general's security detail this morning," the voice explained. "You need to report to *il'capu, stat'*."

"*Il'capu?*" I questioned.

"*Il'capu* . . . the boss . . . Labienus *Legatus*," came the answer out of the gloom. "*Stat*!"

I got to the *praetorium* just as the trumpet signaling the end of the fourth watch sounded. Labienus was standing in the outer area in full kit—officer's *lorica*, plumed helmet under his arm.

When Labienus saw me, he said, "Ah, Insubrecus . . . *bene*!"

He put his arm around my shoulders and guided me to a quiet corner. "Your job this morning isn't security . . . We have enough goons in purple sashes to take care of that . . . When these Gauls show up, just watch and listen . . . See what you can pick up . . . anything to help the general understand what these people are really up to . . . Got it?"

"*Compre'endo, Legate*," I told him.

"Good lad," he said, patting my back. "*Bene*! Let's get this circus started, boys!"

Labienus ducked into his cubicle. I could hear some muffled conversation back there. Then, Caesar *Imperator* appeared in full regalia, with a bright red *sagum* over his shoulders. Someone called the room to attention, but Caesar immediately put us at ease.

"*Bene*! We're ready," he stated. "Let's move out, Labienus, and see what these Gauls want."

When Caesar spotted me, he gestured me over to him. "Ah . . . Insubrecus . . . Walk with me."

We proceeded up the *Via Principalis* toward the *Porta Principalis Sinistra*. I was surprised how some of the legionary squaddies treated the general with calls like, "Give 'im hell, *Calve*, Baldy!" and "Remember, you get the gold, and we get the women, Boss!" Caesar just smiled, nodded at some of the callers, and even waved at a few.

"This may sound strange to you, Insubrecus," he shared with me, "but this is how the boys show they like me. If they said nothing as I passed . . . just stayed silent and sullen . . . I'd be in big trouble."

When we finally wound our way through the gate, I saw a large pavilion erected in the field. Underneath the tent, Caesar's *sella curulis*, his curule seat, indicating his possession of the *imperium* of the Senate and the Roman people as the proconsul of the *provincia*, stood alone. In the field beyond the pavilion, I could see a group of men and horses being guarded by a detail of praetorians.

Our guests had already arrived.

I heard Caesar say to Labienus, "They're on time . . . They must consider their business with me urgent . . . *Bene* . . . Let's take our time with this . . . Delay is to our advantage . . . whoever seems to have the least to lose, wins."

Caesar walked slowly to his chair and carefully arranged his red cloak as he took the seat. He inclined his head in my direction and whispered, "*Observa et ausculta*! Anything you can pick up will be helpful."

Caesar then inclined his head toward the commander of the security detail and gestured that he should let the Gallic delegation approach.

To me, these approaching Gauls were like Gallic warrior-heroes, emerging from one of Gran'pa's tales of our heroic past. They were huge men, giants, each well over six *pedes* in height, barrel chested, and broad shouldered with heavily muscled arms. They seemed to overshadow the members of Caesar's security detail, who themselves were selected for their intimidating physical presence. Most of the praetorians barely measured up to shoulder height on these men. How could we Romans fight such men? They had the stature of gods.

They approached the seat of Caesar with long, confident strides. They all wore luxuriant, thick moustaches reaching down to their chins: some red, some blond, others black. They approached Caesar's seat bareheaded. Some kept their long hair wild and unbound; others had braids interwoven with brightly colored ribbons reaching down their backs. Under his left arm, each warrior carried a bronze helmet, brightly plumed with horsehair and feathers.

They walked in a flurry of colors, with capes, sashes, and trousers of garish red, verdant green, and deep blue. On their left shoulders, the men wore large, ornate, golden *fibula* pins that secured the brightly colored cloaks, which seemed to flutter behind them as they strode forward. Around their necks, the warriors wore thick, golden torcs. I remembered Gran'pa telling me that the kings and chiefs of the Gah'el wore their wealth into battle to attract worthy opponents to combat.

Their bright chainmail cuirasses reached down to their knees and were secured by wide leather belts adorned with gold and silver decorations.

On their left sides, they wore long, Gallic swords suspended from ornately embellished baldrics.

Their groupings and tartan designs indicated three distinct factions approaching Caesar's chair. When they were about three paces from the pavilion, they stopped. The leading warrior from a group of four men in blue and green plaid livery stepped forward to address the general. He held up an ornately carved wand of white wood for Caesar to see. From Gran'pa's stories, I knew it to be a wand of negotiation. It indicated that the warrior came to speak, not to fight. It held the holder inviolate at the cost of five times his head price.

"*Ave,* Caesar," the speaker began in accented Latin, "I am Duuhruhda mab Clethguuhno, tribal king of the People of the Goddess of the Dark Moon, Aine Du, the Aedui to you Romans."

As the king spoke, I examined his entourage. Each man carried the white wand to indicate his diplomatic status. One, by his bearing and the richness of his equipment, was obviously a noble of some standing within the tribe. He had a natural sneer to his smile, and his eyes were what Mama would call "shifty." There was something about him that screamed deceit. I took an instant dislike to the man. The other men carried wooden staffs. These were the king's *drui*, I realized, one for the laws of the gods and the other for the laws of the people.

The king was addressing Caesar, reminding him of the bonds of friendship that existed between the Aedui and the Roman people and of how Caesar's refusal to let the Helvetii cross the Rhodanus at Gennava had sent the Helvetii into the lands of the Aedui and of how hordes of Helvetii were now stripping the fields and storehouses of the Aedui.

I decided there was nothing to be gleaned by my listening to a set diplomatic speech in halting Latin, so I eased over to where the Gauls had left their horses. There, the entourage of the Gallic chiefs was gathered. They were the bodyguards of the kings, the *gwarchodourai*. They weren't listening to the king's speech. I doubt any of them understood Latin. I got as close as I could without arousing their suspicion. Surprisingly, I could follow most of what they were saying to each other.

Most were joking about the Romans in Caesar's security detail: Romans wore skirts like women; they looked like beardless boys; such small men could never satisfy a woman.

Then, I heard one comment on how the king of the Aedui went on and on with his speech like a woman complaining to her neighbors about her monthly cramps.

His companion, one of the Aedui by his tartan, added that the king was trying to lure the Romans across the river.

His companion asked why, what purpose did having Romans in lands of the Aedui serve?

The Aeduan snorted, "The enemy of our enemy is our friend! If the Romans fight the Helvetii, regardless of who wins, there will be fewer Romans and fewer Helvetii for the Aedui to kill."

Then, another of the Aedui said, "This 'Caisar' of the Romans . . . his own people hate him . . . They have paid our king handsomely . . . in Roman gold and silver . . . to lure him to his destruction beyond the lands of the Romans."

The first Aeduan hushed his companion. Then, he looked around and spotted me hovering close by. That was enough to silence the men. I knew I would get no more from them.

When I wandered back to where I could hear the deputation, one of the warriors, a dark-haired man in a red tartan was saying, "Our fields should not be destroyed; our children should not be carried off into slavery; and our towns should not be assaulted when your army is within our sight. It is not possible for us to defend our people from the onslaught of so large a host. Soon, we will have nothing left except the dust of our fields."

When the warrior was finished speaking, Caesar rose from his *sella curulis* and addressed the assembly, "Caesar has heard the complaints and the entreaties of the allies and friends of the Roman people. You will have my answer in the morning!"

With that, Caesar turned and walked back toward the gate of the *castrum*. Labienus and I fell in behind him. We followed him back to his quarters in the *praetorium*. He tossed his helmet on his table and ordered his body slave to assist him in removing his cuirass.

While this was happening, he asked Labienus, "Where do our *exploratores* place the enemy?"

Labienus walked over to one of the maps and pointed to a spot near a squiggly blue line. "They're here, moving west toward this river, the Arar, and taking their time about it. The scouts say that at these points, they're crossing the river on boats and rafts."

Caesar, now free of his armor, walked over to the map and asked, "How long before they get across the river?"

"Late tomorrow . . . maybe the next day," Labienus shrugged.

"What's here?" Caesar asked, pointing to where two blue lines converged.

"That's the confluence of the Arar and the Rhodanus," Labienus answered. "There's a settlement there on our side of the river . . . an *oppidum* . . . a fortified town of the *Sequani* . . . This symbol indicates that there's a bridge across the Rhodanus at this point . . . Looks to be no more than four, maybe five, thousand *passus* south of where the Helvetii are crossing the Arar."

"Perfect!" Caesar said. "Absolutely perfect . . . issue orders . . . three legions . . . the Seventh, Ninth, and Tenth . . . We pull out at midnight . . . We march straight for that bridge . . . Then, we move to catch the enemy at those fords . . . We should catch them divided by the river . . . We can chew up their rear guard, and the rest won't be able to support them . . . Send out an engineering detail with cavalry support to check that bridge . . . I want it capable of supporting our crossing when we get there . . . What is it, Labienus?"

"Caesar, when you cross the Rhodanus, you leave the *imperium Romanum* . . . Without the authorization of the Senate, your command does not reach into *Gallia*," Labienus cautioned.

"Don't be such an old lady, Labienus," Caesar dismissed his counsel. "*Audacibus favet Fortuna*! . . . Fortune favors the bold! You keep this up, and I'll have to appoint you to the Senate with the rest of those old women . . . The Helvetii are a clear and imminent threat to our *provincia,* and our *pietas* demands that we support our friends and allies on the other side of that river . . . We may not get another opportunity like this."

"Yes, Caesar," Labienus conceded.

"*Bene*! Issue the orders!" Caesar continued. "Have the *quaester* visit our Gallic friends in the morning, after we've pulled out . . . We will be out-marching our supplies . . . We'll have them feed our army while we're destroying their enemies . . . Fair trade, I think."

I saw a thought flitter across Caesar's eyes. He looked over to where I was standing. "Insubrecus . . . *veni*!"

"Yes, *Patrone*," I responded.

"I saw you near that Gallic bunch over by the horses," he said. "Did you pick up anything useful?"

"The Aedui want us to exhaust ourselves against the Helvetii so they will have an easier time dealing with us," I offered.

"That makes sense," Caesar agreed. "Anything else?"

I thought of how best to tell Caesar the other news. Then, I remembered Labienus' advice: be direct. "*Patrone*, they were saying that Romans paid their king to entice you to go over the Rhodanus. They want the Helvetii to destroy you and this army."

Caesar looked at me for a few heartbeats, then asked, "Are you sure you heard that part correctly?"

"*Recte audivi, Patrone*," I answered. "Yes, I did!"

Caesar shrugged, "No matter . . . The Helvetii are not going to destroy this army . . . *Bene gesta* . . . Well done, Insubrecus." He patted me on the shoulder.

Then, he turned to Labienus, "Issue the orders . . . We move out at midnight . . . three legions!"

We did move out at midnight. My legion, the Tenth, was the vanguard, followed by the Seventh, then the Ninth. I rode with Caesar's praetorian detail near the head of the column. Valgus, my *decurio*, still had no confidence in my riding abilities and told me just to stay close to him during the march.

Once we cleared the hills around Leminco, our progress was swift. Caesar wanted to reach the bridge at the Rhodanus as quickly as possible, but he didn't want to exhaust the troops doing it. He expected a battle at the end of the march.

By dawn, the army had fourteen thousand *passus* under its boots, and it was marching down a valley past a village called Laviscone. With the sun up, we picked up the pace. To keep them fresh along the route of the march, Valgus had us walking the horses for a thousand *passus*, then riding for a thousand.

We turned north. By the fifth hour, we were another fifteen thousand *passus* down the road, passing a pisshole of a place with the grandiose name of Aosta Salassorum, Aosta of the Salassi tribe, where we turned west and followed a river up another valley.

By the ninth hour, we were close to forty thousand *passus* out of Leminco, about five thousand *passus* east of Bergusium. Despite wanting to press on, even Caesar realized he had to halt or his army would be too clapped out to fight.

When he ordered the halt, the Tenth Legion, the First Cohort boys in the van, started chanting, "Ten thousand more! Ten thousand more!"

But, the general yelled back, "Save some of that for the barbarians!"

"We got plenty!" the boys in the Tenth yelled back.

"I'm sure you do, *m'infantes*!" Caesar answered them. "But, I'm an old man and need my rest!"

"Then, we'll stop for you, Calve!" some wag yelled back.

Caesar rendered a dramatic gesture of thanks to the men in the vanguard. Then, I heard him say to Labienus, "Bring those *exploratores* to me . . . *stat*!"

Caesar called, "Insubrecus! With me!" Then, he rode to where a group of legionary slaves were already erecting his headquarters tent.

When we dismounted, I saw Labienus leading a motley group of Gallic horsemen to Caesar. Caesar said, "Insubrecus . . . talk to those people . . . Find out where the enemy is."

I approached the group and spoke in Gallic to the one I took to be their leader, "*Uh prif duhmuno gweebod bleh mae'r Helvetii uhn cael eu?*"

I saw a look of surprise pass across the face of the rider I approached. "The Roman puppy speaks our tongue!" he said.

"Puppies don't kill. I have," I told him. "Now, answer the question!"

The man gave me a long stare, then said, "You are right. I am being rude. I am Athauhnu mab Hergest of the People of Soucana, a Leader of Ten. To whom do I have the pleasure of speaking?"

"The Romans call me Gai," I answered him. "Among my people, the Insubreci, I am called Arth Bek, Wuhr Cunorud, *mae milour Rhufeinig*, a soldier of Rome."

"Well, Arth Bek, Grandson of the Red Hound," Athauhnu continued, "the Helvetii dogs have reached Soucana's river at the valley of the white pines. That is half a day's ride north from the Dun of Lugus. There are no fords in that place, so they are crossing on boats."

I turned to Caesar, "The enemy has reached the Arar about fifteen thousand *passus* north of a place called Lugdunum . . . They have begun to cross on boats."

"Ask him how long it will take the Helvetii to cross!" Caesar snapped.

"*Pah mor hir uh buhth uhn ei guhmruhd ar guhfer uh Helvetii i groesi'r afon?*" I translated.

I watched Athauhnu calculate in his head. "Three . . . maybe four days," he guessed. "They have women and children . . . and much baggage."

"They're loaded down," I told Caesar. "He estimates three or four days."

Then, Athauhnu said, "Tell the Roman chief that their foraging parties are across the Rotonos, and they have *Almaenwuhra* with them."

Caesar caught the word *Rotonos*, and asked, "What did he say about the Rhodanus?"

"There are Helvetian raiding parties on our side of the river," I told him. "And, he says they have Germans with them."

"Germans?" Caesar said. "How many?"

"*Faint o Almaenwuhra?*" I asked.

Athauhnu shrugged, "Not many . . . not few."

"He doesn't know," I told Caesar.

I saw Caesar considering this response. He decided not to press it. "Tell him thanks, Insubrecus. Tell him he's welcome to food—and water and feed for his horses."

I passed on Caesar's gratitude, but then Athauhnu asked me, "Does the Roman chief intend to continue on the Roman road all the way to the dun of the Allobroges on the Rotonos?"

I wasn't sure that I should share our route of march with the man, so I asked, "Why do you want to know that?"

"The Helvetii are burning our farms, raping our women, and murdering our children," he said. "If the Roman chief marches on the Roman road to the Rotonos, he is going out of his way . . . He is giving those Helvetian pigs more time to kill my people . . . There is a shorter route direct to the Dun of Lugus . . . The road is not as good . . . but it will cut almost a day out of the journey."

"*Imperator*," I called to Caesar, "this man says he knows a shorter route to the bridge over the Rhodanus at Lugdunum than through Vigenna . . . He says our army can pass over it, and it will cut almost a day out of the march."

This immediately got Caesar's attention. "This man is familiar with this road?" he asked me.

"*Noscit, Imperator*," I replied. "Yes, sir!"

"*Bene*!" Caesar said. Then, "Labienus . . . the Tenth's cavalry is up with us . . . Tell their *primus pilus* I need a *turma* for a route reconnaissance . . . *Stat*!"

Then to me, "Insubrecus, ask your man there if he will show us the way."

"*Uhn eich arwain ein marchoglu dros uh fhorth?*" I asked Athauhnu.

Athauhnu shrugged, "Yes . . . of course . . . just give us some time to rest and water our horses."

"As soon as their horses are ready, *Imperator*," I told Caesar.

We were on the road by the eleventh hour. Caesar sent me along with the *turma* from the Tenth Legion because none of the Romans spoke Gallic. There were twenty-five Roman cavalry troopers commanded by a *decurio* called Rubigo, "Rusty," because of his red hair.

About a thousand *passus* east of Bergusium, Athauhnu led us north and west away from the Roman road. We rode almost two thousand *passus*, passed through a narrow valley, and then found ourselves following a small river down a broad valley that the army would have no problem marching through.

Around sundown, we had to climb up through a narrow pass from the valley floor. At worst, the army could pass through it marching two abreast. When we climbed the valley, we found ourselves riding across a broad plain, which would offer no obstacle to our march.

We rode for what seemed like hours. The young moon rose, dimly lighting our way. Soon, off to the north and east, we could see what seemed to be bonfires burning in the night.

Athauhnu halted our march.

"It's worse now," he told me. "Those are the settlements of my people . . . The Helvetii and those German pigs are burning everything."

"Ask him how much farther!" Rubigo interrupted.

I translated for Athauhnu. He shrugged, "Not much farther. The south branch of the Rotonos is to our front. The bridge your Caisar wants is to the northwest . . . It is downstream from where the branches of the river join together and just below the bluff where the dun of my people sits."

"It's not much farther to the northwest," I told Rubigo.

"All that jabber to say 'not much farther'?" the *decurio* complained. "These bloody wogs love the sound of their own voices."

I didn't think it appropriate to point out to Rubigo that I was one of those "wogs."

"*Da!*" I told Athauhnu. "Good! Let's go!"

In less than an hour, we were on a hill overlooking the Rhodanus. Below us, we could make out the bridge spanning the river and the fires of the Roman engineers Caesar had sent out to strengthen it. On the other side of the Rhodanus, on a facing bluff, the torches set on the ramparts of the Dun of Lugus, the seat of the Sequani, were visible.

"We rest the horses," Rubigo said. "Then, we get back to the army. The wog's right. We can be on the banks of the river by tomorrow night."

"*Beth a wnaeth uh un coch uhn ei thweud?*" Athauhnu asked. "What did the Red One say?"

"He said thanks," I told Athauhnu.

"So many words to say thanks," Athauhnu commented shaking his head. "These Romans wag their tongues like old women."

We rode as hard as our tired horses could tolerate to get back to the army. The fires in the north and east seemed to have gone out, leading me to hope that the enemy had withdrawn its raiding parties back across the river.

Erratum. I was wrong.

We were no more than ten thousand *passus* back from the hilltop where we saw the bridge when we literally collided with another group of horsemen in the dark. A rider, no more than a pace or two to my left, grunted, "*Hwa gange ðær?*"

I didn't understand what he said, but immediately the image of a blond giant guarding the blue doorway of a *lupinarium* in Mediolanum appeared in my mind.

"*Germani!*" I yelled drawing my gladius. "Germans!"

I pulled my horse's head hard to the left into the German rider. He was slower to react than I was. I felt my gladius bite home; where, I wasn't sure. The rider grunted and went down.

The rest of the fight was a mad free-for-all in the dark. I could sense, more than see, figures swirling around me; I heard the sounds of steel on steel, the grunts of the wounded. Then, there was silence—silence except for the sound of a woman weeping somewhere in the dark.

I heard Rubigo call, "Insubrecus! *Ub'es tu?*"

"*Adsum!*" I responded.

I felt him ride up next to me. "Thank the gods! The general would have my hide if those Krauts got to you."

"I hear someone crying," I said.

"Prisoners," Rubigo explained. "Those Kraut *mentulae* were dragging their captives along with them. Your wog buddies are seeing to them. Tell them to hurry. We have to get back to the army."

I dismounted and found Athauhnu. He was with a cluster of his men and the freed captives.

"Young women and a few young boys," he spat. "They're from a settlement near the south branch of the Rotonos. The German pigs burned everything ... killed everyone else except these few ... they have value as slaves ..."

"The Red One wants to get back to the Romans," I said. "How soon can you move?"

"He's right," Athauhnu agreed. "The faster the Caisar arrives with his warriors, the faster these pigs will flee from our lands ... I will send two of my men to bring these captives to the Dun of Lugus ... then we will go find your army."

We were quickly back on the road. We arrived at the site of the Roman *castra* during the fourth watch, about an hour before dawn. The army was already awake and pulling down their fortifications. We found Caesar and the command group with the Tenth Legion.

Rubigo reported to the *Imperator*. "The route is open all the way to the bridge at Lugdunum, maybe twenty, twenty-one-thousand *passus*," he said. "One narrow spot along the way but the rest is wide open, dry and fairly flat. The enemy has patrols and raiding parties in the area, nothing big enough to threaten the army."

Caesar was silent for a few heartbeats. Then, he responded, "*Bene gestum, Decurio*! Well done! Stand your men down until the third hour, then follow the army through to the bridge."

Caesar turned to Labienus, "Titus, collect two *turmae* of cavalry from the Seventh and Ninth and one from the Tenth and have them report here at the head of the column!"

"*A'mperi'tu', Imperator*," Labienus responded. "Yes, General."

"Rubigo, I have a favor to ask of you," Caesar said to the cavalry *decurio*.

"Anything, General," Rubigo responded.

"I know you're tired, lad, but you know the route up to the bridge," Caesar told him. "So, I need you to get a fresh horse and guide my cavalry detail along the route ahead of the army."

"*A'mperi'tu', Imperator*!" Rubigo snapped.

Then Caesar called over to a group of officers clustered about three paces off, "Pulcher! I need you!"

"*Quid vis tu, Caesar*?" the man responded walking over to where we were. "What do you want, Caesar?"

"Pulcher, I'm giving you command of five *turmae* of legionary cavalry," Caesar instructed the officer. "Your mission is twofold. First, mark the route of march for the army. Have your troopers collect some of the markers the engineers use to survey the marching camps, and use them to mark the route. Is that clear?"

"*Compre'endo*!" Pulcher responded.

"*Bene*," Caesar continued. "The redheaded *decurio* from the Tenth . . . Rubigo's his name . . . he knows the route. Second, I want you to screen our route of march . . . Keep those barbarian *cunni* off our tails as we move up to the river . . . The threat is basically from the north and east along the route, but don't be surprised if you run into stragglers . . . Grab two *tribuni* to assist you—a couple of those fuzz-faced *angusticlavi* attached to the Tenth who don't seem to know what to do with themselves . . . I doubt the men will miss them . . . Any questions?"

"*N'abeo*," Pulcher answered.

"Good man!" Caesar encouraged him. "As soon as the cavalry *turmae* are assembled, brief them, and get on the road!"

"*A'mperi'tu', Caesar*," Pulcher said and walked over to where Labienus was assembling the cavalry detail.

I heard Caesar mutter at the man's back, "'Caesar,' he calls me . . . in front of the troops . . . like we were a couple of housewives discussing the price of fish in the middle of the forum . . . *Iste pedans mentula Claudianarum!*"

Then, he noticed me standing there, "Ah! Insubrecus! Enjoy the ride?"

"Yes, *Imperator*," I started, "at least most of it. We ran into a German raiding party on the way back."

"Germans?" Caesar questioned. "How many? How'd you know they were Krauts?"

"They spoke German, *Imperator*," I explained. "We counted eight bodies when we were done . . . Don't think any of them got away."

"Germans on this side of the Rhenus?" Caesar mused. "Not good . . . not good at all . . . What do you make of our Gallic friends?"

"They're on our side as long as we're fighting their enemies," I told him. "*Hostes hostium meorum—*"

"*Amici mei*," Caesar finished my sentence. "The enemies of my enemies are my friends. . . . Best we could hope for . . . As long as we can, keep the tribes divided—" Caesar stopped himself from continuing that thought, then asked me, "Think you can stay in the saddle for another day?"

"*Possum, Imperator*," I agreed.

"Good lad!" Caesar said. "Have Valgus find you a fresh horse. I want to be on the Rhodanus before nightfall."

And, we were. The van of our army was on the river and digging in by the seventh hour. Our engineers had reinforced and widened the bridge so that we could cross quickly at any time.

A delegation of brightly attired Sequani crossed the bridge from Lugdunum. We were quickly informed that the main body of the Helvetii were still crossing the Arar about fifteen thousand *passus* to the north. The Sequani offered to lead us to the site.

I believe Caesar was tempted to move the army right out, but he knew that the soldiers would be too exhausted to give battle when they arrived. So, he decided to rest them in the relative security offered by the bluffs on the south side of the Rhodanus. He did send a detachment of legionary cavalry ahead with the Sequani to locate the enemy, survey the ground, and find a route of march for the infantry.

I was so exhausted that my body ached. As soon as I could square away my mount at the horse stables, I found a quiet place in the back of the praetorians' tent to sleep. I felt as if I had just shut my eyes when I felt someone kicking my foot.

"Whaa . . . *qu'accidit?*" I mumbled still half asleep.

"Rise and shine, sunshine!" It was Valgus. "We're moving out."

"*Quot'orarum?*" I mumbled.

"Midnight," Valgus said, "signal for the third watch just sounded . . . Move it, Insubrecus . . . The old man's looking for you!"

I dragged myself up to a sitting position. I felt as if I had taken a beating. Every muscle and joint in my body was screaming. Outside, I could hear the activity of an entire legion in motion. I knew any minute the tent I was in would be coming down on top of me. Still, I searched for my boots in the dark before I realized I hadn't taken them off before I fell asleep.

When I finally stumbled over to where the *praetorium* should have been, the tent was already down, but I soon spotted Labienus briefing some *angusticlavi* tribunes. They looked like boys; I was beginning to have difficulty remembering that I was only sixteen myself.

When Labienus saw me, he said, "Give me a little time here, Insubrecus, and I'll be with you."

The meeting finally broke up with a mixed, "*A'mperi'tu', Legate,*" and Labienus walked over to where I was waiting. He threw his arm around my shoulder and steered me toward the horse lines.

"Big doin', Insubrecus!" he started. "Our *exploratores* got back about an hour ago. The Helvetii left one of their septs . . . a subtribe really . . . stranded on the east side of the Arar. But, that's not the big news . . . The bunch they stranded are the Tigurini . . . You got any idea what that means?"

"*Non cognosco, Legate,*" I answered.

"Didn't think so," Labienus continued. "The old man . . . and every Roman in this army, for that matter . . . has a score to settle with those *cunni* . . . About fifty years back, they slaughtered a Roman army . . . killed a consul . . . one of his legates, Lucius Calpurnius Piso Caesoninus . . . The old man is related to him through his wife . . . so this is personal . . . Caesar's *pietas* demands he avenge Calpurnius and all those poor Roman *muli* who were massacred by those long-haired Gauls. . . He pulls this off, and they'll be shouting Caesar's name in the forum for months!"

I wasn't sure how to react to this. *Pietas.* That was the same reason some Senator's brat was trying to have me killed. In this case, it meant an entire Roman army was crossing the Rhodanus to catch a bunch of Helvetii trapped on the wrong side of the Arar.

We arrived at the horse lines to find Caesar briefing his legates.

"Pulcher, you'll remain in command of the cavalry," Caesar was saying, "three *turmae* of legionary cavalry and a bunch of Sequani . . . They know the ground, so let them take the lead . . . You're to open the way for the infantry . . . Find a good place to engage the enemy . . . There's a lot of broken ground north of the river . . . forests . . . Find a place where I can deploy three legions . . . *acies triplex*, if possible . . . the standard triple battle line . . . But do not allow yourself to become decisively engaged with the enemy . . . Is that clear?"

"*Compre'endo, Imperator,*" I heard Pulcher reply.

I noted that he had used the title *imperator*. Caesar must have had a talk with "that bloody Claudian mentula."

"Bene," Caesar continued, "Cotta, you're commanding the Tenth Legion, the vanguard; Vatinius, the Seventh; Pedius, the Ninth. Crassus, you will continue to act as the army's *quaestor*. You will remain here until the rest of the army has come up with the supply train. Keep that bridge over the Rhodanus open in case the army needs it to withdraw south. Any questions, gentlemen?"

There were none. Caesar spotted Labienus and me standing to the side.

"Get enough sleep, Insubrecus?" he asked.

"*Satis superque, Imperator,*" I lied. "More than enough, sir!" There is never enough sleep for a soldier.

"*Bene!*" Caesar clapped me on the shoulder. "I'm detailing you to Pulcher . . . He has about a hundred Sequani horsemen under his command and doesn't speak a word of their language. . . . You're to act as his liaison with the Gauls."

"*A'mperi'tu', Imperator!*" I responded.

"Good lad!" Caesar continued. "Pulcher can be . . . well . . . a bit difficult. . . . He's real red-boot Patrician . . . and what's worse, a Claudian, and wants everyone to know it . . . I've let him know that you are *sub patrocinio meo* . . . That should account for something. . . . I've given some thought to what you told me about the Gauls saying there are Romans working against me here . . . so I want you to watch and listen."

"*A'mperi'tu', Imperator!*" I responded again.

"Good lad!" Caesar said clapping me on the shoulder. Then, he was off to whatever needed his attention.

"My advice is to stay clear of Pulcher as much as possible," Labienus was saying. "Even for a patrician, he's a right bastard and there's history between his clan and the *gens Iulia* . . . But right now, Caesar needs the good will of his brother, Appius, in the Senate down in Rome. . . . If anyone were working to undermine the old man out here, he'd be my lead suspect."

I had no idea what Labienus was talking about, other than Pulcher was a *podex*, but a *podex* whose goodwill Caesar wanted to maintain, and as Caesar's client, I shouldn't rock the boat.

I found that one of the stable slaves had saddled my horse; it was the black with the white snip that Valgus had me ride previously. I checked the saddle and bridle. Then, I tied down my *spatha* to the left side of my saddle and my *loculus*, the leather bag with my field rations, to the rear. I tied down my woolen cloak to the front of my saddle. I didn't know if we would have to sleep rough. I mounted and adjusted my *parma*, so it hung comfortably on my back. I walked my horse a bit, just to check the saddle again, then went off to find Pulcher and the command group.

They were gathering outside the camp's *fossa*. There were two groups, the Roman legionary cavalry and a group of Sequani horsemen who remained detached from the Romans. I spotted a group of Roman officers in the vicinity of Pulcher and rode toward them. Pulcher seemed remote, distant even, from his own officers; none of them seemed to be willing to get any closer to the patrician than ten *pedes*.

I rode up to him and reported, "Gaius Marius Insubrecus, *miles*, reporting to the *legatus* as ordered!"

Pulcher gave me a long stare. His blue eyes were as cold as a frozen pond in *Ianuarius*; his face looked as if he had unexpectedly gotten a whiff of an overused latrine.

"Insubrecus," he said, seemingly without moving his thin, bloodless lips, "you're Caesar's boy . . . the little Gaul he picked up."

Then, Pulcher turned his head and called over to his officers, "Agrippa! *A'veni!*"

A mounted tribune separated himself from the group and road over to us. "*Ti' adsum, Legate?*"

"Agrippa," Pulcher said, as if he were already bored with having to talk to underlings, "this is Caesar's . . . Caesar's interpreter for the barbarians . . . Collect him up, and take your post."

I noticed the narrow, purple stripe on Agrippa's tunic. He was an equestrian, an *angusticlavus*, a narrow-striper.

Pulcher pulled his horse's head around abruptly, as if to escape the stench of social inferiors, and joined the knot of Roman officers. The tribune who rode up to me seemed to have an open, honest face, the kind which is trusted implicitly. He leaned out from his saddle and extended his right hand to me. "Lucius Vipsanius Agrippa," he announced, "just call me Agrippa. And, you are?"

He spoke Latin with a wide, country twang, which told me he wasn't from Rome—not the city anyway. I took his offered hand, "Gaius Marius Insubrecus, *Trib* . . . I mean, Agrippa."

We rode over to where the Gauls had congregated. Agrippa said, "I'm a bit anxious about all this . . . Pulcher expects me to command this group . . . I don't expect they'll welcome my . . . my involvement."

"Let's see what mood they're in," I started. Then, I saw Athauhnu among the riders.

"Athauhnu," I greeted him in Gallic, "it is good to see you again, my friend!"

"Ah . . . Arth Bek," he responded sourly, "did the Caisar send you and this other one to ensure that the people of Soucana would behave themselves in their own lands?"

"No, my friend," I hedged, "we are here solely to help with communication between the people of Soucana and their Roman allies."

Athauhnu snorted at that response.

"What is he saying, Insubrecus?" Agrippa tried to interrupt, but I held my hand up asking for his silence.

Athauhnu continued, "My people can be great liars when they feel the need, but none can equal you Romans . . . Come . . . You will need to speak to the *penn uh marchoglu*."

"*Penn uh marchoglu*?" I stumbled. "Oh . . . the troop commander . . . Yes . . . lead on, Athauhnu."

As Athauhnu turned to lead us, I said to Agrippa, "He's taking us to their commander."

Athauhnu led us to another rider. By his armor, equipment, and trappings, I assumed he was of the Sequani nobility.

Athauhnu said merely, "These are *our* Romans!"

The man gave us a long look, then responded in accented Latin, "*Salvete*! I am Madog mab Guuhn. I am *rex gentium* . . . people-king of Sequani . . . I am also *dux*, leader of cavalry."

I did not respond, but nodded to Agrippa, who said, "*Salve, Dux*. I am called Agrippa. I am the tribune of the Roman legate, Pulcher, the leader of the Roman cavalry."

Madog nodded at Agrippa, then asked, "And who is other with you?"

"This is *contubernalis meus*," Agrippa responded. "He is called Insubrecus."

Madog said to me in Gallic, "You speak our language. Of what people are you?"

"I am of the Insubres, from over the Alps," I answered in Gallic. Then I repeated myself in Latin for Agrippa: "*De Insubrecis trans Alpes.*"

Madog nodded. Then, Agrippa stated, "The legate Pulcher requests that you lead us to the Helvetii."

Madog seemed to have some difficulty following Agrippa, and I couldn't imagine Pulcher *requesting* anything of a Gaul—or a Roman, for that matter. I was just about to translate, when Madog said, "We go! But, I show you something . . . interest of Romans?"

Madog reached into his saddlebag, pulled something out, and offered it to Agrippa. Agrippa took it, examined it for a heartbeat, and handed it to me. It was a *quadriga*, a denarius coin, a new one, hardly used, no nicks or shavings. It had a small hole driven through it.

"Madog," Agrippa asked, "where did you get this?"

"Helvetii," Madog responded. "A dux of cavalry . . . He wear ten on neck . . . How do you say?" Madog looked over to me and asked, "*Sut ur udych uhn dwed 'muclis' un Ladine?*"

"*Monile*," I told him. "Necklace."

Madog grunted, "He wear necklace . . . I kill him . . . I take necklace."

I looked closely at the coin. The one side had the expected image of the *quadrigae*, the chariot team of four horses. I flipped it over and saw the image of the goddess Venus, the patroness of *gens Iulia*. Then, I realized that the coin was minted only last year, while Caesar was consul. How would a minor Helvetian chief have ten new denarii?

I asked Madog, "May I keep this?"

Madog shrugged, "I gift you . . . We friends . . . I have more."

"Is this significant?" Agrippa asked me.

"I'm not sure," I answered. "It may fit in with something I overheard."

Just then we heard Pulcher's voice, "Agrippa . . . are you going to get those barbarians moving, or are you planning a state breakfast for them?"

Madog gave no sign that he understood what Pulcher said. Agrippa said to him, "*Eamus, Dux*! Let's get going, Chief!"

Madog grunted and started shouting orders to his troop. As they began to move off into the night, Agrippa asked me, "This Madog . . . he's king of the Sequani?"

"King of the Sequani?" I repeated. "No . . . he's one of their *brena leygo* . . . a leader of a community . . . The Gauls call their leaders *brena* . . . '*rex*' in Latin . . . Technically, my father's a *brena qwartego* . . . *rex pecoris* . . . a 'cattle king' because he owns a herd."

"*Compre'endo*," Agrippa muttered. I doubt that he did.

Our approach to the enemy was uneventful. They didn't bother screening their position at all. By the end of the fourth watch, when the sun was still below the horizon but there was already enough light to see over short distances, we were on a wooded ridge overlooking the encampment of the Tigurini. There were no signs of any security or fortifications around their encampment. The night fires were smoldering heaps, and nothing in the camp seemed to be stirring except some hungry dogs. We watched as a man sleepily stumbled out of a lean-to tent, urinated just beyond its exit, and then reentered, presumably to go back to sleep.

Madog grunted at us, "They pigs . . . Helvetii . . . They dirt my sword to kill."

By the end of the first hour, Caesar and his command group joined us on the ridge. He quickly surveyed his objective. There still wasn't much activity in the valley below. Some of the Tigurini were milling about on the river's edge where they had tied up some boats and barges. But, their ferrying operation had yet to start. We could see no sign of any activity on the far side of the Arar. The rest of the Helvetii had apparently moved on and expected this bunch to catch up.

Caesar quickly surveyed the ground and assessed the capabilities of the enemy.

"We'll attack on a narrow front from our route of march, straight up the river valley from the south," he was saying to Labienus. "One legion, I think . . . The Tenth is in the van . . . so they go in . . . *acies triplex* . . . four cohorts in the front rank, then three and three . . . We'll use the cavalry to screen the right flank . . . The river will seal the left."

"That will leave the enemy's rear open," Labienus pointed out. "Do you want to move some of our troops around to seal it?"

Caesar thought about that, then said, "No . . . that will take time, and the enemy might detect the maneuver . . . Besides, even a rat is dangerous when it's trapped . . . I *want* them to be able to escape . . . As soon as we hit them, half their troops will run if they believe they can escape . . . The rest will break as soon as they know the women and children are safe . . . I want to break this bunch, not annihilate them."

Labienus nodded, and said, "*Compre'endo, Imperator.*"

"*Bene!*" Caesar concluded. "We'll keep the Seventh and Ninth in reserve behind the Tenth. Issue the orders to the legates. I want to know immediately when the Tenth is in position."

"*A'mperi'tu', Imperator!*" Labienus said.

Labienus retreated back into the woodline. Caesar remained on the ridge, surveying the enemy in the valley below. Then, he spotted Agrippa and me.

"Ah . . . Insubrecus!" he started. "How did you enjoy your midnight ride? And you are . . . Agrippa . . . Lucius Vipsanius Agrippa? . . . You're one of the new *angusticlavi tribuni* attached to the Tenth? You're an Umbrian . . . from Asisium, I believe?"

"*Recte, Imperator!*" Agrippa snapped. "I am privileged that the *imperator* knows my name!"

"Privileged?" Caesar repeated the word. "It's the duty of a commander to know his officers, Agrippa . . . Remember that if you're ever given a command . . . Know all your officers . . . and all your men for that matter."

"*His meminero, Imperator,*" Agrippa agreed.

"*Bene,*" Caesar muttered, then seemed to retreat into his own thoughts as he watched the doomed Tigurini in the valley below.

"*Imperator,* a word?" I interrupted his musing.

"*Quid vis tu?*" he responded.

I handed him the coin. "Madog, the chief of the Sequani cavalry, gave this to me."

"It's a *denarius,*" he said. Then, he flipped it over. "One of mine . . . What's the point, Insubrecus?"

"Madog took it from a dead Helvetian . . . a minor officer . . . but the man had ten of these, *Imperator*," I began to explain.

"So, what you're saying is that if a minor officer of the Helvetii had ten of these, then the enemy possesses quite a few more?" Caesar interrupted. "And, they're of a new minting . . . one of mine, ironically . . . so the Helvetii came into possession of these recently."

"*Certe, Imperator*," I agreed.

Caesar continued, "And, you believe this is consistent with the rumors of Roman influence on the Helvetii and a possible conspiracy by Romans against me and this army?"

"*Credo, Imperator!*" I again agreed.

Caesar stared silently at the coin in his hand. Then, he flipped it back to me, saying, "You may be right about this, Insubrecus. I'm not completely convinced, but I am intrigued . . . Keep your eyes and ears open . . . Let me know immediately if you discover anything relevant."

I was just about to respond when we heard a bugle signal from the valley below. We watched the Tigurini freeze.

"*Al'iact'est*," Caesar stated. "The die is thrown, Insubrecus! *Cornucen!*"

A bugler appeared from out of the woodline.

"Signal 'Tenth Legion' and 'Attack'!" Caesar ordered.

As the man complied, Caesar shouted, "Horse!"

A member of the praetorian detail came forward with Caesar's white stallion. Caesar quickly removed his red cloak from the saddle and draped it over his shoulders. Then, he leaped up on the horse.

"The men should know their general is watching them, Insubrecus," he said to me. Then, he rode forward to the edge of the ridge.

By this time, the encampment of the Tigurini in the valley below was swirling in chaos as if someone had kicked a beehive. To my left, I saw the first ranks of the Tenth Legion clear the woodline. At first, there were only two cohorts on line. The left-most cohort had its flank anchored on the riverbank. As the Roman line moved forward into the widening valley, a third cohort swung on line around the right flank of the advancing legion.

"Malleus knows how to maneuver men according to the terrain," Caesar said to no one in particular.

There was some order emerging in the Tigurini camp. I could see warriors beginning to form a battle line on the southern edge of the encampment, facing the advancing legion. Others—men, women, and children—were fleeing toward the woods to the north.

I heard Labienus say to Caesar, "We have an audience!" He was pointing across the Arar.

I looked where Labienus was pointing and saw a group of Gallic horsemen.

"*Bene*," Caesar grunted. "Let them report what they see to the rest, and we may finish this campaign before the new crops break through the soil."

The Tenth already had four cohorts on line, facing the enemy. The second line had also emerged from the woodline. The front line advanced to within twenty paces of the Tigurini warriors. Then, the first two men across the entire Roman front launched their *pila* at the enemy. Then, the next two, then the next! Before the third volley of *pila* had hit, the Roman front ranks, their *gladii* bared, were charging into the enemy.

It wasn't much of a battle. The legionaries mowed through the ill-prepared Tigurini. Even from where I stood, I could see the legionaries advance through the enemy ranks with a combination of punching shields and stabbing short swords. Isolated knots of Tigurini warriors would temporarily hold out against the relentless advance of the Roman battle line, only to be surrounded and overwhelmed. The cohorts had pushed the barbarians about a third of the way across their encampment before they finally broke and began fleeing for the safety of the wooded hills to their rear.

When this happened, Caesar again summoned his *cornucen* and commanded, "Signal 'Tenth Legion' and 'Halt'!"

The troops in the valley below executed Caesar's order. I could hear them cheering across the battle line.

Caesar called for Pulcher. "*Legate*, take your cavalry and seal the enemy in from the north and west . . . Do not engage unless you're attacked, but do not become decisively engaged . . . Withdraw and send back for infantry reinforcement if they attempt to punch through you . . . I just want them contained!"

"*A'mperi'tu'*, *Imperator!*" Pulcher's grasp of military courtesy seemed to be steadily improving.

"Labienus!" Caesar summoned. "Detail the *fabricatores*, the engineers of all three legions, to bridge the Arar! I want this army across by sundown!"

"*A'mperi'tu'*, *Imperator!*"

"Agrippa! Are you still here?" Caesar demanded.

"*Adsum, Imperator!*" Agrippa responded.

Caesar ordered, "Get down there to the Tenth . . . Find Malleus, the *primus pilus* . . . Tell him I want his second-line cohorts, all three of them, across the river to screen the bridge building . . . They can use the Tigurini's boats to get themselves across . . . You're in command of that detail . . . Questions?"

"*N'abeo, Imperator!*" Agrippa snapped.

"Good lad!" Caesar encouraged. "Get it done! Insubrecus!"

"*Adsum ti', Imperator!*" I responded.

"You stay with me," Caesar directed. "Pulcher should be bringing in some prisoners soon, and I want to be sure they understand my will."

VII.

De Clementia Caesaris et Offensione Antiqua
CAESAR'S CLEMENCY AND
AN ANCIENT PROVOCATION

Divico respondit ita Helvetios a maioribus suis institutos esse uti obsides accipere non dare consuerint.

"Divico answers that from the time of their ancestors, the Helvetians have been accustomed to take, not give, hostages."

(from Gaius Marius Insubrecus' notebook of Caesar's journal)

*C*aesar had the bridges built and three legions across the Arar by nightfall. At the first hour of the next day, he dispatched a strong cavalry scout west under Labienus to locate the main body of the Helvetii, and by the fourth hour, the rest of the army came up from the Rhodanus and began crossing the Arar.

118

The first Gallic embassy appeared at the sixth hour while Caesar was supervising the deployment of his trailing legions west of the Arar. A rider from Pulcher's cavalry detachment, a *tribunus angusticlavus*, approached Caesar.

"*Ave, Imperator!*" the tribune saluted Caesar, "The legate, Caius Claudius Pulcher, sends greetings and reports that a delegation of nobles from the Tigurini tribe is requesting an audience with the *imperator*. The legate believes they have come to surrender and wish to beg for clemency."

"You're Tertius Nigidius Caecina, nephew of the Senator, Publius Nigidius Figulus, are you not?" Caesar responded.

"*Sum, Imperator!*" the man responded.

"I've read your uncle's *Commentarii* . . . Quite impressive . . . Is he still dabbling in Etruscan augury?" Caesar asked.

"Yes, *Imperator*," Caecina answered with a laugh. "My aunt is always complaining of the stinking sheep livers he constantly drags home from the gods know where to stink up the house."

"*Foro viri, foco mulieres regnant*," Caesar chuckled. "Men rule in the forum, women in the home . . . Please convey my compliments to the legate, and ask him to deliver the Tigurini delegation to me at the site of their former camp."

Caecina rode off to deliver Caesar's message. Caesar then turned to Valgus, who was commanding his mounted praetorian detachment, and said, "Post a man on this side of the river where he can see the delegation arriving from the north. When the Gauls appear, he is to alert me."

Valgus complied while Caesar continued supervising the crossing and quartering of the army. No more than half the hour had passed before the praetorian returned to report the approaching delegation.

Again, Caesar summoned Valgus. "*Decurio*, take twenty men and cross the Arar. I want you to take up a position just south of where yesterday's battle was fought, so the Gauls will have to ride past it," Caesar instructed. "Then, wait for me there."

"*A'mperi'tu', Imperator!*" Valgus snapped.

Caesar dawdled on the west side of the Arar for a while longer, then finally crossed the bridge to receive the Gallic legation. As we rode to where Valgus had established himself, we realized that we were far enough away from yesterday's battlefield that the flies, now feasting on the bodies of the dead Tigurini, would not be a great nuisance. We could see the Gallic embassy and their Roman escort waiting some fifty paces away. They also didn't seem too eager to get close to yesterday's butchery of their comrades.

Caesar halted about twenty paces away from the Gauls. He turned his head in my direction, and asked, "What should I expect, Insubrecus?"

I thought about the question for a few heartbeats, then responded, "If they ride up to you, they expect to negotiate with you as equals. If they dismount and walk to you, they're surrendering."

No sooner had I said that than the leader of the delegation, a tall warrior, with gray streaked through his black hair, dismounted, removed his helmet, and held up his wand of negotiation for all to see. Then, he strode forward to where Caesar remained seated on his horse.

"*Rwy'n cuhfarch uh Caisaro meoun hedouch,*" the warrior said.

Caesar recognized his own name and asked, "Why does this man address me by my name?"

"He means no disrespect, *Imperator*," I cautioned. "He said *uh Caisaro . . .* He thinks that 'Caesar' is your title."

Caesar grunted, then said, "Tell him Caesar welcomes him. Ask him what he wants."

I translated this for the man, who then launched himself into a long, rambling Gallic oration. I kept up as best I could. The man was an under-chief of the Tigurini, but now found himself in command of the entire host since both the high-chief and his *etifeto*, his heir, fell in yesterday's battle defending their people. He understood that there was a debt of blood between his people and the Romans, since the Tigurini had destroyed a Roman army almost a generation ago. The man suggested that yesterday's battle had satisfied that debt, and now the Tigurini and the Romans should live in peace. He offered to obey the Roman Caesar and do whatever the Roman Caesar now requested of him. Then, there would be peace between their people."

Caesar thought about what the man had said, then said to me, "Tell me . . . What is his name, Insubrecus?"

I asked the Gaul, "*Mae Caisaro uhn gofun bet uhou eich enou, Prifo?*"

The man responded, "Please, tell the Caisar that I beg his pardon for my discourtesy. I am Tewdour mab Owain."

I told this to Caesar. He responded, "Tell Tudurmapowin this: First, he is to return his people to this place. Second, they are to bury their dead. Third, they are to return to their homeland. This is the Caisar's wish. Then, the *lemures* of our dead and his dead will rest, and there will be peace between our people."

I told this to the chief. The look of relief was apparent on his face. He had anticipated humiliation, decimation, and slavery for his people. Caesar's terms were more than generous.

We were just about to terminate the negotiation when Tewdour raised his wand of negotiation to get our attention.

"The Caisar's clemency is great!" he began. "Let me grant him a gift in return. Tell the Caisar that the People of the Dark Moon are not his friends, although they pretend to be. Their desire is his destruction. It was they who invited the Helvetii to migrate into their lands. It was they who encouraged the Helvetii to devastate the lands of their enemies, the People of Soucana. It was they who invited the Germans over the Rhenus with promises of fertile land and loot. Also, tell the Caisar, when the People of the Dark Moon first came among the Helvetii, in the time when Owain mab Aflon was the *orgorix*, Romans came with them, Romans bearing silver for the war chief of the Helvetii."

I translated this for Caesar. He showed little surprise at this information. "The *orgorix*," he mused. "That must be the one we call Orgetorix . . . That would have been back when Messala and Piso were consuls . . . Piso has connections to the Claudii."

Then Caesar said, "Can he describe these Romans?"

I conveyed Caesar's question to Tewdour, but he just shrugged his shoulders. Then, I spotted the tribune, Caecina, waiting in the distance with the Roman cavalry escort.

"I have an idea," I told Caesar. "Would you ask Caecina to join us?"

Caesar shrugged, then called, "*Caecina! Ad me venias!*"

The legate joined our group. When he was next to me, I slapped my chainmail *lorica* then his plate *lorica*, and asked Tewdour, "Can you tell me what armor the Romans wore?"

Tewdour said, "Most wore armor like yours . . . good ringed iron . . . but one wore a breastplate like the other . . . hammered bronze."

I reached out and grabbed the bottom of Caecina's tunic, and asked, "The one in bronze . . . was his tunic like this one?"

"Like that," Tewdour affirmed, "but the stripe was wider."

I told Caesar, "There was a Roman officer with the group, a *laticlavus*, a wide-striper."

Again, Caesar grunted. "A senior tribune . . . a senatorial . . . Ask him how the Orgetorix died."

When I did, Tewdour just shrugged and said, "He just died."

When I translated the response for Caesar, he just shook his head. "Sometimes men just die . . . It is their fate . . . Tell him we are done here . . . I expect to see his people gathered in this place by sundown."

I told Tewdour Caesar's wishes. He made no move to depart.

"Why isn't he going about his business?" Caesar asked me.

"He doesn't want to be rude," I told Caesar. "You have precedence here. It is for you to depart first."

"Very well," Caesar said and pulled the head of his horse around toward the bridges on the Arar. "Caecina, with me!" he called over his shoulder.

When we were a few paces away, Caesar instructed Caecina, "The Twelfth Legion is approaching the crossing. Go to their *primus pilus* . . . Nerva is his name . . . Tell him to detail four cohorts to remain on this side of the river and guard the Tigurini . . . I will give them two days to bury their dead and rest . . . Then, I want them heading east, back to their homeland . . . The four cohorts from the Twelfth and two *alae* of their cavalry will form a *vexillatio*, an independent detachment, to escort them . . . You will command it."

"A'mperi'tu', *Imperator*!" Caecina responded, obviously pleased about being given his first independent command.

"And, Caecina," Caesar continued, "the Twelfth is a new legion . . . Most of the men haven't been blooded . . . Tell Nerva to detail one of his more experienced centurions to you . . . Sanga, I think . . . the *pilus prior* of the Third Cohort . . . Yes . . . Sanga will fit the bill nicely."

Caecina rode off to find Nerva and the Twelfth Legion. Caesar led us back toward the bridge. As we rode, he asked me, "Are you surprised by my treatment of the Tigurini?"

"I can't say I understand it, *Patrone*," I answered.

"Why force a man to do what you want when you can convince him it's what he wants?" Caesar answered.

"I'm still not sure I understand," I admitted.

"With a large enemy force ahead of us, it makes no sense tactically to have another large enemy force in our rear," Caesar lectured. "And, I don't have the time or the manpower to police them all. Even if I were to do that, logistically speaking, what would I do with all those prisoners until I could unload them on the slave traders? No . . . better to be done with them . . . The real threat is still ahead of us."

Caesar didn't wait for my response, but continued, "Strategically speaking, the only way to secure the *imperium* is to keep the Germans east of the Rhenus . . . and the best way to do that is to maintain an alliance of strong Gallic tribes along the river . . . Even if they are not especially well-disposed towards Rome, they will not allow the Germans to cross and steal their lands . . . Rome needs the Tigurini back on the Rhenus and needs them strong enough to resist German incursions."

At the time, I had no idea why Caesar was sharing these thoughts with me. I have since learned that great men often make decisions based on instinct, and only later do they try to understand why they did what they did. Weak men fail to act and claim the issue was too complex.

When we crossed one of the bridges to the west side of the Arar, we encountered Labienus, back from his reconnaissance of the Helvetii.

"Ah, Labienus!" Caesar greeted him. "What news?"

"The main body of the enemy is no more than five thousand *passus* to the west," Labienus reported.

"Five thousand *passus*?" Caesar repeated. "They are certainly in no hurry to escape."

Labienus almost sighed, "*Imperator*, I don't think they see the need to escape . . . We couldn't get an accurate count, but there must be tens of thousands of them on the march . . . They fear us no more than an elephant fears a gnat."

Caesar did some quick calculations, "A hundred thousand Gauls . . . Fifty thousand are male . . . Twenty to twenty-five thousand of fighting age . . . No more than ten thousand warriors . . . The rest are just *pagani* with sharp sticks . . . We have six Roman legions . . . I have almost twenty-seven thousand troops in the field, according to this morning's strength report . . . What need do I have for caution?"

"There may be more than one hundred thousand out there on the march . . . many more," Labienus answered. "We need to get an accurate strength assessment before we decide to be too aggressive."

Caesar seemed to mull that over for a few heartbeats. "*Recte*," he acceded. "With that many out there, we're not about to lose them . . . and at their rate of march, they will not outrun us . . . We will follow at a safe distance until we have a clear idea of their intention and strength . . . Hopefully, we can entice them to attack us on terrain of our choosing."

Labienus nodded, then said, "We detected a small band of them heading back in our direction. We think it's some sort of delegation."

Caesar looked at me questioningly.

"If they want to talk, they'll be carrying the truce wands like the others," I told him.

Caesar looked over to Labienus, who just shrugged. "We didn't get that close, *Imperator*," he said.

Caesar grunted in response. "We'll see what they have to say, Titus," he said to Labienus. "Perhaps we can finish this thing here and now, the way we convinced the Tigurini to return to their lands on the Rhenus. When they arrive, lead them to a spot where they can see what we are doing here . . . There's a small hillock between the *castra* of the Tenth and the Seventh Legions . . . That would be perfect . . . I will meet their delegation there . . . Perhaps the sight of Roman power and competence will convince them to return to their homeland."

The Helvetii delegation arrived at the ninth hour. This time, Caesar remained mounted, waiting for them on the hillock, overlooking his legions on the west side of the river. The Helvetii could also see the bridges over the Arar and beyond the river, the remnants of the defeated Tigurini. The message was clear: in one day we defeated one of your tribes and accomplished a river crossing that took you weeks.

The leader of the Helvetian delegation was a giant of a man on a black stallion. His long, flowing gray hair hung freely from his bare head; his long, gray chin-length mustachios seemed to bristle with pride and defiance. As he waved his wand of negotiation negligently in our direction, the sun glinted off the golden armbands that circled his bulging biceps.

He rode directly at Caesar. At two paces away, he pulled his horse's head abruptly to the right; the animal reared a bit and exposed the warrior's long, Gallic sword in a gold-wired scabbard hanging down his left side. He stilled his mount and stared directly at Caesar with cold, piercing blue eyes for a few heartbeats.

It was then I realized that over his chainmail *lorica,* his chest was festooned with Roman *phalerae*—gold and silver sculpted disks awarded to centurions and rankers for acts of valor. No legionary would willingly surrender such treasures. They were trophies taken from Roman dead.

"So, Roman, you are the one called Caesar?" he said in Latin.

Caesar remained silent, perfectly still.

"Are you surprised I speak your language?" the warrior continued. "I learned it from my slaves, who were once soldiers in the army you sent against us many years ago, when we killed your chief, the one you called 'consul.'"

I heard Labienus suck in his breath when the warrior said that. This was not a negotiation, I realized. This man had come to challenge Caesar, to provoke him into combat.

"I am Dewi mab Coel . . . Divico to you Romans . . . Know that it was I who was *orgorix* of the Helvetii the day we slaughtered the Romans and took ten thousand heads."

"*Orgorix?*" Labienus whispered to me.

"Slaughter-king," I translated for him. "War chief."

"*Podex,*" Labienus hissed and spit on the ground.

"The whitened skulls of Roman dead decorate our feasting halls and lodges to this day . . . And now you have the temerity to attack us? Know you, Roman, the fact that you were able to ambush and slaughter one of our minor clans, while they were trapped against a river and burdened with women and children, does not impress us . . . Roman deception and cruelty has been known to us for many generations . . . We will offer you this . . . The valleys of the Rhodanus are wide and fertile . . . We will accept any of them and settle there . . . Know you, Roman, the Helvetii have learned from their ancestors to rely on valor and strength, not on deceit and ambush . . . Unless you want to make of this ground, on which we now stand, another monument to Roman defeat and shame, you will give us the land we demand and withdraw your soldiers across the Rhodanus . . . Then, there will be peace between our nations."

"Quite an oration," Labienus hissed. "He couldn't provoke Caesar more if he tried."

I looked over toward Caesar. His face was as white as a candidate's toga. His lower jaw was set slightly forward, and his thin lips were drawn tightly across his face like a knife scar. I later learned that this expression was the only telltale sign of his rage. Caesar was too controlled ever to demonstrate it, especially when facing an adversary.

Finally, Caesar spoke, "Well, do I remember that of which you speak. No Roman will ever forget the tragedy that befell our nation and the army of Lucius Cassius Longinus . . . Many families still mourn that day . . . Many still desire blood vengeance to appease the restless *lemures* of their murdered ancestors . . . You say that the Helvetii are a people of valor and courage . . . I tell you that you are a liar . . . You defeated Longinus only by deceit and ambush . . . You feigned friendship with the Roman people and delivered treachery at the end of a spear . . . Know you, Divico of the Helvetii, that, although members of my own *familia* lost their lives on that fateful day, I, Gaius Iulius Caesar, proconsul of the Roman people, commander of this army, offer you these terms for peace . . . First, you will return to the lands you abandoned on the Rhenus . . . Second, you will give restitution to the allies of the Roman people whose lands you have pillaged and destroyed . . . Third, you will surrender hostages to me to ensure your submission and good behavior . . . Only then am I willing to let the Helvetii leave this place in peace . . . And also know this, Divico of the Helvetii . . . The gods despise hubris . . . They do seem, at times, to grant their favor, but they do so only to heighten despair when they withdraw it. What is your answer, Divico?"

Divico's eyes glared at Caesar like burning blue embers. "Roman! Since the time of our ancestors, the Helvetii are accustomed to taking hostages, not surrendering them!"

He held up the wand of negotiation, broke it in two, spit on the pieces, and threw them at the feet of Caesar's horse. He pulled back on his reins, causing his black stallion to rear and turn, then galloped off the hillock, followed by his entourage.

Caesar calmly watched Divico ride off. Then, he turned to Labienus and said, "It appears that our negotiation with the Helvetii has ended. Come with me. We have work to do." Then, he rode off toward the *castrum* of the Tenth Legion.

Caesar had established his *praetorium* with the Tenth Legion. When we arrived at the headquarters tent, Caesar said, "Accompany me, Insubrecus!"

We entered Caesar's operations area; the maps were already hung, and soldiers were busy making notations. I could easily see the location of our army on the left side of a squiggly blue line that ran down from the top of the map. The Arar, I assumed. It led downward to another, thicker blue line that seemed to plunge toward the bottom left corner of the map: the Rhodanus. About a *cubitus* to the left of our location was a large red marker: the Helvetii.

While Caesar's body slave was helping him out of his armor, he was talking to Labienus. "That was the best theater I've seen since I left Rome! Divico! He could easily upstage Plautus' braggart. Did you see the size of that sword? How does the man walk without tripping?"

Labienus, his helmet under his arm, answered, "Could he have really been the Helvetian commander when they ambushed Longinus? That would make him what . . . sixty, if he's a day? No one could look like that at sixty."

"What did you think of that act, Insubrecus?" Caesar asked me.

"He was trying to provoke you, *Patrone*," I said stiffly.

"Of course he was," Caesar answered. "I sometimes forget how young you are, Gaius . . . You haven't had time to develop a sense of irony yet."

I too was beginning to forget how young I was.

Caesar stood staring at the situation map. "I feel a bit like that boy in the children's story . . . the one who thinks he's captured a lion because he has ahold of its tail," he was saying. "I can neither let go nor continue to hold on."

At his side, Labienus just grunted his consent.

Caesar continued, "Our first priority is to assess the enemy's intention. I assume they will continue moving west across Aeduan territory, but if they were to turn and attack us with our backs to the river, it could get messy. So, let's get a strong cavalry screen between us and them."

Again, Labienus nodded his agreement.

"Second, we need to assess their fighting strength," Caesar said. "That's going to take some aggressive reconnaissance. Do we have enough cavalry?"

"We have the legionary cavalry," Labienus calculated. "That gives us fifteen *turmae*, about 450 troopers . . . There is a scattering of native cavalry . . . They come and go as they please . . . I can only estimate their numbers."

"Are there any auxiliary cohorts available?" Caesar asked.

"The *Prima Gallica* is still near Gennava," Labienus estimated. "And, there's a Syrian outfit down near Massalia."

"Leave the *Prima Gallica* where it is," Caesar instructed. "The Allobroges are not reliable. I want an effective Roman force sitting on them while we're tied down with the Helvetii. Send down to the Syrian unit. Have them send up their cavalry cohort . . . *stat'* . . . What about that native cavalry?"

Labienus rubbed his chin. "It's difficult to give an exact count . . . Between the Aedui and the Sequani, there must be at least three hundred mounted troops."

"Insubrecus! Will the Gauls submit to Roman military authority?" Caesar asked.

I shrugged, "As long as they fear the Helvetii more than they resent us . . . they'll cooperate . . . How much *authority* they'll accept . . . that's difficult to say."

Caesar addressed Labienus, "Organize the natives into *turmae,* according to tribe . . . say, three *alae* each . . . We'll assign an experienced Roman tribune to each cohort . . . Who do we have available for senior commanders?"

Labienus stared at the ceiling of the tent, thinking. "There's certainly Publius Considius—"

Caesar interrupted, "He's not senior enough for overall command of the cavalry . . . plenty of experience, but not of *laticlavus* standing . . . And he's getting a bit long in the tooth! *Verpa Martis!* The man served under Sulla! I'm thinking Crassus as my cavalry legate . . . I'm sure he's fed up with pushing mules."

Labienus' eyebrow shot up. "Publius Licinius Crassus?"

"Yes," Caesar confirmed, "let's see if the boy has some grit hiding below all that flash . . . He's proven a competent enough *quaester* . . . We'll assign Considius to him and . . . what was the name of that *angusticlavus* from the Tenth who commanded the advance party across the Arar? . . . Agrippa . . . yes . . . Assign Lucius Vipsanius Agrippa to him, too."

"*A'mperi'tu',*" Labienus agreed. "And, who replaces Crassus as quartermaster?"

"Pulcher," Caesar said without hesitation. "I think a healthy dose of mule shit is just what that Claudian twit deserves . . . Yes . . . Pulcher is perfect for pushing the baggage . . . Insubrecus!"

"Yes, *Patrone?*" I responded.

"You get along with Agrippa, do you not?" Caesar asked.

"Yes, *Patrone.*"

"How long have you been *sub aquilis?*" Caesar asked.

I had to think. I was beginning to feel as if I had always been a soldier. "Just over three months, *Patrone.*"

"Just over three months," Caesar mused a bit and seemed to chuckle. Then, he said, "I'm appointing you to the rank of *decurio* . . . at least while you're assigned to Crassus' command . . . Do a good job, and you can keep the appointment."

Labienus slapped me on the back, "Congratulations, *Decurio!*"

"I'm parched . . . Being scared to death by a blowhard Gallic giant is thirsty work," Caesar announced. "*Scriba!*"

I heard a voice from the other side of the partition, "*Quid vis tu, Imperator?*"

"*Vinum!*" Caesar ordered.

"*Merum?*" the voice called. "Straight up?"

"No . . . *mixtum* . . . bring a pitcher of water," Caesar instructed. "We still have work to do," he said to us and winked.

"Back to our discussion . . . the cavalry . . . The Eleventh and Twelfth are mostly Gallic units . . . Let's send over to the *primus pilus* of each . . . We need Gallic speakers who can ride . . . like Insubrecus here . . . good troopers who are considered promotable . . . We'll make them *decuriones* and assign one to each of the native turmae."

I heard Labienus mumble, "*A'mperi'tu!*" I looked over at him. He was scribbling notes on a *tabula*.

Caesar continued, "Enemy intention and strength are our first two priorities. I need to know whether to avoid contact with the Helvetii or provoke it. We can establish our main supply depot at Lugdunum . . . That will give us access to both rivers . . . But my fear is that the Helvetii are going to move straight across country, away from the navigable rivers. That will stretch our supply lines . . . We may need to draw rations and fodder from our allies."

"That could prove a problem, Caesar," Labienus cautioned. "This far north, it's the beginning of planting season, and I doubt the Gauls have a great store of food left over after the winter."

Caesar seemed to think about that for a moment, then shrugged, "It doesn't matter . . . If the enemy moves into the hills, we can have each man carry five-day's rations . . . jerky, *buccellatum*, grain . . . same rations for the officers . . . I'm not burdening the supply train with their luxuries . . . We need the mules and wagons to carry rations, fodder, and the legionary artillery . . . Leave our siege equipment at Lugdunum . . . At least five-days' rations for each man on the legionary mules . . . The fodder's going to be more of a problem . . . The fields cannot yet support our mounts . . . The Gauls must be supplying their own people . . . They can supply us as well."

Caesar's slave entered with the wine and water. Caesar looked up. "Ah . . . *bene* . . . Go ahead and leave it . . . We'll pour ourselves."

Then, he noticed me standing there. "You look like you're on parade, Insubrecus . . . Sit down . . . Relax . . . My man will help you with your *lorica*."

Caesar poured the wine and left us to mix our own water. "Where was I?" he began. "Yes . . . supply . . . Pulcher's first priority will be to arrange grain and fodder from the Aedui as we move across their territory . . . Until we have a clear idea of enemy strength and intention, we will not draw any closer to them than five thousand *passus* . . . Another mission for the cavalry is identifying defensible terrain for the daily marching camps and identifying battle sites should I decide to provoke battle . . . a ridge . . . maximum four-legion front, *acies triplex* . . . good flank security . . . sun in the enemy's eyes . . . wind at our backs . . . You know the drill, Labienus . . . We'll keep the Eleventh and Twelfth in tactical reserve until they get some seasoning."

Labienus looked up from his notes, "Do you want me to assemble the commanders for a briefing?"

Caesar took a long draft of wine. "Yes . . . the *legati*, of course . . . all the *tribuni laticlavi* . . . and the *primus pilus* of each legion . . . We'll be dependent on our centurions for tactical leadership and control until our senior officers have more experience."

Labienus wrote on his *tabula*. "*Quot'orarum?*" he asked.

"Eleventh hour," Caesar said. "I want the officers back with their units by nightfall . . . We'll maintain full alert for the first and fourth watches . . . Keep a strong cavalry screen between the Helvetii and us . . . Having my back to the river is making me a bit nervous."

With that, Caesar dismissed Labienus, but requested that I stay behind. I waited while Caesar poured himself another cup of wine.

Then, he began, "Insubrecus . . . your mission with the native cavalry is to be my eyes and ears for our . . . what shall we call them . . . *socii nostri* . . . our allies. . . . I want to know their attitudes toward us . . . our presence here, north of the Rhodanus . . . and how they react to our officers. . . . If there're any problems, I need to know right away. . . . We're swimming in a sea full of dangerous and unreliable creatures . . . I don't want the Aedui suddenly deciding we're less welcome than the Helvetii and turning on us . . . I need someone who understands the Gauls . . . someone I can trust."

"*Ut vis tu, Patrone,*" I answered.

"*Bene!*" Caesar responded. "And, don't think I'm ignoring the information you've already brought me . . . about Romans influencing the Helvetii and the other Gauls . . . To imagine there was no influence would border on delusion . . . but assuming there's some plot against this army would be a bit paranoid . . . So, keep your eyes and ears open for any indication of Roman influence among the tribes . . . You can trust Labienus, but besides him, you speak only to me about this matter . . . Understand?"

"*Compre'endo, Patrone*," I responded.

Caesar got up from his camp chair and walked over to a wooden chest next to his field desk. "*Adveni, Insubrece*," he said, unlocking the chest. "I want to show you something."

I walked over to Caesar, and he showed me a collection of *tabulae*. "These are my notes on the campaign so far," he said, handing me one of the *tabulae*. I opened it and saw the first line, "*Gallia est omnis divisa in partes tres . . .*"

"That one's mostly a paraphrase of the Greeks . . . the geographies," Caesar explained. "My concept was to keep a journal of the campaign and periodically send the entries down to Rome to be read out to the people in the forum . . . This would be in addition to the official reports, which are prepared by my staff and sent down to the Senate . . . The journals for the people would need to be written in a simple, straightforward style . . . a blunt military report of what we are doing up here . . . That way, if there is some resistance by the *Optimates* . . . the aristocratic faction in the Senate . . . I'd still have the people behind me . . . So, these reports would have to be written in the people's Latin . . . I simply do not have the time to command this army and do justice to these journals . . . So, I'd like you to serve as my *ad manum* . . . You observe, notate, write the journal, and review the text with me . . . Politically, this journal is as important in Rome as a military victory in Gaul."

"*Patrone*," I stammered, "*non existimo me dignum* . . . I don't think I'm up to—"

Caesar held up his hand to stop me. "You were tutored by Gabinius' greekling . . . the same as his own children . . . That's good enough for me . . . Which reminds me . . . I will dispatch a personal message to the consul about . . . about your issue with his family . . . I will let him know that you are part of my personal staff . . . *et sub patrocinio meo* . . . That should put an end to any more *incidents* like the one in Aquileia."

That was perfectly clear. Caesar's offer was protection for writing his journal. "*Ut vis tu, Patrone*," I responded.

"Good lad!" Caesar said, actually tussling my hair. "Get with Valgus . . . Tell him I want you riding like a trooper by the end of the week . . . I don't want to lose my *ad manum* on the end of some Gallic lance!"

VIII.

De Calamitate Prima
THE FIRST DEBACLE

Quo proelio sublati Helvetii quod quingentis equitibus tantam multitudinem equitum propulerant.

"When the Helvetians push back a great number of our cavalry, with only five hundred of their own, they are encouraged by their success."

(from Gaius Marius Insubrecus' notebook of Caesar's journal)

We badly misjudged the response of the Aedui and Sequani to our call for cavalry. We thought we could raise a few hundred. By the sixth hour of the next day, some two thousand had gathered near our camps.

At Caesar's bidding, I questioned the assembled Gallic riders. Some said they came to defend their homeland; some, to loot the Helvetii; some were simply following their chiefs; some were out for the adventure. When pressed by Caesar for some common reason for their enthusiasm, all I could say was that there had been years of peace in the lands of the Aedui and Sequani. It was now the beginning of the fighting season, and the young warriors were spoiling for a fight, any fight. In short, they were bored.

Earlier, during the second hour, our legionary cavalry screen had reported that the Helvetii were on the move into the highlands west of the Arar. Caesar was content with allowing some distance to grow between his army and them; he still wasn't sure what size of a force he was dealing with.

While Crassus was being briefed by Caesar on his new responsibilities as *legatus equitium*, chief of cavalry, Labienus struggled to organize the Gauls into *turmae* and to integrate Roman leadership over them. The Gauls, especially the Sequani, wanted revenge for the burning, pillaging, and slaughter the Helvetii and their German allies had visited on their people. They could hardly be restrained from immediately attacking the enemy. As time passed, more Gallic bands slipped off to the west to pursue the Helvetii independently. By the seventh hour, the rest of our Gallic cavalry initiated a general, headlong pursuit—as if the Helvetii were defeated and fleeing. What Roman leadership Labienus had managed to integrate into this mass of horsemen were more dragged along than leading the way.

I again found myself riding with Athauhnu and the Sequani. He was commanding an *ala* of about twenty men under Madog, who led a hundred riders. Agrippa was the *angusticlavus* assigned to advise him. We had another trooper, a Padus-Valley Gaul from the Twelfth Legion called Flavus, "Whitey," because his hair was as blond as a Kraut's eyebrows. The rest of the unit was somewhat divided into three *alae*, but except for family and clan groups who tended to stick together, the organization was quite fluid. And, they were all fired up to get at the Helvetii.

"I no can to hold back," Madog was complaining to Agrippa. "Young men . . . very eager of going . . . want revenge . . . We lose maybe twenty already . . . They just go . . . We go too."

"Madog," Agrippa was cautioning him, "we don't know how many Helvetii are out there or what their tactical deployments are . . . We could be riding into a massacre."

"Bah . . . Helvetii girls," Madog dismissed Agrippa's advice. "We kill all."

Madog shouted to get his men's attention. When he had it, he waved his *spatha* over his head and whipped the Sequani into a blood frenzy. Then, he screamed, "Follow me!" in Gallic and led them galloping out toward the hills.

We three Romans just sat there in the dust of the Gauls' sudden departure. Agrippa looked over to me and said, "Did you catch what he said? What's his plan?"

"Plan?" I shrugged. "His simply told them to follow him and they will kill all the Helvetii they can find."

Agrippa stared at me for a long heartbeat, then shrugged. "We better catch up to them," he said. Then, he turned his horse and rode toward the hills, following the dusty trail of our Sequani.

Flavus and I rode after Agrippa. Catching up to the Sequani wouldn't be easy. Although their horses were smaller than ours, they had good stamina, especially in the hilly country of their homeland. Also, the Sequani rode lighter than we did. Most did not wear armor. Of those that did, many wore hardened leather as *loricae*, not the heavier chainmail armor and helmets that we were wearing. Many of the Sequani riders were armed with nothing more than small hunting spears. Only the richer Sequani had steel swords or even shields.

I was carrying two swords: my legionary *gladius* strapped on my right hip and a long *spatha* tied down on the left front of my saddle. I had my *pugio* on my left hip. Although I was carrying a small cavalry shield, a *parma*, strapped behind my left shoulder, I had decided not to carry the light cavalry stabbing spear that Valgus called a "Greek lance," the *dory*.

I was still not comfortable riding into possible combat against experienced riders. In the little time we had had, Valgus tried to teach me critical combat riding skills, mostly controlling my mount with my knees and legs so I could use my hands to wield my weapons: the shield in my left hand and the *spatha* in my right. Army mounts are trained for leg control, and Macro had shown me some military riding techniques back home. But, I had no doubt that in the confusion and terror of actual mounted combat, my riding skills would be far from adequate.

During my drills the night before, Valgus had told me a story about a *tiro* cavalryman, who lost control of his mount and was carried into the enemy formation. "A one-man charge!" Valgus chuckled. "Didn't work out well for the poor son of a bitch!"

I didn't want to be that guy, but I wasn't sure I could prevent it.

The other problem was using weapons while mounted. As an infantryman, I was taught to leverage the power of my attack from the balls of my feet. This was the essential technique of the power behind the basic infantry attack with shield and sword, the *percussus*. But, a rider "floats" in the saddle; his feet are literally dangling at the sides of his mount. Not only could I get no leverage to power a sword blow, but if I overreached, I'd lose my seat and find myself on the ground.

Again, I didn't want to be that guy.

Madog's *turmae* weren't difficult to follow, but they were difficult to overtake. We pursued them west across the narrow river valley and up into the highlands. Several times as we were riding, I was aware that we were just three Romans riding alone through hostile territory. If the Helvetii discovered us before we overtook the Sequani, it would not go well for us.

At about the eighth hour, we were some nine thousand *passus* out from the legionary camps. We were riding south up a small river valley with a wooded ridgeline to our west. As the sun shone through the trees at the top of the ridge, I noticed the silhouettes of riders.

I called ahead to Agrippa, "Tribune! We are not alone. Look to your right!"

Agrippa quickly spotted the riders. "Who are they, *Decurio?*" he asked.

It took me a few heartbeats to realize he was talking to me. I wasn't used to my new rank yet.

"*No'scio, Tribune!*" I answered. "I'll challenge them. Be ready to ride like the Furies if they're hostile!"

I rode over to the edge of the woods, which only served to make the men on the ridgeline less visible. Realizing there was no help for it, I yelled a challenge at them in Gah'el: "*Ar uh bruhnu! A uhduhch uhn gyfaillo i Rhufeinig?*"

After a few nervous heartbeats, I heard Athauhnu's voice from the top of the ridge in answer, "Little Roman! What kept you? Come up and join the fun!"

I shouted over to Agrippa and Flavus, "It's Madog's *turma*! They want us to come up!"

We found a track up the ridge and were soon with the Sequani. When Madog saw us, he pointed to another broad valley to the west under our ridgeline. "Good fighting," he said in his broken Latin. "Sending many Helvetii to Land of Youth."

Below us was a swirling brawl of native horsemen—hundreds of them. I could not separate Helvetii and Kraut from Aedui and Sequani. Men were hacking at each other from the backs of horses. On the ground, there were individual duals, small groups attacking other small groups, and all were wrapped in choking gray-brown dust. Periodically, I could recognize a Roman by his armor, but it was obvious that we were exerting no control over our allies or the battle.

"Good fighting!" Madog repeated. "Horses rest . . . Then, we go!"

That delay may have saved us.

Flavus suddenly pointed across the valley. "Tribune! The woodline!"

I peered in the direction that Flavus had indicated. The far woodline was in shadow because of the declining sun, but soon I was able to detect some movement in the gloom.

I began to ask Madog who it was, but I was interrupted by a burst of cacophonous trumpeting from across the valley.

"Helvetii come!" Madog exclaimed.

Immediately, from across the valley, Helvetian infantry, hundreds of them, mostly spearmen, charged into the cavalry melee.

Suddenly, Agrippa yelled, "*Vi'te*! Look there!"

Another large force of enemy infantry had worked its way undetected along the east side of the valley and was now rushing to block any escape route for our Gallic allies trapped in the valley below.

Then, another series of trumpet calls sounded; these were somewhat different from the first. A body of the Gallic cavalry disengaged itself from the battle and fled headlong down the valley to escape the onrushing Helvetian infantry.

"Aedui pigs!" Madog yelled at them. "They run from good fight like children!"

Agrippa reacted. "Madog! Follow me! We must open the road for our men!"

Agrippa moved down the ridge without waiting for Madog to respond. Flavus and I followed behind. We picked out a trail which led us down through the woods to the valley floor. I was relieved when the Sequani followed behind us.

I could see the battle below as we descended. The Helvetian spearmen were decimating our cavalry. I saw more than one Roman go down as the Helvetii stabbed up at them from the ground with their long spears. The Romans were wearing chainmail *loricae*, very valuable booty for the Gauls. I knew that those injured and dying were the newly minted *decuriones* from the Eleventh and Twelfth Legions. Once they were unhorsed and on the ground, follow-on Helvetii infantry surrounded them hacking and stabbing with whatever weapons they had brought to the fight: some swords; many knives; a few clubs; even hoes, billhooks, and scythes—anything that could kill.

Presently we reached the valley floor. The second mass of Helvetii had not seen us. They were loosely strung across the valley exit, expecting little opposition except for the few horsemen who might have escaped the main battle.

Agrippa rode out into the valley floor from the tree line, then yelled back, "Insubrecus! On my right! Flavus, my left!"

We rode out to comply. At that point, the Helvetii down the valley noticed us. I saw a few of them pointing and gesturing toward us.

"Madog!" Agrippa ordered. "Your *ala* is with me. The other two split, one with Insubrecus, the other with Flavus!"

I heard Madog relay the instructions in Gallic, and the riders gathered behind us.

Agrippa, "Form wedge!"

Madog repeated the order, and the Gauls formed behind us as best they could. I suddenly realized that I was the point man in the right-flank wedge, the first man in.

Agrippa yelled, "Right and left flanks, follow ten *passus* behind my center . . . at the WALK . . . FORWARD!"

Our *turmae* began to move toward the Helvetian blocking force. I could see them in the distance, less than three hundred *passus* away. They were beginning to coalesce into a line facing us.

Agrippa, "*Cornucen* . . . SOUND ATTENTION!"

There was some confusion as Madog relayed the order. Finally, a Sequani bugler sounded a series of cacophonous notes to get the attention of our allies engaged across the valley.

Agrippa, "At the TROT . . . FORWARD!"

We picked up the pace of our advance toward the enemy. They now stood shoulder to shoulder, facing us. Their officers and chiefs were adjusting their line, shouting encouragement.

Agrippa, "*Cornucen* . . . SOUND, WITHDRAW!"

That was the signal for our men across the valley to disengage from the enemy and follow us out of the valley.

Agrippa, "At the CANTER . . . FORWARD!"

At that, I could feel my mount's excitement grow. She seemed to be straining to get at the enemy. I had my shield off my shoulder and drew my *spatha* from its sheath. I was guiding my mount as best I could, using only my legs and knees.

Agrippa raised his own sword and screamed, "*TURMA* . . . CHARGE!"

The horses stretched forward into a dead run toward the enemy line. Over the pounding of the hooves, I heard the war cries of the Sequani.

I heard myself screaming in Latin, "*Fortuna! Bona Fortuna m'ames!* Goddess of Good Fortune! Favor me!"

Looking forward, I could see a solid, dark line of enemy infantry. As we closed, I could distinctly see faces, equipment, and spear points leveled directly at us. Suddenly, I remembered Valgus saying that Roman cavalry is not meant to engage infantry. We pursue; we scout; we screen. But we cannot stand up to infantry. Across the rapidly shrinking space, I spotted one Helvetian. He was looking directly at me. His spear was leveled at *me*. He intended to kill *me!*

Abruptly, out of nowhere, there was movement in the Helvetian line. A man dropped his spear and fled to the rear, then another, then more. My would-be killer looked to his right and saw his mates breaking and beginning to flee. He looked back at me. There was doubt in his eyes, then fear. Suddenly, he dropped his spear. He broke to his left. He was trying to get past our flank.

When I hit the Helvetian line, it was no more. We thundered past it. We hacked down the Helvetii spearmen fleeing to the rear, trying to outpace our mounts. Some fell to the ground, hoping to avoid our swords. Others turned at the last moment in a futile attempt at resistance.

We killed them.

About a hundred paces past the Helvetian line, we were out of the valley and in a bowl-like area where three valleys seemed to converge. Agrippa halted our advance and turned us around, facing the line of our own charge. About a hundred paces behind us, we could see what was left of our cavalry, riding to follow us out of the trap.

Agrippa yelled, "Spread out! Let them pass through us!"

Madog repeated the order in Gallic, and the Sequani did their best to comply. Their effort was adequate. Our escaping comrades managed to pass through our lines with little confusion. They did not halt to assist us.

When they had cleared us, Agrippa yelled, "Prepare to receive the enemy!"

Agrippa rode along our front with Madog in his wake, tightening our line, adjusting our positions, encouraging the men. In the distance, I could see a force of enemy cavalry about twice our size coming forward rapidly. My mount was still struggling to regain her wind.

Agrippa commanded, "If they attack, we move forward into them . . . We cannot allow them to hit us at a standstill . . . We cannot give them momentum . . . initiative."

Madog struggled to relay Agrippa's orders. I had no idea how he was coping with Latin words like "momentum" and "initiative."

In the distance, the enemy force was coalescing into individual riders. I was trying to detect their speed. I imagined that they would want to hit us at the gallop, but they seemed content to trot toward us.

Athauhnu appeared suddenly at my side. "Enjoy the ride, Little Roman!" he chuckled. "Soon the gods will give us more Helvetii dogs to kill. I'm happy the People of the Dark Moon did not remain with us. We will not have to share the glory with those pigs."

As I watched the enemy mass approaching, I was not at all sure that I appreciated Athauhnu's humor.

Agrippa and Madog assumed positions in the center of our line. The enemy continued to approach at a trot. They were less than two hundred *passus* from us. Agrippa knew he had to maintain enough distance to get our horses to a run before we made contact. He had just raised his sword to start us forward when the enemy halted.

For many heartbeats, we just sat there, looking at each other across a flat, grassy field. Then, one of the Helvetii riders came forward a few paces. He was wearing a high, plumed helmet and a chainmail *lorica*; he held up a large, battered, red shield. He raised a long Gallic *spatha* over his head. He was yelling something across at us. I could only pick up a few words: "dogs of the Romans . . . many heads taken . . . drinking mead out of your skulls!"

When he was done with his tirade, the Helvetii behind him raised a racket, screaming and hitting their shields with their swords and lances.

They seemed to be working themselves up to attack. At my side, Athauhnu said nothing. It seemed that his odd sense of whimsy had escaped even him.

Agrippa was strangely paralyzed by the outburst. He just sat there on his horse. In my mind, I both urged him to order the advance before it was too late and prayed to *Fortuna* that he would not.

Then, the Helvetian chief made an unmistakable, insulting hand gesture in our direction and spit on the ground. He turned his horse and rode back into his own troop. The entire Helvetian horde seemed to collapse backward, following their chief away from us. Soon, we were staring at the backs of a withdrawing enemy.

I could see Agrippa's shoulders sag with relief. Unless he were foolish enough to pursue, the fighting would be over for the day. I suspected Madog wanted to continue, but Agrippa reached over to Madog's mount and steadied both man and horse. We were finished for that day.

Finished, except for having to explain this debacle to Caesar.

We discovered the legionary *castra* less than five thousand *passus* from the site of the battle. Caesar had moved most of the army forward to shadow the Helvetii. Agrippa settled the Sequani in a protected position between the camps. Then, we Romans and Madog went in search of Caesar's *praetorium*. We found it again in the *castrum* of the Tenth Legion. When we approached the *praetorium* tent, we spotted Labienus directing some soldiers.

"Agrippa, what in the name of Hades happened out there?" he demanded as soon as he saw us. "The Gauls are all in an uproar about some ambush . . . a massacre . . . They're saying the Helvetii are coming, and they're all running off into the hills!"

We dismounted and approached Labienus. Agrippa asked, "Do you want me to give my report to you or to the *imperator*, *Legate*?"

Labienus thought about it for a moment, then said, "Let's go in and brief the boss. Crassus is already in there with him. How bad is it, Agrippa?"

Agrippa shrugged, "Not good . . . Could have been a lot worse . . . but not good."

Again, Labienus stared at him briefly, then gestured to the tent entrance saying, "Let's go see Caesar. Insubrecus! Come with us!"

Caesar was studying his maps. Crassus was with him, looking like he had just walked in from inspection parade. Clearly, the cavalry commander did not participate in his own unit's battle.

When Caesar heard us enter, he asked Labienus, "Titus, how confident are you that the six remaining cohorts of the Twelfth can hold the bridgehead against the enemy?"

Labienus shrugged, "Six cohorts of trained Roman soldiers fighting from well-prepared, defensive positions on good terrain should be able to hold back a sea of barbarians, *Imperator*! Agrippa has returned. He has a report about the cavalry battle."

"*Bene*," Caesar responded, walking away from the map. "*Nuntia, Tribune!* Report!"

Agrippa, his helmet gripped firmly under his left arm, assumed a stiffer position of attention. "*Imperator*, I commanded three *alae* of native cavalry . . . Sequani. . . . We encountered an enemy force of both cavalry and infantry, approximately—"

"Infantry?" Caesar interrupted. "There was infantry? How many? How equipped?"

Agrippa answered, "Approximately a cohort . . . maybe as many as eight centuries . . . lightly armored . . . principally with spears . . . some farm implements . . . a few swords."

Caesar nodded, "This is the first I've heard of infantry . . . About six hundred, you say?"

"*Nuntio recte, Imperator*," Agrippa answered.

Caesar seemed to mull this over. Then, he said, "*Bene* . . . Please, continue your report."

Agrippa continued, "We encountered a force of infantry and perhaps ten *alae* of cavalry approximately six thousand *passus* to the west . . . When we arrived at the eighth hour, the enemy cavalry was engaging our cavalry—"

"Why did you not immediately attack the enemy, Tribune?" Crassus interrupted. This was more of a challenge than a question.

Agrippa turned his head to face Crassus. "Legate, initially we were not in position to attack, and our horses were still winded from our advance—"

Caesar interrupted him, "We can get to that later, Crassus. Agrippa, continue your report!"

"*A'mperi'tu', Imperator!*" Agrippa responded, again facing Caesar. "At a given signal, the enemy infantry attacked our cavalry in two wings from concealment. One wing attacked our men directly; the other tried to seal off their escape—"

"Do you think this was a planned attack, Agrippa?" Caesar asked.

Agrippa hesitated. Caesar was asking him to commit himself on a military matter, use his tactical judgment, in front of his commander.

Finally, Agrippa stated, "*Existimo esse rectum, Imperator!* I believe that's the case! There was a prearranged signal given to initiate the infantry attack. I believe the Helvetii deliberately ambushed our cavalry and attempted to annihilate them."

"Bah!" Crassus exclaimed. "Those barbarians are not that sophisticated—"

"That's probably what Longinus believed right up until the time one of those unsophisticated barbarians was sawing off his head!" Caesar silenced him. "I want to hear the tribune's report, Crassus . . . After all . . . he was there!"

Crassus blanched at Caesar's swipe, then remained silent.

Agrippa continued, "My three *alae* attacked the enemy blocking force, allowing the survivors of our cavalry force to escape the trap. I estimate three or four *turmae* of friendlies escaped from the valley. The enemy chose not to continue the engagement and withdrew north, up the valley. We then returned here to report."

There was silence as Caesar digested what he was just told. Suddenly, Madog whispered, "Tell the Caisar that coward Aedui run away from fight."

"Who's this?" Caesar asked, seeming to notice Madog for the first time.

Agrippa responded, "*Imperator*, this is Madog mab Guuhn, leader of the Sequani cavalry, *equitatis Sequanianis dux.*"

"*Salve, Dux,*" Caesar nodded toward Madog. Then, he turned back to Agrippa. "What is this about the Aedui running from the battle?"

"*Imperator*," Agrippa reported, "when the Helvetii sprung their ambush, about three *alae* of Aeduan cavalry withdrew from the battle before the enemy could block their escape."

Caesar was just about to respond when Madog interrupted again, "No, Agrippa . . . that not Aedui horseman . . . that . . ." Madog's Latin began to fail him, "important man soldier . . . protect."

Caesar looked intently at Madog, then at Agrippa. Finally, he noticed me. "Insubrecus, can you tell me what this . . . this Madapguinus fellow is trying to say?"

I asked Madog in Gah'el, "Who were those horsemen, Lord?"

Madog responded, "They were *fintai,* the personal bodyguard of Deluuhnu mab Clethguuhno. I recognized their standards. He is the *dunorix* of the People of the Dark Moon, the commander of the king's stronghold, Bibracte. He is also the brother of the king, Duuhruhda mab Clethguuhno!"

I translated this for Caesar. He shrugged and said, "Then, we are fortunate that this . . . this *dunorix* person escaped. If he had been killed, it would have been a disaster for us and for the Aedui."

Madog picked up enough of what Caesar said to explain further. "The Caisar does not understand! The *fintai* of the *dunorix* would have led the horsemen of the People of the Dark Moon into that valley. Perhaps, Deluuhnu himself commanded them! They would never leave the place of battle while their people were in peril. It would be unthinkable! Shameful! They led their own people into that ambush and left them to be slaughtered!"

Again I translated, and again Caesar seemed inclined to dismiss the warning. "Just bad luck . . . It happens."

Again, Madog, "Surprised and ambushed by the Helvetii in their own lands? Impossible! They had to know! They led them into it."

After I translated that, Caesar challenged "*Qua causa?*"

Madog shrugged, "The *dunorix* is married to a Helvetian woman, the daughter of the former *orgorix*, the war chief of that tribe, the one who planned this invasion. Through his mother's people, he has formed marriage bonds with all the major clans of the Helvetii. With others, he has exchanged silver and hostages. He plots not only the destruction of the Caisar's army, but the destruction of his own people. He is not satisfied with being a mere *dunorix* of a single tribe; he plots to be the *dumnorix* of the Gah'el!"

It took me a few heartbeats to sort that out. Madog had constructed a clever pun: *dunorix*, the "fortress-king" of the Aedui, and the *dumnorix*, the "universe-king" of the Gauls. I translated all this for Caesar, translating *dumnorix* as *rex Gallorum*, king of the Gauls.

Caesar was now interested in what Madog was saying. "Ask him if the king of the Aedui, Diviciacus, knows of this," Caesar demanded.

Madog understood Caesar's question. He shrugged, "Diviciacus . . . Duuhruhda mab Clethguuhno . . . How could he not know what is happening in his own house?"

When Caesar heard this answer, he nodded. "Insubrecus, tell this Madicus . . . uh . . . tell the *Dux* he has done a great service to the Roman people . . . Tell him we are grateful . . . I will direct my *quaester* to issue his *turma* rations . . . equipment . . . whatever they need if he will continue to serve the *populi Romani*."

When I translated this for Madog, his eyes widened. A single, worn-out chainmail *lorica* was enough to assure the loyalty of one of his riders for a lifetime—a well-forged sword, two lifetimes. Caesar had just bought the loyalty of Madog and his troop for as long as he needed them.

Madog bowed. "*Me' Caesar . . . gratias ti'ago . . . maximas gratias . . . Tu' vir sum, ego!*"

Madog departed. He was going to cash in on Caesar's promise before the general could change his mind.

Caesar seemed a bit amused. "It's just a few battered *loricae* and a few rusty swords! Are you Gauls always this enthusiastically grateful?"

I decided to ignore Caesar's "you Gauls" characterization and explained, "*Imperator*, iron armor and weapons are valuable to these people. By putting them in Madog's hands, he can ensure the loyalty of his soldiers for the rest of their lives. You just made him one of the most powerful *orgorixa*, war chiefs, among his people. Even his own king must now give him respect. In fact, you are now his *orgorix* . . . his war chief. He will never cease being Sequani, but now he is, as he said, *vir tuus, miles Caesari* . . . your man, a soldier of Caesar."

Caesar stared at me briefly, then said, "*Simil'est clientela*? Like clientage?"

"*Recte, Imperator*," I affirmed, "but to the death . . . He is honor-bound to you."

"An important lesson, Insubrecus," Caesar responded, nodding. "What do you think of all this, Labienus?"

Labienus shrugged, "I don't know where to start. It seems we cannot trust the Aedui. What concerns me is that we are about to enter their territory and will be dependent on them to supply the army with food and fodder."

Caesar seemed to become impatient, "Yes . . . yes . . . Agrippa . . . what happened today? From your point of view . . . what went wrong?"

Agrippa stiffened a bit. He was a mere *angusticlavus* and on the spot again before the *imperator*, his chief of staff, and his own legate, Crassus.

He tried to cage his response, "*Imperator* . . . uh . . . there were many . . . uh . . . variables . . . things no one could foresee."

Caesar had no patience for this evasiveness. "Come now, Agrippa . . . You're a Roman soldier . . . an officer . . . We're all comrades here . . . Nothing matters except this army and the interests of the Roman people . . . You were out there on the ground . . . If you were me, what would you have done differently?"

Agrippa nodded, "*Imperator*, it was a matter of command and control. Once the Gallic cavalry rode off, they did what they wanted to do. None of us could control them. There were too many of them, too few of us, and too little time to integrate leadership among them."

"So, you're saying this was *my* fault?" Crassus accused.

"No! No, Legate!" Agrippa attempted. "No one could have—"

Caesar interrupted, "Please . . . gentlemen . . . if it were anyone's *fault*, it would be mine. I am the commander of this army. I cast my *pilum* before I had a mark. No . . . if anyone is to blame for this . . . this . . . *calamitas* . . . this debacle . . . it's me. Thank you for your *libertas*, Agrippa, your candor. It's a Roman virtue, and I appreciate it. Now, gentlemen . . . please, leave me . . . except for you, Labienus. I need some time to think."

As we left Caesar's *praetorium*, Crassus intercepted us. "Tribune!" he summoned Agrippa.

"*Adsum ti', Legate,*" Agrippa responded, coming to attention.

"Tribune!" Crassus started. "You will never . . . I repeat . . . never speak out of line in or out of my presence again! You will report to me and only to me! If the *imperator* needs to hear anything you have to say, he will hear it from me. Do you understand me clearly, Tribune?"

"*Perspicue, Legate!*" Agrippa almost shouted.

"*Miss'est, Tribune!*" Crassus dismissed him. Then, he noticed me.

"*Tu,*" he started. "*Tu! Si tu non deliciae Caesari Galliculae . . .* You . . . you . . . if you weren't Caesar's little Gallic bitch, I'd have your guts for boot straps! I can't stop you from telling the *imperator* anything you want, but as long as you're assigned to my command, you stay away from me. I don't want to see you, hear you, or be reminded that you as much as exist. Do you understand me, boy?"

"*Compre'endo, Legate!*" I shouted.

"You'd better! If I have any more trouble with you, *boy*, even Caesar won't be able to save your sorry ass!"

With that parting shot, Crassus stomped out of the *praetorium*.

I waited a moment before following him out. I was halfway through a string of expletives, "*verpa . . . mentula . . . fututor canibus . . .*" when I noticed Agrippa standing outside the tent. I immediately stiffened to attention.

"Tribune!" I stammered. "I didn't see . . . I mean . . . I—"

"Don't worry about it, *Decurio*," Agrippa said, putting his hand on my shoulder. "We've had one hell of a day. I'm parched. Would you happen to know where we could find a nice jug of wine, or maybe some *posca? Coleonibus Martis!* I'd even settle for some of that horse piss the Gauls call *cooru.*"

IX.

Lente Festinamus
WE HURRY SLOWLY

Caesar suos a proelio continebat ac satis habebat in praesentia hostem rapinis pabulationibus populationibusque prohibere.

"Caesar held his troops back from battle. For the time being, he considered it adequate to prevent the enemy from looting, foraging, and plundering."

(from Gaius Marius Insubrecus' notebook of Caesar's journal)

We pursued the Helvetii for the next ten days.

Pursuit is perhaps too aggressive a word to describe what was happening. After the debacle with our cavalry, and the continuing uncertainty of the enemy's strength, Caesar refused to allow any of his units to become engaged with the Helvetii.

Our cavalry tried to maintain contact with the enemy. On its face, this mission was not much of a challenge. We were following a massive horde, tens of thousands of men, women, and children. They were dragging everything they possessed along with them, with some of it on their backs, some strapped to beasts of burden, and the rest piled into slow-moving wagons. We could follow them from their trail: a path of crushed grass, burned huts, dead livestock, and uprooted foliage almost a thousand *passus* wide.

Also, our infantry, which could easily march twenty thousand *passus* a day without breaking much of a sweat, was barely moving ten. By the standards of the Roman army, the pace was leisurely. By the seventh day of our "advance," the Twelfth Legion had caught up with us, having tucked the Tigurini back in along the Rhenus and having pulled down the bridges over the Arar. Caesar could now deploy all five of his legions against the enemy.

At the same time, the enemy was becoming quite aggressive. Not a day passed without an attack on one or more of our cavalry patrols. From a tactical point of view, this made perfect sense. Tacticians called it "preventing reconnaissance." The enemy cavalry was screening the main body from our reconnaissance patrols.

Athauhnu, by then all decked out in his Roman chainmail *lorica* and shining brass cavalry helmet, told me that the Helvetii were too thoughtless and rash to execute an actual strategy. Most of the attacks on our cavalry were carried out by minor Helvetian war chiefs seeking heads, horses, and booty. Unfortunately, as it would prove, many of our senior officers believed this theory, too.

However, these incessant spoiling attacks by the Helvetii were taking a toll on our Gallic allies. There was no booty to be had and much danger to be anticipated. Unlike the Roman army deserters, who would sneak away alone or in pairs in the dead of night, the Gauls just left. Entire *turmae* rode away to return to their homes. When I asked Madog about it, he just shrugged. If there was no glory to be had, no riches to seize, why remain? By the tenth day, I doubted we could field five *turmae* of native cavalry against the Helvetii.

The most pressing problems, though, were the men's rations and the fodder for the horses. The legions had gone through the ten-day marching rations that they had been carrying, but no resupply had arrived from our allies, the Aedui, whose territory we were marching across. Caesar had managed to bring up one supply column from Lugdunum back at the confluence of the Rhodanus and the Arar. But, we had advanced almost one hundred thousand *passus* away from that supply depot. Although the legions had cleared a passable road along our route of march, Labienus was still doubtful as he calculated the amount of time the *impedimenta* took to make the trip and its carrying capacity. The inescapable conclusion was that we could not adequately supply the army along that route. Unless the Aedui made good on their promises to supply the army, the men would have to be placed on reduced rations—sooner rather than later.

Caesar was resisting the recommendation to reduce his men's rations. He knew that Roman soldiers would tolerate many hardships on campaign—their officers' arrogance, harsh discipline, even at times tactical incompetence—but they would not tolerate logistical bungling for long.

Never botch the men's rations!

On the afternoon of the eleventh day, after returning to the legionary *castra* from patrol, I was summoned to Caesar's *praetorium*. I was still riding with Agrippa and Madog's Sequani. Agrippa was proving to be a good officer and a good companion. During one of our rides, he shared with me his desire to pursue a career in the army, not politics down in Rome. He was concerned about being subordinate to Crassus and his arrogance. But, avoiding Crassus while on active field duty didn't prove much of a challenge. The man didn't seem interested in doing anything that might tarnish his armor. Agrippa was also aware of my relationship with Caesar, but he never brought it up in any of our conversations.

One afternoon, Agrippa shared with me that he had a little brother named Marcus back home in Asisium. Their father had died when both boys were young, and Agrippa had to assume the role of *pater familias* for his brother, younger sister, Vipsania, and their mother. Marcus was only fourteen, five years younger than Agrippa. Marcus idealized his older brother and wanted to follow him into the army when he was of age.

With a start, I realized that, as we were riding with Madog's Sequani through the lands of the Aedui, thousands of *passus* north of the Rhodanus in *Gallia Comata*, trying to avoid being ambushed by enemy war bands and trying to make contact with a large and menacing enemy force, I would be turning seventeen on my next birthday.

I reported to Caesar's *praetorium* as ordered. When I arrived, Labienus and Caesar were conferring in front of the operations map. Caesar was asking, "What if we attempted to shorten our supply lines by moving the supply depot down the Rhodanus to a position directly south of our location? Surely, we could float our supplies and equipment down the river on barges. That would also shorten the route from our port in Massalia."

"That would shorten our supply lines," Labienus agreed. "And, if the Helvetii continue to march west, we may eventually have to do just that. But, that will not solve our immediate problem of feeding the men and the livestock. Also, we'd have to reconnoiter and establish supply routes south to the river. That would strip away part of our infantry force, while at the same time we are facing a numerically superior enemy. No! The only solution is to draw supply from the Aedui—either with their help, as they promised, or despite them."

Caesar seemed to ruminate over what he had been told, finally asking, "What are your recommendations, Titus?"

"I see only two options, Caesar," Labienus answered. "One, we send out foraging parties and take what we need from the surrounding settlements. Granted, we could pay for what we take, but we need food and fodder immediately. Second, you summon Diviciacus and demand he make good on his promises. Threaten to take hostages if need be, but you've got to put his *colei* in the vice and get him moving!"

Caesar thought about that for a few heartbeats. "What if we strip our ranks for *venatores* and send them out to bring back game?"

Labienus shrugged, "*Venatores* would be useful to augment our rations with meat, but I doubt that they can supply the entire army with food. Besides, even if most of the hunters manage to avoid being picked off by enemy cavalry, how much game do you think they'll find within ten thousand *passus* of our army after the Helvetii have gone through and stripped everything? And, hunting does nothing to alleviate our fodder shortages."

It was then that Caesar noticed me. "Ah! Insubrecus! You ride with Agrippa's Sequani. How are the Gauls feeding their horses?"

I shrugged, "They let them graze when they're in a secure location and far enough off the line of march so that there's foraging available. Sometimes, they just go into an Aedui village and demand food and fodder for keeping the Helvetians moving away. The farmers aren't altogether pleased with it, but with Helvetii and German raiding parties in the area, they recognize the necessity of keeping the Sequani on their side."

Caesar thought about this briefly. Then said, "*Bene*! There's our answer, Labienus. We'll put Diviciacus' balls in a vice, like you say. Summon him to me here. Meanwhile, we'll send out a limited number of foraging details to the nearby villages . . . detail the Eleventh and Twelfth. There are plenty of Gallic speakers among the soldiers in those legions. Remind the Gauls in the villages that it's the Roman army that's keeping the Helvetii and Germans at bay, and the Roman army needs to eat. We will pay for what we take. Detail a member of the *quaester*'s staff to accompany each detail. He'll designate what's useful to the army . . . Have him draw funds from the treasury for payment . . . standard rates for anything taken. Take care to leave the Gauls enough to survive until the next harvest. Rome is their friend, not their oppressor. Put a junior tribune, an *angusticlavus*, in charge of each detail, with a *centuria* of *muli* from the legions. We must use moderation in this. The men will only take action to defend themselves or the supplies. I want no incidents with the friendlies. We are swimming in a sea of Gauls, so stirring up a storm is not in our interest. In fact, I will personally brief all the *angusticlavi* and centurions before they go out. The message to Diviciacus should be clear: fulfill his promises to supply the army, or we'll take what we need."

This was a classic Caesarian performance: take in information, process it quietly and quickly, and then deliver an explosion of decisions and instructions.

While Caesar spoke, Labienus was muttering, "*Bene . . . bene*," while furiously taking notes on a *tabula*.

Finally, Caesar asked, "*Habesne quaestiones ullae, Labiene*? Any questions?"

"*N'abeo*," Labienus muttered, still writing.

"What do you think, Insubrecus?" Caesar asked me. "How will the Gauls react?"

I shrugged. "Difficult to say, *Patrone*. Armed Roman soldiers are entirely different from Gallic cavalry to these people, but payment will help. The *quaester* will need to pay the village headman, not the individual farmers. Also, it may be good to barter a bit. The Gauls consider that more . . . uh . . . gracious . . . more civil than just forcing a fixed price."

"Good point," Caesar agreed. "Did you get that, Titus?"

"Barter a bit . . . more civil," Labienus muttered not looking up from his *tabula*. Finally, he stopped writing.

"Titus," Caesar began, "thank you! Go arrange the foraging details with the *quaester* and the *primi pili* of the Eleventh and Twelfth. Detail the tribunes yourself. That lad, Caecina—the one who commanded the *vexillatio*, the detail that escorted the Tigurini back to the Rhenus—he'd be a good choice for this. But only our 'brighter lamps,' eh? Initially ten teams: five north and west, five south and west. Stay clear of the enemy. Also, find Agrippa and that Madocus *Dux* who commands the Sequani cavalry and have them report to me. I want them to shadow the foraging details going north."

"*A'mperi'tu', Imperator!*" Labienus said.

"*Bene!*" Caesar acknowledged. "Insubrecus! You stay! I need to talk to you about something."

Labienus and his *tabula* left the *praetorium* on his mission, and Caesar gestured me over to his field desk. He gestured to a chair, "*Sedeas, Insubrece!*"

Caesar picked up a couple of the *tabulae* stacked on his desk. "I've reviewed the work you've done on my journals, and I'm pleased . . . quite pleased. I've made a few minor changes."

He handed me the stack. I opened the first and recognized the opening lines of the first entry, "*Gallia est omnis divisa in partes tres.*" Then, I noticed where Caesar had inserted a correction. Caesar wrote, "*nostra*, in our language, they are called Gauls."

"*Patrone*," I said, "we call ourselves *Gah'ela*, which is close to the Latin word used in the text, '*Galli*,' so there's really no need—"

"I understand that," Caesar interrupted. "But, this book is not meant for language scholars and geographers. It's meant for the *plebes* in the forum. The word *Galli* represents the things of Roman nightmares: giant, bloodthirsty, invincible savages from the dark forests of the frozen lands to the north . . . and these are *our* victories . . . *nostra*. Subtle, I agree, but sometimes *suggesting* is more powerful than *stating*."

I nodded my agreement. Caesar went on, "But, that's not the reason I asked you to stay. I received a response from Consul Gabinius, about . . . about our little problem."

With that, Caesar had my complete attention. I replaced the *tabulae* on his desk.

"I'm actually quite surprised at how quickly the consul responded," Caesar continued. "Almost as surprised as I was by the response. In short, Gabinius denies all knowledge of any attempt on your life."

"*Patrone! Sed igitur quis?*" I began.

Caesar held up his hand to silence my protest. "I believe the consul. He has no reason to lie and every reason to tell the truth in this matter. Since I made it clear to him that this was a matter of *patrocinium*, and therefore a matter of the *dignitas* of my family, he could very well have brought up the *dignitas* of his family. You did put a shameful mark on his son's face with that *pugio* of yours, and the consul could have horse-traded for some political advantage. But, he didn't. He simply said he and his son were not involved in this thing."

"I was only defending myself, *Patrone*—" I protested.

Again, Caesar stopped me, "I know that, Gai. I believe Gabinius understands that, too. But, I also believe this line of inquiry is a dead end."

As I was mulling that over, Caesar said, "There is one more thing."

"What is that, *Patrone?*" I responded.

"The consul has asked me to take on his son as a *tribunus militium*," Caesar stated. "It seems that his posting to Greece . . . well . . . that fell through. Gabinius had to make some deals and pull in some markers to get elected, and that soured his son's posting to Greece. It seems that Gabinius and the proconsul to Greece are no longer in the same political camp. But, Gabinius is an associate of Pompey, and I need Pompey's good will in supporting my interests in Rome. So, I really have no choice but to—"

"*Sed, Patrone!*" I burst out.

Caesar again raised his hand to silence me, "Gai! I have little real choice in this! It's politics! Besides, there's an old Roman saying, '*Vincinia amici teneantur hostes magis.* Keep your friends close, your enemies closer.' I'll find something to keep young Gabinius busy in the supply depot. He can keep Pulcher and the pack mules company. Or, I need someone to command the military port in Massalia. You'll never see him, and he'll be firmly under my thumb. His father and I both understand *patrocinium* and *dignitas*. There will be no problems having him with the army . . . none . . . I will not allow it."

It made sense, but I was not totally convinced.

Caesar changed the subject. "I've been giving some thought to what you told me about the possibility of Roman interference with the Helvetii."

"*Audio, Patrone*," was all I could muster. My mind was still trying to sort out the Gabinius news.

"Ambitious Romans have been known to provoke barbarians on the borders of the *imperium* for the sake of military adventures," Caesar explained. "According to your sources, while Piso and Messalla were consuls, Orgetorix took Roman silver from a senatorial in order to provoke the Helvetii to abandon their homeland. Messalla is not a soldier, and Piso expected to be given the Syria province, not Gaul. Rome's golden boy, Pompey, celebrated his triumph for defeating Mithridates that year. Even he is not so ambitious that he would provoke a war in Gaul so soon after returning from Asia. That leaves Crassus. He certainly had enough gold to buy a mere Helvetian chief, and he was still smarting after Pompey stole his glory in the slave wars. The Senate only awarded him an *Ovatio* for defeating the slaves, not the Triumph he desired. He had the opportunity and the motive, I think. Defeating the tribe that played a leading role in the destruction of Longinus' army would have assured him a Triumph. All he had to do was convince the Helvetii to invade our *provincia* and then convince the Senate to give him the command. He had more than enough gold to accomplish both."

I just nodded. All this was a bit beyond me, but I did recognize the name Crassus. The dressing down that Crassus Iunior had given me over the recent cavalry debacle was still fresh in my mind.

"That still begs the question why Romans would be still involved with the Gauls, now the Aedui, it seems," Caesar continued. "Crassus' attention has turned east toward Parthia, so who is trying to buy betrayal from the Aedui, I wonder?"

I correctly understood this as a rhetorical question and kept silent.

"There are two distinct possibilities," Caesar continued. "Pompey could be trying to engineer my defeat simply to take me down a few notches. He's protective of his reputation as Rome's premiere soldier, and he's not the type of man who shares his glory with anyone . . . But, no . . . he's now my son-in-law . . . married to my Iulia."

I realized Caesar was talking simply to hear himself out, so I remained silent.

"Then there are the *Optimates* in the Senate, the last, sorry vestiges of Sulla's excesses. They would do anything to bring me down. Cicero and Cato are too traditional to engineer the defeat of a Roman army in the field. Lucullus is filthy rich from the booty he brought home from Asia. He could buy half of Gaul, and he's still smarting from being relieved from his command so that Pompey could finish off Mithridates and celebrate a Triumph. But, he's an old man now. He seems content with his building projects and his fishponds. Bibulus has never forgiven me for upstaging him during our consulship. He tried to block my appointment as proconsul to Gaul. Pompey even thinks Bibulus is trying to assassinate him, but I doubt he's capable of a complex plot. He can hardly plan his day competently. Then there's Brutus. He's young, but not without ambition. And, Pompey killed his father. But, no . . . that can't be . . . He's Servillia's son . . . That would be close to patri—"

Caesar suddenly interrupted his own monologue. He seemed to come out of his musings and return to his *praetorium* in the hills of *Gallia comata*. He again noticed me sitting in front of his desk.

"This issue bears watching, Gai," he said. "I think our friend, the one whose men ran from the cavalry battle, what did you call him? The *dumus rex?*"

"Deluuhnu mab Clethguuhno," I offered. "The *dunorix* of the Aedui, the king's brother."

"That's the one!" Caesar agreed. "He bears watching. He may be the key to this." Then, Caesar seemed to have an idea. "And, he may be just what I need to put pressure on his brother."

At that point, Caesar's *scriba* stuck his head into the *cubiculum*, "*Imperator!* The tribune, Agrippa, and his Gaul are here as ordered."

"*Bene*," Caesar responded. "Send them in!"

I rose as Agrippa marched into the room in full kit, helmet tucked under his left arm. He assumed a stiff position of attention and reported to Caesar, "*Imperator, Lucius Vipsanius Agrippa, Tribunus Militium, defert ut imperatus!*"

I noticed that Madog hung back, watching the Roman show.

"*Laxa, Tribune,*" Caesar responded. "Sit down here. Madocus *Dux*! Please . . . sit! I wish to talk to you about a mission. Please sit, all of you."

We sat, and Caesar called out to his clerk, "*Scriba!* A jug of *posca* . . . and four cups!"

"*A'mperi'tu', Imperator,*" responded a bodiless voice from beyond the tent flap.

I wondered briefly how Caesar managed to have a supply of *posca* while many of the legionary *muli* were considering boiling their boot straps for soup.

As we all settled in front of Caesar, he began, "While we're waiting for the *posca*, tell me how things are going out there."

Always an awkward question to answer in front of the commander, especially considering how prickly the absent legate, Crassus, was of his "prerogative."

Agrippa, as the senior officer on our side of the desk, waded in. "*Imperator*, the main body of the enemy continues to move slowly west, as you know. We notice that their depredations have lessened considerably since they left the lands of the Sequani."

Madog audibly grunted when Agrippa stated this.

"We believe that it is due to the pressure our army is putting on them . . . We are still experiencing aggressive counter reconnaissance, mostly from their cavalry . . . But small infantry units, usually no more than a *centuria* in size, have, at times, attempted to engage us. According to your orders, we have avoided contact whenever possible—"

Caesar interrupted Agrippa's report, "*Bene* . . . What about you, Madocus? What are you seeing out there?"

Madog shrugged, "Agrippa, to be truthful . . . very dangerous . . . Helvetii and German everyplace . . . want fight."

"*Bene*," Caesar agreed. "But, I heard you react when Agrippa said that enemy damage has lessened since the enemy entered Aedui territory. Why do you think that is?"

Madog shrugged again, "Aedui buy them, I think . . . Give Helvetii silver . . . No burn, no steal . . . Give Helvetii food . . . maybe you food . . . Kill Sequani . . . No kill Aedui."

Caesar's clerk entered the *cubiculum* with a pitcher of *posca* and cups. As he set them down on the desk, Caesar asked, "Were you sure to test the *posca*, Ebrius? Is it up to your standard?"

"I assure you it is, *Imperator*," the clerk responded without batting an eye. "And, I guarantee it's not poisoned."

"Glad you're looking out for me," Caesar responded. I assumed this was a well-rehearsed routine between them. "You may go. We'll pour ourselves."

As the clerk, Ebrius, left, Caesar asked, "Will you do the honors, Insubrecus?"

As I poured, Caesar began his briefing. "Tomorrow, I'm sending out ten foraging details . . . wagons and a century of *muli* from the Eleventh and Twelfth Legions. There'll be an *angusticlavus* in command and a centurion with the infantry. I'm sending one detail straight north. They'll be the most exposed team . . . close to the enemy . . . hilly country . . . perfect for ambushes. I want you to screen them to the west and make sure they have a clear route out and back . . . Pretty standard cavalry mission. They'll pull out at first light tomorrow when the signal for ending the fourth watch sounds."

When Caesar finished, we all took the opportunity to sip the *posca*. Ebrius was right. The *posca* was prime. It hardly burned the back of my throat at all as it went down; it had a nice aftertaste of honey and herbs.

Caesar continued, "One of my goals is to test the attitudes of the Aedui toward us and to find out why they haven't come through with the supplies they promised us. If there is any evidence of a conspiracy between the Aedui and the Helvetii, that's where you come in, Insubrecus. I want you to be my fly on the wall. Pick up any intelligence you can from the villagers."

"*A'mperi'tu'*, *Imperator!*" I acknowledged, putting my cup down on the desk.

"I have summoned Diviciacus, the king of the Aedui," Caesar continued. "I expect him no later than tomorrow afternoon, but I plan to let him cool his heels, at least until the day after. I need to be briefed by you on what you find out in the field *before* I face him. In fact, your information will go a long way in my planning a strategy for dealing with the Aedui. So, I expect to see all three of you in my *praetorium* tomorrow—no later than the first night watch."

Both Agrippa and I muttered "*A'mperi'tu'!*" Madog just nodded.

Caesar took a long draught from his cup. He was enough of a trooper that the *posca* didn't seem to affect him at all. But, then again, if anything affected Caesar, he gave little indication of it.

He continued, "By the time you get back in, I expect the *castra* to have moved about ten thousand *passus* west of this location. But, your best bet is to return to this location and follow our trail out. If for any reason the army doesn't relocate tomorrow and you go directly to where you expect us to be, you'll run right into the Helvetii."

We had already figured that one out, but we all nodded as if Caesar had given us sage advice.

"*Quaestiones ullae?*" Caesar asked. "Any questions?"

"*N'abeo, Imperator,*" Agrippa and I answered. Madog just shrugged and grunted.

"*Bene,*" Caesar said. "*Miss'est* . . . Get some sleep! You have an early start in the morning. Insubrecus . . . stay behind, please!"

I rose as Agrippa and Madog left. As soon as they were gone, Caesar said, "Gai, I'm posting some dispatches, instructions to one of my *comites,* my deputy down in Aquileia. The courier departs tomorrow at first light. I understand that you come from a small farm just outside Mediolanum. Perhaps you'd like to write a short note to your parents? Let them know you're safe . . . what you're doing. I know military service can be worrisome, especially for mothers. What's her name? Valeria, is it not? My clerk can fit you up with some papyrus and a pen. Place your message in the dispatch bag, and I'll see that it's delivered. Your parents will be proud of your promotion. I'll give instructions for the courier to wait for a response."

"*Multas gratias, Patrone!*" I stammered.

I was staggered, not only by Caesar's kindness, but also by the fact he actually knew where my home was, and he knew my mother's name. Later, many who claimed to know Caesar well, certainly better than I did, claimed this was all part of an act, an elaborate ruse to instill loyalty and devotion in those around him.

I never learned the truth of it. Caesar was certainly a consummate actor, always on stage, but he was also a man, a human being. And, a kindness imitated is still a kindness done.

On my way out of the *praetorium*, I did scribble out a quick note to my parents, mostly to mama. After all these years, I don't remember what I wrote. Probably some bromides about being well, about the weather being warm and dry, about having plenty to eat, about being in no danger—the sort of stuff a young soldier thinks his mother should hear, the sort of stuff I wrote to her until the day arrived when writing home didn't make sense to me anymore.

Mama has long since gone to the Land of Shadows. A hundred Orpheuses with a hundred lyres cannot bring her back. What I wouldn't give to be able to write one more message to her and have the courier wait for her response. I'm sure I'd take the opportunity more seriously than I did that evening in Caesar's *praetorium*.

Before dawn the next morning, I joined Agrippa and the Sequani cavalry. The foraging parties were assembling in a secure, open area between the legionary *castra*. In the dark, the assembly was a confused mass of dark, moving shapes, alive with the creaking of wagons, clanking and scraping of armor and weapons, jangling of harnesses, whickering, snorting and stomping of horses anxious to be on their way, complaints and curses in Latin and Gallic, and the smell of the ever-patient mules.

We sorted things out and found the foraging party we were supposed to screen. It was commanded by the *angusticlavus*, Caecina, who had commanded the *vexillatio*, the detail escorting the surviving Tigurini back to the Rhenus. He was again paired with Sanga, the centurion from the Twelfth Legion. I stood back as Agrippa sorted things out with them.

I found Athauhnu's *turmae* and was surprised when he greeted me in Latin, "*Salve, Decurio!*"

"Finally assuming some civilized manners, Chief?" I responded in Gah'el.

"Latinly, *Decurio*" he responded again in broken Latin. "Madocus *Dux* to say we Roman soldier . . . to take Roman gift . . . sword . . . silver . . . now to speak Roman word."

"*Bene!*" I encouraged him. I had gotten used to Madog's fractured Latin, even Spina's Aventine-Hill gutter patter. Figuring out what Athauhnu was trying to say shouldn't prove too much a challenge. "I'll call you Adonus *Decurio* from now on when we speak Latin."

"Adonus," Athauhnu tried his new Roman name. "Is *bene* . . . Adonus *Decurio!*"

I heard Agrippa call for us, and we found him at the northern edge of the assembly. The eastern sky was beginning to turn dark purple. We needed to get this show on the road if we were going to cross the departure line according to Caesar's wishes.

When we found Agrippa, Caecina was standing with him; Sanga was hovering behind him, the silhouette of his helmet's transverse crest identifying him as a centurion.

"The tribune and I have worked out a plan," Agrippa began nodding toward Caecina. "Madog, we need to split up your cavalry . . . Insubrecus *Decurio*, you will accompany Att Owen's *ala*."

"Adonus *Decurio, Tribune*," Athauhnu corrected him.

Agrippa hesitated for a heartbeat, not sure what had just happened. I was about to say something when he shrugged and continued, "The *ala* of Adonus *Decurio*. Our target is the small *vicus* we scouted the day before yesterday, the one with the large, round building or barn in the center and the perimeter fence built from brambles. Your mission is to scout the route directly to the village for Caecina's foraging party. But, do not enter the village. When you reach it, move around it, preferably to the west if the terrain and the situation permit. Seal its flank and rear . . . No one in, no one out. I don't want them hiding the cattle and trying to carry off the grain . . . *Compre'enditis vos?*"

"*Compre'endo, Tribune!*" I answered. I wasn't sure how much of this the newly minted Adonus *Decurio* was getting.

"You are to avoid contact with the enemy," Agrippa continued. "If you detect the enemy, fix their position and move south back to Caecina's force. We'll let the *muli*, the legionary grunts, sweep away the trash."

I heard Sanga guffaw and slap the hilt of his *gladius* when Agrippa said this. Agrippa continued, "I will be with Madocus *Dux* and the two remaining *alae*.

We will be paralleling the ridgelines to the west of the route of march to seal it off from enemy reconnaissance or raids. Standard visual and aural signals remain in effect. *Quaestiones?*"

"*N'abeo, Tribune,*" I responded.

Athauhnu said nothing. I was positive that the Latin terms "paralleling," "reconnaissance," and "standard visual and aural signals" were well beyond his Latin. I could hash it out with him in the saddle.

"I assume the same order of march on the return," Agrippa finished. "But, we'll talk again when we're on the objective. Insubrecus *Decurio* . . . are you and . . . and . . . Adonus *Decurio* ready to move out?"

"*Parati, Tribune!*" I answered.

"Bene!" Agrippa said. "Stay in contact with the foraging party all the way to the objective. You lead out. I'll follow and peel off to the west before we enter the hill country to the north. Caecina, as we discussed, lead out your foraging party about a quarter of the hour after we depart, about when the eastern sky starts to go from red to orange. That should put us a few hundred *passus* in front of you."

"*Constat, Agrippa!*" Caecina said.

"Let's mount up, Insubrecus!" Agrippa concluded. "May *Domina Fortuna* favor us this day!"

In the darkness, I heard mutterings, "*Domina Bona . . . Fortuna . . . Dea Bona.*" I found myself patting my *lorica* where my medallion hung.

Initially, we made good time, despite the darkness. I was again riding the black mare with the white snip, on which Valgus, my *decurio* in Caesar's praetorian detail, had trained me. Valgus believed that man and horse were a team; they trained together, and they fought together. Like *gemini*, they had to trust each other completely. I felt I was getting to that point with my horse, Clamriu. I could feel her moods, sense her enthusiasms, her fatigues, and her fears as we rode. She responded easily to the reins or to my knee and leg directions.

Valgus didn't believe in Roman soldiers giving their mounts names; he considered it *alienus Romanitati, barbare*, as he put it. But, all the great heroes of Gran'pa's sagas rode noble steeds with their own identities. So, I named my mare Clamriu after one of Arth Mawr's mounts. Even then I knew it was a childish affectation, but one I still wished to embrace.

We reached the hills, and Agrippa's detail moved off to the west. We had to go more slowly now. Not only because of the darkness, but also because this was terrain that favored close ambush. Athauhnu sent *exploratores*, a two-man point detail, out about twenty paces ahead of the main body. It was still too dark to make flankers practical, so we were vulnerable as we made our way slowly over the narrow trail. Before the encroaching hills had obscured the eastern sky, I noticed that the horizon was revealing itself in a golden glow. Caecina and his foraging party should be well on their way from the assembly area.

"Adonus *Decurio*," I called to get Athauhnu's attention.

"*Quid volare tu?*" he responded in Latin. "What to fly you?"

I realized quickly that he meant to ask what I wanted. I switched to Gah'el. "I think we should leave two riders at the trail head to make sure the foraging party doesn't miss it."

"Good idea," he responded. "Damn Romans could get lost between a tent and a latrine."

I didn't think to remind 'Adonus *Decurio*' whose side he was on at the moment. The fact that he had stopped referring to me as "Little Roman" and seemed to except me from the innate disorientation of all Romans marked a major advance in our relationship.

As soon as there was adequate light, Athauhnu posted two riders out on each side of our column as flank security. Where the terrain was open and flat, they ranged out almost fifty *passus* from our line of march; when the terrain closed in, they virtually rejoined our column.

Our "command group" consisted of Athauhnu, me, a trumpeter with a hunting horn hanging strapped across his chest and chinking against his chainmail lorica as he rode, and a *vexillarius*, carrying a bright red pennant attached to a long spear. We rode at the head of the column, about twenty passus behind our two-man point element. Occasionally, when the terrain flattened and the trail ran straight, we caught sight of the two riders. The rest of our *ala*, twelve troopers, rode in a staggered formation along the trail. To our rear, two riders kept contact with Caecina and the wagons.

We were an *ala* of twenty-four riders, small by Roman standards, but considering the Gauls' peculiar sense of *officium et fidelitas*, quite adequate.

Again, by the standards of the Roman army, we appeared to be a motley collection of troopers, a band of Gallic brigands. We sported an assortment of bronze and steel helmets: some conical, some round, some with cheek guards, some without. About half the men wore chainmail; a few wore leather; and several had nothing more than padded jackets. Most of the men wore Gallic long swords; the rest had short Roman *gladii*.

I noticed a couple of our troopers were carrying *iacula*, light javelins, in long quivers behind their saddles. To me, such weapons didn't seem to serve any purpose; they seemed too light to be of any use in combat against armor. I asked Athauhnu about it.

"Ah," Athauhnu answered, "we call that *uh gae*. It's a weapon given to my people by the god, Lugus, when we departed from the Land in the Skies."

I recognized the word. In Gran'pa's stories, the ancient heroes had magical weapons called *gaea* that dripped gore, glowed with anger in combat, and once thrown, always tasted enemy blood. I had never actually seen one before. I was expecting a substantial weapon, something worthy of Homer's epic—a long, heavy ash shaft thrusting a long, black, razor-sharp, steel blade. These javelins that the Sequani troopers were carrying seemed insubstantial, flimsy.

Athauhnu noticed my skepticism. "Lend me your shield, Arth Bek," he requested, holding out his hand.

"What?" I questioned.

"Your shield," Athauhnu insisted, "let me have it."

I shimmied out of my shield, which was hung across my back, and handed it over.

"Emlun! To me!" he called out to one of his troopers.

A rider from the middle of our column came forward. He looked to be a boy of about my age, maybe a bit younger. He had a round, bronze helmet bouncing on top of his head, and he wore a padded jacket. His *spatha*, hanging across his chest by a leather baldric, looked to be at least two sizes too big for him.

"Yes, Athauhnu . . . uh . . . Chief," he said to Athauhnu.

"Emlun," Athauhnu instructed, "take this Roman shield up the trail about a hundred *passus* and hang it facing us on a tree right next to the trail."

The one called Emlun stared at Athauhnu for a couple of heartbeats, not sure what was going on. Then, he shrugged, took my shield, and rode ahead down the trail.

Athauhnu watched him go. "My cousin," he explained, "my mother's sister's son . . . a good lad . . . Needs some seasoning."

We watched Emlun pound down the trail, finally stopping to hang my shield on a tree. Even from that distance, I could see the red boar of the Tenth Legion painted around its center. Emlun waved to us when the shield was secure.

Athauhnu waved his cousin back to the column. As Emlun was cantering back, Athauhnu called out again, "Guithiru! To me!"

This time, one of the veteran troopers rode up to Athauhnu. He was arrayed in Roman chainmail, the cheek-pieces of his bronze *galea* helmet secured tightly under his chin.

"Yes, Chief!" he saluted.

Athauhnu pointed down the trail to my shield. "The boar . . . kill it!"

Guithiru grinned, "Where do you want me to hit it?"

Athauhnu shrugged, "You kill a boar by spearing its heart!"

Guithiru nodded. He reached behind his saddle and extracted one of his *gaea* from a quiver. He waited a few heartbeats for Emlun to clear the trail and rejoin the command group. Then, he shouted and kicked his heels back into his horse's flank. His gray, dappled stallion exploded down the trail, gaining speed as he approached his target. I watched as Guithiru rose up off the saddle with his knees locked into his horse's flank. This was a signal for the stallion to increase his speed. Guithiru's hand and arm holding the *gae* came up, then thrust forward in a blur. Even from a hundred *passus* away, I could hear the sharp thwack as the javelin punched into its target. Guithiru pulled his stallion up some thirty *passus* beyond my now transfixed shield. He waved back toward Athauhnu.

"Let's go see if Guithiru killed his boar," Athauhnu invited.

We cantered down the trail. As we approached the tree, I could see that Guithiru had indeed "killed the boar." His *gae* had pierced the image of the red Tenth Legion boar just behind its front legs, right where the animal's heart would have been. The javelin had punched completely through my shield and had pinned it fast to the tree.

"That is how deadly a *gae* is in the hands of a warrior!" Athauhnu remarked.

Guithiru rode up to inspect his handy work. "Perhaps we should just leave it there like that as a warning to our enemies," Guithiru suggested.

Athauhnu shrugged, "The Romans would force our *decurio* to buy a new one."

Guithiru laughed at the folly of Roman quartermasters and dismounted. After a few twists and pulls, he managed to extract his javelin from the tree, but he had to cut it out of my shield with his *pugio*. He handed the round *parma* back up to me. There was a small, jagged hole in its middle, straight through the heart of the red boar.

"Hold it away from your body if we get into a fight, *Decurio*," Guithiru suggested. "Maybe your chainmail will be enough to stop the point." Then, with a laugh, he resumed his position back with the column.

I inspected the ruin of my shield. I had been considering trading it for an oblong, Gallic cavalry shield. It would be a bit heavier than my *parma*, but it would give better protection for the upper legs and head. This little demonstration convinced me.

About an hour later, crossing our trail, we discovered fresh tracks left by an unknown force. Since there was no reason for friendlies to be in the area, we had to assume they were hostiles.

We were crossing a small valley split by a stream running toward the southeast. We could easily see our two scouts on the other side of the stream, some fifteen hundred *passus* ahead of the column. They had stopped, and one of the scouts seemed to be examining something on the ground while the other remained mounted and alert. Suddenly, the mounted scout whistled to get our attention and beckoned us forward.

Athauhnu acknowledged the summons. He whistled to get the attention of our flankers, who were operating some thousand *passus* up and down the valley on either side of the trail. He signaled them to halt; then he indicated that they should be vigilant to their front.

Then, he called for Guithiru.

"What do you wish, Chief?" the warrior asked when he joined the command group.

"Our scouts have found something," Athauhnu explained. "We're going forward. Keep the men here until we get back. Keep them alert."

"*Uhr wuhf ifitho, a pen*," Guithiru acknowledged. "Yes, Chief!"

Athauhnu and I rode forward to meet the scouts. As we approached them, the mounted scout, a rider named Alaw, greeted us: "We found a trail . . . riders moving up the valley."

We dismounted and walked over to the scout, who was examining the ground.

"What is it, Rhodri?" Athauhnu demanded.

The one called Rhodri rose, "About twenty riders . . . moving northwest . . . not in a great hurry . . . Horses are shod . . . heavy burdens . . . Armored men, I think."

"How long ago?" Athauhnu asked.

Rhodri shrugged, "Not long . . . dawn . . . a little earlier. I'll follow the trail through the grass. Maybe I can find some fresh droppings."

"No need," Athauhnu said. "Shod horses and armored riders, you said?"

Rhodri nodded.

"Not Helvetii," Athauhnu said to me. "Not all their horses are shod, and most of their cavalry aren't equipped with heavy armor like the Romans."

"Not Helvetii?" I questioned. "Then who?"

Athauhnu shrugged, "Maybe People of the Dark-Moon . . . a group of Aedui . . . This is their territory. If it were a rich noble's *fintai* he would equip his bodyguard with armor and equipment."

"There's no Roman cavalry operating up here," I affirmed. "We'll assume they're hostile, Helvetii or not."

Athauhnu nodded.

"What's off in that direction?" I asked Athauhnu, gesturing to the northwest where the riders had gone.

Athauhnu shrugged. "I don't know. There seems to be a ridgeline leading off to the north. Bibracte, the Dark-Moon king's fortress is to the northwest . . . I don't know . . . Our objective is directly north from here . . . maybe another seven or eight thousand *passus*."

I looked up to the northwest where the valley twisted into a heavily wooded ridgeline. "We're probably under observation out here in the open," I said to no one in particular.

"*Uhr wuhf uhn cuhtino,*" Athauhnu answered. "I agree. We should push on to the village."

"We should," I agreed. "But, I need to send a rider back to the Roman column with a message."

Athauhnu nodded; he whistled to get Guithiru's attention. "Send my cousin up to me!" he called.

Soon Emlun galloped up to our position. "The *decurio* has a job for you," Athauhnu informed him.

"What is it, *Decurio?*" Emlun asked.

"I want you to ride back to the Romans with a message," I began. "Report to the tribune, Caecina. He's the officer wearing plate armor with a red plume in his helmet. Tell him we believe there is enemy cavalry operating in the area . . . a group of twenty to thirty, heavily armed, positioned on the high ground to the northwest. Repeat that for me."

Emlun did. I continued, "Approach the Roman column carefully. They'll probably have a *contubernium,* eight infantry . . . to their front, walking point. Most of them can't tell the difference between you and a *Helvetius* . . . and they don't much care. They'll unload a few *pila* at you, then issue a challenge."

Emlun laughed. "If I can't get close to Romans without being seen, I should just go back to my father's farm and help the plant the summer crops."

"Be that as it may," I cautioned, "just be careful! Some of those troops speak *Gah'el,* so you'll be understood. Now, repeat the message again for me."

Emlun did, and I sent him galloping down the trail toward the Roman foraging party.

We saw no sign of any threat for the next hour. Emlun rejoined our column to say that Caecina had acknowledged my message. We were climbing the last ridgeline before reaching our objective. I estimated the Aeduan *vicus* to be no more than a few hundred *passus* distant.

Suddenly, Rhodri appeared at the top of the ridge ahead of us and whistled sharply. Then, he pointed to the northwest. There, in a small clearing at the top of a hill, where our ridgeline twisted up into the highlands, were four riders.

Athauhnu and I cantered to the top of the ridge to get a better look. The riders remained stationary. They were obviously observing us and felt no need to remain hidden.

"Who are they?" Athauhnu demanded of Rhodri when we reached the top.

"*Ni Rhufeinig*" Rhodri shrugged. "Not Romans . . . Well-armed . . . Dark-Moon warriors, I think . . . king's men . . . *fintai*."

I looked toward the group. They were carrying no standards or pennants, but the sun glinted off their armor. "They seem interested in us," I said to no one in particular.

"Indeed, they do!" Athauhnu agreed. "And that village we're trying to reach."

"*Edruhch, a pen!*" Rhodri said suddenly, pointing east into our line of march. "Look, Chief!"

When I looked, I could see a smudge of grayish-black smoke staining the sky about where the village should be.

"That can't be good," I muttered. Then, I whistled back to our main column. "Send up Emlun!"

Athauhnu's cousin soon joined us. "I have another message for the Romans," I told him.

Emlun acknowledged me, and I began my report, "Tell Caecina that we have made visual contact with an unidentified force of cavalry approximately one thousand passus to the northwest on the high ground . . . four riders, well-armed and armored. Also, there is evidence of hostile activity at our objective. Repeat that back to me."

He did, so I continued, "Take an escort with you . . . another warrior for security. Be careful! We're under enemy observation. Don't get ambushed!"

Emlun nodded vigorously. "I'll take Idwal with me, if you approve, Chief," he said. He was excited to be in contact with the enemy.

Athauhnu grunted in the affirmative.

"Repeat the message again!" I ordered.

Emlun did. "*Redi guhvluh!*" I told him. "Ride quickly, but keep your eyes open!"

Emlun flashed me a wide grin. Then, he was off down the hill.

"He still thinks this is a game," Athauhnu commented.

This time I grunted in the affirmative. Emlun and I were of an age, but somehow I had changed.

"Rhodri!" I called to get the scout's attention. "You and Alaw get as close to that village as you can without being detected. Then, get back to us. I want to know what we're riding into."

Rhodri quickly glanced over to Athauhnu, who nodded. Then, he rode off toward the *vicus.*

Athauhnu whistled down the hill and gestured the column to join us.

"I didn't mean to 'ride your horse,'" I told him, "with Emlun and Rhodri, I mean."

Athauhnu just shrugged, "You're a warrior . . . *uhn pen* . . . a chief . . . You're doing your job. You must be able to act without the approval of others. You must be willing to take responsibility for what happens. Emlun's a good choice. He rides light, and if we get into a mess down the trail, he's better out of it. And Rhodri knows his job. If the *poblo r'avon* or any of their *cuun almaeneg,* German dogs, are waiting for us down the road, he'll see them before they see him."

"*Poblo r'avon?*" I questioned. "*Gentes fluminis* . . . River People?"

"That's what we call the Helvetii," Athauhnu said. "*Poblo r'avon.* When this is over, I'll be glad to drown every last one of them in that bloody river of theirs, the Rhenus."

We rode forward down the ridge, toward the Aeduan village. The smudge of dark smoke in the sky became increasingly larger as we approached. We had covered about two-thirds of the distance when Alaw met us on the trail.

"Report!" I snapped, not waiting for Athauhnu.

"We rode to a spot overlooking the village," Alaw said. "The smoke is from the large round house in the center. It's been burned . . . yesterday . . . no earlier . . . still smoldering. No sign of any enemy activity in the village. Can't tell what's going on in the hills to the north, but it seems quiet up there too."

"Where's Rhodri?" I asked.

"He's watching the village from concealment," Alaw answered. "If anything happens, he'll get back to us before we ride into it."

"What do you think?" I asked Athauhnu.

He was about to respond, when Emlun rode up to us from the column.

"Did you report to Caecina?" I asked him.

"I did!" Emlun said. "The Roman chief says we continue with the mission unless prevented."

I looked up toward the northwest. Our watchers had disappeared. I wondered if Agrippa and the rest of Madog's riders had spooked them—or maybe they were up to something else.

Athauhnu brought me back from my musings. "Arth Bek! I want to see that village with my own eyes before our band arrives. We should ride forward with Alaw."

I nodded to Athauhnu, then said to Emlun, "*Diolkh*! Thanks! Rejoin the column! Send Guithiru up to us!"

Again, Emlun flashed his boyish smile and turned back toward the column. I heard his whistle and his calling out to Guithiru. So much for operational security! Now every Helvetian and Kraut within two hundred *passus* knew we were there.

"I suppose you've noticed that our friends on the hill have left us," I said to Athauhnu.

He nodded and said, "A while back."

Guithiru approached us.

"The *decurio* and I are going forward to scout the village," Athauhnu told him. "When we send back to you, I want you to bring the rest of the band up to us."

"*Uhr wuhf ifitho, a pen*," Guithiru acknowledged. "Yes, Chief!"

"Take us in, Alaw!" Athauhnu said.

Alaw nodded and turned his horse back up the trail.

We followed Alaw at a slow trot for about five hundred *passus* down the winding trail. The forest closed in on both sides. When we came to some rising ground, Alaw pulled up. He looked around for a few heartbeats and seemed to see what he was looking for.

"We dismount here," he told us, hopping down from his horse. "Rhodri's just ahead."

We pulled our mounts off the trail, and I saw Rhodri's bay. We dropped our reins. The horses were trained to war. They would not move. Alaw led us up the hill, along an almost invisible path. We were just about to the top when Rhodri's voice challenged us.

"Rhodri," Alaw answered, "I have the chief with me."

Rhodri suddenly appeared out of the brush. "Come! Look!" he said and gestured us forward.

Rhodri led us to his well-concealed observation point. "Helmets," he hissed at us.

We removed our helmets so they would not betray our presence by reflecting sunlight. Then, we looked down into a small valley. In the middle, along a running stream, was the village. In its center stood a blackened, smoldering ruin of what had once been a large round-house—a chief's hall or a storage barn. There were other, smaller round-houses and huts in the complex, but they seemed untouched. The cluster of huts was surrounded by a barrier of brush and bracken. I could see the outline of what had once been a defense ditch around the entire settlement; it had eroded into a grassy indentation by seasons of wind and rain. Beyond that, the village fields and grazing lands stretched to the edges of the forest.

"I've seen no movement down there," Rhodri hissed at us. "No signs of life . . . no cattle or fowl . . . not even dogs . . . nothing."

"If they were massacred, there'd be bodies," Athauhnu mused. "We'd see those . . . and the dogs. They never get all the dogs. They'd be back to feed on . . . feed on the leavings."

"Any activity to the north?" I asked Rhodri.

He shrugged. "Too many trees. Anything could hide in that forest. The birds show no alarm. This time of day, they like to stay close to the nest."

"Our orders are to bypass the village and screen it," I said to Athauhnu. "Do you see any reason why we shouldn't continue?"

Athauhnu was silent. He was scanning the treetops to the north. Suddenly, he grabbed Rhodri's arm and pointed to the northwest, "Look, there!"

I looked in the direction that Athauhnu was pointing, but saw nothing.

"Something's disturbed them," Rhodri agreed with Athauhnu.

"What do you see?" I asked.

"A flock of birds rose from the trees there," Athauhnu pointed out over the village. "It's too far for an ambush on the village. Could be nothing. But, that is where we should look."

I nodded, then said, "Alaw! Ride back to the troop and have Guithiru bring the men forward!"

Without a word, Alaw moved back to where we left the horses.

Athauhnu was talking, "I think we should bypass the village to the west and work around it. It's the long way round, but it will position us uphill from whatever's spooking those birds."

"*Uhr wuhf uhn cuhtuno!*" I nodded. "Agreed!"

Guithiru soon brought the rest of the men up. I left two troopers behind— Emlun and his friend, Idwal—to lead Caecina and the foraging detail into the village. The rest of us worked our way around the village to the west.

It was not cavalry country. We had to dismount and lead our horses up along narrow paths through the woods and brush. As we moved through the forest, the horses snorted; they were reluctant to move forward; their eyes darted about, examining the forest around them. Athauhnu said that horses had an innate fear of the forest. Somehow, they knew wolves hunted among the trees in packs. And, big cats, rarely seen but deadly killers, lurked in the shadows. On open ground, wolves were no match for horses. But here among the trees, the wolves were the masters.

We were making so much of a racket, trying to work our way around the village, I doubted any self-respecting wolf would be caught within a thousand *passus* of us. As far as cats big enough to take down a horse, I didn't want to think about that.

Horses weren't the only creatures made nervous by these dark, northern forests.

We finally reached a position we believed to be directly above where we suspected human activity. The village was invisible, down the sloping ground to our southwest. We had cleared most of the perimeter around the village, so I was confident that Caecina and the foraging detail weren't marching into a trap. But, we had to ensure there was no enemy threat to our front. I sent Alaw and Rhodri ahead on foot to scout the area.

Alaw soon returned. "There's a clearing about fifty *passus* down the hill. We can see people—"

"People?" I interrupted. "Enemy soldiers?"

"No," Alaw said. "Mostly women and children . . . some old men . . . The missing villagers, I think."

"No sign of weapons . . . armor?" I pressed.

Alaw shrugged, "They have planting tools."

"I think we should move forward," I said to Athauhnu. "But, we need to be careful. These woods could hide an army. They may be using the women and children to bait us."

Athauhnu nodded, and we moved forward.

Alaw guided us to the edge of the clearing where Rhodri was waiting. I was just about to begin to deploy the *ala* to sweep into the clearing when we heard a voice from down below.

"Are you oafs going to snap every shaggin' branch and crack every shaggin' twig you can find in those damned woods before you show yourselves? I could smell you and your shaggin' horses a thousand *passus* away. Show yourselves, and get your arses out here!"

I stood up and exposed myself. Luckily, I wasn't greeted with an arrow in the chest. I saw a large man standing in the clearing below me. He sported bushy, gray Celtic mustachios that reached down to his chin—rather a cascade of descending chins—and he was wearing an old-fashioned domed helmet that floated on an aureole of bushy gray hair. His leather *lorica* struggled to contain his belly. There was, however, nothing comic about the sword he was holding, a long, Gallic *spatha*, whose recently honed edges caught the sunlight; it glowed like *Durn Gwin* White-Hilt, the lightning sword Lugus.

"So, who the hell are you?" he challenged me in Gah'el.

I puffed out my chest and tried to channel all my Roman *dignitas*, answering, "I am Gaius Marius Insubrecus, *decurio* of the praetorian cavalry of Caesar, *imperator*—"

"You look like a shaggin' Roman, alright," he interrupted. "But, those wankers standing next to you are no more Roman than my hairy bottom! By their colors, they look like *Soucanai* to me! What the hell is a Roman puppy and a gang of *Soucanai* sheep-shaggers doing on my lands?"

"Are you chief here?" I asked him.

"Chief? I'm the king around here . . . twice over, you Roman pup!" he spat back. "I am Cuhnetha mab Cluhweluhno, *buch'rix* of these lands and *pobl'rix* of the *Wuhr Tuurch*!"

I understood the words 'cattle king' and 'clan king.' *Buch'rix* meant that Cuhnetha was the leader of this settlement, which was prosperous enough to have at least a modest herd of cattle. I wasn't at all sure about the meaning of the *pobl'rix* of the *Wuhr Tuurch*, the clan king of the Descendants of the Boar.

"Who are the *Wuhr Tuurch*?" I asked him.

Cuhnetha looked at me as if I were something nasty that just dropped from a tree into his path. "Tuurch Mawr was the first king of the Aineduai, the Dark-Moon People—Aedui to you Romans. He led the people down from the Land in the Skies into these valleys in the time before time. He defeated the *Pobl oh Danu*, the People of the Dark God, and took these lands for the Aineduai. He rode as a chief at the right shoulder of Arth Mawr when the Gah'el rubbed the noses of *uh Chellinai*, the Greeks, and you Romans as well, in dog shit. Now, he feasts with the gods in the Land of Youth! Enough of your questions, Pup! What are Romans and these *Soucanai* dog-turds doing in my lands?"

Athauhnu answered, "After we *Soucanai* have destroyed the River People and the *Almaenwuhra* that you Aiduai run from, even in your own lands, and the Romans go back to their grape farms, we are going to make dogs of your women and shit on the heads of your sons, oh *pobl'rix* of cows and sheep!"

"Our women alone are enough to drive you sheep-shaggers back into your shit-ridden swamps!" Cuhnetha laughed. "What are you called?"

"Athauhnu mab Hergest," he answered. "*Pen cefhul* of Madog mab Guuhn, *pobl'rix* of the *Wuhn* clan of the *Soucanai* and *Dux* of the Roman Caesar."

"I should have guessed that a *Soucanai* king would attach himself to a Roman's arse, oh Horse Chief of Madog!" Cuhnetha shot back. "But, unless we're going to fight, the law of our ancestors demands I offer you hospitality, and all this talking has given me a terrible thirst. So, come down out of those woods and join me!"

Cuhnetha pulled off his helmet and walked away back into the clearing. "Rhonwen!" he shouted. "Some *bragawt*! The good stuff! *Medd coch* . . . the red mead! We have guests!"

I looked over at Athauhnu. Despite all the insults hurled back and forth, he was laughing. When he saw me looking, he gestured toward the clearing.

"Come, Arth Bek!" he invited. "The King of Blowhards has offered us hospitality and is now honor bound for our safety. And he's right! Insulting him has given me a terrible thirst and a few cups of his *bragawt* sounds like just the thing to slake it!"

We followed Cuhnetha down into the clearing. For the Gah'el, hospitality is sacred. The host is responsible to the king for the comfort and safety of his guests. If a guest should die, through no fault of the host or his people, the host would have to pay his head price to the king. If a guest were killed or murdered through no fault of the host, three times the head price. Should the host himself harm a guest in any way, the host's rank and honors would be stripped and he would be exiled.

Near the center of the clearing, Cuhnetha had a pavilion set up, a lean-to of leather sheets, not unlike those of a legionary tent. There were some rickety-looking wooden stools. Cuhnetha gestured for us to sit.

"The women will take your horses," he told us as he struggled out of his *lorica*. "They'll also serve your men. Your nags look as relieved as you do to get out of those woods. We don't have much . . . some *bragawt*, cheese, and yesterday's bread."

Athauhnu got the men situated and came back to the pavilion, where a tall, lissome red-haired girl of no more than seventeen winters was pouring a reddish-orange liquid into clay cups.

"We call this *medd coch*," Cuhnetha said, grabbing one of the cups. "Our bees produce the richest honey in all the lands of the Aineduai. Drink!" Cuhnetha took a long, noisy draught from his cup.

We drank. I was cautious, and that proved a good thing. Cuhnetha's *medd coch* didn't have quite the bite of the *dur* my father distilled out behind our storage sheds, where Mama wouldn't see, but it was hard to taste the difference. The fumes rose up into my head, making my eyes water, and the liquid burned like fire going down my throat.

"*Dur uh buhwuhd*," Cuhnetha said as if he were reading my mind. "The water of life." He smacked his lips and held up his now empty cup to the red-haired girl.

The red-haired girl was obviously accustomed to Cuhnetha's act. She filled his cup, placed the pitcher on the ground next to his stool, and walked out of the lean-to.

Cuhnetha caught me watching her as she walked away.

"*Fuh nith*," he said. "My sister's daughter!" That was Gah'el guest-talk for, "Don't think about it; she's family."

"So," Cuhnetha started after another long pull from his cup, "you never explained what a Roman and a band of Soucanai pig-thieves are doing in my woods."

"Your king promised us food if we fought the Helv . . . I mean . . . the River People for him," I said. "We've come to collect."

Cuhnetha laughed at that. "Well, you've come a day too late, Little Roman! All the food's gone!"

"Gone?" I said. "You mean the raiders took it all?"

"Raiders?" Cuhnetha snorted. "There were no raiders here . . . You and your Soucanai friends excepted, of course."

"No, raiders?" I questioned. "Then who burned your barn?"

"Barn?" Cuhnetha shot back. "That was no bloody barn! That was my hall! And, it was the men of that gob-shite of a *dunorix* who burned it. They took the food!"

"The *dunorix*?" I stammered. "The commander of the king's fortress? Deluuhnu mab Clethguuhno? The king's brother? Your own people burned your bar—I mean, your hall?"

"Right and wrong, Little Roman," Cuhnetha shot back, taking another long drink. "The *fintai* of the *dunorix* set the blaze alright! But, Deluuhnu mab Clethguuhno is not 'my own people'! He's the snot-nosed, treacherous, piece of shit of his usurping, twice-bastard father, Clethguuhno mab Grefhuhtha.

May he rot in the latrines of Annuhfn while worthy men piss on his head for all eternity!"

While Cuhnetha was refilling his cup, I asked, "'Usurping, twice-bastard'? Are you saying he's not of the royal clan? Who is the legitimate king of the Aiduai, then?"

"I am!" Cuhnetha almost shouted. "I am the *pobl'rix* of *Wuhr Tuurch*! The high kingship of the Aiduai has always been founded in the *Wuhr Tuurch*! Since we descended from the Lands in the Sky, the descendants of *Tuurch* have always ruled the tribe! That was until Clethguuhno poisoned my grandfather. My da was only a boy, then, not yet of the age. Clethguuhno convinced the Council of the Three Generations that the gods had killed my grandfather—not the concoction of Greek weeds he put in his beer. And, with hordes of *Almaenwuhrai* rampaging through our lands, the Aineduai needed a strong man . . . a warrior . . . ruling the tribe. My grandfather's death was a sign that Clethguuhno should rule. Then, when the Germans left us to go south and kill Romans, Clethguuhno's breeding bitch gave him two strong sons . . . heirs. He convinced the Council to recognize his oldest, Duuhruhda, as his heir."

Ranting was thirsty work. Cuhnetha held up the now-empty pitcher and bellowed to Rhonwen for more. From somewhere out among the milling Aineduai and our Soucanai troopers in the clearing, I heard a woman's voice yell back, "Wait your turn, old man!"

"No respect, I get!" Cuhnetha complained. "From my own blood!" Then, he looked at me, "Don't ever marry a red-haired woman, boy! She'll be the death of you!"

I didn't take his advice, and after thirty-some years, I'm still alive—bruised somewhat, but still alive.

"So, now the *Wuhr Blath* rule the tribe," he started.

"The Wolf People?" I questioned.

"That's Duuhruhda's clan," Cunetha said, while glaring out into the clearing as if that would bring Rhonwen faster. "The shaggin' descendants of the shaggin' wolf. It was they who came here yesterday with their carts, demanding all our stored food. It's for the king's *dun*, Bibracte, they said. I asked them how we were going to eat until the crops were in. Eat your seeds, they laughed. They're already in the ground, I said. They just laughed. Then, they burned my hall. It was a message from their bloody *dunorix*, that gob-shite brother of that gob-shite usurper . . . Deluuhnu mab Clethguuhno."

Rhonwen finally arrived with a fresh pitcher of the *bragawt*.

"It's about time!" Cuhnetha grumbled. "A man could die of thirst waitin' on the likes of you, girl!"

"Shut ya gob, old man!" she shot back. "And just be thankful I pay ya any mind!"

As she turned to leave, Rhonwen gave me a smile and a wink. I felt both in my heart.

"Where is your *fintai, pobl'rix*?" I heard Athauhnu ask as he leaned forward for Cuhnetha to fill his cup. "Why did your warriors allow this?"

Cuhnetha snorted, "My son led our sixteen warriors and five boys to Bibracte weeks ago, when that usurping, pretending king—may he wipe backsides in Annuhfn for all the ages—summoned them. Now they're all cowering behind those nice, thick walls up on top of those high hills, while the River People and Krauts do whatever they want to the rest of us. When those worthless followers of the *dunorix* set the fire, my people fled to the woods. When it's safe, I have to bring them back . . . start rebuilding . . . decide how I'm going to feed them until the harvest. A king's responsibility is to his people . . . to the land! When the land burns, the king burns. That's how we did it in the old days . . . Kill the king; choose another!"

Cuhnetha drained his cup to that sentiment.

Remembering Caecina and his foraging detail, I stood. Athauhnu did also.

"*Diolch i chi am eich cletuhgaruuch, A Argluuhth*," I pronounced the ritual of thanks.

"*Riduhch chi bab amser uhn cael eu croesauu uhn fi, A Argluuhth*," Cuhnetha rose unsteadily and completed the ritual. "You are always welcome at my hearth, Lord . . . at least, as soon as I rebuild the shaggin' thing," he added.

X.

Scaena Caesaris

CAESAR'S DRAMA

Diviciacus multis cum lacrimis Caesarem complexus obsecrare coepit ne quid gravius in fratrem statueret quod si quid ei a Caesare gravius accidisset cum ipse eum locum amicitiae apud eum teneret neminem existimaturum non sua voluntate factum qua ex re futurum uti totius Galliae animi a se averterentur haec cum pluribus verbis flens a Caesare peteret.

"In tears Diviciacus embraced Caesar and began to implore him not to condemn his brother further. If Dumnorix were severely dealt with by Caesar, no one would believe that it had been done without Diviciacus' concurrence since Caesar held him in such regard. All Gaul would turn its favor away from him if such a thing were to happen. Weeping profusely, Diviciacus begged these things of Caesar."

(from Gaius Marius Insubrecus' notebook of Caesar's journal) e found Caesar and the army by the eleventh hour. They had moved less than ten thousand *passus* to the west, still following the lumbering mass of the Helvetii.

Caecina was not a happy man. His wagons were empty; he felt that he had failed in his mission. When Athauhnu and I descended to the village from Cuhnetha's encampment, Agrippa and the other two *alae* of Madog's Sequani cavalry had already returned from their screening mission in the west. Caecina's foraging detail had also arrived from the south; his wagons were assembled in the center of the village, while Sanga's infantry had secured the perimeter.

Obviously, there was no food, and no Aedui, to be found.

I briefed the tribunes and Sanga on what Athauhnu and I had found and on what Cuhnetha had told us.

Caecina wasn't satisfied, "I suggest we send Sanga and his *centuria* back up the hill and squeeze that cow king's balls. He must have some grain hidden away! And what about cattle? Did you see any sign of livestock?"

Agrippa shook his head. "Even if we do, I don't imagine we'll get enough food to make a difference. The Aedui have had more than enough time to hide any remaining supplies not stolen by their own people. I'm more concerned with what this *dunorix* bastard's up to. It seems as if he's stripping the countryside to starve us, when he's supposed to be gathering food to feed us."

"Caesar will not be pleased if we return with empty wagons," Caecina insisted.

"You can't squeeze wine out of raisins," Agrippa countered. "We will at least be able to offer Caesar information that he may find useful. If the Aedui, or some faction within the royal household, are plotting against us, Caesar will need to be informed. I recommend that we rest the men and animals until the eighth hour. Then, we return to the army."

The men were sullen on the way back. Not only did they think that their mission had failed, but they were also not looking forward to the expected food shortages and reduced rations.

When we reached the legionary camps, we discovered that we were not the only foraging party to return empty-handed. All the foragers who had marched north and northeast found empty barns. The ones coming in from the south and southeast had had better luck because the Helvetii and our army had screened these settlements from being stripped by their own people in Bibracte.

We again found Caesar's *praetorium* in the camp of the Tenth Legion. Labienus was outside the tent with his *tabulae,* taking reports from the returning foraging parties and instructing them how to distribute their takings.

When he saw us, he said, "Agrippa . . . Caecina . . . you marched due north . . . Let me guess . . . Our Aeduan allies beat you to the food."

"*Recte, Legate,*" Agrippa responded. "We came back empty."

Labienus grunted and scratched something into his *tabula.* Then, he seemed to notice me, "Ah . . . Insubrecus . . . Caesar wants you. He needs you to make sense out of those daily journals he's collecting. The rest of you are dismissed. You did a good job today . . . Not your fault it didn't work as planned . . . not your fault at all."

I asked Athauhnu if he would have someone look after Clamriu, my horse. He nodded. "I'll have Emlun look after her for you. He'll bring her back to Valgus after she's groomed and had a chance to cool down."

When I entered Caesar's *cubiculum,* I saw the *imperator* standing over by his operation maps in a heated discussion with four officers. They wore chainmail *loricae* and had their swords hanging on the left—centurions. Each wore a broad, red sash, designating their status as *primi pili,* the *de facto* commanders of Caesar's four veteran legions—despite any *legatus* Caesar might assign to tag along.

Caesar was stripped down to his *subarmalis* jacket; his plate armor *lorica* and helmet were tossed in a corner. His hair was plastered down on the top of his head by the weight of his helmet and the sweat of the day.

When Caesar spotted me, he called over, "*Bene,* Insubrecus . . . the *tabulae* are there by my field desk. I'll be finished here soon."

I did my best not to eavesdrop on Caesar's conversation: rations needed to be distributed to the men soon; break off contact with the enemy; march south into the *provincia*; resupply from Massalia—or attack now and finish the enemy.

Then, I heard Caesar say, "*Satis! Me Taedet!* I command here! I will decide what this army will do!"

I couldn't help but look over. The four centurions stood stiffly, braced at attention before their commander.

Caesar recovered his composure. His jaw relaxed, and the Caesarian mask was back in place. "Excuse me . . . gentlemen . . . It's been a long, frustrating few days. I will consider everything you've said. I know you are motivated only by what's good for the Roman people and for this army. Please . . . leave me now . . . I have much to consider."

The centurions' positions of attention seemed to loosen around the shoulders, just slightly; their chins seemed a bit less braced. They muttered, "*A'mperi'tu',*" and they began moving away from their commander.

One of them noticed me. It was Malleus, "The Hammer," *primus pilus* of the Tenth Legion. He came over to where I was sitting. Since Caesar was the ranking officer in the tent, I did not rise, but I sat up stiffly.

"Insubrecus," Malleus said, noticing my decurion sash, "or, should I say, Insubrecus *Decurio*. Moving ahead in the world, I see. Congratulations on your promotion! If your career continues at this pace, I'll be working for you by the end of this campaign."

I knew Malleus was pulling my leg, but I wasn't quite sure of his point. I decided to play it safe. "*Gratias ti', Centurio!*"

Malleus nodded in reply. "Your old centurion, Strabo, is back on his feet and still with the Tenth Cohort. I may be moving him up to the *acies secunda* soon. You should pay a visit. I'm sure he'd be glad to see you."

"*Gratias ti', Centurio,*" I repeated.

Malleus nodded again. He had a slight smirk on his face. "Don't let too much of that *tabula* wax rub off on you . . . It's not good for soldiering. I may want to get you back in the Tenth to do some real soldier's work."

With that, Malleus left the tent.

After a short while, Caesar wandered over from the maps. "Another day . . . another ten thousand *passus* . . . day after day. I don't know how exciting you can make that sound in your report, Insubrecus."

Caesar seemed to be prattling a bit. With him, that meant he was talking about one thing while his mind was processing something else. "When senior centurions think they must give advice to their commander, things are not good.

The men must be getting restless . . . worried about their rations . . . tired of avoiding an enemy they think they can beat . . . Ten thousand *passus* a day and then build another marching camp. That doesn't tire them out enough. They have too much extra energy to stew and fuss . . . too much time to be anxious about getting this thing over with . . . Uneasy about rumors . . . running out of food . . . wondering what the purple-striped chump in the command tent is doing . . . No good for discipline."

Suddenly, he came out of his ruminations. "*Scriba!*" he yelled.

"*Imperator!*" answered the voice of his clerk from the outer *cubiculum* of the tent.

"Get me Labienus!" Caesar ordered. "*Stat'!*"

"*A'mperi'tu!*" the voice responded.

"Insubrecus," he said to me, "hand me those reports . . . No . . . not those . . . Today's . . . the dailies . . . yes."

I handed Caesar a stack of tabulae. He had just started trying to examine them when Labienus entered.

"Ah! *Bene!* Labienus," Caesar started. "What's our battle-line strength? How many infantry can we deploy against the enemy?"

"Just legionaries?" Labienus responded without missing a beat.

"Yes . . . yes," Caesar said, still trying to balance the tabulae in his arms while looking through them.

Labienus reached over and plucked one of the tabulae from Caesar. He opened it and began to read, "Seventh Legion . . . they had a strength of 4,327 . . . seven on leave . . . twenty-seven detached for detail . . . forty-two on sick call."

"Just bottom-line it for me, Labienus!" Caesar interrupted.

"Yes . . . yes," Labienus muttered, reviewing the daily strength report. "The four veteran legions, the Seventh, Eighth, Ninth, and Tenth, 15,552 effectives, give or take a dozen or so. The new legions, Eleventh and Twelfth, 8,736. If we put everyone in the battle line, 24,288."

"24,288," Caesar repeated. "What are our intelligence estimates of enemy strength?"

Labienus placed the current *tabula* on the desk and reached over and removed another *tabula* from Caesar's tenuous grasp. "Bottom-line it again?" he asked.

"Yes . . . yes," Caesar said.

Labienus began to examine the new tabula. "This isn't an exact science," he muttered as he read. "Since we separated the Tigurini from the other clans, forty, maybe fifty thousand maximum. Of those, no more than fifteen thousand fully equipped warriors. The rest are just tribal musters. That includes both cavalry and infantry. We can't get a good fix on the Germans. We think no more than ten thousand total, maybe three thousand warriors. So, we're facing less than twenty thousand warriors of battle-line strength; the rest would be just dirt farmers and swine herders with pitchforks and scythes."

"If we engaged them tomorrow, could we beat them?" Caesar asked.

Labienus shrugged, "Almost twenty-five thousand trained Roman infantry . . . eighteen thousand barbarian warriors supported by a herd of sword-fodder . . . We pick the ground . . . Can't see why not . . . Yes . . . we could win that fight."

"How many days on full rations do we have?" Caesar shot.

Again, Labienus took one of his *tabulae*. "We haven't fully tallied what the foraging parties brought in, but . . . three days, full rations . . . maybe, stretch it to four. That's a conservative estimate. Three days, I'd say."

"We could reach the Rhonus from here in one long day," Caesar said. "About thirty thousand *passus* . . . one and a half days at a regular march . . . another day to gather supplies from the *provincia*. So, we have to decide now. We break off the pursuit and march to the Rhonus, or we go right at the Helvetii and resupply ourselves with their food, or we go hungry waiting for these Gallic *verpae* in Bibracte to deliver on their promises."

"*Patrone*," I interrupted.

"*Quid dicere vis tu, Insubrece?*" Caesar said.

"Bibracte, *Imperator*," I answered. "There's plenty of food in Bibracte. The Aedui have been stockpiling it there, and it's no more than twenty thousand *passus* north of here . . . one day's march."

"That is consistent with what many of our foraging parties have reported, Caesar," Labienus confirmed. "The Aedui seem to be stripping their own villages of food and livestock and bringing it into their fortress at Bibracte."

"Why would they do that?" Caesar asked.

Labienus shrugged, "Feed the garrison . . . deny it to the Helvetii—"

"Or, deny it to us," I interrupted.

Caesar stared at me for a few heartbeats. Just when I was convinced that he was going to reprimand me for interrupting a senior officer, he asked, "So, you're suggesting we could march on Bibracte and resupply there?"

Labienus made a noise and Caesar asked, "What is it, Titus?"

"That may be our most dangerous option, Caesar," he said.

"*Cur?*" Caesar demanded, "Why?"

"That would put the army between the Helvetii and the Aedui, with no clear line of withdrawal to the Rhonus," Labienus stated. "We'd have over eighteen thousand barbarians on our asses. Only the gods know how many Aedui would be to our front, and we'd have a fortified position to crack—with our siege equipment back on the Arar. I'm not sure that's the battle we want."

A light seemed to go on in Caesar's mind. "A trap . . . the food is the bait . . . Roman silver encouraging the Helvetii and interfering with my alliance with the Aedui . . . That seems to be a stretch, Labienus, but I see your point."

"*Patrone*," I said, "there is another thing."

When I had Caesar's attention, I explained what I had learned from Cuhnetha about the dynastic issues among the Aeduan clans.

After listening, Caesar rubbed his hands together. "This is getting as intricate as the plot of a Greek play. The *dunorix*'s men burning out a rival's village . . . rumors of Roman silver and purple-stripers riding with the enemy . . . a poisoned king . . . our allies withholding supplies . . . and a horde of barbarians seemingly beckoning us farther on to our destruction. A Greek melodrama, Labienus. All we need is a pirate king and a kidnapped virgin. The Aeduan king . . . he is to be here tomorrow . . . correct?"

"*Recte, Imperator*," Labienus nodded.

"*Bene*," Caesar continued. "Summon my senior officers . . . all my *legati* . . . the *centuriones primi pili* of the legions . . . the senior military tribunes, *the laticlavi*, too. I'll conduct a council of war to discuss our situation . . . Do we provoke a battle with the Helvetii . . . break off pursuit and withdraw to the *provincia* . . . or turn north against Bibracte?"

The next day, during the third hour, Caesar was in his *praetorium*, waiting for the arrival of the Aeduan king, Duuhruhda mab Clethguuhno. Our *exploratores* had reported the Helvetii on the move, but the legions remained in camp. What Duuhruhda had to say was critical to Caesar's next move.

The council of war the night before had been stormy.

To a man, the senior centurions wanted to close with the Helvetii and destroy them. They claimed this was the only option the men would accept. Withdrawing to the *provincia* was a retreat, a shameful defeat of a Roman army by a crowd of *pilosi*—shaggy barbarians in plaid breeches. Caesar would be shamed in the army and in Rome. Enough of the talk. Enough of the delay! Catch up to them . . . Kill them . . . Eat their food . . . Take their gold . . . Take their women . . . Have done with it!

The legates were a bit more circumspect. After all, they were civilians, not soldiers, and politicians at that. They were along on this campaign to enhance their public careers in Rome, not to decorate some barbarian's hut with their bloody heads. Certainly, a great victory would go a long way to their winning the next lap of their political careers, the race along the *cursus honorum*. Some of them had their eyes on a consul's chair in the foreseeable future. A retreat back to the *provincia* was not especially helpful to them, but their political careers could survive that. They could blame the defeat on Caesar. But, the bloody defeat of a Roman army would be the end of their political lives—maybe quite literally.

The broad-stripe tribunes, the *laticlavi*, didn't say much. They were of the senatorial class, but many were extra sons who didn't have much of a political or financial future in Rome. Their home was in the army, unless they were lucky enough to have an older brother die prematurely and were summoned home to take his place. Some were actually committed to a military career. So, they did not want to cross the *primi pili* for military reasons and did not want to oppose the *legati* for fear of losing possible political favors in the future.

The upshot of it was that, if the Helvetii offered the opportunity of a battle on favorable ground in the next two days, the army would attack. Caesar had sent out his *exploratores* at first light with orders to locate a possible battlefield.

If, however, the opportunity did not arise to attack the Helvetii, the army would return to the *Rhonus* and resupply from the *provincia*. They would bridge the river and establish their *castra* on the north bank, so technically they weren't retreating back into the *provincia*. There, they would watch and wait. When the enemy settled down, they would renew the offensive.

The option of turning north against Bibracte was rejected as too risky. None of the officers wanted to be trapped against a fortified enemy position, low on rations, with the Helvetii across their line of withdrawal.

The wild card in this game was Duuhruhda.

Caesar planned to confront the Aeduan king aggressively concerning his promise to supply the Roman army. If the king could be forced to make good on his promises, the crisis was over. The Roman army could continue pursuing its current strategy of attrition against the Helvetii. Caesar believed the key to the king was his brother, the *dunorix*, and his family's tenuous claim to the throne.

Caesar wasn't quite sure how he would use that as leverage.

Labienus entered Caesar's *cubiculum*. He was formally attired as a senior Roman officer. He wore a highly polished, muscled, bronze *lorica* with a Medusa image engraved high on his chest. He had a bronze *galea* helmet sporting a bright-red, horse-hair crest and highly polished cheek pieces fastened tightly under his chin. Hanging from a polished leather *balteus* on his left side, he carried a *gladius* in a leather scabbard wrapped in gold wire. His legate's red sash was tied about his waist.

"Caesar, the scouts report that the Aedui are approaching," he said.

"How far out are they, Labienus?" Caesar asked.

Labienus shrugged, "By now, less than five hundred *passus*."

"Has the escort detail arrived at the *Porta Praetoria*?" Caesar enquired.

"*A'venere*," Labienus answered. "Yes! Five *contubernia* from a first-line cohort . . . Third *Centuria* of the Second Cohort, I believe . . . Under arms with shields and spears . . . Under the command of their centurion . . . a . . . uh . . . Mettius . . . uh—"

"Mettius Atius Lupinus," Caesar filled in. "He's a Roman . . . from the *subura*, I believe. His father's a *fullo*, a fuller. Because of that, some of the boys call him *Lotium* . . . Piss. But, only behind his back—unless they want the *medicus* trying to put their jaws back together."

"Uh . . . yes," Labienus agreed, "that's him . . . Mettius Atius Lupinus. He'll bring the king and his brother here to you. Also, he'll allow no more than ten members of the king's . . . uh . . . What do you Gauls call *praetoriani*, Insubrecus?"

"*Fintai, Legate*," I answered.

"Yes . . . *fintai* . . . ten members of the king's bodyguard detail with their swords and daggers only."

"*Euge*," Caesar agreed. "The bodyguards remain outside with the legionary detail. You and Lupinus escort the king and his brother in here to me. Is Valgus standing by with my *praetoriani*?"

"*A'sunt*," Labienus affirmed. "They're in my cubicle. The Gauls will not see them when they enter."

"*Bene*," Caesar nodded. "Insubrecus, you remain here as my *ad manum*. Take notes of our conversation. But, if the king should suddenly develop problems understanding my Latin, you interpret for me. Let's get this *spectaculum* started!" Caesar rubbed his hands together.

Labienus left Caesar's cubicle. Very little time passed before I heard footsteps and voices approaching the entrance. Caesar was sitting in his chair of state, the *sella curulis* of a Roman magistrate possessing the *imperium* of the Senate and the people. Caesar sat straight as a spear on the backless chair, which he had positioned to face the entrance of his *cubiculum*. His red *sagum* was draped over the chair. Around his head, he had affixed his *corona civica*, a golden chaplet of oak leaves woven to form a crown. I noticed how well the gilded oak leaves covered his thinning hair and receding hair line. His highly polished bronze *lorica* reflected the lights of the many lamps he had burning around his *cubiculum*. But, from my perspective, the brightest light in the room seemed to shine coldly from Caesar's pale blue eyes.

Duuhruhda mab Clethguuhno, King of the Aedui, was first to enter, followed closely by his brother, the tribal *dunorix*, Deluuhnu. Both men seemed a bit disoriented, uncomfortable at being in the middle of a legionary camp surrounded by thousands of Roman soldiers and uneasy at having to leave their bodyguards outside Caesar's tent.

I could tell by the way the men were equipped—their finest armor and weapons, the bright colors of their cloaks and *bracae*, their golden torques and armbands—that they had intended to overawe their Roman ally. I was sure that they had ridden into the camp on the two largest stallions from their herds, but the horses were now out of sight, impotently munching grass somewhere outside our camp.

The Aedui stood before Caesar, Deluuhnu a pace behind his brother. Labienus and the centurion, Lupinus, slipped in behind them and stationed themselves between the Gauls and the exit, as Caesar had instructed.

Caesar did not rise. He said, "*Salve, Diviciace, Rex*! And greetings Prince Dumnorix, brother to the king!"

I winced a bit at Caesar's butchering of Gallic names and titles, but clearly this was not the time to launch into a pronunciation lesson.

Caesar continued, "I have summoned you here to demand that you explain why my army has not been resupplied as you promised. I thought I'd give you the courtesy of explaining your failure before I turn away from my pursuit of those I thought were our common enemies and march on your *oppidum*, Bibracte, and take what has been promised me!"

Duuhruhda now clearly understood why he and his brother were standing alone in front of Caesar, surrounded by Caesar's army. Unless they could give a satisfactory answer, they were not leaving this place.

"Caesar—" Duuhruhda began.

"It is customary to address a Roman magistrate by his office, *King*!" Caesar interrupted. "In my case, you will address me as *imperator*."

"Caesar . . . I mean . . . *Imperator*," Duuhruhda started, "this is not Italy! We have long winters and cool springs. The crops have not ripened—"

"*Me tadet specium*," Caesar interrupted. "If I wanted a lesson in agriculture, I would have read Cato. My troops need to be fed!"

"*Imperator*," this time Deluuhnu, the king's brother, spoke, "my men are collecting what food is left among our people after a hard winter. These things take time—"

"Insubrece!" Caesar interrupted him, calling my name, "Insubrecus! That report!" He held his hand out to me.

I had no idea what Caesar was talking about! I took a step toward him to ask discretely what he meant. But, as soon as I was within arm's reach, he snatched the *tabula* in which I was scratching my notes.

"My sources tell me," Caesar pretended to read, "that there are powerful men among the Aedui who are preventing the villages from gathering the grain. If the Romans defeat the Helvetii, they say, Rome will subjugate the Aedui and all the rest of Gaul. These men claim that if the Aedui cannot rule Gaul, it is better to be ruled by Helvetii than by Romans. My sources tell me these same men are betraying my plans and the movements of my army to the Helvetii. They plot the defeat of my army by starvation or by battle. And, the ringleader of this cabal of treasonous filth is . . ." Caesar looked up from the *tabula* directly into the eyes of the king, "Dumnorix, your brother!" Caesar slammed the *tabula* shut.

Duuhruhda recoiled as if struck. Deluuhnu's face went ghostly pale. His right hand seemed to inch closer to the hilt of his sword. Then, he remembered where he was, and the two Roman officers standing directly behind him. His hand relaxed and fell back to his side.

"What have you to say to this . . . *King?*" Caesar spit out the last word into Duuhruhda's face.

I almost felt sorry for the man. He was trapped in the middle of a Roman legionary camp and entangled in a drama of Caesarian cunning. It was a magnificent piece of stagecraft. He didn't have a chance.

"*Imperator*," the king stammered.

"I am not finished reading my charges against your brother," Caesar announced, as if he were a *praetor* trying a criminal case in front of the forum mob. He reopened his all-knowing *tabula*.

"*Item*," Caesar began, "Dumnorix is the tribal *exactor*, the tax collector, and as such, *he* is responsible for the collection of the foodstuffs that were to be distributed to my army. And, this collection effort, by your own admission, has failed! I blame this failure on Dumnorix and his desire to weaken my army."

Caesar paused. I was glad that neither Gaul realized that no *tabula* could possibly contain so much information.

Caesar again looked down at the *tabula* and seemed to place his finger on another non-existing charge. "*Item*, Dumnorix is married to a woman of the

Helvetii. Because of these marriage bonds, he favors the Helvetii and desires their victory over Rome and even over his own tribe!"

Caesar again paused for effect, then continued, "*Item*, Dumnorix has created strong political ties with the ruling classes of other Gallic tribes through the marriages of his mother's sisters and other close female relations. He does this in order to establish himself as the ruler of the Aedui, the Helvetii, and eventually all Gaul, once my army has been destroyed. He has gone so far as to exchange hostages with the Helvetii to assure mutual cooperation in this plot against me!"

Caesar was not done with this crucial scene. "*Item*, Dumnorix engineered the defeat of a Roman cavalry force by luring it into an ambush and then ensuring its defeat by withdrawing his personal cavalry forces once the engagement began. This treachery led to the deaths of a score of Roman citizens."

Caesar again closed the *tabula* and fixed the king and his brother in the cold, blue steel of his glare. "The final offence alone justifies a summary judgment and his immediate crucifixion!"

Caesar looked up toward Labienus. "Labienus! Has the king's escort been neutralized?"

"*Gestum, Imperator!*" Labienus snapped.

"*Bene!*" Caesar answered. "Summon my *praetoriani!*"

Labienus called for Valgus, and immediately he and ten members of Caesar's praetorian cavalry entered the room in full rig.

"Seize that man!" Caesar ordered, indicating Deluuhnu. The praetorians had the king's brother in their grasp before either Gaul could react. Valgus pulled Deluuhnu's hands roughly behind his back and began to bind them while one of his troopers removed the *dunorix*'s weapons.

"This is an outrage, Roman!" the king shouted, forgetting Caesar's demanded protocol. "We came here in good faith! You are responsible for our safety! My people will not stand for this . . . They will rise against you . . . They will join with the Helvetii."

"And, who will lead this insurrection, *King*?" Caesar asked in a low voice.

"I shall!" Duuhruhda shot back. "I, as their king."

"Which brings me to the next item of business," Caesar told him. "Insubrecus, hand me that communique from Rome . . . the one that arrived by consular courier last night." Caesar gestured toward his field desk, on which lay a number of *tabulae* and pieces of papyrus.

I had no idea what Caesar was talking about. No special courier had arrived last night. Then, I remembered that I was playing a part in Caesar's drama. The *tabulae* and *papyri* were just props. I pretended to search through the papers and finally selected one that was covered with Labienus' scribbles.

"Here it is, *Imperator!*" I announced, handing it to Caesar.

Caesar took the piece of papyrus and pretended to review it. "This is an urgent message from my colleague in Rome, Gnaeus Pompeius Magnus, who serves the Senate and the Roman people with Marcus Licinius Crassus and me, as a *triumvir*. You've heard of Pompeius, have you not, Dumnorix?"

The king's brother blanched as if having his arms tied behind him and being in the grasp of two of Caesar's *praetoriani* was suddenly the least of his worries.

Caesar continued, "Pompeius writes . . . oh . . . but before we get to that, did you know, Diviciacus, that Pompeius is also my son-in-law . . . married to my daughter, Iulia? I hope he will give me a grandchild soon. We Romans take our familial obligations very seriously."

Caesar let that snippet sink in, then continued. "Pompeius has complained to me, both as his father-in-law and as a Roman magistrate, to look into an injustice done to one of his clients . . . a member of your tribe, a king . . . by the name of . . . Cuneda . . . Did I pronounce that correctly, Insubrecus?"

I leaned in over Caesar's papyrus and pretended to read, "That's Cuhnetha, *Imperator*, Cuhnetha mab Cluhweluhno."

Duuhruhda's face went white when he heard that name.

"Yes," Caesar affirmed, "Cuhnetha . . . It seems that Pompeius wants me to look into his client's complaint . . . nasty business, too . . . He claims that your father murdered his grandfather and stole the throne from him . . . Claims that he's the rightful king of the Aedui."

"Pompeius would never have written such a letter," Deluuhnu suddenly contradicted. His speech was cut short as Valgus smashed him across the face.

"Gag the prisoner," Caesar ordered. Valgus forced a piece of cloth into Deluuhnu's mouth while one of his troopers bound it fast with his *sudarium*.

"What would a condemned, treasonous, sack-of-shit barbarian know about what Pompeius Magnus would or would not have written to a Roman proconsul?" Caesar charged.

Caesar looked over to where I was standing, and I swear he winked at me.

Caesar then noticed that Deluuhnu was bleeding from his nostrils. "Make sure he doesn't suffocate, Valgus!" he ordered. "I don't want him to cheat the cross!"

Caesar turned back to the king. "My colleague and son-in-law, Pompeius, has asked me to look into his client's complaint that he is the rightful king of the Aedui. And, *you* . . . you are standing here in front of me, after failing to provide me with the food that you promised me, the food I need to feed my troops . . . after harboring and abetting a traitorous plot against the Roman people by your own brother . . . and after threatening to lead the Aedui in revolt against me . . . Insubrecus!"

"*Ti' a'sum, Imperator!*" I snapped.

"Cuhnetha mab . . . uh . . . whatever that name was . . . Didn't I recently see that name in a report?" Caesar asked. "I seem to recall that one of our foraging parties reported that his village was burned . . . his crops stolen . . . his livestock run off?"

That was a bit of an embellishment, but it was theater after all. I responded, "Yes, General, and the man claimed it was done by Aedui, the *fintai* of the *dunorix*, the king's brother, Deluuhnu." I was getting into my part.

Caesar turned to the king. "You see, Diviciacus. I have already begun my investigation for my colleague and son-in-law . . . Perhaps I should dig into this matter more deeply while you remain here as . . . as my guest. That way you can witness your brother's execution."

The king had stood motionless before Caesar. Then suddenly, he fell to his knees, placing both his hands, empty and upright, on Caesar's knees. This was the Gah'el ritual of submission.

In tears, the king of the Aedui begged, "I implore you, *Imperator!* Spare my brother! No one is more ashamed of his actions than I am! But, he has great influence with the Aedui and over the neighboring tribes. He has even tried to use his influence to undermine me, his own brother! But, he *is* my brother.

When I look at him, I see my father's eyes staring back at me. And, he is still a youth. When we were young and full of our own importance, deceived by a belief in our own immortality, who among us has not done what we should not have done, tried what we should not have tried? If you move against Deluuhnu, no one in the tribe will believe I was not complicit; no one will believe that I did not betray my own brother, and among my people that is an unforgivable crime. The very gods would turn against me! To remain loyal to a fratricide would surely invite the wrath of the gods."

Caesar, like most Romans, did not know how to react to this sudden outpouring of Gallic grief and emotion. He glanced at me over the king's bowed head.

Somehow, I sensed that this was Caesar's endgame. He had Duuhruhda exactly where he wanted him. Discretely, I gestured to Caesar to place his hands in those the king was holding open on his knees, thus showing that he accepted Duuhruhda's submission.

Caesar nodded at me and did so, saying, "I accept your reasoning, King, and I accept your submission to the Roman nation. Rise! I release you to return to your *oppidum* at Bibracte, and I command you to collect the promised rations needed by my army and deliver them to our *castra* by this time tomorrow."

Duuhruhda rose, but kept his head bowed. "I thank you for your clemency, *Imperator*, and will do what you command. My brother—"

"Dumnorix will remain here with me . . . as my *guest*," Caesar stated. "I will stay his execution as long as *you* remain a faithful and dependable ally. You may tell your people that he remains here at my side as a trusted advisor. When we have defeated the Helvetii and the threat to your lands and mine is removed, I will decide what is to be done with him. But, for now, he is safe."

"*Multissimas gratias, Imperator*," Duuhruhda mumbled. "Do I have your leave to depart?"

"*Abeas, Rex!*" Caesar stated.

Duuhruhda wasted no time in escaping from Caesar's presence. Labienus and Lupinus followed him out. Caesar abruptly realized that the battered, bound, and gagged Deluuhnu was still standing before him in the grasp of his *praetoriani*.

No play can end until all the actors have made their exits and all the props are removed from the stage. And, Deluuhnu was a prop in Caesar's play. Surrounded by thousands of Aedui, on whose cooperation Caesar depended, he had had no real intention of executing the man. He was merely leverage over his brother, the king.

"Take him away!" Caesar ordered almost absently. "And, keep a close eye on him. He's valuable to me!"

Valgus nodded and gestured the prisoner and the *praetoriani* out of the tent.

Now that the play was over, Caesar seemed to droop a bit in his curial seat. "*Scriba!*" he yelled.

"*Ti' a'sum, Imperator!*" the voice from the other room responded.

"*Vinum,*" Caesar ordered, "a large pitcher . . . and four cups!" Then, before the clerk could ask, he added, "*Merum!* No water!"

"Nicely played, Insubrecus," Caesar said softly, "nicely played, indeed. I'll make a Roman politician out of you yet."

I took my bow just as Labienus returned to the cubicle.

"The king's gone," Labienus reported. "He took off out of here so fast, you'd think his horse's tail was on fire. Lupinus is marching his detail back to their tents."

Before Caesar could respond, his clerk entered with the wine. Caesar asked him, "Is the wine up to your standards, Ebrius?"

"*Certissime, Imperator,*" the clerk answered. "You know I wouldn't let any of the cheap stuff get by me."

Ebrius placed the pitcher and the cups on the field desk, then left.

"Would you pour, Insubrecus?" Caesar requested.

As I was pouring the wine, Caesar asked, "What did you think of the performance, Labienus?"

Labienus took a cup of wine from me, and answered, "I'm wondering if we didn't do that pompous king a favor by keeping Dumnorix here?"

"*Quo modo?*" Caesar asked.

"If Dumnorix is causing his brother problems with the Aedui," Labienus explained, "we just removed the *podex* for him."

Caesar grunted, took a sip of his wine, and then said, "Did you see the way Dumnorix reacted when he heard Pompeius' name? He damn near admitted that he's working as his agent."

Labienus shrugged, "That's possible, Caesar. He certainly didn't believe that Pompeius would support the claims of uh . . . what's that other Gaul's name again, Insubrecus?"

"Cuhnetha, Legate," I offered.

"Quite," Labienus agreed. "Cuhnetha . . . Dumnorix certainly didn't believe that Pompeius supported Cuhnetha's claim to the throne. But, concluding from that that Pompeius is actively colluding with our enemies is a bit of a stretch."

"Pompeius interfering with the Gauls would explain many of the rumors of purple-stripers and Roman silver," Caesar mused. "My daughter has written me from Rome saying that Pompeius is keeping strange company these days . . . dinner parties with Cicero and Bibulus . . . inviting Milo to his home for hushed conversations over jugs of wine. He even took a meeting with Cato. How he despises the man!" Caesar grimaced over some memory filtering through his head.

He continued, "I imagine he'd claim he was just greasing up the *Optimates* . . . looking out for our mutual interests in the Senate. But, we are in too precarious a situation up here to take any chances. It's far better to confirm than to trust."

All at once, Caesar was back in the room, focused. "Labienus, I want you to do a bit of research. I want a list of any officer in the army who has any possible connection with Pompeius . . . anything . . . family . . . clientage . . . recommendations . . . prior service . . . anything!"

Labienus asked, "How far down do you want me to dig?"

"Right down to the bottom!" Caesar snapped. "Even if the man is serving as an *optio* in a third line cohort, I want to know."

"Caesar, our veteran legions are originally from Spain! They served under Pompeius there!" Labienus protested.

"True," Caesar agreed. "But, I doubt Pompeius was cultivating the *muli* back then, except to keep them fed, paid, and busy. Concentrate on the older, more senior officers, anyone who was a junior centurion when Pompeius was in command . . . especially anyone he promoted."

"Do you doubt the loyalty of our senior centurions?" Labienus asked. "You're talking about *primi pili*, even the *praefectus castrorum*!"

"Doubt?" Caesar puzzled. "No . . . I don't *doubt* them . . . I just want to be *sure* of them . . . *absolutely* sure."

Labienus was just about to say something when Caesar's clerk, Ebrius, entered the cubicle. "Forgive the interruption, *Imperator*," he announced. "But, I have an officer outside who claims to have urgent information for you."

"An officer?" Caesar questioned. "Who?"

An *angusticlavus*, a narrow-striper, one of the *exploratores* you dispatched this morning—" Ebrius began to explain.

"One of the scouts!" Caesar exclaimed. Ebrius now had Caesar's undivided attention. "Send him right in, Ebrius! I want to hear what the man has to report!"

"*A'mperi'tu', Imperator!*" the clerk obeyed and left the tent.

A few heartbeats later, Agrippa entered Caesar's *cubiculum* followed by Madog. Caesar greeted them eagerly, "Agrippa! Madocus *Dux*! *Beneventi*! Please! Help yourselves to some wine!"

Both men poured some wine into cups. Agrippa drank deeply. Madog sniffed his. He saw his companion drinking, so he did likewise. He grimaced a bit. The Sequani chief had yet to develop a taste for the grape.

Caesar waited while Agrippa drank, then asked, "What do you have to tell me, Tribune?"

"*Imperator*," Agrippa began, "we have found your battlefield. You can trap the Helvetii!"

Agrippa now had Caesar's full attention, "*Mi' dicas*, Agrippa!"

"They hardly moved today, *Imperator*," Agrippa continued. "They seem to be consolidating some of their stragglers and letting their livestock rest and feed. They're spread out in a valley no more than ten thousand passus west of here with high ground on three sides. They've made no move to secure that high ground or to screen its approaches with their cavalry. We were able to move in above their encampments without being detected."

Madog was nodding along with Agrippa's briefing. His wine cup was almost empty. "True . . . true," Madog agreed, "very stupid Helvetii . . . fear nothing."

"Less than ten thousand *passus*, you say?" Caesar was nodding. "Little security . . . *bene* . . . *bene* . . . What's the slope of the hills? Can our infantry negotiate it?"

"There's high ground on their flank," Agrippa continued. "A hillock, really. It's flat on top and could easily accommodate two legions arrayed in the *acies triplex*. The slope down to the valley floor is open and not too steep."

"Wait a moment, Agrippa!" Caesar said. Then, he called out, "*Scriba*! Ebrius! To me! Quickly!"

Caesar's military clerk appeared, "*Ti' a'sum, Imperator*!"

Caesar ordered. "*Celeriter*! Quickly! I need a sand table . . . a terrain model. Can you round something up for me?"

Ebrius shrugged, "*A'mperi'tu', Imperator*!"

Caesar also realized that he had removed the campaign maps from his headquarters in preparation for his confrontation with the Aedui. "And, have a couple of your assistants set my maps back up!" he instructed. "*Age, Miles*!"

Caesar had the bit between his teeth, so Ebrius shot out of the tent like a *ballista* bolt.

Caesar looked about the room, then ordered me, "Insubrecus! My desk . . . bring me a piece of that papyrus . . . There should be some charcoal over there, too . . . Bring me a piece!"

I ran over to the field desk to collect the items. Madog was observing all of the Roman turmoil while he poured himself another cup of Caesar's wine. His Gallic distaste of the insipid Roman grape-mash was clearly becoming a thing of the past. There was some hope that *Romanitas* could be brought to *Gallia comata*!

I brought Caesar the papyrus and charcoal. He handed it to Agrippa, ordering, "Sketch the terrain so I can see it, Agrippa . . . Less than ten thousand passus, you say?"

"No more, *Imperator*," Agrippa nodded as he drew. "They hardly moved at all . . . just sitting there."

Madog leaned in, almost as interested in what Agrippa was doing as he was in the wine.

While Agrippa drew his map and briefed Caesar, Ebrius returned to the tent with two legionary *muli* carrying their *dolabrae*, entrenching tools. "Right here!" He pointed to a spot on the ground in front of where a couple of his assistants had begun to set up the campaign maps. "About ten *pedes* by ten *pedes* square . . . through all the grass, right down to the dirt . . . Make it smooth, and be sure you take all the spoil out of here with you . . . Use your helmets if you can't find buckets."

The grunts started whacking at the turf. Caesar looked over to where they were working, and said, "Scrape it clean for me, boys! Ebrius'll give you some *posca* to replace all the sweat!"

"Smooth as a baby's bottom, *capu'*," one of them grunted between swings with the entrenching tool.

While they worked, a couple more *muli* came through carrying some cut logs. Ebrius directed them to stack their load at the back of the tent.

As they were leaving, I heard Ebrius tell them, "Grab up the buckets outside the tent and take 'em down to the water point . . . Fill 'em with sand from the stream bank . . . the dry stuff . . . and bring it back here . . . on the double . . . *il' capu'* is in a hurry!"

Caesar, Labienus, and Agrippa were bent over Agrippa's map. Madog hovered behind the group with his half-emptied cup of wine.

Caesar was questioning Agrippa closely concerning the details: "Is there a stream between those two ridges? How steep is that slope? You're sure they haven't ringed their wagons? Show me again where you saw the horses grazing."

The two legionaries in the back had finished their digging. One was carrying the spoil out in a bucket, while the other began to fit the logs around the cleared space.

I heard Caesar say, "What do you think, Labienus?"

"I think we got them where we want them," Labienus affirmed. "We couldn't ask for a better set up than this."

"*A'sentior*," Caesar nodded. "I agree. But, I have to see the terrain myself. Agrippa! You and Madocus *Dux* will lead me out there."

"Shall I alert Valgus?" Labienus asked.

"My praetorian detail? No! Too many Romans," Caesar stated. "Too much activity . . . I don't want to tip my hand to the enemy. I'll go alone with Agrippa . . . and you too, Insubrecus! You're with me."

We rode to where Agrippa had located the Helvetii. As per Caesar's instructions, our Sequani cavalry took us in from the north. Caesar was anxious to see whether there was a negotiable avenue of approach for his infantry around the enemy's flank. He had left his red general's cloak behind and wore the ruddy-brown *sagum* of a *mulus*. He strapped his helmet to his saddle in order to prevent it from being recognized as Roman and to avoid the possibility of any reflection of the afternoon sun, which might alert the enemy of our presence.

We got ourselves into position in a little over an hour. We left our mounts in a stand of woods, guarded by one of the cavalry troopers. Athauhnu's *ala* was deployed to our rear as a screen to ensure that an enemy patrol didn't surprise us from that direction.

During the ride, Athauhnu practiced his latest attempts to learn Latin on me. Phrases like "trees to be green being good" and "horse to be running prompt when field to be flat" were still ringing in my ears as I crept forward behind Caesar, Agrippa, and Madog to get a glimpse of the enemy. The cavalrymen of Madog's remaining *ala* were fanned out around us as we advanced toward the lip of a flat hilltop.

As we neared the edge, I could hear the hum of activity from the valley below. We advanced on our hands and knees. To this day, when I see one of Caesar's heroic statues standing magnificently on a gilded marble plinth in one of his temples, I grin as I remember him that day, his thinning hair plastered flat to the top of his head, a streak of mud running down his cheek, and his breath labored as we crawled through the long grass to get a look at the Helvetii.

And what a sight we saw!

The entire valley below us was teeming with people, animals, tents, wagons, campfires, and equipment, all seeming to swirl about in smoke, noise, and colors. There must have been tens of thousands of them down there: men, women, and children—all seemingly without a care and behaving as if they were on some spring holiday. There was no sign of any military preparedness, no fortifications, no sentries, and no formations of armed men. Women went about their chores, many with babies on their hips; children chased each other about in mindless patterns; and the men seemed content to laze about around the fires and the tents.

Caesar had his hand-drawn map out and was making corrections and notations with a piece of charcoal. "If I had two legions up here now, I could finish this thing by sundown," I heard him whisper to Agrippa.

"You see where the valley narrows a bit to the east?" he continued. "That's where we want their main body to assemble. We want all their attention focused right there. Then, we sweep down on their flank and rear from this hill."

We remained in place for about half an hour before Caesar indicated he had seen enough. We withdrew from the hill and returned to the legionary *castra*.

As soon as we got back, Caesar immediately set his plans in motion. He directed Labienus to summon his senior officers to a war council at the tenth hour, all his legates, the broad-stripers, and the *primus pilus* of each legion.

While Labienus was about that, Caesar studied his maps and supervised Ebrius and his assistants in building in the sand table an accurate terrain model of what we had just observed. Caesar then had Ebrius' clerks cut and paint a number of wooden blocks to represent military formations: red for Roman, with numerals indicating legion designation; black for the Helvetii, each representing five thousand warriors. Caesar arranged and rearranged the blocks on his sand table as he hypothesized various scenarios. When Labienus had finished arranging the war council, he joined Caesar at his sand table, and they discussed the various options.

The council of war that assembled later that day in Caesar's *praetorium* was very different from the previous meeting.

Caesar began by announcing to his officers, "Gentlemen, we have located the main body of the enemy in a valley approximately ten thousand *passus* west of our location. It is my intention that this army will advance on the enemy, attack at dawn tomorrow, and destroy the Helvetii."

With Caesar's pronouncement, I looked up from the *tabula* in which I was scribbling notes. There was absolute silence among the assembled officers, but I could see the knuckles of the senior centurions whiten as their grasp tightened around the hilts of their swords. After a few heartbeats, they began to nod in agreement. Caesar's legates and the broad-stripe tribunes remained perfectly still.

Caesar, standing over his terrain model using a *sudis* as a pointer, continued, "We are located approximately here. The enemy is spread out for about two thousand *passus* in this valley, here. They do not seem to be aware of, nor do they seem to care, about our proximity to them. They have made absolutely no defensive preparations."

When Caesar said this, I noticed that two or three of the senior centurions shook their heads and smirked. No Roman army would permit itself to be caught out in the open in enemy territory.

Caesar continued, "It is my intention to attack using the basic hammer and anvil tactic. Labienus will command the 'hammer,' a task force of two legions, the Seventh and Eighth. I will command the 'anvil,' four legions, the veteran Ninth and Tenth and the two new legions, the Eleventh and Twelfth . . . Yes, Malleus?"

"*Imperator*, what are your estimates of enemy strength in the valley?" the *primus pilus* of the Tenth Legion asked.

Caesar smiled slightly and nodded. He knew where Malleus was going. He answered, "Our intelligence indicates that the Helvetii and their allies can field between twenty-five and thirty thousand trained warriors . . . probably twice that number in tribal levies. My observation of the enemy position this afternoon supports those estimates. Are you worried that there aren't enough of them out there for each of your Tenth Legion boys to get at least ten each?"

Malleus grinned broadly as he said, "No, *Imperator* . . . my boys'll earn their ten copper *asses* a day . . . That's a penny for each of those shaggy *comati* they stick. My concern is that we seem to be dividing our forces in the face of a numerically superior enemy. It seems to me that's the way Caepio and Maximus screwed up against the Cimbri back in the day . . . No offense, *Imperator*."

Caesar leaned forward on the *sudis*. "And none taken, Malleus. As a senior centurion, your job is to keep the purple-striped nobs Rome keeps sending up here from totally screwing the pooch. Caepio and Maximius put a river between their two armies and did not exercise unified command. In fact, those two political *stulti* did everything they could to work against each other, and many good Roman soldiers died as a result of their arrogance and ambition. I have no intention of allowing that to happen to this army. The two wings of our army will always be under my command and will not become so separated that they cannot support each other should the enemy decide to attack. In fact, luring the Helvetii into attacking one of the columns is my plan. Allow me to continue."

Malleus nodded his credence to Caesar's explanation. Caesar continued, "Labienus' division will depart from this location at the beginning of the third watch. He will march along this northern route and get behind the enemy's left flank by occupying this hill, here. Their primary goal is to reach this hilltop, which is their assault position, undetected. They will remain there in a concealed position until our main force has engaged the enemy's front, here."

There were no questions, so Caesar continued, "I will lead the main body along this route, entering the enemy-occupied valley just before dawn at this point. We will advance toward the enemy and deploy across this narrow ground here . . . three legions forward in the *acies triplex* . . . the Tenth on the right flank, the Ninth in the center, and the Eleventh on the left. The Twelfth will serve as my reserve, deploying in a line of cohorts across the rear of the forward three legions. The objective of my division is to get the Helvetii to attack our line. The optimum point of contact is here, along this line, where our flanks will be secured by high ground. When the enemy has committed itself to that attack, Labienus' division will advance from its concealed assault position and attack the enemy's rear. These *hursiti*, hairbags, do not have the discipline to sustain a two-front battle. They'll crumble when Labienus attacks. Then we finish it. Questions, gentlemen?"

There was silence for a few heartbeats while the officers absorbed what Caesar had told them. Then Spurius Hosidius Quiricus, the *primus pilus* of the Ninth Legion, known around the camps as *Quercus*, the "Oak," spoke up: "*Imperator*, I see you have one of the new legions, the Eleventh, on the battle line. Are you sure they're up to it? No offense, Iudeaus!"

Quercus was apologizing to Marcus Sestius, the *primus pilus* of the Eleventh. Sestius was an old hand who had served with Pompeius in the east and was wounded in a skirmish in eastern Syria. A Greek hoplite had tried to drive his spear into Sestius' left thigh but missed his aim slightly. Ever since then, the boys referred to the centurion as Iudaeus after one of the eastern tribes which practiced some bizarre ritual on the penises of the males of their tribe. Iudaeus didn't seem to care about the nickname and always asserted that, despite the wound, the *mulieres castrorum* never complained.

"None taken, Quercus," Iudaeus answered. "My boys're up to it."

As Quercus nodded, Caesar said, "I expect the Helvetii to send in their tribal levies first to soften us up for the warriors. I expect that they'll falter after our first volleys with the *pila*. Before their chiefs can rally them, Labienus should be down on them. Then, the *acies prima* can move forward into the valley and clean them out."

The officers nodded. As Caesar said, it was a classic tactic: hammer and anvil.

Caesar continued, "That's where you and your cavalry come in, Crassus!" With his *sudis*, Caesar pointed to a round, red block on the left flank of the legionary line. "I'm concentrating the legionary cavalry on the left flank. That way they won't get tangled up with Labienus' boys, who will be in front of our right flank. The cavalry will advance apace with the infantry front line—until I give the signal from my position on the right flank. At that signal, you will attack down the valley. Stampede them, Crassus . . . Kill as many as you can . . . Panic them! The limit of your advance is here where this small stream crosses the valley, or when I signal the recall. I want you to position yourself in front of the main body of the cavalry, Crassus. Right up with the forward edge of the infantry line. If you spot an opportunity, an opening, you go! Even if I haven't signaled the advance, you go! Can you do that for me?"

"*A'mperi'tu', Imperator*," Crassus responded. I smiled to myself as I noted down his response. Looked like that pretty boy was finally going to get some mud on his boots.

"*Bene*," Caesar acknowledged. "I'm deploying the auxiliary cavalry on our flanks for security." He pointed to another round, red block positioned to the north, saying, "Madocus *Dux*, I want your boys on the northern flank, watching the approaches from Bibracte. I want no surprises from our *socii*, the Aedui, during this operation."

"*A'mperi'tu', Caesar!*" I heard Madog's voice among the crowd of Romans.

"*Bene*," Caesar said. "Assignments for the legates . . . Labienus, you're with the Seventh . . . Cotta, you go in with the Eighth in Labienus' division . . . The rest will march with me . . . Pedius, the Ninth . . . Rufus, the Eleventh . . .

Vatinius, the Twelfth . . . Crassus, you have the cavalry. I'm with the Tenth. The boys'll march light . . . basic combat load . . . one day's rations and water. We won't be pulling down our marching camps here when we pull out. Each legion will detach its tenth cohort to secure their *castrum* and their baggage. Pulcher, you'll be in charge of the *castra*. If you're attacked by an overwhelming force, you can consolidate the cohorts in one of the camps until we can relieve you. But, you are to hold this position . . . *Compre'endis?*"

Caesar was ensuring that the army had somewhere to retreat to in the event that the beehive he was about to kick over proved more dangerous and powerful than he had estimated, especially now that he could no longer rely on the good will of the Aedui.

"*Compre'endo, Imperator!*" I heard Pulcher's voice sound. Pulcher had been on his best behavior since Caesar had relegated him to the ash and trash detail.

"*Bene*, gentlemen!" Caesar concluded. "Labienus' division pulls out at the beginning of the third watch. My division, an hour after that. Remember, Asellio writes, '*Audaces amat Fortuna!* Fortune favors the bold!' Let's finish this thing! Return to your commands! *Miss'est!*"

I am glad that at that point in my career, I hadn't yet read the *Rerum Gestarum Libri* of Sempronius Asellio, the histories of the Third Punic War, because then I would have known that he also wrote, "No military plan survives the first step of its implementation."

After the officers had left, I waited while Caesar gave some directions to Labienus. "Titus, it's absolutely imperative that you get your legions in position without being detected by the Helvetii. Also, do not reveal yourself to them or commit yourself to the attack until you're absolutely sure that my division is in position. We should be visible from your position, and you'll hear my attack signals. Your two veteran legions, even on high ground, may not be enough to withstand a determined attack by that horde. Despite what I told Malleus, if the enemy gets between me and you, I'm not sure I can get to you, and we want no repeat of the Cimbri disaster. If you're detected by the enemy during your approach to the assault position, break off and return here. Warn me by cavalry couriers, and I'll withdraw my division. But again, you're to initiate no attack unless I'm in position. Wait until you see their backs; then you go in."

"*Compre'endo, Caesar,*" Labienus responded.

"Good man!" Caesar responded, clapping Labienus on the shoulder. "Get your boys ready, and I'll see you before you pull out."

Labienus walked away, and I offered Caesar the *tabula* with the meeting notes for his review. "I don't need to see that, Insubrecus," he said. "Just give it to Ebrius for the file."

Then, after a moment, he said, "I'm sending you up north with Agrippa and the Sequani. Sorry. You're going to miss the big show, but whatever the Aedui are up to is critical to me. I'm as interested in who enters Bibracte as I am in who departs . . . Those *cunni* are up to something, and I'm convinced now that someone down in Rome is pulling their strings. Agrippa knows to keep a low profile up there, but if you can grab hold of someone who can help me understand what in the name of Nemesis is going on . . . I don't care if it's a Roman, an Aeduus, a Helvetius, or a blue-painted Briton . . . Grab him up, and bring him to me in a condition in which he can still talk."

XI.

Calamitas Itera
ANOTHER DISASTER

Multo denique die per exploratores Caesar cognovit et montem a suis teneri et Helvetios castra movisse et Considium timore perterritum quod non vidisset pro viso sibi renuntiavisse.

"Finally, after most of the day had passed, Caesar discovered from his scouts that the mountain was occupied by his forces and that the Helvetians had moved their camps. Caesar now understood that Considius had lost his nerve, and what he had reported to Caesar as having been personally seen by him, he had not actually seen."

(from Gaius Marius Insubrecus' notebook of Caesar's journal)

 t the time, I was not sure whether I was disappointed or relieved—disappointed about missing what Caesar called "the big show," or relieved knowing that I wouldn't be trapped in a narrow valley up to my ass in frenzied hairbags screaming for my blood. By the end of the second watch that night, while the Roman camps were in a maelstrom of movement and noise, I was mounted and moving north with Agrippa and the Sequani cavalry. We encountered no enemy counter-reconnaissance patrols. It was as if the Helvetii just didn't care that a Roman army was less than ten thousand *passus* away from their main camps.

We rode hard and arrived at a wooded ridgeline overlooking a broad valley by dawn. From there we could see the dark, hulking mass that was the *dun*, the royal fortress-city of the Aedui, Bibracte.

The *oppidum* sat on a double hill, a higher summit to the east with a lower summit to the west and north. It was surrounded by two walls. The lower, which seemed to surround the entire bottom of both hills, was almost fifteen *pedes* in height and built of stone reinforced with logs. The second, which stretched higher along the slope around the double peaks of the hill, had a sturdy, log fronting. I assumed the logs held a thick core of soil and spoil, like the walls of a permanent legionary camp. From where we stood, we could see a road leading from the south and west, entering the fortress through a large, well-guarded, and fortified gate.

"That not main gate," Madog was telling Agrippa. "That on the north side of *oppidum*. But, if Aedui talk to Helvetii, that road runners to use."

"*Bene*," Agrippa agreed. "Let's put an *ala* across that road. I expect that when Caesar attacks, the Helvetii will send a courier up to inform Diviciacus. If that happens, we'll let the courier pass. If a response is sent, that's the one we'll intercept. But, we'll want the courier alive."

"Maybe response from Aedui is attack Romans," Madog cautioned.

"Then, we don't need the messenger," Agrippa said. "We ride south and warn Caesar."

Agrippa noticed me looking away to the south. "You see something, *Decurio*?" he asked.

"*Aliquid non cerno, Tribune*," I answered. "No, sir. I was just wondering why we can hear nothing from the south."

Agrippa shrugged, "The army's in a valley over twenty thousand *passus* away. We may not hear the battle here. So, let's stay focused on our own mission."

I nodded. Still it seemed strange to me that two huge armies were locked in a decisive struggle a few thousand *passus* to the south, yet here, there was no indication of it.

Madog was talking, "Other gate for north road; we need watch."

Agrippa grunted his assent. "Where is it?" he asked Madog.

"To north," Madog answered, pointing, "other side hill that direction."

Agrippa nodded. "That's your job, Insubrecus. You and Athauhnu work your way around there without being seen. Get a good, concealed observation position. Same deal. You see any known enemy couriers, snatch them up on their way out, though I doubt you'll see any Helvetii north of here. And, if the Aedui move south, they'll probably come this way. Greek or Roman merchants, you see any of them, stop and question them. Hold them until you withdraw. I want you back here by the sixth hour. By that time the battle in the south should be decided. I'll stay in this area. Madog, will you take the south road?"

Just before Athauhnu and I pulled out, Agrippa said to me, "Take a good look at the defenses, Insubrecus . . . any weaknesses you can see . . . places where the walls need repair . . . gaps . . . low spots. Pay special attention to water breaks, sewers, or streams. I have a feeling we're going to be back here in a couple of days and the boss is going to want to take this place apart."

It took Athauhnu and me the better part of an hour to work our way around to the north. We passed a few farmsteads, to which we gave a wide berth. We had a nervous few moments when a farmer's dog took a noisy and somewhat passionate interest in our presence. But, for the most part, the land around Bibracte was quiet and sparsely inhabited.

By the second hour, we were on well-wooded, high ground from where we could see a road winding down from the north and another coming in from the northwest. They met at a large gate piercing the lower wall of Bibracte. It was as Madog said. This gate was larger, more formidable than the one in the south. Dressed in the red-plaid tartans of the Aeduan royal house, a detachment of about ten Aedui warriors were guarding the double portal and collecting tolls from those wanting entry and duties from those leaving. We guessed there were more troops concealed in the gatehouse.

We split the *ala* into three sections: one kept watch on the roads and gate; another provided security around our position; the third slept. Athauhnu volunteered to take the first command shift and let me take a nap after having ridden most of the night. I found myself a warm, shady spot on top of some springy pine needles just over the reverse slope. I kept my *lorica* secured, but loosened by boots. I rolled my *sagum* into a pillow and lay back. I felt like I had no more than closed my eyes when I felt someone shaking my shoulder. It was Athauhnu's nephew, Emlun.

"Come with me!" he whispered. "Athauhnu . . . I mean, the chief, wants you to see something."

I rubbed my eyes open, then tightened my boots. With my *sagum* rolled up and under my arm, I followed Emlun over the crest of the low ridge to where Athauhnu was crouched behind some trees. When he saw us approaching, he signaled us into a crouch. When we reached his position, he pointed down toward the north road.

There, I could see a group of riders, ten warriors by their armor and weapons. They were followed by an entourage of servants and baggage. This was obviously not a war band. The leader was arrayed to impress: a tall, conical helmet; gold arm bands; a polished, chainmail *lorica*; a rich cloak swept back to reveal a long, Gallic *spatha* in a rich gold-wrapped leather scabbard. I caught a glint of gold around his neck, the golden torc of a noble.

"They are not River People, not Helvetii," Athauhnu was saying. "I do not recognize their tartan."

Athauhnu gestured one of his warriors over to him. It was the scout, Rhodri. "Do you recognize the colors?" Athauhnu asked him.

I focused on the colors that the riders were wearing. Their *bracae* and cloaks were in a blue and white plaid that I had never seen before. A *signifer* riding immediately behind the noble was displaying a banner of long blue and white strips, which stretched back and flapped in the light breezes.

Rhodri nodded, "Blue and white . . . they are Barisai from the north. I went on a cattle raid into their lands two . . . three winters ago . . . Nasty place . . . too cold . . . Cattle are thin. They built their *dun* on an island in the middle of a river . . . Nasty place . . . Floods every spring. Nothing worth taking in their lands . . . not worth the horse fodder to raid them."

Athauhnu nodded and whispered to me, "You Romans call them Parisi."

"Parisi," I repeated. I had heard the name, but knew nothing about them. "What are they doing down here?" I asked.

Athauhnu just shrugged. "By his gold, he's one of their chiefs . . . a noble. It must have something to do with the king, with Duuhruhda."

As we watched, one of the noble's *fintai* handed him something. He held it up to examine it. It was a white wand, the sign of a diplomatic mission. He had come to negotiate with the king.

As the Parisi rode to the north gate, the noble raised the white wand so the guard detail could see it. I saw the officer of the guard point in a direction and bow. The rest of the guard detail stepped aside and let the Parisi enter Bibracte.

I didn't know what all this meant, but I was sure Caesar would be interested. By that time, I was wide awake, so I let Athauhnu get some sleep. I rotated our security detail and checked the horses. Everything was in order. I checked the position of the sun. It was still well before *meridies*. I settled down to watch the roads.

I spent my time examining the fortifications. Back then, I had no experience or training in evaluating the strength of fortress walls. Since then, I have studied the treatises of Aeneas Tacticus and participated in a number of sieges, from both sides of the defensive walls. Back then, I had only been in the army long enough to note that there was no defensive ditch protecting the walls of Bibracte. Otherwise, the walls looked strong for the most part and in good repair. I noticed that the walls dipped down into a small valley between the north gate and the double-peaked hill in the south. From the look of the terrain within the double walls, there seemed to be a stream that flowed down from between the hill tops and must have come through both walls where they crossed that small valley.

By the shortened shadows, it was about the fifth hour when I noticed movement on the north road. I hissed over to the trooper closest to me, Alaw, to go get Athauhnu. By the time Athauhnu joined me, the shapes of the riders on the road were resolving themselves. It was another group of warriors.

When I pointed them out to Athauhnu, I heard him hiss the word, "Belgai!"

These warriors were not as well arrayed as the Parisi. Their clothes were dark colored, varying shades of black, brown, and gray. Most of their armor was hardened, boiled leather; their faces were bearded; great gouts of hair escaped from underneath their helmets. Their horses, though, were magnificent, black and dark gray, larger even than the horses that the Roman army preferred, which came from Spain and the east, the land of the *Arabiani*. The mounts of the *Belgae* pranced and snorted as they moved down the road, as if constantly challenging the control of their riders.

Their weapons were equally impressive. Each warrior carried a long lance with a flattened iron head, almost two *pedes* long and a *palmus* broad in the center, pointed and sharpened on each edge. This was a formable weapon, capable of stabbing and slashing. Each wore a long *spatha*, hung from a dark leather baldric and secured at the hip by a wide leather belt. Their shields were round with a dark iron boss; each displayed the totem of a red wolf's head.

These were the *Belgae*, a nightmarish race of fierce savages clinging to the frozen edges of the known world on the shores of *Oceanus*. Even the *Germani* from beyond the *Rhenus* feared these people, and now they were here, among the Aedui, less than twenty thousand *passus* from our army.

"What are the *Belgai* doing in Gaul?" I heard myself say in Gah'el.

"They're not all *Belgai*," I heard Athauhnu say as he pointed down toward the head of their column.

I looked where Athauhnu had indicated and noticed a rider who had been partially obscured by the Belgic leader. He was a smaller man, bareheaded and clean shaven. His hair was cut short, like a Roman. I noticed that under his reddish-brown military cloak, he wore a short sword on his right hip, a Roman infantry *gladius*.

"A Roman?" I questioned.

"*A Rhufeinig!*" Athauhnu agreed.

I watched as the party approached the gate. Since *Belgae* do not observe Gallic protocols, they carried no wand of negotiation. But, they were obviously expected. The Aeduan guard detail passed them through into the *dun*.

I heard Athauhnu snort.

"What's so funny?" I asked him.

"Belgai and Barisai despise each other," he answered. "A blood feud since the Belgai came across the Rhenus and pushed the Barisai off their lands. I would love to be a bird in the rafters of Duuhruhda's hall when those two meet."

"Enemies become friends only when they have a common enemy," I quoted.

Athauhnu grunted his agreement.

It was close to the seventh hour, almost time to pack it up and head south, when another party arrived, this time down the road from the northwest. Alaw, who had been posted up that road as a scout, alerted us.

"*A Pen*," he reported to Athauhnu. "Chief! A merchant and his party are approaching the city."

"How many?" Athauhnu asked.

Alaw shrugged and calculated, "The merchant . . . his woman . . . two bodyguards . . . a slave . . . four pack mules."

"How far out?" Athauhnu asked again.

Again, Alaw shrugged, "Maybe five hundred *passus*. He's in no hurry."

"Let's intercept!" I suggested.

Athauhnu grunted his agreement, then hissed, "Guithiru! Mount five!"

Then, he turned to Alaw, "Is Rhodri keeping an eye on him?"

"'Tis, Chief!" Alaw nodded.

We walked our horses down off the reverse slope of the ridge and hit the road out of sight of the city gate. There we mounted and followed Alaw to the northwest. We spotted the merchant's party less than four hundred *passus* up the road. He halted when he saw us. His two guards attempted to look as menacing as they could in the face of nine well-armed riders.

We halted about ten *passus* away. Almost immediately, Rhodri joined us from behind the merchant's party, and now they faced ten. I held up an empty right hand to show him I was not holding a weapon and asked in Latin, "Are you bound for the fortress of the Aedui?"

The man hesitated for a few heartbeats, then answered in a halting Latin, "*Romani vos?*"

I answered, "We are from Caesar's army. Are you not a Roman?"

"*Non Romanus. Graecus,*" he answered.

"Να μιλούν την ελληνική γλώσσα," I said. "I can speak Greek."

The man stared again, then smiled, "Like a Roman schoolboy trying to recite Homer for his tutor," he said in Gah'el.

"Then Gah'el it is," I agreed. "Where are you bound?"

"This is the road to Bibracte, is it not?" he shrugged.

"'Tis," I agreed. "Where are you coming from?"

The man shrugged, "I am coming down from the lands of the Senones, but I have been as far north as the Ocean, among the Veneti."

I could tell Athauhnu and the men were uneasy about being out in the open while we talked, so I said, "We would like to hear your tales of the Senones and the Veneti. Perhaps we can talk out of the sun, over in those trees."

Now it was the merchant's turn to be nervous about being waylaid by a band of brigands pretending to be Roman soldiers—or about being waylaid by actual Roman cavalry who might be looking to augment their wages. So I spoke again, "I am Gaius Marius Insubrecus, *decurio* in Gaius Iulius Caesar's *praetoria*. And, this is Athauhnu mab Hergest, *pencefhul* of the Soucanai, in the service of Caesar and the Roman people."

The man's eyes widened a bit at that. "Romans this far north and Soucanai this far west! These are indeed interesting times." Then, he looked up at the sun. "You are correct, young man, this sun is hot. A short rest under the shade of some trees would be welcomed."

We moved over to a grove of trees to the north of the road. Alaw and Rhodri moved farther north to screen the road. Athauhnu dispatched Guithiru and two men to the south. The rest of our troop spread out, securing the area.

As we dismounted, the merchant announced, "I am called *Gennadios Haw Emporos*, Gennadios the Trader. The woman is called Evra. She claims to be from an island beyond Britannia, where the dead live. Years ago, when she was a girl, she was taken in a raid by the Veneti. Now she's my woman."

"Not *that* long ago, Merchant!" she spat.

Athauhnu's eyes widened at that. "A woman from the island of the dead! Then, that place exists!"

Gennadios shrugged, "She claims she never saw the dead feasting in golden halls. According to her, it's a place of pigs, cattle, and salmon the size of *tiuunai*, tunnyfish, in the rivers. No! No walking dead. Just drunks, pigs, and fat farmers. Eh, *Meli Mou?*"

The woman gave a dismissive grunt as she adjusted the pack straps on one of the mules.

"Ah! Where are my manners?" Gennadios said. "Wine! Evra! The skin of retsina! Three cups!"

Then he turned to us, "I doubt you've ever tried retsina. We use pine resin to preserve the wine. It travels well!"

Gennadios' woman from the Isle of the Dead handed us cups, then poured the wine. It was golden yellow as it flowed from the wine skin. I could smell the pine resin. When all the cups were poured, we acknowledged our host and drank. I was surprised. It was light, delicious.

Gennadios smacked his lips, then said, "I had heard that Caesar had moved north of the Rhonus, but I hadn't expected to see his men this side of Bibracte."

"Really?" I said. "Where did you hear that news of Caesar?"

"From the Roman delegation to the Senones—" he began.

"Romans! Among the Senones! Who—" I began.

Gennadios held up his hand. "Yes! A Roman delegation arrived in the Senones' *dun*, Agedincum . . . When was it? About two . . . three weeks ago. They had a broad-striper leading them . . . a noble or a senator . . . A real nob, he was. The rest looked military . . . Bodyguards, I would think, led by a narrow-striper. They had an audience with the *uucharix*, the tribal king, Caswalu, but they spent most of their time with his *dunorix*, Dramaelo. No love lost between those two, I can tell you. Dramaelo is older, but Caswalu seems to have favor with you Romans."

"Do you know what these Romans wanted?" I interrupted.

"Wanted? Oh, yes . . . They told the king that Caesar did not have the Roman Senate's authorization to cross the Rhonus . . . that the Aedui were still friends of the Roman state."

"They specifically mentioned the Aedui?" I interrupted again.

"They didn't have to," Gennadios tutted. "They had an escort of Aedui riders from the *fintai* of the Aeduan *dunorix*."

"Deluuhnu?" I asked.

"The same," Gennadios confirmed. "Why are you surprised? Didn't you know that Dramaelo is married to Deluuhnu's sister?"

"His sister?" I said.

"Oh, yes!" Gennadios continued. "In fact, many of Dramaelo's troops are Aedui. Makes his king right nervous."

"Did the Romans encourage the Senones to attack Caesar's army?" I asked.

"Attack them?" Gennadios answered. "No . . . not in so many words. But, the impression they gave was, if the Senones joined with the Aedui in defending Aedui territory against Caesar's unauthorized incursion, the Senate would understand."

Evra, who was sitting with the two bodyguards over by the mules, called over to Gennadios, "*Labhair tú i bhfad ró, fear d'aois. Roinnt lá beidh go bhfaigheann mharaigh tú.*"

I didn't understand what she said, but some words sounded familiar, almost recognizable.

Gennadios chuckled. "She's telling me to keep my mouth shut," he told us. "The women of the Gaelige . . . that's what they call themselves on the Isle of the Dead . . . Gaelige . . . sometimes the people of Eriu . . . that's their goddess of love . . . Aphrodite. You'd never know it from Evra. Their women are like the women of the Gah'el, but ten times worse. They just do what they want . . . say what they want. When I get back to Massalia, I'd keep Evra locked up, but she wouldn't stand for it. She'd tear my place apart, and me along with it." He chuckled again.

"Gaelige," I said absently. "Almost sounds like Gah'el . . . but back to the Romans."

"Yes, the Romans," Gennadios said, filling his cup and offering more wine to Athauhnu and me, which we gratefully accepted. "Quite generous they were too, especially to the *dunorix*. All nice, new silver, too."

Gennadios reached into his *marsupium*. He pulled out a silver coin and handed it to me. It was unworn and shiny, a newly minted *quadriga*, a *denarius* coin. I flipped it over and saw the image of one of this year's consuls, my erstwhile patron, Aulus Gabinius.

Gennadios was talking, "It worked out well for me. Usually there's not much hard currency among the tribes. I sometimes have to resort to bartering . . . swatches of eastern cloth and pottery for chickens . . . that sort of thing . . . Useless when I get home. A man needs silver to live in Massalia."

I handed the coin back. "You didn't happen to hear the name of the purple-striper did you?" I asked.

"Hear it!" Gennadios exclaimed. "I did better than that! I sold a skin of wine to his tribune. The man had a ghastly scar across his face . . . still red and puckered in places . . . Said he got it in a skirmish with the Belgae last season. I hadn't heard anything about Romans fighting the Belgae. He told me the man's name was something like Pompius . . . That's it . . . Gaius or Gnaeus Pompius. When Simathemeni . . . that's my name for the scarred Roman . . . "Scar Face" . . . when this Simathemeni got a bit drunk, he referred to his companion as Minus. That means 'The Lesser,' doesn't it? I never understood you Romans' sense of humor."

I certainly thought I recognized the name. Pompius or Pompeius. That was the name of Caesar's colleague, one of the *triumviri*. But Pompeius Minus? Pompeius was called Magnus, "The Great." Was he one of Pompeius' freedmen? No, a freedman wouldn't dare wear a broad, purple stripe, regardless of who his *patronus* was. Did Pompeius Magnus have a son? If so, wouldn't he be called Pompeius Iunior—or was "Scarface" making a sarcastic joke, like Gennadios thought?

Before I could ask, Guithiru came into the grove. He addressed Athauhnu, "Chief! A messenger came up from the Roman tribune. We're to withdraw and meet him south of Bibracte."

I sensed something important was up. Was it the battle in the south? Had Caesar been defeated? Were we cut off?

I stood up. "We thank you for your hospitality, Gennadios. We must depart."

I thought to tell him not to inform the Aedui of our presence, but telling a merchant not to share gossip and information made as much sense as asking a stream not to flow.

I reached into my *marsupium* and found a small, silver *mercurius* and handed it over to the merchant. "For the wine and the conversation, *phile mou*," I told him.

Gennadios made the coin disappear into his own purse. "*Vobiscum fortuna sit, mi amice!*" he said in Latin.

"*Et tecum*," I responded, unconsciously rubbing my *lorica* where my medallion rested.

I looked over to where Evra was sitting. The woman from the Isle of the Dead was glaring at me with the soulless, black eyes of Hecate.

Unconsciously, I made the *cornucellus*, the little horn, with the fingers of my right hand to ward off the evil eye.

We rejoined Agrippa, Madog, and the rest of the Sequani troopers at the rendezvous point south of Bibracte. Agrippa told me briefly that a full *ala* of the *dunorix*'s *fintai*, almost forty riders, had sallied out of the south gate a little less than an hour earlier. At first, Agrippa feared that his troop had been detected and the Aedui were going to attack him. But, the Aedui rushed past his position without as much as a wink. They pounded down the road to the south, toward where our army was engaged with the Helvetii. Agrippa sent five *exploratores* to follow the Aedui while he waited for my *ala* to return from north of Bibracte.

"Any word of the battle?" I asked him.

He shrugged, "*Nil!* Not even a sound!"

We rode south in the tracks of the Aedui. We had gone about ten thousand *passus* when we found our scouts. They were in a narrow wooded cut between two low hills. Two had been killed by arrows; two more had been brought down with stabbing wounds to the abdomen, typical of a close ambush by infantry; one scout was missing. Their horses were gone. All the bodies had been stripped of their armor and weapons.

A trooper from our point element was examining the ground around the bodies.

"What happened here?" Madog demanded.

The trooper shrugged. "Men on foot . . . maybe fifteen . . . twenty at the most . . . They hid in the brush along the trail . . . went off in that direction . . . leading riderless horses."

I translated for Agrippa.

"Where is Ailwuhnu?" Madog asked after the missing man.

Again the trooper shrugged. "He's not here. Maybe they took him?"

Our other point man came back down the trail. "They had horses just over the rise," he reported. "They retreated south toward the Helvetii."

"The Aedui we're tracking?" Madog demanded.

"No," the trooper said. "The horses rode light. The Aedui had steel armor. These men did not."

Madog was just about to respond when there was a commotion to our rear. One of our men was leading a horse carrying a wounded man. It was our missing *explorator*. He was doubled forward in his saddle. There was blood down his saddle and his right leg.

Madog recognized the man, "Ailwuhnu! What happened here?"

The man gathered his strength to face his chief. "Ambush, Lord," he gasped. "They came at us . . . up out of the brush." His companion steadied him in the saddle.

"The Aedui?" Madog began.

"No!" the man gasped. "*Almaenwuhra*! Germans!"

I translated that for Agrippa. "There are Krauts with the Helvetii?" he said to no one in particular. "What are they doing up here?"

The Sequani were helping Ailwuhnu down from his horse. I was no *medicus*, but the man had a deep stab wound in his lower right abdomen. His chances were not good. And, he could suffer for days.

"Bring up the *medduhg*!" Madog called down the line of riders. Then, he turned to Agrippa and said in Latin, "We have *medicus* for horse. He do what he can."

While the Sequani were trying to make Ailwuhnu comfortable, Agrippa said, "We need to get back to the army; Krauts this far north is not a good sign."

"I am same," Madog nodded. "I leave companions here. Take care of thing. Then we go."

Madog dismounted and walked over to where the *medduhg* was treating the wounded trooper. I saw Madog take the hand of the wounded man as they spoke. Then, they embraced briefly. Madog touched the man's cheek as a father saying farewell to his child, then he remounted.

A rider came up beside me. It was Athauhnu.

"Ailwuhnu is Madog's sister's son," he said. "This is not a good thing."

"What will they do?" I asked.

Athauhnu shrugged, "What they can. If he cannot travel, the *medduhg* will give him drugs to make him comfortable before the *cuhthraulai*, the daemons, possess his gut. Then he'll help him to *tir ieuenctid*."

"The Land of Youth," I echoed remembering Gran'pa's tales. "You mean the *medduhg* will . . . he'll kill him?"

Athauhnu nodded. "*Ie*! It is . . . *un drugaretha* . . . a mercy. There is no honor for a warrior to die drenched in his own piss and shit after hours of agony. The *medduhg* will send him to the feasting hall of heroes. It is an honorable death."

Athauhnu left me to follow his *ala* down the trail. I looked back to where the *medicus* was attending to Ailwuhnu. He was propped up against a tree. His eyes were closed; his face was pasty white, almost greenish, covered with sweat. He would be feasting with the heroes before the sun was down. For the first time in my career as a soldier, a thought formed clearly in my mind: *fortunae deae gratias ago*. I thanked the goddess Fortuna that it was not me. I turned my horse and followed Athauhnu.

Since we did not know the outcome of the battle, Agrippa led us to where the camps had been when we departed that morning. They were still there, but the legionaries, who had been left behind, were dismantling them. Agrippa found the legate, Pulcher, and asked him for news of the battle.

"Battle!" Pulcher snorted. "There was no battle. Our *imperator* allowed the barbarians to escape right out from under his ample snout. Those hairy Gauls are still laughing themselves sick over the incompetence of—" Then, Pulcher thought about what he was about to say and continued, "There was no battle. The army's in camp ten thousand *passus* to the west. You'll find Caesar there."

Agrippa was about to walk away, when Pulcher spoke again, "When you see the *imperator*, tell him I have obeyed his order and released the Aeduan prisoner, Dumnorix!"

We found Caesar's *castra* along a ridgeline south of where the battle with the Helvetii was to have taken place. As we entered the camp of the Tenth Legion, we could sense the sullenness and resentment of the soldiers. Through no fault of their own, the enemy had escaped. So, the halfhearted pursuit of an enemy they believed they could have defeated would continue. And still, no new rations had been issued. The men had long ago exhausted their supplies of fresh meat and wheat; even their marching rations of jerky and *buccellatum* were gone. Even worse, the *posca*, their beloved sour wine, was a memory. To fill their stomachs, they could look forward to nothing but barley and water, usually a punishment ration, while their enemy ate well and had been allowed to walk out of their trap, with nothing but contempt for them. They blamed their officers; they blamed Caesar.

We found Caesar's *praetorium* in the center of the camp. As we dismounted, we saw Ebrius, his clerk, standing outside the tent.

"You might want to think twice about going in there," he warned us. "The boss is not having a good day."

Agrippa ignored the *scriba* and entered. Madog and I followed. Even in the outer *cubiculum*, we could hear Caesar's voice, "I don't care what his excuse is . . . whether he lost his nerve . . . whether he's blind . . . or whether he's just bloody incompetent. He's relieved of his command! He's not fit to serve in this army! I want him out of camp before the sun sets!"

We slipped into Caesar's office. Labienus seemed to be in the line of fire of Caesar's tirade. He was still dressed in his battle armor, his helmet locked under his left arm.

Caesar looked over and saw us. "Agrippa," he said, "I suppose you have more good news for me?"

Before Agrippa could answer, Ebrius entered the tent.

"Pardon my interruption, *Imperator*," he apologized, "but the senior centurions are outside as you ord . . . er . . . requested."

Caesar nodded. "You are dismissed, Labienus, but don't go far. Agrippa! I need some time with my officers in private; then we'll talk."

When we got outside, Agrippa turned to Labienus, "What in the name of *Dis* happened, sir? Why are we still here? What happened to the enemy?"

Labienus held up his hand to silence Agrippa. I could see the fatigue and frustration in his eyes.

"It was a good plan, and it should have worked," Labienus began. "But, it turned into a complete cluster. I got my two legions into position above the enemy a good hour before dawn. The Helvetii had no idea we were up there. They must have detected Caesar approaching just after dawn because we could see the camp begin to stir. A battle line was forming down toward our left front, just like Caesar planned. The warriors were forming up the musters and pushing them forward. The enemy had their backs to us . . . no idea we were there. Then, it all just came apart. The Helvetii began to melt away from the intended battle position and began to move to the west as if there was no threat approaching. They must have detected our presence up on the hill because a group of them began pointing up toward our position. Luckily, there wasn't enough discipline down there to organize an attack, or we could have been *immerda*. A bunch of the Helvetii dropped their *bracae* and showed us their backsides before they walked away . . . really pissed my boys off. They wanted to run down there and stick their *pila* through the Helvetians' *bracae* ... I had all I could do to keep them together."

"But what happened?" Agrippa persisted.

"I'm getting to that," Labienus continued. "I sent riders to find Caesar. He was digging in here, wondering what the hell had become of me. It seems that when he was coming up the road toward the Helvetii, he had sent some *exploratores* forward to make contact with my division . . . an *ala* of Roman cavalry under an *angusticlavus* named Considius. He couldn't have chosen a worse officer for that assignment. Considius has been with the army since the time Marius was fighting Sulla. The man is as blind as Homer . . . can't see past his own nose, and all of his cronies have been covering for him. He reported to Caesar that my hill was occupied by the enemy and my division was nowhere to be found. So Caesar halted the advance and veered off to the south to find some high ground in case the Helvetii attacked him. By midday, I was sitting on my hill, watching the dust of the enemy escaping to the west, and Caesar was on his hill, wondering where I was . . . all because of a blind scout. A blind scout! It would be damned funny if I had any sense of humor left."

About that time, the six *primi pili* of the legions left Caesar's tent. I had seen men look grimmer, but that was at a funeral. Ebrius beckoned us into Caesar's office. "The *imperator* will see you now," he intoned.

Caesar was sitting in a slouch beside his field desk, legs extended in front of him. He was staring intently at the ground. "My senior centurions tell me that after today's *calamitas*, they cannot guarantee the loyalty of my troops," he said as we entered. "What good news do you boys have for me?"

Agrippa reported what we had seen and heard around Bibracte. Caesar said nothing. He just rubbed his forehead and shook his head.

When Agrippa reported the ambush by Germans and the death of Madog's nephew, Caesar said, "Germans . . . that's all I need . . . Germans this far west of the Rhenus. My condolences to you and your family, Madocus *Dux*. Your nephew died in the service of Rome. His name will be remembered."

"Thank you, Caesar," Madog responded. "He died like a warrior . . . a good death." Madog's voice sounded hollow, exhausted.

"Parisi and Belgae delegations in Bibracte . . . A Roman riding with a Belgae war band . . . Renegade Aedui horsemen somewhere in my rear . . . A Roman senatorial telling the Senones that if they attack us, Rome will not take offense. Do I have it all, Agrippa?" Caesar asked.

Agrippa nodded, but then said, "One more thing, *Imperator*! Pulcher reports that he has released Dumnorix, according to your order."

When Agrippa said this, Caesar's head jerked up. He stared at Agrippa for a few heartbeats, then said in a low voice, "*Quid dicebas tu?*"

"*Imperator*," Agrippa responded, "Legate Pulcher reports that he released the Aeduan, Dumnorix."

"He did what?" Caesar shouted jumping to his feet. "*Iste stulte* . . . that . . . that *verpa*! He did what?"

"Released Dumnorix . . . the Aeduan," Agrippa stammered.

"*Cacat*!" Caesar shouted, his fist slamming down on the desk. "Labienus! Send a detachment of my *praetoriani* back to those camps . . . bring that *podex*, Pulcher, here . . . to me! *Stat*! *Iste fellator* . . . That *half-wit* better have a good explanation, or I'll crucify him!"

Suddenly, Caesar's eyes became unfocused. He stumbled, barely able to steady himself on the field desk. Labienus rushed forward and took his arm. Without taking his eyes off Caesar, he said, "Insubrecus . . . quickly . . . find Spina, the *medicus* . . . Bring him here! Agrippa! Madocus! Wait outside!"

I flew out of the tent, past a startled Ebrius. I ran over to the medical tent, less than thirty *passus* away. "Spina! Spina, *Medice!*" I shouted.

I heard his thick, Aventine accent from one of the rear compartments, "Who's dat? Whadda you want? I'm ovah hee'ah!"

"Medice!" I shouted. "I'm here to bring you to—" Then, I stopped myself. Yelling out that the commander of the army was near collapse was not conducive to morale, especially after a day like this.

Spina came out of the back. "You callin' for me, or what?" he asked.

"Yes, *Medice*," I said, lowering my voice, "please accompany me to the *praetorium . . . stat'.*"

"The *praetorium?*" Spina started. Then, he whispered to me, "Is da boss havin' one of his spells?"

I nodded at him. He nodded and then went back into the tent where jars of herbs and drugs were stored. He packed something into a *loculus* and said, "Okay, let's get adda hee'ah!"

As we walked back to the *praetorium*, he recognized me, "You're dat *tiro* I patched up a while back, ain't cha? Duh one who got stabbed by duh slave who wasn't a slave, right?"

"*Recte,*" I confirmed.

"How's dee ahm?" he asked.

It took me a heartbeat to realize he was asking me how my arm was. "Good as new," I told him.

"*Bene!*" he said. "Looks like yaw getting up in duh world. A *decurio* in less than a year . . . a praetorian to boot! Dat's impressive!"

By that time we were at the *praetorium*, Spina was immediately passed straight through to Caesar's *cubiculum*. I saw Agrippa and Madog still standing outside.

"What's this all about?" I asked.

Agrippa just shrugged, but he looked worried.

Madog said in his broken Latin, "Sometimes gods enter in man's anger—" Then, he stopped. Either his Latin or his knowledge had failed him.

After a bit, Spina came back out. "Youse can go back in now. He wants to tawk to yas. Not too long. He needs to sleep." Then, he walked back toward the medical station, whistling some tuneless sounds.

We reentered Caesar's *cubiculum*. He was sitting at his desk, drinking something that smelled of wine, vinegar, and something else—something sweet and cloying. He seemed relaxed, his eyes lidded and heavy. Labienus was standing next to him.

Caesar looked up at me and asked, "Insubrecus, are you familiar with the story of the Gordian's Knot?"

I remember the Stick telling us the tale during a class on Greek culture. I recited, "When Gordias became the king of Phrygia, his son, Midas, dedicated a chariot to Zeus and tied its shaft with an intricate knot of cornel bark. He declared whoever could undo the knot was the rightful king of Phrygia. Later, Alexander arrived in Phrygia, when it was a province of Persia. When challenged to prove himself worthy of the throne by undoing the knot, Alexander sliced it in half with his sword. That night, there was a violent thunderstorm. Alexander took this as a sign that Zeus was pleased and would grant Alexander many victories."

Caesar nodded. "Not lyrical, but accurate, Insubrecus. All these stories and reports of Romans, Belgae, Krauts, and whatnot have become a knot I do not have time to unravel, so I'm just going to slice it open!" Caesar announced. "Tomorrow at dawn, this army marches on the Aeduan capital ... we march on Bibracte!"

XII.

BIBRACTE

Et quod a Bibracte, oppido Haeduorum longe maximo et copiosissimo, non amplius milibus passuum XVIII aberat, rei frumentariae prospiciendum existimavit; itaque iter ab Helvetiis avertit ac Bibracte ire contendit.

"The town of Bibracte, by far the largest and most prosperous settlement of the Aedui, was not more than eighteen miles away. Since Caesar estimated that the town would provide him a supply of grain, on the next day, he diverted his route of march away from the Helvetians and toward Bibracte."

(from Gaius Marius Insubrecus' notebook of Caesar's journal)

uring the fourth watch, Caesar assembled his six legions in the dark valley north of the camps. I was again assigned to Agrippa and Madog's Sequani cavalry. Our mission was to screen Caesar's advance to the east. Once we came abreast of Bibracte, we were to swing around it to the east and seal its northern approaches. Caesar hoped he could trap any Gallic deputations still in the *oppidum* and any Romans accompanying them. My mission was to ensure that any prisoners we took were delivered to Caesar's interrogators in a condition to talk.

As we rode through the darkness, my head was fuzzy from lack of sleep and a bit too much of Caesar's *posca* the night before. I don't know what strange and exotic herbs Spina had dosed Caesar with, but it put the *imperator* into one of his rare loquacious moods. He kept Labienus and me up well into the second watch, talking about his vision for Rome and his frustrations with the antiquated, doddering machinery of the *res publica.*

"These old fools in the Senate just don't understand Rome's position through the extension of our *imperium*," he was saying. "They think they're still ruling a city and the farmlands around it. Marius . . . even Sulla . . . taught them the foolishness of that. One strong man with the support of the army can set their whole house of straw ablaze."

"But, Caesar," Labienus protested, "these institutions . . . our laws . . . the Twelve Tables . . . prevent too much power from falling into the hands of a single man. Our ancestors understood this from the tyranny of the kings. The *mos maiorum*, the tradition of our ancestors, is sacred."

Caesar retorted, "The *mos maiorum* didn't stop Sulla from killing hundreds of his enemies for their estates, did it? He just ignored it, and the Senate quaked in their red boots while he did it. Why? He had an army to back him up, an army loyal to Sulla's purse, not to the Senate."

"We have restored the *res publica* since Sulla—"

"Bah!" Caesar snorted. "The sacred *mos maiorum*! When *fides* and *pietas* encounter silver and greed, they melt away! And there is the heart of it! Rome is not ruled by *virtus*; it's ruled by *avaritas* . . . and Rome's greed seems to have developed an infinite desire for plunder. So she extends the *imperium*, grasping more and more. We do not rule our provinces; we rape them! We say we send out proconsuls and propraetors to protect the interests of the *res publica* . . . to bring *Romanitas* to the barbarians . . . But what do they really do? They enrich themselves and their masters in the Senate! The only difference between a Roman army and a pack of brigands is size and discipline. If you encounter either, they'll strip you bare and leave you bleeding!"

I continued to wonder what Spina had put in Caesar's drink.

"Look at Insubrecus, here!" Caesar went on. "*He* represents the future of Rome! He's one generation out of a round hut; his grandfather wore trousers just like the Helvetii we're chasing across *terrae comatorum*, the lands of the hairbags. But, he is the future of Rome—not those over-educated, inbred senatorials down in Rome who think they have the right to rule the world because some boot-licking, scroll-sniffing charlatan told them they're descended from Romulus! Bah!"

Labienus was sweating freely by this time. He was devoted to the legendary Rome of Mucius Scaevola, Scipio Africanus, and Cato the Elder. Or, at least he was devoted to the legends of these heroes from the dim chronicles of our history.

"When I return to Rome from this command," Caesar continued, "I plan to introduce legislation to offer the franchise to *Gallia Cisalpina* and all of *Italia*—"

"Certainly, that will not pass the Senate!" Labienus protested.

"Politics, my dear Labienus! Politics!" Caesar snorted. "As long as I, and my tame, plebian tribunes, support land reforms for Pompeius and oppose debt reduction for Crassus, it will pass. Believe me! Those doddering old fools in the Senate love their luxuries and fear the gangs of Clodius and Milo more than they cherish their *mos maiorum*. And that's only the beginning!"

Caesar went on like that well into the night, until the wine and drugs finally took hold of him. As we were sitting in that tent that summer night about twenty thousand *passus* south of Bibracte, we had no idea how Nona was spinning out the threads of our destinies: the death of Caesar's daughter, Iulia, and his split with Pompeius; the death of Crassus in the land of the Parthians; Labienus' death while fighting against Caesar in the civil wars; Caesar's own death at the hands of those to whom he had granted his *clementia*. No! As we sat and drank *posca* that night in *Gallia*, all of that lay well in the future.

Caesar's plans for Rome and the fumes of the *posca* I had drunk the night before were fogging my head as we pounded north into the darkness on our way to Bibracte.

Before I returned to my quarters the night before, Labienus had confided in me that Pulcher did, in fact, possess a written directive apparently issued by Caesar's headquarters, ordering the immediate release of the Aeduan prince, Dumnorix. Pulcher claimed that the directive had been delivered to him by an *angusticlavus*, a narrow-striper whom he did not recognize.

Regardless, Pulcher was finished in the army.

Labienus advised him to pack his kit and be on the road to Massalia before Caesar remembered his threat to crucify him. Not that even a proconsul with full *imperium* could, or would, execute a citizen, a patrician, and a senatorial, like a slave, but why test the theory? Labienus told Pulcher to be on a ship to Ostia before Caesar had a chance to try to make good on his threat.

The issue that really worried Labienus was that there were obviously Roman officers serving within the army who were actively engaged in undermining Caesar and his efforts to bring the Helvetii to heel.

By dawn the Sequani cavalry *turma* was positioned across the only major avenue of approach from the east that could cut across Caesar's line of advance. It was more of a pathway than a road that travelers had created following a tributary river up from the Rhonus Valley.

Agrippa and Madog had advanced as a recon in force some two to three thousand *passus* down the narrow, wooded valley. Athauhnu and I were positioned where the road from the east broke out of a valley and joined the road from the south we had taken from Caesar's camps. From there, both roads ran toward the west, up into a broader valley, which we expected our army to cross on its way to Bibracte. We weren't expecting any problems. We assumed the main body of the enemy was well to the west.

As usual, Alaw and Rhodri were deployed a few hundred *passus* down the road to the east. Guithiru was deployed with five of our troopers to screen our rear. The morning sun was beginning to warm me and diffuse the fumes in my head. Athauhnu seemed quite amused by my damaged condition.

"I have known men who had to drink for courage before battle," he joked, "but you're the first one I've ever known who gets drunk the night before so he's hungover *for* the battle!"

"Not today," I dismissed him. "I'm in no condition."

Athauhnu reached into his *marsupium* and handed me what looked like a dried out twig. "Here! Chew on this. It will clear your head," he offered.

I took the stick and examined it.

"Go ahead, Arth Bek!" Athauhnu encouraged. "I wouldn't poison you."

I chewed a bit on the twig. It did seem to help a little.

"Madog is concerned about the Caisar," I heard Athauhnu say.

"Concerned about the Caisar?" I questioned. "In what way?"

Athauhnu shrugged. "Madog says that last night, Caesar had a . . . a spell . . . and when he recovered, he decided to go to Bibracte."

"Caesar knows what he's doing," I defended my *patronus*.

Again, Athauhnu shrugged. "At times the gods send madness to cause a man to destroy himself. We march north, with the Helvetii behind us and the Aedui in front of us. If things go badly, we Soucanai will go east back into our own lands. You should come with us, Arth Bek. The Aedui will show no mercy to defeated Romans."

I had no idea how to respond to that. In the case of a defeat, escaping to the east made sense. But, that would mean abandoning Caesar and the Roman army, to which the *sacramentum* bound me until dismissal or death.

Before I could formulate a response, two riders came pounding up the trail from the east. It was Alaw and a trooper that had gone forward with Madog. They pulled up in front of Athauhnu. "*A Pen! Uh doucliau geluhnai!*" Alaw reported. "Chief! The enemy's coming!"

"*Uh geluhnai?*" Athauhnu questioned. "The enemy? The River People . . . the Helvetii?"

"*Na, Pen!*" the man responded. "*Almaenwuhra!* Germans!"

"How many?" Athauhnu asked the man.

The messenger shrugged. "The valley is narrow . . . the road twisted . . . They advance without fear. Madog believes there are many."

"Cavalry?" Athauhnu pressed the man.

"We have seen only mounted men," the man confirmed.

Athauhnu nodded and walked over to his horse. He took a hunting horn that had been attached to his saddle and blew some discordant notes to assemble his *ala*.

Then, he surveyed our position. "See that rise there?" he asked the messenger, pointing to where the ground rose to meet the road from the south. "Tell Madog I will assemble my troop there."

The Alaw nodded, and he and his companion turned back down the road. He passed Rhodri riding in, in response to Athauhnu's summons. Soon, Guithiru and his detail returned.

Athauhnu mounted and quickly briefed his men: "The enemy approaches from the east. Germans! We do not know how many. Madog is withdrawing to our position. We will move west up the valley. We will stay above the Germans, between them and the Romans. When they reach this point, they will have to deploy . . . spread out. Then we will see how many we're dealing with."

"*A Pen*, the sun will be in our eyes!" Guithiru observed.

"It can't be helped," Athauhnu stated. "We will keep the higher ground. They are mounted! If there are too many to fight, we will escape to the west, toward the Romans."

Guithiru grunted.

We withdrew to the top of the rise and deployed, in line, facing the opening of the road below. There we waited. To our rear, the valley rose gently toward the north and west. Whoever these Germans were, they were heading right into the flank of the advancing Roman army.

We seemed to wait for an eternity before we spotted movement on the road below. I could sense our troopers tense as the first riders became visible below us. They were ours! Athauhnu signaled to them with his hands. They quickly joined us, assembling in line on our left flank. Their leader approached Athauhnu. He was a veteran warrior called Ci, the "Hound."

"*A Pen!*" he reported to Athauhnu, "the Germans advance . . . Madog has engaged but withdraws before them."

Athauhnu grunted and nodded. Ci rejoined his troop.

Again, we waited. At least the flies that started buzzing around in my stomach made me forget about the pain in my head. Suddenly, I realized that I had thoroughly chewed the twig Athauhnu had given me earlier. I spit it out.

Athauhnu kept his eyes on the opening of the road below us, but said to me out of the side of his mouth, "This is the worst time . . . just before the enemy comes. Once they are here, we won't have time to be afraid."

I nodded, grateful for Athauhnu's use of the word "we."

Soon, Madog's men came up the road. Again, Athauhnu waved and pointed to our right flank. Madog and Agrippa were the last riders to emerge. Madog had a man behind him on his horse. I heard Athauhnu mutter, "Two missing."

Athauhnu waved again. Agrippa and Madog joined us in the center of the Sequani line. The man riding behind Madog dropped off the horse. Then, I saw that he had the stub of an arrow protruding from his thigh.

Madog caught me looking at the man. "German horsemen do not carry bows," he said in Gah'el. "There are warriors on foot down there."

"*Pedes?*" I responded in Latin. "Infantry?"

Agrippa heard me. "*Pedes, Insubrece!* I don't think this is a raiding party coming in from the east. I need to get an idea how many Krauts are coming up that road, then warn Caesar."

Alaw pointed toward the road below us. "*Pen! Maint uhn dod!* Chief! They're here!"

German riders were emerging from the valley and filling the field below us. They saw us but didn't seem at all concerned. There didn't seem to be any organization. They milled around in the field below us, some pointing toward us, with others just roaming about.

Their equipment wasn't impressive. Some had bronze helmets, others leather, some none at all. I could see no chainmail, but I did see some leather *loricae*. Most of them carried either lances or stabbing spears.

I heard Madog spit, "Farmers on horses!"

Then, another group of warriors emerged from the narrow valley. These men were well-equipped, with steel helmets, chainmail, and large, round shields with the image of what looked like a red oxen with long horns painted over the boss. Each had a red, horsehair topknot trailing from his helmet. One rider, a giant with a red beard, emerged from the trail. Directly behind him rode a mounted warrior carrying a totem on a spear shaft, with long, black oxen horns and a skirt of a black pelt below it.

"That one must be their *eorle*," I heard Athauhnu use an unfamiliar term.

"What's an *eorle*?" I asked out of the side of my mouth, afraid to take my eyes off the giant below us.

"That's what the Germans call their *penai*, their chiefs," Athauhnu answered. "The riders with him are his *gedricht*, his *fintai*. He equips them, feeds them, and they are sworn to protect him in battle or die with him. The Germans believe that any member of the *gedricht* who survives a battle in which their chief dies is cursed to wander the middle lands alone, an outcast."

Madog interrupted us, pointing down at the Kraut standard. "That is the totem of the Aurochs. They are Germans . . . the People of the Aurochs . . . You Romans call them *Boii* . . . the 'cow people.' And that is no *eorle*! That is their *ciuning* . . . their tribal king . . . look. There are at least fifty riders in his *fintai*. No *eorle* could support so many. That is the tribal muster coming up the trail . . . Thousands would be my guess."

As he spoke, well-armed warriors on foot emerged from the valley. They didn't march in step or in any recognizable formation as did the legions. They just poured out onto the open area below us. The men wore bronze or steel helmets, many with cheek guards and some with bands of metal extending down over their noses. Some carried spears; some war axes. Each wore a long sword on his left side and a shorter sword on his right. Every one of them carried an oversized, round shield. They poured out of the valley in the hundreds.

"Those are *cnihtas*, the professional warriors of the tribe," Madog said. "They are *dugath*, *veterani*, blooded warriors. They form the *scilde wealle*, the shield wall, in the center of the battle line. Behind them march the *iougath*, the young warriors, boys who have yet to be blooded. They stand behind the shield wall. And, behind them, the *fiurd*, the tribal muster. They form the flanks of the battle line in the defense. When the Germans attack, they're the shock troops. They disrupt the enemy's line so the *dugath* can get in among them and do the real killing. That's a tribal assembly down there. The Boii are going to war against the Caisar."

It was just then that we heard a trumpet call in the distance behind us.

"Caesar?" I asked.

"It must be," Agrippa answered, "but, if the army's on the march, why would it be sounding trumpet signals?"

Down below we could see the Boii king haranguing his cavalry and pointing up the slopes toward us.

"I think that big Kraut down there with the red beard wants us out of here," Agrippa observed.

I translated for Madog, but he had understood most of it. "Tribune right. Time go away for us," he announced in Latin.

Madog made sure that the wounded man had been mounted behind another warrior. He was about to signal his riders to withdraw to the west when Agrippa said, "We can't leave yet."

Madog froze. Then, he said in Latin, "Stay here, madness! Why no go?"

"Where are the Tulingi?" Agrippa asked. "The Tulingi were marching with the Boii. Where are they?"

Before Madog could answer, we could see the German riders begin to move toward us. There was no order to their advance, just knots of three to six riders beginning to move up the slope toward us. They didn't seem to be in any hurry to attack uphill into what appeared to be a disciplined and well-equipped Roman cavalry detachment.

Madog quickly snapped out some orders. Athauhnu and Ci were quickly to withdraw five hundred *passus* to the west. Madog's *ala* would screen the withdrawal from the German cavalry. I translated for Agrippa, who nodded and said, "You stay with Athauhnu. I'm with Madocus!"

Before I turned my horse, I looked down the hill. The German *dugath* was still emerging from the valley. They were milling about down there, waiting for their horsemen to clear us off the ridge. There had to be almost two cohorts of them below us.

Athauhnu gave Ci the order to withdraw. We cantered our horses back to our new position. There was no point in winding them; we didn't know what was in store for us. We followed the valley floor as it gently rose toward the northwest. When we arrived at our new position, I could clearly hear Roman signal trumpets away to the west. I remembered some of the signals from my training. I thought I heard "assemble." And, the only reason I could think of to sound that command while on the march was contact with the enemy. But, which enemy: Helvetii, Aedui, or both?

To our east, Agrippa and Madog withdrew slowly toward our position. The German cavalry followed cautiously, without any semblance of purpose or organization. They maintained a healthy distance from the Sequani riders. Finally, Agrippa and Madog joined us. The Germans continued to maintain a safe distance. They halted in small groups of seven to ten riders about a hundred *passus* to our front. There were no more than fifty of them below us. There was no sign of the German infantry cresting the ridge to the east.

I reported to Agrippa: "I can hear our army. They seem to be no more than three to five thousand *passus* up the valley. I think they're engaging the enemy."

"Is the enemy between us and the legions?" Agrippa asked.

I hadn't thought of that. "I . . . I don't know, Tribune. There is no sign of enemy troops to our rear . . . just the sound of Roman trumpets."

Agrippa stared up the valley for a few heartbeats, then shrugged, "Can't worry about that now. We're not finished here yet . . . Madocus *Dux*!"

Madog sidled up next to Agrippa, "*Quid vis tu, Tribune?*" he asked. "What do you want, Tribune?"

"We're going to teach those arrogant *verpae* a lesson. We attack!" Agrippa said, pointing toward the motley assemblage of German riders.

Madog nodded and called for Ci. Athauhnu was mounted beside me.

"Three wedges," Agrippa instructed. "Madocus' *ala* center, Adonus left, and Caius right. I'm with Madocus. Insubrecus with Adonus. We advance no farther than our last position on the ridge."

I translated for Athauhnu and Ci. Athauhnu spoke up, "They are too close. We will not be able to get the horses to the gallop before we're among them."

I translated that for Agrippa. He nodded and said, "You are correct, Adonus *Decurio*, but I do not believe that will make much of a difference with that rabble. They'll run as soon as they see us advance. I want one last look at the Kraut infantry. I want to see if we can locate the Tulingi down there with the Boii. And last, I want the German cavalry terrified that their infantry will have to advance blind, with no cavalry screen. That should slow them down some."

I translated. Both Athauhnu and Ci grunted and eagerly nodded in agreement. There was a blood debt. The Germans had raided their lands, burned their homes, and raped their women. Now they must pay.

Agrippa wasted no time. He and Madog trotted back to their band of riders and almost immediately moved forward toward the Germans. Athauhnu and I moved our men to Agrippa's left; Ci moved to the right. The cavalry wedges formed naturally as we advanced. But, I heard Agrippa give the command, "*Alae . . . ad . . . cuneum*! Troops . . . form . . . wedge!" I shrugged my shield off my shoulder. Strapping it to my left arm, I fell in behind Athauhnu on his left.

I heard Agrippa's voice again, "*Alae . . . equiis . . . citatis*! Troops . . . to the canter!"

Madoc signaled the Sequani by pumping his right fist twice, and the horses broke into a canter.

Ahead of us, I could see the Germans take notice and stiffen, but they seemed frozen in place. They didn't know what to do.

Again, Agrippa, "*Alae . . . spathas . . . stringite*! Troops . . . draw . . . sabers!"

Finally, in ones and twos, the Germans began to turn their horses away from us. They began to retreat back toward their army. Some remained in place, frozen.

Agrippa, "*Alae . . . equiis . . . currentibus*! Troops . . . to the gallop!"

We were just beginning to pick up some speed when we ran into those few Germans too foolish to run. One appeared directly in front of me. His eyes seemed to be the size of *denarius* coins. He dropped his spear and raised his arms up, as if to protect himself. I saw Athauhnu's sword slice into his face just above his mouth. His body tumbled to my left. I felt a brushing impact with his horse. Then, I was past him. Nothing but empty fields and fleeing German horsemen were to my front.

We were about a hundred *passus* away from our objective when Nemesis struck.

The mounted *gedricht* of the German *ciuning* began to crest the slope in front of us—whether alerted by their own fleeing cavalry or following the king who wanted to see the terrain in front of him, I could not tell. The *ciuning* was riding in the center of his troop.

Madog ran directly at the German king. Athauhnu changed the direction of our gallop so we would crash into the Germans' right flank.

I heard the crash as Madog's troop collided with the Krauts. I had no time to look. We hit the German flank immediately after. My horse, Clamriu, crashed into a German's mount. I saw her bite down into the other horse's neck. The rider was thrown off away from us. He never rose. His horse collapsed and rolled where the rider fell. I saw a face in front of me, bearded. I stabbed at it and felt an impact up through my sword arm. I glimpsed a tightly packed group of Germans protecting a wounded man, leading him down the slope away from the battle. It was their king.

Then Clamriu reared back. I almost tumbled over her rump. She was kicking and biting at another horse. The Kraut rider was trying to get control. A Sequani reached over and plunged his sabre into the man's arm pit. He went down into the scrum. The German riders seemed to be melting away back down the hill. Somewhere to my right, I could hear a Gallic hunting horn. Our troops were pulling back toward it. The tangle of men and horses was unraveling. I stole a look down the ridge. The ground was covered with German infantry. A chief on a horse was trying to rally them up the ridge toward our position. I could sense some movement in our direction. Again I heard the Gallic signal to assemble. I moved back to where our troop was gathering.

Agrippa was still in the saddle. He had a slicing wound across the ridge of his nose and his left cheekbone. Madog and Athauhnu seemed winded, but unbloodied. Ci was not there. Then, I saw him sorting out our troops as they rode back from the point of contact.

Agrippa grabbed my arm. I realized I hadn't sheathed my *spatha*. I raised it and realized the point was bloodied. I wondered how I could clean it off before returning it to the sheath. I heard Agrippa's voice in the distance. "Are you listening, *Decurio?*"

"Uh . . . *audio? Te audio, Tribune!*" I heard myself say.

"You are to ride back to the army!" Agrippa was saying. "Find Caesar . . . Tell him there's an entire Kraut army on his flank . . . at least ten thousand . . . probably more . . . Boii and Tulingi . . . They're marching west . . . *Compre'hendis tu?*"

"*Compre'endo, Tribune!*" I said snapping out of it.

I still didn't know what to do with my bloodied *spatha*.

Athauhnu handed me a bloody rag. "Use this," he told me. "The German who wore it doesn't need it anymore!"

I cleaned off my *spatha* and returned it to the sheath on my saddle.

"Emlun and Rhodri will ride with you," I heard Athauhnu say.

"Rhodri without Alaw?" I questioned.

Athauhnu shot me a dark look. "Alaw feasts with the heroes in the Land of Youth," he said.

The three of us ran west as fast as our tired mounts could take us. Most of the way, we didn't dare to go faster than a canter. Ahead, I could hear the Roman trumpets clearly. The last signal I heard was a general call for close ranks. That could only mean the enemy was advancing on the legionary line.

Ahead, there was a wooded ridgeline that advanced across the valley from the south. Beyond it, I could hear a noise, a noise like powerful waters running and the murmur of thousands of voices.

Rhodri suggested we climb the ridge and not go around it to the north. I agreed. That decision probably saved our lives.

When we crested the ridge below us, we saw the enemy, the Helvetii, tens of thousands of them, moving north across the open valley. We were *behind* the enemy horde!

To my right, on a gently rising slope along the north wall of the valley, was Caesar's army. Four legions in *acies triplex*, the triple line, were facing the Helvetii. Above them, I could see the remaining two legions in *acies duplex*, two battle lines with open ranks, matching the flanks of the forward legions.

The Helvetii were rushing straight toward Caesar like a wall of water when a damn breaks. I wondered briefly if our army could withstand such a massive flow of warriors.

I did feel a momentary surge of relief, realizing that the Germans would arrive on the battlefield in front of our troops. Then, Rhodri grabbed my arm and pointed to a long slope about five hundred *passus* to our left.

"The Helvetii are forming a shield wall there!" he said.

I peered in the direction Rhodri indicated and could easily make out enemy troops forming ragged battle lines on the forward slope.

"Look there!" Rhodri said again. "The king has set himself near the hilltop!"

Again, I could see a cluster of heavily armed, mounted warriors where Rhodri indicated. There was a cluster of enemy standards among the riders.

"This is not right, Arth Bek," Rhodri started.

"Not right? What do you mean?" I asked.

"Their *brenna aw frouuhdrau*, their war chief, is holding his best troops back from the attack," Rhodri explained, pointing toward the enemy standards. "Only the tribal musters advance. The warriors led by their war chief should be advancing behind them under the tribal standards. When the musters open the Roman lines, the warriors must be in position to attack through the gaps. Something is wrong!"

Just then, the Romans began their attack.

The forward edge of the enemy advance had begun to climb up toward the Roman front line. When it was about thirty *passus* away, I heard the Roman trumpet signal *pila ponite*, "present spears!" There wasn't much movement along the Roman line; most of the *muli* in the front line had already assumed the position by the time the enemy reached the bottom of their hill.

Then, as the enemy closed to twenty passus, *pila parate* was sounded, "ready spears." Even at this distance, I could see movement and reflections of light as the *muli,* almost in a single motion, brought their throwing spears to the ready position.

Then, the trumpets sounded *pila iacite*, "open fire." This was followed by three blasts of the horn, three rounds. The soaring spears looked like a fast-moving, black cloud rushing from the Roman lines into the front edge of the enemy, some fifteen *passus* away. Before the first volley struck, a second was in the air, then, a third.

The effect of the spear volleys was devastating.

The natural reaction to a volley of spears is to raise shields for protection. But, the Roman *pila* are weighted, designed to punch through a shield with enough force to penetrate even the thickest protective padding, even hardened leather.

Most of the Helvetii muster-men wore nothing; in fact, many had attacked bare-chested to show their contempt for the enemy. They were mowed down like wheat under a scythe.

Even if a warrior were lucky enough to have chainmail to blunt the point of the *pilum*, the impact of the blow would be enough to knock him down, and the spear would have rendered his shield useless. The Roman *pilum* is designed so it cannot be extracted from a shield, leaving a man naked before the short, Roman stabbing sword, the *gladius*.

No sooner had the third volley of *pila* risen into the air than the Roman trumpets signaled *acies prima*, "Front line!" Then, *gladios stringite*, "Draw swords!" Across the valley, all along the Roman front line, light flashed as thousands of short swords were drawn from their scabbards.

Behind me, I heard Emlun calling my name. I didn't want to take my eyes off the drama unfolding in front of me.

The Roman trumpets called *impetum facite*, "Attack!"

The entire Roman front line descended on the muddle that was once the front edge of the Helvetian attack. It was no contest. The Romans slaughtered any of the Helvetii foolish enough to try to stand their ground.

Then, from the hill to our left, the Helvetian trumpets blasted out a cacophonous strain. Immediately, the thousands of Helvetii in the field below us turned and ran from the Roman advance. At that time, I was too inexperienced to realize that the maneuver I was seeing was impossible for a barbarian army, unless it had been planned.

Again, Emlun called to me.

"What is it?" I called back.

"*Madog un dod!*" he answered. "Madog comes!"

"Signal him up here to us!" I instructed.

As the Helvetii fled south, the Roman trumpets blasted "general call." Then, *signa proferte*, "advance the standards." Immediately, the second and third lines followed the first down the ridge and began crossing the valley in pursuit of what Caesar believed was a defeated and fleeing enemy. I noticed that the two legions near the top of the ridge held their position.

Agrippa was suddenly at my side. He was speechless for a few heartbeats as the panorama of the battle unfolded below him.

Off to the north, I saw the Roman cavalry advance across the enemy's left flank, led by an officer mounted on a white horse and a bright red *sagum* trailing behind him.

"*Venatum Caesar ducit ipse, Tribune!*" I said to Agrippa. "Caesar leads the pursuit himself, Tribune!"

We watched as Caesar and most of our cavalry disappeared behind the edge of a distant hill heading toward the enemy's rear.

Suddenly, Agrippa exclaimed, "*Verpa Martis! Quae calamitas!* This is a disaster!"

"*Pro qua dicis tu?*" I sputtered, forgetting all military protocol.

Agrippa turned and grabbed me by my shoulder armor. I thought he was going to deliver *castigatio* for being insubordinate.

But instead, he said, "Don't you see it, Insubrecus? That Kraut horde is less than an hour behind us. They will arrive *here*, right where we're standing. By that time, they will be on the flank and rear of our army and in position to attack. And, our *imperator* is on the wrong side of the battlefield, out of position, chasing after easy kills and plunder! Over ten thousand Germans will be pouring down this hill right onto the back of our army! It will be the massacre of Arausio all over again!"

Agrippa noticed the two legions still positioned on the ridgeline to the north. "Those must be the Eleventh and Twelfth," he concluded. "Caesar must be holding them back so the army will have a position to retreat to. There must be a senior officer up there with them. I hope he has a set of *coleones*! We have to turn the army around!"

"Madocus *Dux!*" Agrippa called.

Madog approached our position. He too was initially stunned by what he saw below us. He too immediately understood the German threat.

"*Immerda sumus!*" he said, for once getting the Latin idiom right.

Agrippa instructed him, "Madocus, your mission is to track the Germans and screen our army. I believe this will be their final coordination line for an attack on the Roman rear. When they reach this point, withdraw down into the valley below. Stay between the Krauts and our army! Do not become decisively engaged with them! You must maintain your freedom to maneuver. I will go below and try to organize a defense. I will look for you on the field of battle. But, if this thing goes wrong, I release you from your *sacramentum*. Do what you can for the survivors, but get your people back to your own lands as best you can. The Aedui will be looking to settle some old debts once we Romans are gone."

To ensure Madog understood, I translated while Agrippa spoke. A few *pedes* away, I saw Athauhnu listening. He looked grim.

Agrippa turned to me. "You're with me, Insubrecus *Decurio*. Let's see if we can pull Caesar's balls out of the vice he's placed them in."

As I retrieved Clamriu from Emlun's care, I felt a hand grasp my shoulder. It was Athauhnu. He looked at me gravely, then nodded his head. "You dress and talk like a Roman," he announced, "but you are still Gah'el. When this is over we will feast together, either in the hall of my father in the lands of the Soucanai or in the Hall of Heroes in the Land of Youth."

"Save me a place on the mead-bench!" I said. "We'll fight over the hero's portion."

We placed our hands on each other's shoulders in the fashion of the Gah'el. I mounted Clamriu and followed Agrippa onto the battleground below.

We rode hard across the battlefield, behind the Roman third line, to the right flank of the army, the commander's position. Agrippa was hoping that Caesar had left someone there with enough *auctoritas* to take command of the army in his absence. We were disappointed.

When we arrived, we found no senior officers. Malleus, the "Hammer," the *primus pilus* of the Tenth Legion, was advancing on foot along with his legion on the right flank of the entire Roman army.

Agrippa pulled up next to Malleus. "Are you in command here, *Centurio*?" he asked.

Malleus shrugged, "I must be, Tribune . . . I'm the senior officer present!"

"Where is the *imperator*?" Agrippa asked.

"Forward with the cavalry," Malleus indicated the fleeing enemy's open flank.

"What orders did Caesar leave you?" Agrippa demanded.

Again, Malleus shrugged, "He said to continue to advance . . . Keep up the pressure . . . Don't let them rally against us . . . The normal shit, Tribune. What's the problem?"

"The Boii and Tulingi are coming in on our left flank, *Centurio* . . . You're walking into an ambush!" Agrippa declared.

Malleus' face blanched. "There's nothing I can do. I have my orders. My authority only extends over the Tenth."

Agrippa nodded. "I will find someone who has the authority. Listen for the signals!"

With that, Agrippa turned his horse, and we galloped toward the two legions still stationed on the hill to the north. As we rode, I wondered who Caesar had put in command on the hill. Unless he were willing to take a risk and use some initiative, we were *perfututi*, absolutely screwed.

We immediately spotted a command standard on the right flank of the Eleventh Legion. It was Labienus. There was hope!

Labienus came forward when he saw us riding up. He knew we were screening the army's flank and sensed our urgency. Agrippa wasted no time in briefing him. Labienus immediately understood the gravity of the situation.

"And Caesar cannot be reached?" he demanded of Agrippa again.

"No, Legate! The *imperator* has gone forward with the cavalry," Agrippa confirmed.

"*Cacat!*" Labienus exploded. "Shit! How soon will the Krauts arrive?"

Together, we all looked across the battlefield to where we had left the Sequani cavalry screen. They had not withdrawn from the hill. The Germans were not yet in position. "My guess, we have less than an hour," Agrippa answered.

I watched as Labienus examined the disposition of forces on the battlefield. Then, he examined the ridge from which we expected the Germans to descend on us. He seemed to make a decision.

"*Fabi! Ad me!*" he called over to his command group.

A broad-striper rode forward. "*Ti' adsum, Legate!*" he reported.

"Fabius, have both legions entrench!" he instructed. "Two camps with enough room to protect the baggage train. Do it now!"

"Sir," Fabius responded, "there's no water on this hill . . . Perhaps I should find a better position?"

"No time, Fabius!" Labienus shook his head. "Have the men fill their water bottles . . . There should be some water carts within the supply train . . . Fill them . . . Fill anything that will contain water . . . but get those camps built! We may not have much time!"

"*A'mperi'tu', Legate!*" Fabius responded.

Fabius turned his horse back toward the standing legions and started to snap out orders to the senior centurions.

Labienus called out again, "Iudaeus!"

The *primus pilus* of the Eleventh stepped forward. "*Ti' adsum, Legate!*" he reported.

"Put one of your flute girls on a horse and send him to me!" Labienus ordered. "I need to borrow him for a while!"

"*A'mperi'tu', Legate!*"

Agrippa spoke suddenly and pointed across the battlefield. "*Legate, ecce!* Sir, look!"

Along the edge of the woods on the ridgeline, where we had left Madog, there was movement.

"We're running out of time," Labienus muttered.

A legionary *cornucen* rode up to our group with his *cornu* draped around his body.

"*Ti' adsum, Legate!*" he said, almost falling off the horse with the effort.

Labienus pointed to the left flank of our advancing army, the point closest to where the Germans would soon appear. "*Illuc!* There! We ride there! *Celerrime!* We haven't much time! Follow me!"

Labienus galloped down the hill, Agrippa immediately behind him.

I looked over to the trumpeter. "You going to make it?" I asked.

The man was holding his reins with one hand, a saddle horn with the other, all the while trying to keep his *cornu* from slipping down off his shoulder.

"I'll make it, *Decurio*," he said, with no sense of certainty.

We galloped across the battlefield. As we rode, I saw the Sequani cavalry break from cover and ride down the slope. They didn't seem to be fleeing, but withdrew in good order. They rode about fifty *passus* from the bottom of the slope and spread out in a screening line between the ridge and the left flank of our army. There was still no movement on the hill above them.

I finally caught up to Agrippa and Labienus. "This will be our right flank, here!" Labienus was saying.

Right flank of what? I wondered.

"I will be positioned here with the *cornucen*. Where is that man?"

We looked back from where we rode. The trumpeter was still barely on his horse, about seventy *passus* from our position.

"*Festina! Festina, miles!*" Labienus shouted. "Hurry!"

Labienus continued, "Agrippa! You will position yourself on the left flank. Don't let them turn you. Bend back in a prevent formation if they overlap us."

There was movement now in the trees on the ridge above us. The Germans had arrived.

The trumpeter finally arrived. Immediately, Labienus ordered, "Signal . . . third rank . . . attention!"

The man tried, but nothing meaningful came out of his *cornu*. It made a sound like a duck farting in a swamp. He gave up on the horse and slid down from the saddle. Finally, planting his feet back on firm ground, he took three deep breaths. When he took his fourth, he raised the trumpet to his lips and blew, "Third rank . . . attention!" I could see the transverse crests of the centurions marching in the third rank of the closest legion turn. I imagined I could hear them echoing the order to their *muli*: "Attention!"

"Order, '*Consistite!*'" Labienus instructed. "Halt!"

The *cornucen* looked at Labienus and stammered, "*Consistite, Legate?*"

"Do it!" Labienus ordered.

The trumpeter blew the signal. The entire third line of the Roman advance, twelve cohorts, came to a halt in two steps.

In front of us we could see the German *fiurd*, the muster-men, pouring out of the woodline.

"Don't let them go right into the attack!" Labienus hissed through his teeth. "Mass them there . . . Give me the time I need."

Then, Labienus ordered, "*Cornucen*! Order . . . third rank . . . *signa conversate* . . . turnabout!"

The trumpeter did as ordered. Across the field behind us, our little army of twelve Roman cohorts turned as a single man. I saw the standards and officers run to reverse their positions: centurions front and right; *optiones* rear and center.

The Krauts seemed to be cooperating with Labienus. The musters were milling about on the ridgeline. The sight of an entire Roman army maneuvering across a battlefield as if on parade will make even experienced soldiers pause.

I heard Labienus mutter again, "Here's where it gets complicated!" Then, "*Cornucen* . . . signal . . . third rank . . . *ad dextram* . . . *aciem* . . . *formate*!"

Labienus gave the order for the entire third rank to wheel right and form their battle line facing the Germans. The trumpeter blew the signal, and twelve cohorts began to wheel into position.

Labienus snapped a command to Agrippa: "Ride across their front! Get on their left flank! Guide them to a line on my position facing the enemy. Move, Tribune!"

Over his shoulder, as he galloped across the advancing Roman front, Agrippa yelled, "*A'mperi'tu'!*"

Then, Labienus was talking to me, "Insubrecus! Ride forward to Madocus *Dux*. He is to withdraw as the Krauts advance. Have the Sequani take a position behind our battle line here. We will only be eight men deep at the most. If any of the Krauts break through, the Sequani are to stop them . . . mop them up. Is that clear?"

"*A'mperi'tu', Legate*!" I confirmed and rode forward, looking for Madog.

As I rode off, I heard Labienus order the trumpeter: "Signal . . . third line . . . *gradus bis* . . . double-time."

I found Madog in the center of the screening line. He seemed bent slightly forward in his saddle. Then, I noticed blood flowing down his right leg.

"Madog, *Pobl'rix*!" I said in Gah'el. "You are hurt!"

"I can still ride, Arth Bek!" he responded somewhat breathlessly.

I related Labienus' commands. Madog nodded. He blew his hunting horn, then led the way to our new position.

Before I followed, I looked up at the Krauts. Well-equipped members of the *dugath* were aligning the ranks of the muster-men. The attack was imminent. I turned my horse to follow the Sequani. I could see the Roman cohorts double-timing up to the battle line. I remembered these drills from my training. The men on the left flank who had the farthest to run would be heaving by the time they got into position.

We rode across the front of the Roman advance and around its left flank. Madog ordered his men into three loose wedges behind the Roman line: Athauhnu on the left, Ci on the right, and himself in the center. As the senior Roman officer, I assumed a position with Madog.

On the ridge, the *dugath* was finalizing the disposition of the *fiurd*. From the looks of it, they wouldn't overlap our flanks. A rider emerged from the woodline, trailed by a *gedricht*, a royal bodyguard.

"Their *ciuning*?" I asked Madog.

"No," Madog gasped. "I've done for that bastard. That's one of his *thegns* . . . his companions . . . what you Romans call *comites*. I left that German *ciuning* with his guts hanging out over his belt."

Madog could hardly catch his breath. He was holding onto his saddle horns to steady himself.

"Do you want me to call for the *medduhg*, the medic, *Madog Pobl'rix*?" I asked him.

"No," he panted, "no . . . my men must stay strong . . . Can't see their king fall out of the saddle . . . not now."

Our cohorts had finally come on line facing the Germans. From my position near the center of the line, I could see some of the *muli* on the left flank doubled over with the exertion of double-timing in full combat kit. The *centuriones* and their *optiones* were trying to straighten the lines and get the men ready for the German assault, but even they were affected by the run they had just made.

The Krauts on the hill made no move to take advantage. From the distance, I could hear chanting, some weird and disturbing sound from the German line: "Wo . . . wo . . . wo."

"What is that?" I muttered out loud.

"They're praying to Woden," Madog responded.

"What's Woden?" I asked him.

"Not what . . . who," Madog began to say. Then, a fit of painful coughing racked him. When he steadied himself, he spit out whatever was in his throat. It was a bog of bloody phlegm.

"They are . . . they are calling on their god, Woden, to send the *Wal Ciurige* . . . the gatherers of the dead . . . to take them to the *Wal Halle* . . . the feasting hall of the dead . . . if they are killed in battle."

Madog started coughing again.

"They will feast there," he continued, "with the heroes of their people . . . until Woden calls them forth . . . for the *rako werdum* . . . the great war . . . at the end of times."

"That sounds like our Land of Youth," I observed.

"Bah!" Madog tried to start, but again a fit of coughing hit him. There was a small trickle of blood running from the side of his mouth.

He finally caught his breath to speak, "They believe that everything . . . everything will be destroyed . . . at the *rako werdum* . . . the end of times . . . Men . . . the gods . . . and the earth will be burned away. *Wal Ciurige* . . . they're only the crows. They strip the flesh off the battle dead . . . nothing more . . . Woden is a god of carrion."

Madog's description of the crows reminded me of a tale Gran'pa had told me of a dark phantom, a goddess, the *Mawr Riganu*, the great queen, who appears on the battlefield in the semblance of a great crow to feast on the blood of the slain. I shuddered. I reached up and rubbed my *lorica* where my *Bona Fortuna* hung.

Athauhnu was right when he said the waiting is the worst.

The straw-headed bastards on the hill were working themselves into a frenzy: "Wo . . . wo . . . wo."

"It won't be long now," Madog gasped.

I could see that our battle line had stabilized, but the main Roman attack force, the first and second battle lines, were still advancing toward the Helvetii. A gap was opening between their left rear rank and our right flank.

I called over to Ci and pointed to the gap opening on our right flank. He nodded and moved his *ala* into it.

The movement of the Gallic horsemen must have caught the attention of the *primus pilus* commanding the legion advancing against the Helvetii on the end of the Roman battle line. I could see from its standards, it was the Seventh Legion. Suddenly, their *acies secunda*, three cohorts, halted, turned about, and aligned themselves in a prevent formation, a line diagonal to their route of march, to protect their left flank against the German threat. Then, the two leftmost cohorts of the *acies prima* executed a smart, three-quarter turn to the right and tucked themselves to the rear of the advancing First and Second Cohorts to reinforce them. All this was accomplished as if they were on parade and not unexpectedly moving into a battle position.

Then, I heard a shout to my front. I looked. The German *fiurd* was charging down the ridgeline at us.

"*Maent uhn dod!*" was all Madog could manage. "They come!"

Suddenly, the entire ridgeline to the north, where Caesar thought the already-defeated Helvetii were cowering, exploded in a cacophony of Gallic trumpets and movement. The Helvetii warriors threw themselves down the ridgeline into our advancing legions.

The ambush was triggered, and we were standing right in its kill zone!

Looking back toward the Krauts, I immediately saw that they had miscalculated. First, our lines were too far back from their ridge for their momentum to take them into us. They would have to run across at least seventy *passus* of flat ground before making contact. That should wind them and slow their attack. Second, the Krauts were headed straight for us and not for the gap opening on our right. Killing Romans seemed more important than winning the battle.

Then, I noticed that the Germans had left about a hundred men deployed across their ridgeline. Archers!

Labienus saw them too. Before the Krauts could launch their arrows, his trumpeter sounded, "*Notate! Ad testudinem!*", "Form the turtle!"

Immediately, the Roman *muli* in front of me closed ranks and lifted and locked their shields over their heads. They were protected from the German arrows, but large gaps opened in the battle line.

I felt a hand grab my forearm. It was Madog.

"We move back . . . out of range," he gasped. I didn't know what was holding him up in the saddle. His face was pasty, almost greenish. There was a patina of sweat across his face.

As we moved back, the German muster-men cleared the hill slope and screened our line from their archers. The archers ceased fire. The *dugath*, the professional warriors, organized themselves into five groups, each about the size of a Roman century. They moved down the slope, spreading themselves out across the battle line. They followed behind the German *fiurd*.

"They follow," Madog panted, indicating the *dugath*. "Wherever the *fiurd* opens the battle line . . . they attack."

Labienus realized that the arrow fire had ceased. He and the *cornucen* emerged from the turtle. Neither of their horses had been hit. The legate remounted so he could see the battlefield, but the trumpeter chose to stay on his feet. At Labienus' command, he again signaled, "*Notate! Aciem formate!*"

Immediately, the turtles collapsed and the *muli* reformed their line. The forward edge of the German *fiurd* was less than thirty passus from our lines.

The trumpet called, "*Pila ponite! Pila parate!*" I saw the arms and javelins of the entire Roman battle line come up.

Labienus waited.

The Krauts closed to within twenty passus, then fifteen, then ten. "*Iacite . . . iacite*," I heard myself mutter. "Throw . . . throw." Then, finally, the trumpet sounded: "*Pila iacite!* Open fire!"

The Roman spears went forward into the German attack. It staggered as men crumbled. Others tripped over the bodies of the dead and wounded. Some stopped running to avoid the growing pile up. Others stopped to try freeing their shields of the Roman spears. The rear ranks piled up on the stalling and staggering front ranks.

There was no second volley!

Then, I remembered that these were *miles aciei tertiae*, third-rank men. They were only carrying one *pilum* each.

Quickly Labienus ordered *gladii stringite*: "Draw swords!"

Then, immediately *impetum facite*: "Attack!"

Labienus was *attacking* a superior force!

Initially, it worked. The Roman *muli* quickly covered the ten *passus* between themselves and the struggling pile of men that had been the forward edge of the German attack. These they quickly cut through. Then, they came into contact with the rest of the horde of Kraut muster-men who had lost all forward momentum. Our advance slowed, but we were still moving forward.

As we moved forward, though, the gap on our right widened.

I heard a cacophonous trumpet call from the German ridgeline. The Kraut *thegn* had stationed himself there so he could see his battlefield. He indicated the gap on our right with his sword. Immediately, one of the formations of the *dugath* turned and moved toward it. As they moved forward, they formed a wedge, like a Roman *cuneus*, a "bore's snout."

I yelled over to Ci, commanding our cavalry on the right, and indicated the threat. He raised his hand to acknowledge. I saw the two cohorts from the Seventh Legion adjust their position in the face of the new threat. But, they stayed well back. Their mission was to protect the rear of their own legion, not pull our balls out of the vice.

I turned to Madog to recommend we reinforce Ci's *ala*. He was off his horse, on the ground, not moving.

"*Medduhg! Medduhg!*" I yelled.

The Sequani horse doctor was immediately off his horse, attending to the king.

"Athauhnu! To me!" I called to our troop on the left.

Athauhnu rode over.

"Madog's down," I told him. "The troop is yours! We must reinforce Ci! The Germans are attacking the gap!"

Athauhnu nodded. He called over to his men, "Guithiru! You are in command! Move center!"

We rode over to the right and joined Ci.

The Kraut wedge was moving toward us, now no more than fifty *passus* from the gap, over sixty warriors, at least, with shields up. They formed a solid, German *scilde wealle* of linden wood, leather, and iron and were determined to crash through us.

Our horses would not attack a shield wall, and there were less than forty of us. I could see the red-horned aurochs totems painted on the round shields as they bore down on us.

Then, I remembered Athauhnu's lesson with the *gaea*, the light hunting spear that had pierced my cavalry shield as if it were *vellum*.

"Athauhnu!" I snapped. "A *gaea* attack!"

"*Gaea* will not penetrate that!" Athauhnu objected.

"They don't have to!" I said. "We just need to weigh down their shields. We have to fight them on foot. Our horses won't stand up to that!"

Athauhnu understood immediately. He gave instructions to Ci, then yelled, "Follow me!"

My Sequani horsemen attacked the German wedge in a file. Each rider approached at an acute angle, turned in front of the wedge, and delivered a single blow with a *gae*.

The *dugath* halted when they became aware of the Gah'el attack. We took advantage of their indecision. The Sequani turned and attacked a second time. The Krauts quickly realized that horsemen couldn't seriously damage them, so they resumed their advance. I could already see many of their shields were held lower, weighed down by our spears.

It wasn't much, but it was all we had.

I dismounted and ran into the middle of the gap. "Form shield wall on me!" I shouted.

Labienus finally noticed the activity on his flank and quickly realized the threat. He bent back his First Cohort to protect his right flank. His only reasonable hope was to safeguard his own formation, which was already heavily engaged with the German *fiurd*. He could do nothing to help us.

The Sequani began to form around me. I had my Roman short sword out. Most of the Gah'el had only the *spatha*, the cavalry long sword—not the best weapon for this type of close-in fighting. We were all carrying Gallic cavalry shields, light and oblong, giving little protection for the throat and legs of dismounted fighters. They also lacked the punching handle of the Roman infantry *scutum*; they were defensive weapons only. I did not have much confidence that they would stand up to the massive German round shields bearing down on us.

The Kraut wedge was less than ten *passus* away. I could hear them chanting a cadence to time their attack. As they got closer, the pace of the cadence increased. They planned to bowl right through us.

Suddenly, the right side of the German wedge collapsed.

The two Roman cohorts on our right from the Seventh Legion had delivered a volley of *pila* in support of us. The Krauts never saw it coming. More than a score of them went down.

"*Illuc!*" I screamed pointing to the hole in the wedge. "*Impetum facite! Illuc!* There! Attack there!"

I suddenly realized I was screaming in Latin, but it made no difference. The Sequani leapt into the gap in the wedge, slashing and stabbing. The Kraut formation crumbled like a rotten wall. German warriors dropped their shields and spears. They began running to the rear. A few tried to hold their ground. They were quickly cut down.

I was still standing exactly where I had originally positioned myself. I had won a fight without as much as striking a single blow, without even moving!

Athauhnu was still standing next to me. "Shaggin' Germans!" he spat. "Only brave when they think they're winning."

I stepped forward and turned toward the Romans who had delivered the decisive blow. I raised my right fist in their direction, and yelled, "*Io! Victoria!*"

"*Io! Victoria!*" they thundered back. The signifers moved their standards up and down in celebration. A centurion raised his fist and saluted me back.

But, the fight wasn't over yet. We were still engaged with the Boii *fiurd* across our entire front. Off to my right, I could also see the dust of our desperate fight with the attacking Helvetii.

"Let's remount the troop!" I said to Athauhnu.

We remounted the two *alae*. I posted Ci's men back in the gap to remind the Krauts that we were still there. Athauhnu and I rode back to the center of the battle line, displacing Guithiru's troop back to the left flank.

Our line was no longer advancing against the Germans, but it seemed to be holding its own. Labienus had had to relieve his first rank and bring the second forward. We were only eight men deep, four pairs of *gemini*. The first line was recovering its strength and reorganizing itself for its expected redeployment. From the look of things, they had lost about a quarter of their strength, killed or wounded.

The legionary slaves, distinctive in their brown tunics and with their small handcarts, were hard at work carrying water to the men in the battle line. From the dead or badly wounded, they were also collecting the equipment, which they dragged back to a collection point located somewhere behind our lines.

The *capsarii*, the legionary medical orderlies, were also up on the line, carrying their *capsae*, boxes of bandages and medical equipment. They were bandaging and stitching up the slightly injured *muli* so that they could stay in the fight.

The more seriously wounded were being triaged. Those who had a chance of surviving were taken directly back to the *medici*, who had established a medical station about fifty *passus* behind us. Some of the *capsarii* were riding horses with a double saddle. The wounded man was lifted up on the saddle in front of the orderly, and they rode back to the aid station.

Those who had little chance of survival waited. Sometimes, if the wound was hopeless and a man was in great pain, the *capsarius* would help the soldier on his journey.

Other slaves were loading the bodies of the dead onto their handcarts and taking them back so the *medici* could confirm that they had indeed crossed the river.

The *capsarii* wore black tunics. I imagined this was to hide some of the blood. As they worked, their hands, arms, and faces became covered with the blood of the dead, dying, and wounded. The *muli* called them *cornices*, crows. They referred to evacuation back to the medical station as *ad cornices ire*, "to go to the crows," or sometimes, *cornices pascere*, "to feed the crows."

I shivered, thinking of these images: the *Mawr Riganu*, the great crow, drinking the blood of the dead; the *Wal Ciurige*, the black carrion goddesses of the Germans; the black-clad *capsarii*, scurrying around the dead and dying on the battlefield.

Where was Madog?

"*Medduhg,*" I called. "*Medduhg*! To me!"

The man rode over from Guithiru's troop. "What is it, Arth Bek?" he asked.

"The king!" I demanded. "Where is Madog?"

He shrugged, "*Uh brana dua* . . . the black crows didn't want to take him, so I brought him back myself."

I looked over to the Roman medical station. I had a bad feeling.

"Athauhnu!" I said. "I am checking on Madog. If anything happens, send a rider!"

I rode back to the medical station. The place smelled and sounded like an abattoir in the depths of Tartarus. It reeked with the stench of blood and fresh-cut meat. The wounded moaned, some screamed, many cried.

Clamriu reared back from the place. I have since learned that, in many ways, horses are smarter than men. I dismounted and approached on foot.

To my left, I saw the *medici* working. A man was being held down on a bloodstained wooden table by two burly attendants. A doctor was cutting on the man's abdomen. The soldier screamed, arching his back. The *medicus* jumped back, removing his hands and scalpel from the man's gut.

"Hold him still, damn you!" he yelled at the attendants.

In front of me were three groupings of men. To the left, farthest from where the *medicus* was working, were the dead. Their only companions were two slaves, who were busy chasing the carrion birds away from an inviting feast. I watched as a slave returned from the battle lines with his handcart and dumped three fresh bodies on the pile. *Cornices pascit,* I thought. He is feeding the crows.

Next were the badly wounded, men not expected to survive. A couple of black-clad attendants walked among them. Some seemed to be treating wounds; others were checking to see if a man had crossed over. I watched as an attendant called over one of the dead-pile slaves and indicated a body for removal.

Closest to the surgery were the slightly wounded. Some were lying on the grass, others sitting up. Most of the attendants worked with this group, checking wounds, bandaging others, giving the men water. I saw a *medicus* come over, wash his hands in a bucket, then indicate a wounded man to an attendant. The attendant stood the man up, walked him over to the open-air surgery, and sat him on a table for the doctor to treat.

It was then that I noticed a man lying by himself off to one side, seemingly belonging to no group. I walked over to him. It was Madog. His eyes were half open; his face was greenish-white; his chest was not moving.

I looked to my left and saw a *capsarius* walking among the badly wounded.

"You!" I shouted at him.

He looked over at me with a trace of curiosity.

"Yes! You, soldier! Get over here! Now!" I ordered.

He scrutinized me for a few heartbeats. From my sashes, he took in that I was a junior officer, a member of some nob's praetorian detail. He decided that he should at least placate me. He sauntered over. His hands and arms were covered with blood, ranging from bright, wet red to crusted black. There were even streaks of gore on his left cheek and forehead.

"*Qui' vis tu?*" he asked with no great interest. "Whadda you want?"

I was in no mood to be placated.

"*Quid vis tu, Decurio!*" I insisted.

He shrugged. "*Si ti' placet* . . . if that's what makes you happy ... What do you want, *sir?*"

"Why is this man not being treated?" I demanded.

The crow looked at me as if I had lost my mind. "For one thing, he's a bloody wog!"

"I know he's a wo . . . a Gah'el . . . He fights for Rome . . . He was wounded fighting for Rome. So why in the name of *Dis* isn't he being treated?" I raged at the man.

"Look around you . . . *sir!*" the *capsarius* came back at me. "We have our hands full treating *Romans.* We don't have time for any of your bleedin' *wogs* . . . Besides," he said, nudging Madog's unresponsive shoulder with the toe of his boot, "somebody made this one a *good* wog . . . He's already dead!"

That's when I hit him.

To this day, I don't remember hitting him. One minute I was watching him kick my dead comrade; the next, he was sitting on the ground with blood pouring from the wreckage of his nose.

Hands immediately grabbed me from behind. The *capsarius'* buddies were trying to restrain me. A wounded officer waiting for treatment intervened.

"Break this shit up!" he ordered. "What are you doing, *stulti*, you idiots? Don't we have enough hairbags and Krauts to fight? Do we have to fight each other?"

The attendant I punched was getting off the ground with the help of one of his friends. "This officer struck me!" he sprayed through the blood from his ruined nose. "I want to press charges!"

"Shut your gob!" the wounded officer retorted, grabbing my elbow. "You deserved it . . . What I saw was an officer delivering a justified *castigatio* to an insubordinate gob-shite of a crow!"

He steered me away from the gathering flock of crows. "What do you think you're doing, *Pagane*?" he hissed at me.

When he called me *Pagane*, I finally recognized him. "Bantus," I answered, "are you hurt?"

Bantus touched the bandages covering his neck and right shoulder. "A Kraut arrow got through our turtle," he explained. "The *capsarius* up on the line couldn't remove the arrowhead, so he sent me back here to feed these crows."

"So, you were with us! You fought with Labienus?"

"That who it is?" Bantus asked. "I was over on the left with the third-line cohorts from the Tenth."

"I'm with the Sequani cavalry," I told him. "That was their *dux* whom that *mentula* kicked!"

"The Sequani?" Bantus nodded. "You guys put up a hell of a fight in the gap. I saw it just before I went to the crows."

I spotted a rider galloping toward us. It was Emlun.

"That's one of mine," I told Bantus. "I have to get back."

I quickly collected Clamriu.

Bantus went on, "Most of your old mates are with the second line now. They're catching shit up on the hill with the rest of the Tenth Legion. They sent Minutus all the way up to the first line because of his size. Strabo's still with the tenth cohort, though. He was still on his feet when I was sent back—"

Emlun rode up to us. "Arth Bek!" he called to me in Gah'el. "Athauhnu says you must return!"

"I'm coming!" I responded, mounting Clamriu.

Then, to Bantus, "*Vale, contubernalis!* Be well, mate! I have to get back to the party!"

"*Vale, Pagane!*" Bantus responded. "Try to stay off the pyre!"

Emlun and I rode quickly back to the battle line. Athauhnu met us about ten *passus* behind our line.

"Madog's dead," I told him.

Athauhnu didn't as much as blink at the news. "I expected it," he said. "No man could have lived long with such a wound. He feasts with the heroes, and we may soon join him. The Germans are massing the *dugath* for an attack."

I looked across the field. The German *thegn* and his *gedricht* had come down off the ridge. He was massing a division of the *dugath* against our center. I tried to count, but it was impossible. The Germans kept no order, no formation. I estimated that the Krauts were massing over two cohorts—about a thousand warriors about seventy *passus* to our front. Fresh troops, well-armed. They should rip through our thin, exhausted cohorts like wolves through sheep.

On each of our flanks, the *thegn* had also assembled about a cohort of the dugath, around five hundred warriors, to prevent us from shifting men to the center.

Across our entire line, our men were nearing exhaustion. They had been engaged with the German *fiurd*, the muster-men, for over two hours. Each fighting pair of *muli*, each *gemini*, had been in the front rank at least twice. One in three were down, dead, or wounded. The rest were trying to martial their last vestiges of strength.

The German muster-men were not pressing hard. They were also exhausted, and they knew that the *dugath* was about to take over the fight. They had done their job. Our ranks were exhausted and whittled to the bone. It was time for their warriors to finish the job—not a time to get killed uselessly.

Suddenly, Agrippa was at my side.

"Didn't you hear officers' call, *Decurio?*" he announced. "Labienus is summoning us."

I rode off after Agrippa, with Athauhnu trailing behind. We met Labienus just behind our right flank cohort, a Seventh Legion unit. He had also assembled the senior centurions from each legionary group.

Labienus wasted no time.

"I assume you men have seen the Krauts massing in our center," he began. "They obviously plan to attack at that point. Our line is six men deep, at the most, and on its last legs. If we let them hit us, we're through."

There was no demurring from the officers. Even the centurions did not baulk. We were looking at a looming disaster.

"I plan to form maniples with the centuries of the Ninth and Eighth Legions at the expected point of enemy contact," Labienus announced.

Labienus could have caused no more surprise with that statement than if he had announced the god Mars was on his way, with a troop of unicorns, to rescue us. No Roman legion formed maniples in combat; Marius had obsoleted the tactic over fifty years ago.

A maniple was a formation of two massed centuries, closed ranks, one behind the other. It was a tactic used to achieve tactical mass back in the days when the phalanx was the state-of-the-art combat maneuver. Basically, two armies would run straight into each other and keep pushing and shoving in a scrum until one broke. But, the maniple formation was rigid; it had no flexibility. The enemy could run right around its flank, or if they had elephants, stomp it flat. The Roman army hadn't seriously employed massed maniples since they were massacred by Hannibal and the Carthaginians at Cannae.

Marius had reorganized the Roman legion into ten cohorts of six separate centuries each. This was possible because all Roman legionaries were trained and equipped to the same standard. The three unequal divisions of legionary infantry—*triarii*, heavy infantry; *principes*, spearmen; and *hastati*, light infantry—were a thing of the ancient past. Also, the cohort-based organization allowed a commander the flexibility to deploy his troops according to the terrain and the nature of the threat on the battlefield, a principle that Labienus himself had demonstrated when he peeled off twelve cohorts from the rear of four advancing legions to meet an enemy threat on their left flank.

Curiously, vestiges of the old manipular system still existed in the training and traditions of the army. Within the cohorts, the first, second and third centuries were known as the *prior*, or front-line centuries, based on what their positions would have been in the maniple. The remaining centuries—the fourth, fifth, and sixth—were called the *posterior* centuries because in the maniple, they would have stood behind the forward centuries in the phalanx. What's more, the prestige of the centurions commanding any cohort is based on whether they are *prior* or *posterior* centurions.

In training and on parade, the command to form maniples was still given. But, this formation was used only to cross up *tirones* during training drills or to put on a show for some visiting nob—not while decisively engaged with an enemy force, as Labienus was about to attempt.

To make matters worse, the only viable way of forming maniples from *acies formata*, the linear battle line formation in which we were currently deployed, was by first forming the *quincunx*, the "five dots."

According to legend, the great Scipio Africanus innovated this maneuver at the battle of Zama. When Hannibal sent his elephants in to destroy the Roman phalanxes, Scipio opened gaps in his front by having his centuries displace and shift behind one another, thus allowing the elephants to pass through the Roman lines.

The only time the *quincunx* was employed in modern warfare was well before contact was made with the enemy, and it was only used in order to allow support troops and cavalry to pass easily through legionary lines. Once the enemy was proximate, the three "posterior" centuries of each cohort were moved forward on line, and the ranks were closed.

No one would conceive of forming the *quincunx* while in contact. In our current deployment, since the posterior centuries were grouped together, this would open two ninety-foot gaps in the middle of our line!

"This will double our depth at the point of attack. I believe with a front sixty-men wide and sixteen deep, we can hold the Krauts main attack back," Labienus concluded. "Any questions?"

"Legate, what about our flanks?" Agrippa asked.

"Good question, Agrippa!" Labienus answered. "The Krauts did us a favor there. In fact, they've done us two favors. The first is that they have exposed their plans. They see no point in stealth. They think they can just walk right over us. The second is to your point. Except for their earlier attempt on our right flank, they have not pressured our flanks at all. In fact, we now overlap *them* on both flanks. You and I will continue to command the flanks. Our mission is to ensure that, when their spoiling attacks hit, they do not turn us. If they do, we're in danger of being enveloped. So we have to hold on the flank. Centurion?"

A centurion I didn't recognize from the Ninth Legion spoke. "Legate, when we form the *quincunx*, what's to keep those *verpae* from charging into the gaps?"

"Good question!" Labienus nodded. "Insubrecus *Decurio*, that's where you and the Sequani come in. Split your command into two divisions. When the *quincunx* opens, you deploy a division into each of the gaps. I don't think the Kraut muster-men have the heart to attack. But, if they try, you stop them. And, you need to protect the flanks of the exposed *prior* centuries when the *posterior* centuries pull back from the line. Just make sure you get your men back before the door closes . . . *Compre'endis tu?*"

"*Compre'endo, Legate!*" I affirmed.

"*Bene!*" Labienus concluded. When we reestablish the line of battle, we will align on the Eighth Legion. That's all! Return to your commands! Listen for the signals!"

I translated what was being said to Athauhnu. I doubt he understood much about maniples and *quincunces*; there weren't even words in Gah'el to express such formations. But, he did understand that we were intentionally opening gaps in our lines to pull off some obscure Roman battlefield dance routine, and it didn't please him. What pleased him less was that we were expected to ride into the gaps and throw ourselves in front of German infantry.

We rode back to our position behind the Roman lines. Athauhnu assembled the Sequani riders and quickly briefed them on what to expect. He then separated them into two divisions: one under me and Guithiru, the other under Ci and himself. I noticed he didn't mention anything about Madog. Each of our divisions assumed a ready position, mine behind the Ninth Legion, Athauhnu behind the Eighth.

Time was running out for us. A gap had formed between our front line and the German *fiurd*; they were starting to disengage. But, the Kraut *dugath*, massing for the attack, were not moving. They were chanting their strange mantra to their god, Woden: "Wo . . . wo . . . wo."

Then, from our right, a Roman bugle sounded, "Attention!"

Then, came a signal for the Eighth and Ninth Legions, quickly followed by, "Quincuncem . . . *formata!*"

Immediately, the posterior centuries of the two legions executed an about-face and began to march in quick time to the rear.

As they began to move off the line, I led my riders into the opening gap. Initially, the German muster-men proved Labienus right; they froze. Then, a few of the bolder ones made to follow the retreating centuries into the gap. We rode at them, and they quickly retreated. I was able to form two lines of cavalry across the gap. The *fiurd* showed no desire to attack us.

Across the field, I noticed movement behind the massed German warriors. The *thegn* realized something was up. Perhaps he feared his prey was retreating from him and he would not get the chance to kill many more Romans this afternoon. He rode in front of his center division, stabbing his sword in our direction. He harangued his elite troops to move forward, to take advantage of the widening gap in the Roman line. But, like all barbarian maneuvers, this one had a momentum all its own that no leadership could alter. The German *dugath* remained still and continued its woeful chant; it would move when it was ready, not before.

The posterior centuries had reached their position in the *quincunx*. They halted and turned about, again facing front. No sooner did the motion of the maneuver cease than Labienus sounded the signal trumpets again: "Eighth Legion! Ninth legion! *Manipulos formate!*"

Immediately, the rearmost Roman centuries executed a right-face and began to double-time behind the forward centuries.

The Germans did react to this maneuver.

The *thegn* may not have totally understood what he was witnessing, but he now understood its purpose. We were reinforcing our lines to meet his attack on our center. Still, his *dugath* would not move forward. He dispatched most of his *gedricht*, his personal bodyguards, to attack the gaps in the Roman line. But, he miscalculated. His own *fiurd*, still milling about on the battlefield, watching the Roman maneuver like a crowd in the arena watching a show, got in their way. His *gedricht* were soon tangled among their own troops, and their attack never arrived.

I looked over to where the German *thegn* was raging at the *dugath* to move, screaming for the *fiurd* to get out of the way, and thundering at his *gedricht* to attack the Roman gap. I saw he had less than a dozen men left to protect himself.

No sooner had that realization entered my mind, than Labienus signaled again, general call: "*Aciem formata!* Form battle line!"

Quickly, I turned my troop, and we rode out of the gap as the Tenth Legion battle line closed with the Ninth. At the same time, the Ninth Legion maniples moved right to close on the Eighth, while the Seventh moved left.

The door had slammed shut! Labienus had pulled off the maneuver!

The Krauts were finally beginning to move. All three divisions of the *dugath* were running forward to attack our lines. Behind them, the German *thegn* and the twelve remaining members of his *gedricht* stood alone in the field.

I had an insane idea!

My military training and discipline told me to hold my position, to block and contain any penetration of our line. But, the Krauts had exposed themselves to a potentially fatal blow, which only I could deliver.

What was it that Caesar had said the other day? *Audaces amat fortuna!* ... Fortune loves the bold! Instinctively, I reached up and touched my *lorica* where my *Bona Fortuna* hung. It seemed strangely warm.

"Athauhnu!" I yelled, turning Clamriu and riding toward our left flank. "*Me sequere!* Follow me!" I quickly realized that, in my excitement, I had spoken Latin, so as I rode past his position on the left, I repeated myself in Gah'el, "*Diluhna fi!*"

I galloped the Sequani around our left flank. I remember catching a glimpse of Agrippa's shocked face as we thundered by. We rode out onto the field, past the right flank of one of the Kraut divisions. A couple of their warriors looked over toward us, but continued their run toward the Roman line. As soon as I cleared the rear of the German *dugath*, I angled right to where I knew the *thegn* was standing.

He was still there, alone except for the small remnant of his bodyguard troops.

I halted opposite, about a hundred *passus* distant. I turned Clamriu toward the Germans, extended my arms out parallel to the ground, and Ci's *ala*, the seventeen men still in the saddle, assembled on both sides of me, facing the Krauts. Athauhnu lined his twenty-two riders up behind us. Then, he rode forward and took a position on my right.

Across the field, the remnant of *thegn's gedricht* began, almost hesitantly, to position themselves between us and their leader, whom they were sworn to protect to the death.

The gods of the Gah'el were about to collect on that promise!

But first, I had one last die to cast.

I rode out a few steps and turned to face the Sequani.

"Warriors of the Soucanai!" I shouted. "Madog, your king is dead!"

I heard a moan go up from the men.

I raised my hands. They became silent.

"The man who killed your king . . . the dog who treacherously cut Madog down after he had slain the king of the Germans . . . and stabbed him from behind in his moment of triumph . . . stands there . . . before you!"

I pointed right at the German *thegn,* who was sheltered behind the thin line of his *gedricht.*

The men were growling.

I drew my *spatha.* "A place on the mead-bench beside Madog in the Land of Youth, and the hero's portion served by the hands of Andraste, the goddess of victories, to the man who delivers the head of that German dog to the tomb of Madog!" I shouted.

I turned Clamriu and charged the Germans.

My Sequani thundered behind me, screaming for German blood.

To their credit, the *gedricht* remained faithful. They died for their oath.

As I galloped toward the Germans, I shimmied my shield off my left shoulder and inserted my forearm through its bindings. I aimed for a gap in the center of the German line. When I hit it, I felt a glancing blow on my shield from the Kraut to my left. I didn't bother with the one on my right. I was through the line and bearing down on the German *thegn*.

As I reached him, I heard a crash behind me as the rest of the troop made contact with the Germans.

The *thegn* pulled back hard on his reins. His horse reared up on his hind legs. Clamriu crashed into her opponent's chest. The German horse began to tumble backward. I felt a massive blow on my helmet, just above my eyes. I tumbled backward into blackness.

When I awoke, Emlun was kneeling over me, and Rhodri was standing beside him. Emlun helped me sit up. That was a mistake. The world seemed to twinkle and spin in front of me. I felt like I would vomit.

When my eyes focused again, Emlun held up my helmet. In the front, there was a dent the size of a small fist.

"Cheap Roman tin!" Emlun shook his head. "A German horse brought you down! You ought to get yourself a new helmet from a good Soucanai smith!"

Clamriu was calmly cropping the grass a few feet away. Behind her, a couple of the Sequani were trying to subdue the *thegn's* riderless horse. Just over to my right, I saw his body with two *gaea* spears protruding from its chest. I puzzled for a moment why the body looked strange. Then I realized; it had no head.

Rhodri gestured toward the *thegn's* horse. "You brought him down, Arth Bek. By our custom, his horse and his armor belong to you!"

"Athauhnu?" I croaked.

Emlun pointed across the field toward the Roman lines.

Athauhnu was galloping across the face of the German horde spinning something over his head. It looked vaguely like a ball, a ball attached by a yellow rope. It was a head, the head of the German *thegn*!

The Germans were standing, watching. I realized that they had dropped their shields and weapons. The Roman *muli* from our battle line were advancing among them, driving them down onto their knees, tying their hands behind their backs, collecting their weapons. Our fight was over.

Emlun was talking: "Athauhnu killed the German you passed. Guithiru and me followed you through their line. By the time we caught up with you, you were already down. So was the *thegn*. His horse rolled over him. He was probably dead already, but Guithiru put the first javelin into him. Then I stuck him. Athauhnu came and took his head for Madog. The honor was his as chief. We'll bury it with Madog. Lay it between his feet. That German dog will be his slave in the Land of Youth for eternity!"

They stood me up. Another mistake. This time I did vomit. Strangely, I felt a bit better after that. Emlun steadied me.

I saw a small group of Roman riders approaching. The leader wore a bright red *sagum* and rode a white stallion.

It was Caesar.

Labienus rode immediately to his left.

I tried to assume some semblance of attention as the *imperator* arrived. Again a mistake. Emlun's steadying grasp was the only thing that kept me from pitching forward into the grass.

"Well, this completes my collection of insubordinates!" Caesar said dryly. "First a senior legate, who won't stay where he's been assigned, but starts his own battle with the Germans, and now a *decurio*, a very junior *decurio* at that, who abandons his assigned post to lead a cavalry attack against a superior force of German infantry. What do you have to say for yourself, soldier?"

"*Nil 'scusationis mi', Imperator!*" I snapped out, as if a *tiro* on punishment parade.

"You have that right!" Caesar snorted. "There's no excuse at all! It's a marvel Rome has survived this long with soldiers like you following her eagles."

Caesar jerked the head of his horse around and rode toward the top of the ridge where his battle with the Helvetii still raged.

Labienus hesitated. Then he said to Emlun in perfect Gah'el, "Trooper! Get this Roman officer to a medic!"

Before he turned to follow Caesar, he winked.

Post Scriptum

A t Bibracte, I survived my first battle.

Only politicians, historians, and generals classify battles as victories or defeats.

Soldiers recognize no victories. Even in the greatest national victories, comrades are lost, and the survivors suffer. They suffer from the wounds they receive; they suffer from what they witness; they suffer from the loss of dear friends. Win, lose, or draw, soldiers just thank *Domina Fortuna* for sparing their lives and pray to her that this will be their last fight.

At the time, I expected that our war was over at least for that year. Having defeated the Helvetii, Caesar would withdraw the army south of the Rhodanus. We would spend the rest of the campaign season in the *provincia,* licking our wounds, collecting rations, and getting ready for the winter.

Erratum! I was wrong. Despite our battered condition after Bibracte, Caesar wasn't done.

I hoped that Bibracte could be my only great battle. I would serve my remaining enlistment in relative peace and safety, and return home to Mediolanum. There, Macro and I would quickly become rich wine merchants, and perhaps then I would win back my beloved Gabi.

269

Denuo erratum! Again I was wrong.

They say that the greatest gift the gods have given to men is they don't see their own future.

I believe that.

Had I known on that day that what lay before me was over twenty years of blood, betrayal, and loss; that after the Helvetian campaign would come years of brutal fighting in Gallia, Aquitania, Belgica, Germania, and that mysterious island across *Oceanus*, Britannia; and then Caesar's wars in Italia, Hispania, Asia, Africa, and Aegyptus; then Octavius' wars against the *Liberatores*, Sextus Pompeius, and finally Antonius; that after the battle at Bibracte would come Gergovia, Alesium, Dyrrhachium, Pharsalus, Zela, Alexandria, the Nile, Thapsus, and Munda with Caesar; then Forum Gallorum, Mutina, Philippi, Naulochus, and Actium for Octavius; along with hundreds of murderous encounters in places too insignificant to be remembered by a name, I believe seeing the course of my future would have driven me *demens*, completely mad.

But the gods at least spared me that.

Agrippa stayed with us in Mediolanum only a few days before returning to his refuge in Italia. He graciously invited us to visit his estates near Asisium. Then, he departed south, carrying with him my answer to Octavius' request.

It seems that our *princeps civitatis* is continuing Caesar's vision of extending *Romanitas* into the provinces. Octavius has appointed a number of provincial citizens, whom the Roman senatorials consider no better than *peregrini*, foreigners, to military and civil positions traditionally reserved for Romans of the proper pedigree. He has even appointed provincials to the Roman Senate.

Octavius also plans to extend Roman citizenship to the provinces by creating *municipia*, cities with citizenship rights in the established provinces and in the major tribal centers of the newly acquired territories. Established cities in the "civilized" provinces, as he terms them, would be granted full Roman citizenship with the right to vote. Other cities and tribal centers would be granted a lesser degree of citizenship, which would grant their residents the protection of Roman magistrates, service in the legions, and of course, payment of taxes and financial levies to Rome.

Mediolanum is planned as one of Octavius' initial "first-class" *municipia* in the strategically important *Gallia Cisalpina* region. Since this is a plan with which the aristocratic elements in the Roman Senate are not pleased, the Augustus is determined that these first grants are successful. In order to do that, he is handpicking the city magistrates.

Octavius has already commissioned the two *duumviri* and the two *aediles* who will administer affairs in Mediolanum. In fact, one of the *duumviri* is my cousin, Lucius Helvetius Naso Quartus, who still runs my grandfather's empire of foundries, garum factories, and wine presses.

Once things have "settled," these positions will become elected annually. But for now, Octavius is controlling and supervising the process personally—which brings me to his request.

First and foremost, I am to be Octavius' "eyes and ears" in Mediolanum. As one of his former officers, he knows that I will report to him what he needs to know—not what I want him to know.

Second, I am to be commissioned as the *praefectus urbis* of Mediolanum. As such, I will have command of all things "military" in the newly minted *municipium*, meaning command of the urban militia cohort, which exists only to collect the tolls and taxes at the city gates. I am also to form a troop of *vigiles*, after the model developed by Lucius' brother, Marcus Agrippa, in the city of Rome.

The primary duty of the *vigiles* would be firefighting. However, they would also serve to maintain civil peace and safety by patrolling the city streets on the lookout for thieves, muggers, burglars, and runaway slaves.

Before Agrippa left, I discussed the offer with my wife, Rhonwen. She asked only two questions: would I get paid, and would the job get me out of the house? When I answered that I would receive a salary from the Augustus' privy purse, five times that of a *primus pilus* in the legions, and would have to establish a *praetorium* near the center of town, from which to run things, she told me I should do it.

Besides, she said, she didn't think I should disappoint such a nice man as Lucius Vipsanius Agrippa after he had travelled so far just to ask me to do this.

So, I find myself about to start a new career, again in the service of the *gens Iulia*. I have decided that, despite my new responsibilities, I will continue to write my memoirs of Caesar's wars in Gaul. While I am waiting for the confirmation of my appointment as the *praefectus urbis* of the new Roman *municipium* of Mediolanum, I have begun to review my journals of Caesar's campaign against Ariovistus and the Suebi. I am dubbing this chapter of my journal, *De Re Suebiana*, "The Swabian Affair."

MILITARY LATIN

Despite the many modern novels, whose setting places the reader among Roman soldiers, and popular movies about the Roman Empire, surprisingly little is known about the day-to-day operations of a Roman legion during the time of Caesar.

Caesar's own works about his military operations in Gaul and the subsequent civil war is perhaps the best detailed surviving sources for that period. But, Caesar's goal was not to write a manual about Roman military operations; Caesar's goal was political self-promotion.

A fifth-century work sometimes called *de re militari*, "Military Operations," attributed to Publius Flavius Vegetius Renatus, survives and presents a representation of the military operations at the height of Rome's power. Although Vegetius claims to have based his treatise on descriptions of Roman armies of the mid to late Republican period from Cato the Elder, Cornelius Celsus, Frontinus, and Paternus, and on Roman military operations during the principate and early empire from the imperial constitutions of Augustus, Trajan, and Hadrian, little of Vegetius' sources survive, and his writings are separated from his primary sources by centuries. Additionally, Vegetius was not a historian or a soldier, and his purpose seems to be more a nostalgic recalling of the glory days of Roman military power than a reporting of what actually happened. So, *de re militari* resembles a somewhat clumsy compilation of materials from various sources rather than a military field manual reflecting the actual standards and practices of the Roman legions.

In order to create a realistic setting for this novel, the author has based the "big picture" on the first half of the first book of Caesar's *de bello Gallico* where he reports his campaign against the Helvetians.

However, in order to create the microcosm of the Roman soldier in training and in the field, the author has channeled his five years of studying Latin and Roman history with his twenty-five years serving in the infantry and rangers. The scenes of Gaius Marius Insubrecus' basic training with the Tenth Legion outside the Roman city of Aquileia are based on the author's own infantry training in Ft. Jackson, South Carolina and his airborne and ranger training in Ft. Benning, Georgia. In the novel, Caesar's Gallic cavalry *alae* conduct road reconnaissance and screening missions based on the same principles of US light-infantry or armored cavalry scout platoons.

Roman legionaries use a vocabulary that modern soldiers would appreciate. Where the author's comrades in Vietnam would describe a particularly unpleasant experience as "being in the shit," Insubrecus' *contubernales* refer to the same as *immerda*. The American soldier refers to a screwed up situation as FUBAR; the Roman soldiers in this book call it *perfututum*.

Military Terminology

Besides the "formal" tactical terminology of the Roman army, little is known about how the soldiers actually spoke. They weren't the types to leave a written records of their conversations.

As was related in the first book of the Gaius Marius Chronicle, *The Gabinian Affair*, the Roman legionary during the time of Caesar was more rustic than urban and more provincial than Roman. So, it is reasonable to believe that they incorporated words, grammatical constructions, and accents from their native languages into the Latin they used as the *lingua franca* of the legions. The author is reminded of the "Army English" he had to learn as an infantry recruit; it sounded more Southern than Yankee and had its own jargon. To "put the quietus" on something was to stop it; the plural of the noun "man" was often "mens"; and combat was described as "hitting the shit." So, it's reasonable to assume that the Roman *muli* in Caesar's time had their own brand of spoken Latin, which would probably have made Cicero weep.

Also, the language used between soldiers tends to be direct, colorful, and, in a strange sense, intimate. That was the character of US Army "rhetoric." Drill sergeants often referred to their charges as "maggots"; so Roman training officers may have called their *tirones, blattae*, "cockroaches." Lazy or incompetent soldiers were referred to as "snuffies"; so the author invented the Latin term *funguli* for legionaries known to cut too many corners in the performance of their duties.

Other than that, the following list of Roman military jargon is perhaps just another example of a traditional, classical education gone dreadfully wrong!

Acies (pl. acies) – edge, battle line

Acies triplex – the triple line, standard battle formation of the Roman legion

Acies prima – The vanguard of the legion on the march or the front line of the legion deployed for battle in the *acies triplex*; the First, Second, Third, and Fourth cohorts of the legion

Acies secunda – the middle line, the Fifth, Sixth, and Seventh cohorts of the legion

Acies tertia – the rear line, the Eighth, Ninth, and Tenth cohorts

Agmen (pl. agmines) – a marching column

Novissimum Agmen – the rearguard of the marching column; the rea, the caboose

Primum Agmen – the vanguard of the marching column, the "bleeding edge."

Ala (pl. alae) – literally, a bird's wing; an element of Roman cavalry roughly equivalent in numbers to forty to sixty troopers

A'mperi'tu' – military jargon coined by the author, short for *Ad imperatum tuum*—"At your command"; this was one of the acceptable responses from a subordinate to a superior's command.

Aquila (pl. aquilae) – literally, an eagle, a bird sacred to Iove; figuratively, the standard of a legion and its *animus*, its "life force, spirit, soul"; the worst disgrace that could befall a legion was to lose its *aquila* to an enemy.

Sub aquilis – literally, "under the eagles"; figuratively, "in the army."

Aquilifer – an officer bearing the eagle standard of a Roman legion; also the "treasurer" of the legion handling payroll and burial club transactions.

Ballista (pl. ballistae) – a piece of Roman artillery that launched a large, arrowlike bolt over great distances

Balteus – a leather baldric used to suspend a sword. It was worn over the shoulder, passing down to the side where the sword was suspended. Enlisted men wore their swords on the right side; centurions and senior officers on the left.

Bestiola (pl. bestiolae) – literally, any small animal; in the jargon of the Roman army, it's a derogatory term used to address trainees, equivalalent to "maggot" in English. (author)

Blatta (pl. blattae . . . there's never only one of these things) – literally, a cockroach; figuratively, a legionary trainee.

Buccellatum – hardtack; part of a *mulus'* marching rations.

Caliga (pl. caligae) – Roman, hobnailed military boots.

Capsarius – army slang for a field medic, one who carries a *capsa*, a box or satchel, which carried medical supplies

Capu' – boss, chief, from Latin *caput*, "head"; modern Italian, *capo*. Military jargon coined by the author.

Carinus – ruddy brown; in this story, the standard color of an enlisted man's *sagum*

Castigatio (pl. castigationes) – a minor military punishment; often a beating with a centurion's *vitis*, his vine cudgel.

Castro' – an "army brat;" *mus castrorum*, a "camp rat"; this is a soldier who was the offspring of a legionary and one of the *mulieres castrorum*, camp followers, and brought up in a legion's *vicus*; these soldiers felt that they were *familia legionis*, members of the legion's family, therefore superior to first-time enlistees; sometimes adopted as the soldier's cognomen, e.g., Lucius Furius Castro or Lucus Fulius De Castris (author).

Castrum (pl. castra) – a legionary marching camp; these were constructed at the end of each daily march.

Cedo alteram, centurio! – "Hit me again, sir!" The expected response of a
soldier undergoing *castigatio*.

Centuria (pl. centuriae) – a sub-unit of a Roman legion consisting of ten
contubernia, eighty legionaries, commanded by a *centurio*

Centurio (pl. centuriones) – a centurion, a Roman officer who commands a
centuria of eighty men

Centurio prior pilus – a senior centurion; a centurion of the first rank;
in this novel, designates a centurion who commands a cohort and so
would stand in the front rank of the cohort in the battle line.

Centurio primi ordinis – in this novel, designates a centurion of the first
rank; a centurion who commands a century in any of the first four
cohorts, which constitute the first rank of the legion in the *acies triplex*,
the "triple battle line," a battle formation favored by Caesar

Centurio primus pilus – "The First Spear"; senior centurion of a legion;
commands the First Centuria of the First Cohors and also commands
the First Cohors; in the absence of both the *legatus legionis*, the
legionary commander, and the *tribunus laticlavus*, the "Broad-Stripe"
tribune, commands the legion.

Centurio secundi ordinis – in this novel, designates a centurion of the
second rank; commands a century in Cohorts Five, Six, or Seven, the
second rank in the line of battle

Centurio tertii ordinis – in this novel, designates a centurion of the third
rank; commands a century in Cohorts, Eight, Nine, or Ten, the third
rank in line of battle; the reserve or "Forlorn Hope" of a legion

Chlamys (pl. chlamydes) – chainmail shoulder pads that fit over the *lorica
hamate*, a legionary's chainmail armor

Cingulum (pl. cingula) – a Roman military belt; this was one of the indicators
of a soldier; it was decorated with an ornate buckle and highly polished
metal bits; this and a razor-sharp pugio gave a mulus a bit of swagger when
he went into town for wine and entertainment.

Cochleare (pl. cochleara) – a mess spoon; part of a legionary's mess kit

Cohors (pl. cohortes) – an element of a Roman legion commanded by a senior
centurion, consisting of six centuries, 480 legionaries

Comes (pl. comites) – a companion; an intimate; used to describe a general's personal staff and / or members of his personal guard.

Contubernium (pl. contubernia) – a squad, a grouping of eight legionaries who share a tent in the field or a squad room in a permanent camp

Contubernales – members of a common *contubernium*, "mates," "squaddies"

Cornex (pl. cornices) – literally, a crow; in military jargon, a field medic (author), a *capsarius*, who wore a black tunic in combat to hide the blood and gore on his uniform.

Cornices pascere – literally, to feed the crows; figuratively, to be evacuated to the aid

station.

Cornu (pl. cornua) – a Roman "brass" instrument about ten feet long in the shape of a musical G-clef; used to relay orders on the battlefield

Cornucen (pl. cornucines) – the horn-blower, a minor officer who carried a *cornu* to signal orders over the field during battles.

Corona civica – Civic Crown, the second highest Roman military decoration, after the "grass crown"; reserved for a Roman citizen who saved the lives of fellow citizens by killing an enemy on a spot not again held by the enemy that same day; the citizens saved must bear witness to the act—no one else could be the verifying witness; any recipient of the Civic Crown was entitled membership in the Roman Senate.

Cuneus – the "boar's snout"; a Roman infantry and cavalry offensive military formation, the wedge

Decanus – a junior legionary officer; commander of a *contubernium*; a squad leader

Decurio (pl. decuriones) – a junior cavalry officer commanding a *turma*, about thirty-five troopers.

Dicto pareo – literally, "to what is spoken I comply"; "Yes, sir!" Another acceptable response from a subordinate when given a command (author).

Dolabra (pl. dolabrae) – an entrenching tool; a versatile axe, pickaxe and mattock; no *mulus* would be caught without his or his centurion would have his guts for shoelaces.

Dux (pl. duces) – this was not a formal military title in the time of Caesar. Literally, the word denotes a leader. In this book, it means "chief" and refers to anyone in a leadership position who is viewed favorably by the troops (author). Also, it's an honorary title given to native leaders of allied bands and auxiliary units.

Expeditus (pl. expediti) – unburdened, lightly armed, ready for combat

Explorator (pl. exploratores) – a scout, spy

Fabricator (pl. fabricatores) – an engineer, construction troop

Fossa – a ditch; part of the standard fortifications of a castrum

Fungulus (pl. funguli) – literally, a little mushroom, a fungus; figuratively, military slang for an incompetent soldier, a "snuffy" (author).

Furca (pl. furcae) – a pole on which a soldier carried his personal equipment on the march

Fustuarium – a severe military punishment; being beaten to death with clubs by the members of one's *contubernium*; this is one of the few punishments inflicted in the Roman army where the victim is not expected to say, "Hit me again, sir!"

Galea (pl. galeae) – the standard Roman military helmet

Geminus (pl. gemini) – literally, a twin; figuratively, military fighting partners (author)

Gladius (pl. gladii) – the *gladius hispaniensis*, "Spanish short sword," the basic Roman infantry short, stabbing sword

Hastae purae – a minor military decoration

Hastile – a wooden staff carried by an *optio*; in battle, the *optio*'s position was at the rear of the century; it is thought that the *hastile* was used to keep the battle line straight, discourage flight, and to beat legionaries back into line should they get some other idea

Immerda – from *in merda*, literally "in the shit": figuratively, a Roman legionary's characterization of a bad situation. *Immerda sumus!* We're in the shit! (author)

Immunis (pl. immunes) – a military status in which a soldier was excused from fatigue details and got extra pay for doing some specialized job, like clerk, blacksmith, forager, etc.

Impedimentum (pl. impedimenta) – equipment, baggage, military kit

Impeditus (pl. impediti) – marching under a full field load or *mulare*, "to mule it".(author)

Imperator – a Roman title given to a victorious commander by acclamation of the troops; a general

Imperium – basically, "power"; it is the power of the Roman state over individuals which in Caesar's time was delegated by the Senate to a magistrate; also refers to the area where Roman law ran and where a Roman magistrate could wield the power of the state, *imperium Romanum*, "The Roman Empire."

Interrogatio – interrogation, inquisition, a grilling; if a slave or non-citizen were undergoing an *interrogatio*, torture would typically be used; legions had *immunis* soldiers, *carnifices*, who were specialists in getting the answers a general wanted from prisoners.

Intervallum – an open area between the ramparts and tents in a *castrum*

Lagoena (pl. lagoenae) – water bottle, a canteen; part of a legionary's field kit

Latrina – privy, water closet; the engineers were careful to place these downstream of the water and bathing point

Latus apertum – the right side; the "open side"; the side of an individual soldier or an entire military formation not protected by shields

Latus opertum – the left side; the side of an individual soldier or an entire military formation protected by shields

Legatus – a legate; a senior Roman officer appointed to assist a Roman magistrate in some manner; usually of the Senatorial order, an equestrian plebeian, or patrician; a political appointee, a client of the magistrate, a political favor, a nephew or an in-law, or someone the magistrate didn't want to leave back in Rome, where he couldn't keep an eye on him.

Legatus Equitium – cavalry commander; an ad hoc assignment.

Legatus legionis – a legate appointed as the army commander's representative in a legion; in Caesar's time these appointments were not permanent assignments but ad hoc based on the situation; tactical control of the legion in combat was usually left to the legion's senior centurion, the *primus pilus*.

Loculus – a military satchel; part of a soldier's marching pack

Lorica (pl. loricae) –upper-body armor of a Roman legionary; during the period of the story, it was the *lorica hamata*, made of iron chainmail for the enlisted men and plate armor for senior officers; men serving in the auxiliary units might wear leather *loricae*.

Medicus (pl. medici) – doctor; army medic

Mercurius (pl. mercurii) – Mercury, a Roman god; military slang invented by the author for a sestertius coin

Miles (pl. milites) – the basic word for a soldier; in this story, it's what *tirones*, trainees, strive to become, *milites Romani*.

Minerva – Minerva, a Roman goddess; soldiers' slang for a bronze triens coin (author)

Mulieres castrorum – women of the camps; camp followers

Mulare – "to mule it"; the Roman equivalent to the US Infantry expression "humping"; marching under a full load. (author)

Mulio (pl. muliones) – teamster, mule driver

Mulus (pl. muli) – literally, a mule; figuratively, army slang for an infantryman, a grunt (author); from the expression *muli* Marii, "Marius' mules," describing legionaries marching *impedimenti*, "loaded down" with their personal equipment, after the Roman general, Gaius Marius, unloaded the mules in the baggage train and loaded the gear onto the backs of the legionaries to improve the mobility of the legions

Murus (pl. muri) – a wall; in the military jargon of the author it describes a close-order defensive formation, a *murus scutorum*, a shield-wall

Nil 'scusationis mi' – "I have no excuse!" One of the five responses authorized for a Roman legionary *tiro*, along with "Yes, Sir!", "No, Sir!", "Sir, I do not know!" and "Hit me again, Sir!" (author).

Obsequar ti' – "I obey you!" Again, another acceptable reponse to a military order (author)

Optio (pl. optiones) – "chosen" one; a junior army officer; second in command of a *centuria* under the centurion

Ordo (pl. ordines) – rank in battle or a social class

Palus (pl. pali) – pole used to practice sword drill

Paratus – "Ready!" The only acceptable response when an officer asks *Parat' tu?*—"Are you ready?"

Parma (pl. parmae) – cavalry shield

Passus (pl. passus) – a complete stride from when the right foot goes down until it comes down again; about five and a half feet on flat ground; the standard legionary daily march was twenty thousand passus

Patera (pl. paterae) – mess tin

Percussus – literally, a blow, strike, punch; in the book it's used to describe a soldier's use of dagger, sword, and offensive shield techniques; also, it means, "hit man," someone who "punches" his victim with a dagger.

Perfututum – FUBAR, totally screwed up! Much worse than *immerda*! (author)

Pes (pl. pedes) – a foot; army slang invented by the author for an infantryman, equivalent to the American military expression for an infantryman, a "leg."

Phalera (pl. phalerae) – a military decoration

Pilleum (pl. pillea) – a cap worn by freed slaves; in the army, a cap worn under the *galea* for stability, fit and cushioning

Pilum (pl. pila) – Roman military javelin; really one of the legions' secret weapons. It was essentially an antipersonnel device, but it was also used to render opponent's shields unusable so the *muli* could close in for their sword work; the shaft bent on contact so the *pilum* could not be extracted from a shield or thrown back at the Roman line; a nasty piece of business.

Porta (pl. portae) – a gate, portal; a Roman marching camp, *castrum*, had four standard *portae*

1. Porta Decumana – the "Gate of the Tenth Cohort," the back gate
2. Porta Praetoria – the main gate
3. Porta Principalis Dextra – right side gate
4. Porta Principalis Sinistra – left side gate

Posca – a drink made from vinegar and herbs; mother's milk of a Roman soldier

Praefectus – commander; a Roman officer, often of the centurion or tribune status, in command of a legionary *vexilliatio* or an auxiliary unit

Praefectus castrorum – commander of the camps; senior centurion of the army

Praetorium – a headquarters

Preatoriani – headquarters security troops

Primus – literally, first; military jargon coined by the author for "Top Soldier," Number One; reserved for senior centurions; in direct address, "*Prime!*" (pronounced PREEM-eh!)

Pteruges – the skirt of leather or fabric strips worn around the waists of Roman soldiers. They were often decorated with metal studs or embossed images.

Pugio (pl. Pugiones) – a knife used by Roman soldiers as a sidearm; along with the military belt, the *pugio* was one of the indicators of a soldiers status; it was considered a "noble" and "Roman" weapon, unlike the *sica* which was used by villains, thieves, scoundrels, backstabbers, throat-cutters, and barbarians from the east.

Quadriga (pl. quadrigae) – literally, a four-horse rig in a chariot race; street talk coined by the author for a *denarius*, a roman coin.

Quaestor (pl. Quaestores) – in Caesar's time, *quaestores* were officials who supervised the treasury and financial affairs of the state; as a proconsul, Ceasar would have had a *quaestor*, or *quaestores*, to help him cook the books in the provinces assigned to him; in this story, the *quaestor exercitus*, is the army quartermaster.

Quincunx (pl. quincunces) – literally, the pattern of five dots on a dice cube; figuratively, a disposition of soldiers or centuries in a military formation

Rudis (pl. rudes) – literally, a stick; a wooden practice sword or knife, weighted heavier than the real thing to build up muscle

Saccus (pl. sacci) – a bag for carrying equipment, food, and loot; part of a soldier's marching pack

Sacramentum – the military oath taken by soldiers

Sagum (pl. saga) – a military cloak, woolen and treated to be waterproof

Sarcina (pl. sarcinae) – military marching pack

Scutum (pl. scuta) – Roman infantry shield

Senior – literally, older; figuratively, "Sir!" (author)

Sica (pl. sicae) – a small, easily-concealable knife with either a straight or curved blade; believed to be of eastern origin, therefore not considered by Romans as a "noble" weapon; favored weapon of the *sicarius* (pl. *sicarii*), the "knife man" or "hitter."

Significatio (pl. significationes) – an indication of approval; in the novel, it is
the ceremony in which *tirones* are accepted as soldiers by their legion

Signum (pl. signa) – the standard of a military unit

Signifer – a soldier who carried a unit's *signum*

Situla (pl. situlae) – a bucket; in the legions, *situlae*, "buckets," was a drill
requiring trainees to carry full buckets over long distance to build upper-
body strength (author)

Socius (pl. Scocii) – an ally

Spatha (pl. spathae) – a long sword, used mostly in the cavalry because a *gladius*
doesn't reach well when one is sitting on a horse

Subarmalis (pl. subarmales) – padded jackets worn under a *lorica* by Roman
soldiers

Sudarium – a soldier's scarf; a "sweat-rag"; served many purposes for a
mulus . . . it kept his *lorica* from chafing his neck on the march; it
cushioned his shoulder from his *furca* when marching *impeditus*; it wiped
the sweat off his face; it was a handy field dressing.

Sudis (pl. sudes) – stakes used as part of army fortifications; antipersonnel
devices

Tegimen (pl. tegimenta) – a covering; a leather carrying case for the *scutum*, the
legionary shield

Tesserarius (pl. tesserarii) – a Roman officer, usually third in rank in a *centuria*;
named after a *tesserae*, a clay token on which was written the daily password

Ti' adsum – "At your service!" Literally, *tibi adsum*—"I'm here for you!"

Tiro (pl. tirones) – the lowest thing on earth, a recruit, a rookie in the Roman
army, a trainee

Tribunus (pl. tribuni) – a tribune, a military and civil officer

Tribunus plebis – tribune of the people

Tribunus militum – tribune of the soldiers, a military tribune

Tribunus angusticlavus – a military tribune from the *ordo equester*, the
knightly class; a junior tribune; a "narrow-striper"

Tribunus laticlavus – a military tribune from the Senatorial or Patrician
class; a senior tribune; a "broad-striper"

Turma (pl. turmae) – cavalry squadron; a cavalry unit of two or more *alae*

Umbo – the boss of a shield

Vagina – a scabbard for a sword.

Venator (pl. Venatores) – a hunter; an *immunis* detail in the legion, a soldier who hunts game for rations

Venatus – literally, the hunt; figuratively, a cavalry advance against a fleeing enemy

Vermiculus (pl. vermiculi) – literally, a maggot; figuratively, a training officer's pet name for a trainee.

Veteranus (pl. veterani) – veteran, an experienced soldier, an "old man"

Vexilium (pl. vexilia) – a banner, flag

Vexilium rubrum – the red flag; symbol of a legion

Vexillarius – a guidearm; one who carries the unit pennant

Vexillatio (pl. vexillationes) – an independent detachment of legionaries commanded by a centurion or tribune; this was considered an "independent command," so it was a desired assignment for any amibitious junior officer

Via Praetoria – one of the standard "streets" of a *castrum* running from Porta Praetoria, the main gate, to the Porta Decumana, the rear gate

Via Principalis – one of the standard "streets" of a *castrum* running from the Porta Principalis Dextra and the Porta Principalis Sinistra

Vicus – village; a settlement of camp followers outside a legionary *castrum*

Vimen (pl. vimenes) – the "basket"; a weighted, wicker practice shield used in training

Virgo (pl. virgines) – literally, a virgin, a maiden; figuratively, a soldier who has not experienced combat, a "cherry" (author)

Vitis (pl. vites) – club, cudgel, swagger stick made from a grape vine; one of insignias of rank of a centurion used to direct military drill and to administer physical punishment.

Roman Military Commands

Again, little is known about Roman unit drill and combat commands. In order to bring the reader into the Roman battle line, the author used his own experience as a combat infantry commander and a liberal use of the commands developed by Roman military reenactors.

In the Gaius Marius novels, the Roman army uses a "shorthand" version of Latin for efficiency. So, in order to command a unit to turn to the right, the normal Latin expression, *ad dextram*, meaning, "toward the right hand," becomes *a' dex'*, and the Latin command to turn, *versate*, becomes *versat'* ... "*A' Dex ... Versat!*"

Some drill commands, like "*Stat'!*"—"Stand up" or "Attention!"—were "signal commands." When delivering these commands, an officer first names the unit for whom the command is intended, then delivers the command for execution by the troops. So, if a *decanus*, a Roman squad leader, wants to bring his *contubernium* of eight legionaries to the position of attention, he says, "*Contubernium . . . Stat!*"

Most Roman military commands are divided into two elements—the prepatory command and the command of execution. The prepatory command is given to warn and prepare troops to execute a specific movement. The actual movement is executed on the command of execution.

So, if a Roman officer wants his detail to turn right, he first calls them to the position of attention by issuing the command, "*Stat!*" He then issues a prepatory command, "*A' Dex'*," meaning "to the right," then the command of execution, "*Versat!*" When the soldiers hear the command of execution, they turn to the right.

The Roman drill and combat commands used in the novels are:

Aciem . . . Format'! – "Form battle line!"

Ad Cuneum! – "Form the wedge!" A Roman attack formation

A' Dex' Aciem . . . Format' – "Form battle line to the right!"

A' Dex' . . . Versat'! – "Right, Face!"

A' Pedes! – "On Your feet!"

Ad Signa! – "Fall In!"

Ad Sin' Aciem . . . Format' – "Form battle line to the left!"

Ad Sin' . . . Versat'! – "Left, Face!"

A' Testudinem! – "Form the turtle!" A Roman defensive formation

A Signis! – "Fall out!"

(Unit) . . . Consistit'! – "Halt!"

Contra . . . Versat'! – "About, Face!"

Dex' . . . Dex' . . . Dex', Sin', Dex' – counting marching cadence, "Right . . . right . . . right, left, right."

Equiis . . . citatis! – "Horses canter!" (cavalry command)

Equiis . . . currentibus! – "Horses gallop!" (cavalry command)

Gladios . . . stringit'! – "Draw swords!"

Gradus Bis . . . Movet'! – "Double-time march!" Increase marching pace to 120 passus per minute.

(Unit) . . . Laxat'! – "Stand at ease!"

Impetum . . . agit'! – "Attack!"

Manipulos . . . format'! – "Form maniples!"

(Unit) . . . Miss'est! – "Dismissed!"

Ordines . . . Densat'! – "Close Ranks!" Close the interval between each man to an arm's length.

Ordines . . . Extendit'! – "Open Ranks!" Extend the interval between each man to two arm's lengths.

Ordines . . . Revert! – "Normal Interval" This command is only given to recover from open to closed ranks; recover the normal interval between each man to one arm-length.

Pila . . . iacit'! – "Cast spears!"

Pila . . . parat'! – "Prepare spears for casting!" At this command, the legionaries place their feet shoulder distance apart, right foot back, shields held slightly up toward the enemy; right arm and hand holding the *pilum* cocked to the rear, the point slightly elevated.

Pila . . . ponit'! – "Present or pick up spears!" At this command, the legionaries place their feet shoulder distance apart, right toe to left heel; shields remain level and to the front in a good defensive position. The right hand holding the *pilum* is held at the level of the right ear, the *pilum* parallel to the ground.

Promov . . . ete! – "Forward March!" Step off on the right foot and march the standard Roman marching pace of sixty full passus per minute.

Quincuncem . . . format'! – "Form quincunx!" Form the "five dots"—a
    formation used to allow a passage of lines.

Scuta . . . erigit'! – "Shields up!"

Signa . . . Conversat'! – Reverse the access of advance, a 180 degree turn; "Turn
    about!"

Signa . . . Profert! – "Advance!"

Spathas . . . Stringit'! – "Draw sabers!" (cavalry command)

(Unit) . . . Stat'! – "Attention!"